The

VISITOR

A magical understanding of uncertainty

The

VISITOR

A magical understanding of uncertainty

KAREN WEAVER

www.serenitypress.org

Serenity Press Publishing books may be ordered through booksellers or by contacting:

Serenity Press Publishing
www.serenitypress.org
serenitypress@hotmail.com

ISBN: 978-0-9872818-1-4 (sc)
ISBN: 978-0-9872818-2-1 (e)

Printed in Australia

For my wonderful gifts:
Dylan, Eithen, Kiera, Saoirse, Eimear and bump.
To my little angel gem, thank you.
I am complete because of you.

*From all negative situations
is the potential for a positive outcome.*

Karen Weaver

PREFACE

When I embarked on this journey, my creativity was at a high, as I had recently given birth to my fourth child. I participated in Nanowrimo in November 2010, and The Visitor was born during that same time.

I also have experienced a miscarriage, and one of the characters is based on my personal experiences. I never knew why I was just expected to accept what had happened, but I couldn't. One day whilst watching The View, it became clear. Whoopi Goldberg told a couple who had just experienced a miscarriage that they should not worry, because this was only a visitor who had come to let them know that the real gift is on its way.

At that moment, the penny dropped. I thought about my own circumstances, and then I just knew I had to write about it all to give hope to other women who endure this painful loss—and who are expected to accept it.

I embarked on an emotional roller coaster with my main characters, and I would like to share that experience with you.

ACKNOWLEDGEMENTS

This book would not exist without the loving, positive support that I received from my dear friends, Sascha and Donna, at buildingbeautifulbonds.com. You are amazing and inspiring women! I am so blessed to have you in my life.

Nyanda, thank you for your positive review at a critical point during the process.

My darling hubby, you unconditionally support my passion for writing. Thank you for being my rock and for being you.

To all of my children Dylan, Eithen, Kiera ,Saoirse, Eimear and any more yet to come - you are my inspiration and my passion. My heart glows for you all every day.

Mum and Dad, my sisters Emma and Lisa, my brothers Jonathan, Mathew and Luke, my Aunty Paddy, and my entire family and friends — thanks to all of you for always believing in me. I would not be who I am today if you were not part of my life.

Tesha, the way my book has touched your heart has affirmed that I am on the right path. Thank you for being wonderful.

Finally, Bill & Bev thank you for gracing my life with your presence, you are very special people.

Life is good to me.

Contents

Prologue

There is a special place, somewhere in the heavenly universe. You may already feel that this place does exist; yet you will never truly know of its existence unless you have experienced the magic that it delivers directly to those chosen few who are its receivers. It is from this place that this journey began.

Five special but significantly different women became eligible to experience the magic of changing their lives to receive the true gift. Because of what they know now, they will no longer see things as "I have a job to do." This is not a pleasant encounter at times. But, in order for the true magnificence of my role to shine through the darkness, I must first endure a tough journey, and so must they.

The women came from all across the globe, but their varied locations are not ever significant, as they are now joined by a bond deeper than most; some may never meet but they will be connected forever through the memories I now hold.

CHAPTER 1

The Meeting

I still do not know why the Boss gave me this role; I still wonder what he saw in me to make him think that I am the best person for the job. He must value my opinion highly to give me control of such a life-changing responsibility. No pressure then! Right. But then again, perhaps not. My mates have started to call me the "Indian", because I give a gift and then take it away. It's all right for them, with their conventional "giving" jobs. Not so for me. The official name for my job is "Visitor"; the definition of which is "a person or thing that enters into someone's life for a short period of time". I am just back after a break between assignments. Each assignment can take a lot out of me. The pressure can be intense, and I never know what to expect. Every assignment is different, from start to finish, so anything can happen.

Ah, Jonnie has just sent me a message:

"Meeting 10 mins boardroom."

That means it's time. Soon I will find out the name of the people I'll spend the next few months with, I always feel nervous and a little uncomfortable at this point. So I must remember to make a stop at the loo on the way to the meeting. As the Boss doesn't like it if we need to leave the room; sometimes these meetings can go on for hours.

I remember what happened to my good friend, Sydney, at the last meeting. She had been out for a curry and a few glasses of wine the night before, and they were doing a conga in her lower intestines the whole way through the meeting. I remember looking at her: the sweat on her forehead and the greenness of her cheeks told the whole story all

3

by themselves. The poor girl was in pain, but I have to commend her. She stuck it out until the end. We didn't see her the rest of that afternoon, and we usually hang out to make sure that we are all in sync when the Boss isn't around.

Outside the boardroom door, we all line up in anticipation, as if we are waiting at the living-room door to see what Santa left for us. As we look in through the small window in the door, I can only describe the room as being spacious, bright and airy. The prominent colour is white — white walls, white table, enormous white fluffy chairs that we all sink into. Sitting in them is like lying on a giant cloud. When you sink in it feels quite luxurious. But they are awkward to get out of, and I have not worked out why. It is all very strange, as this room is not one that you would expect the Boss to have had an influence in designing; yet, apparently, it was his vision. Boss is quite loud and sharp; when he talks he has everyone's attention. Quite a bulky, strong man, not anything like me — I could fit twice into his pants. He has the utmost respect from everyone. No one has ever questioned his decisions, as he has never faltered; I would trust him with my life. I suppose, in a way, I have.

We hear a loud "Come in!" So we all enter the room and take our seats at the large white desk, where our assignment files await us. I am dying to take a peek, but I decide to wait until it is time to read about the people I am going to encounter. I love meeting new people; I love delving into the soul of their lives in order to find their true being. What makes them tick? Do they already know, or are they to find out in the future? Human behaviour has always intrigued me.

Boss gives us all the usual spiel: start afresh; forget the past assignments; take a fresh approach; all the usual get-in-the-zone focus stuff that helps us build a brick wall between assignments. And then comes the moment we have all sunken into our seats to await.

"Well, what are you all waiting for? Open your files. Have a look, and if you have any questions that I can help you with before the end of the meeting, all the better. If not, you can take your time to look over them tonight, and be at my office early, because dispatch starts at 9.00 sharp. Got it?" says Boss.

In unison, whilst we all reach for our files, we agree, "Got it, Boss"..

On this assignment I have five different candidates to observe, and I have five special gems assigned for me to pick up in the morning before I dispatch. The gems are not designed to last long, but they will have an unimaginable effect on those who encounter them. It never seems to baffle me how everyone deals with these situations in his or her own unique way. Over the thirty-four years that I have had this role, I believe I have seen it all—but, hey, maybe not. I never take things for granted; definitely not here, anyway. Once I have done my duty, I am not allowed to interfere; I must only observe for the immediate reaction and then report my findings to Boss and the others.

I am always asked how I am able to do my job. Well, my answer to that is that someone has to do it, and I feel that I do it properly by ensuring that, although the gift I deliver is taken away, there are only so many gifts to give, and I help in the process of choosing the best candidates in each assignment group.

Scanning my files I see that my first candidate is a thirty-year old, blonde-haired, blue-eyed woman named Carrie. As I look at her picture, I see that her sparkle is hidden—still there, but hidden behind a dark cloud. Her profile says that she had always lived life to the fullest until having her first child, which was at the same time that her partner encouraged her to give up her work and her studies, and focus on her family commitments. She has applied for a visa to move to the other side of the world, far away from her friends and family, in order to focus on the family unit that she is creating with her partner.

All of this, and yet she hasn't considered having any more children! I am intrigued to know why. I delve further into her profile. Ah! Now I see the reason. About a year ago a violent attack inside her home traumatised her, and she suffered the symptoms of post-traumatic stress, which she is still trying to overcome. I try not to judge others, as it is by means of a combination of different circumstances that we each make dramatic choices. A lot more to discover here, I imagine.

Next is a thirty-eight-year-old woman named Tracy. Based on her appearance, she has had a rough life and has let herself go somewhat. It is amazing how the pressures of life can really reflect on someone's face. She has brown short hair and is wearing jeans that are too tight for her, which creates a muffin-top effect around her waist. Let's see what her profile says. Oh, she has a medical condition which she has not discovered yet. A miracle sent to her four years ago allowed her to conceive her son. She has been trying, to no avail, to have a second child, and she has had many miscarriages. She also takes care of her mum, who is not as mobile as she once was and thus needs a lot of care. Tracy's family has had its fair share of trauma, which has led her to become quite cautious and sometimes anxious. People perceive her as being a negative and dull person who often feels sorry for herself, regularly vocalising her sadness over losing another pregnancy.

Because some people can feel uncomfortable with the taboo subject of miscarriages, they avoid her. This leaves her feeling isolated, which only adds to her anxiety and paranoia, especially after a playgroup session. Again, I do not judge. I will take the time to encounter people for myself so that I can understand the lifetime of circumstances that have brought them to this place in life where they now stand.

The third candidate is a twenty-two-year-old model named Bethany. She is very beautiful, with long brown locks that flow elegantly over her slender shoulders. Her eyes are as brown as the darkest mocha, but she is so thin that her bones show through her tanned skin. Her profile says that she has a boyfriend who is also famous. They are regular partiers. Some in society have presumed that they are together in order to get more publicity, as the paparazzi have followed their every move since their dating status became "news".

They seem to be what people perceive as a "perfect couple" — if there is such a thing! She is Australian; he is American. What more could the world want than the hunky American actor and the glamorous Australian beauty. Ever since birth, Bethany has won every "bonny baby" contest and beauty pageant available. Yet people have only seen her beautiful appearance, not who she is inside. But I can see that she is in love, as she has a twinkle in her eye that it is not love for herself. It is true love for her soul mate. Again, I am intrigued to learn more about her life. My job becomes so much easier when I am interested in learning more.

Next is another thirty-eight-year-old woman. This one is named Kath. She looks a lot younger in her picture, which indicates a stress-free life; maybe she has not yet had children. She has a toned physique. Her hair is blonde and her eyes are blue. She seems to have a confident presence, which I can discern by her posture and facial expression. The profile says that she has always been focused on her career and has always planned everything in her life in advance. Time has moved swiftly since Kath was in her twenties, and she has worked hard to become a highly successful fitness instructor. She appears regularly on daytime television and has produced numerous fitness videos.

She has had neither the time nor the space for children, as she storms through life at an ever-increasing pace, exercising and exercising and exercising some more. Kath is obviously very successful; but, is she happy? That is what I would like to know. I read on to discover that, over the past few years, she has tried — unsuccessfully — to fall in love. Now she has started investigating a sperm donor, as she feels that it is her only option; her biological clock ticks louder and louder, and she has not yet found the right person — the man she would love enough to partner with to create a family. Many a debate goes on all over the world, through different lands, religions and cultures, about medical intervention when it comes to having children. Is it better to start a family when a woman is young and her body is in its prime? Or is it better for a woman to wait until she has secure job and is more mentally and emotionally prepared for raising a child responsibly? I still am out on this one. So many pros and cons exist for both; and, from my experience, each individual is exactly that: individual, and, therefore, having her own positives and negatives. We must always remember that no one is perfect. However, decent with some moral standards are preferred "qualifications."

The fifth and final file. This will be interesting; the Boss usually saves the best until last. Well, her photo shows a woman who takes care of herself. She is very petite and has fiery-red hair tied back tight from her face. "Let your hair down, girl" comes to mind immediately. She has a killer-instinct look in her eye. Not much softness here, and her choice of clothing is a very businesslike suit with killer heels—must be to match her killer look. I don't see a ring on her finger, and I suspect she doesn't know what is coming. Let's see what her profile reveals. Her name is Siobhan, she is thirty-four years old, and has never wanted to get married or have children. Siobhan's sole focus in life has been to secure the top job at Maximus Corporations, a powerful law firm. There seems to be no limit to what moral hurdles she will jump through in order to achieve that goal. I have no inkling at all as to how this is going to end up. However, I am intrigued to discover how this ambitious go-getter has arrived at this pinnacle.

"Rupert, are you still with us?" I hear Boss shouting in the distance.

Oh, that's me! "Yeah, Boss. Sorry, I was just scanning my files."

"I see that Rupert, but what I want to know is if you have any questions to ask."

"No, Boss. Everything seems to be in place."

"All right. If that is all that I can do for you all, I will get back to my office. I trust that everything will run smoothly then." He said this as he intensely scanned the room.

Everyone agrees, and then we all look back at each other under our brows. We all know that the Boss has a lot of responsibility, but we all work voluntarily for this cause because we believe that what we do is for the greater good of mankind. Do we look for anything in return? No. I suppose we do live very comfortably when we are not on an assignment, but it is not as if we don't earn it.

There I go again. "Stop!" I say to myself. Where is my optimism? I do love it here—it is so heavenly, and everyone is in the same boat, so we have a sense of camaraderie. Syd, Jonnie and I are good mates, and we help each other out a lot; each of our roles allow us to interact all the time, and people who have been through as much as we have been through together tend to get close to each other.

"Hey, Roo, what's up with you? You're off in a world of your own."

"Sorry, Syd, you know me — just afloat in another thought bubble. What do you think of these assignments?"

"Yeah, pretty standard really — well, apart from assignment five, of course; it will be interesting to see how that progresses. We will have to work closely on that one I think. Are you okay about that one? She looks quite like…"

"Who? What do you mean, Syd?"

"No one, Roo. You know me: I just jump to conclusions without any justification at times. Please don't pass any remarks. Do you fancy catching a coffee later?"

"Yeah, sounds great, Syd. Will need to be early, though. I want to get prepared for dispatch in the morning. You know I am always first to go."

"Let's say six at my place this time? I'll pick up some heavenly delights from Dave."

"How can I resist such an offer, then? Are you gonna tell Jonnie, or will I?"

"He said to confirm a time via message. He has had to rush off to get some form signed from the Boss."

"Oh shit! I need my dispatch form signed, too; otherwise, I can't get the gems released. There is no way that I am going running around in the morning."

I quickly jump up, grab my files, and run around to the other side of the desk, where Syd is trying to get out of her chair. So I bend down, meeting her halfway and giving her a friendly thank-you kiss.

"Syd, what would I do without you?" I say.

"But I just said... Oh, well, you are welcome, then," she replies, as she tries to get up whilst watching me dash out the door.

Outside the door I have the unfortunate encounter of bumping right into Jayden.

"Whoa, Rupert, you are in a hurry! Did you forget something important? Maybe you forgot to take back the gift you gave 'Indian boy.'"

I just ignore him, as I don't want to fuel the fire that he is trying to ignite. I start to walk away, and he continues to shout after me, for all to hear.

"If you can't handle that job of yours I can always take it of your hands! Make sure you tell Boss that when he discovers how incompetent you can be."

Oh, he does rag me sometimes, but he is just jealous. Although I understand that is where his fire is coming from, it doesn't justify how he expresses his frustration. But I know the day will come when he moves on, so I will bide my time until then. I stand glorious in the knowledge that I am what he wants to be, and it is he who has issues, not I.

I make it around to Boss's office in good time and knock lightly at the door.

"Come in, Rupert," he calls loudly.

I hate it when he does that! He makes me feel that he knows my innermost thoughts.

"Take a seat. Would you like a drink?" he asks, whilst making himself an espresso in his fancy espresso machine.

"No thanks, Boss. I am meeting Syd and Jonnie for a coffee later, and I don't want to overdo it. I will never sleep tonight!"

He takes a seat right opposite me in his big, white-leather chair, which he fills completely; it would take four of me to fill it.

Keen to move on after a moment of awkward silence, he says, "Have you got the dispatch form there, Rupert?"

"Oh, yes, the form. It's right here," I reply, fumbling in my bag.

Ah, got it—thank goodness. As he signs the dispatch forms, he says, "Are you looking forward to this assignment, Rupert?"

"Yes, Boss. I will look over the files in more detail tonight, of course, but it all seems intriguing,"

"Case five has very close similarities to…"

"I know what you are going to say. And, no, that is not a problem, Boss."

"Remember the profile, Rupert, because what is inside is not the same."

"Yes, Boss, and it is what's inside that matters the most. If that's all, Boss…"

"Yes, Rupert, that's all. I hope that your dispatch goes smoothly, and I will check in with you at some stage."

"I will look forward to that!" I say sarcastically, as I quickly move towards the door.

"Rupert!" I hear, just as I reach my exit. I roll my eyes and turn around to see the Boss with his hand raised high, holding up my signed dispatch form. I can see that he now knows I've been distracted. No point in digging a bigger hole for myself, so I just grab it, smile my glowing smile, and leave as quickly as possible.

CHAPTER 2

Dispatch

Syd's quarters are across the corridor. On her door she has a big diamond number eight, and she feels that it is her destiny to live there, as that has always been her favourite lucky number. I am not a real believer in all that kind of stuff, but if it encourages positivity, what harm can it do? Especially for Syd, as she tends to imagine the worst-case scenario, even though she always has good intensions.

I close my white but nonetheless dull-looking number-seven door, and then I walk across the corridor to Syd's place. She must have a sensor on me, as she opens the door before I knock.

"Ah… great! Just in time, Jonnie is on his way. And Dave has just made his delivery; I think that Jayden is onto our secret meeting. Apparently, he asked Dave a lot of questions."

"Jayden does have issues. You know that, Syd," I say as I take a seat.

Inside is not any less glitzy than her door. Diamonds and crystals on every wall, and a giant crystal Cupid statue sits right in the middle of her glass-topped coffee table, which has legs shaped like Roman pillars. I do not know why, but every time I go for a cuppa, Cupid is always pointing at me. Believe me, I avoid it! The last thing that I need in my life is for Cupid's arrow to strike me. It struck me before, with detrimental effects on my behaviour, as I totally devoted myself to, and sacrificed everything for, love. But let's be optimistic — at least there is a substantial plate of Dave's heavenly delights beside it.

"Yeah, I know, Roo. What is the deal with you and him? Is he after your job? I always thought that he was suited to the power he had as head of

13

dispatch, but he is obviously not. I wonder what lengths he will go to. You may not be safe...."

"Oh, stop it, Syd! None of us can go to the loo without the Boss knowing it. Let's be realistic; any issues Jayden has are his problem to solve, not mine. I have a very important assignment to focus on."

"You're right, I know, but there is no harm in being cautious around Jayden, Roo—especially after dispatch. Boss can't watch everything then."

"All right. I promise that I will be more aware. Now can we get into the coffee and heavenly delights? I need a sugar rush."

"We better wait for Jonnie. You know what he is like if we start without him!"

"Well he had better be quick."

"There he is now," she said a full beat before we heard the knock on the door.

"How do you do that, Syd?"

She just gives me a cheeky smile as she gets up to answer the door.

Jonnie comes in, all apologetic—as usual. He will pass himself someday, if he hasn't already.

"Hi, Roo! Have you and Jayden been at it again? It's the talk of the lower domain."

"What are you talking about, Jonnie?"

"The argument that you guys had in the big corridor after today's meeting."

"Does an argument not need two people to participate?"

"Well, yes, I think so. What do you think, Syd?"

"I think that it takes two to tango"

"That doesn't help, Syd."

'Well, if you don't like the answer, Jonnie, don't ask my opinion."

"Okay, you two. See, that could be considered an argument. I didn't answer Jayden today, so I did not have an argument. Can we please get some coffee now, Syd?"

"Coming right up. Large, fluffy-dream espressos all around?"

Our eager nods show our delight in and need for caffeine. Syd is back in an instant, and three of us are silent for a few moments as the espresso enters our caffeine-starved bodies. We all then indulge in a delicious heavenly delight.

"Wow! I so miss these when I am away," I say as I lick the lightest, fluffiest cream from around my mouth. I giggle as I look at Syd; as always, the cream is all over her nose and mouth. Not gonna tell her, I think to myself. From the smirk on Jonnie's face, I suspect he isn't either.

For the next hour we drink coffee, eat heavenly delights, and go through each file — but there is only so much we can talk about without speculating. Our meetings are really a catch-up and support group for each other. So much can happen so quickly around here that it is good to have mates to catch up with.

"I might head on now, as I will be getting up super early."

"Yeah, I might head on now, as well, Syd. We'll let you hit the sack, too."

"All right, guys. Great to catch up! We must not leave it as long the next time."

We all wish each other well with our dispatches, and then Jonnie and I each head back to our own quarters to wind down.

* * * * *

Well, I don't sleep very much at all. I never do the night before dispatch. It all seems so unnatural — I suppose it is, really; it is a process that was created. I never will fully understand it, and maybe I should look into it more. "Knowledge is key", after all.

Anyway, I better get up. I set my alarm for 6.00 a.m, which would give me three hours to get ready, but I have already hit snooze a few times, and so now it is 6.25 a.m. I hop out of my bed, which is quite big and comfy. It is the main luxury that I possess. I am not into clutter; I'm more minimalistic. I suppose that is what you could call my style. Keep things simple, as life is complicated enough at times without adding to it.

Wiping the sleep from my eyes I think about what lies ahead. I must keep a clear focus on the target destinations of my assignments. I hop into the shower; maybe this will wake me up. I take one last read through the files and then head for the dispatch department.

When I arrive, there is a bit of a commotion. Jayden comes towards me in a very determined manner.

"Where have you been? Your dispatch has been brought forward. Hurry up!"

"What? Why? What's going on? I haven't even collected the gems yet."

"I have them ready for you here. Sign this and get going, or you will hold everyone else up."

"But the Boss didn't inform me of any changes."

"He did try to contact you last night, but you weren't in your quarters. As it was just a fifteen-minute change, and you are usually ready to

16

dispatch early, he thought that it wouldn't be a problem. Trust you to take your time this morning! You'd better hurry."

"Oh, right, thanks. Will do," I say as I sign the form, take the wooden box containing the gems, and head to dispatch room as fast as I can. Something else must be happening today to cause such an upheaval. I am just surprised that I wasn't told sooner. Boss is usually meticulous. Something doesn't feel right, so I call Syd on my way to hear what she thinks. I know she will imagine the worst-case scenario, but, together, we may come to some conclusion. I have tried ringing but get no answer, so I will send her a message:

"Hi, Syd. Jayden acting strange @ dispatch — made rush through entry & pickup. Call soon... Roo."

Maybe I am just reading too much into it all; he is just trying to unsettle me so that I am not focused on the dispatch, which could make me navigate to the wrong setting. It is just not like him to help me.

Down the corridor, which is bright white, there are many doors, which are all also white — if not for the numbers or signs on each door, you would not even notice them. I do not know what goes on behind these doors, but some of them have signs, "Strictly No Entrance", so, quite possibly, I will never discover what happens there. I have, on occasion, wondered if there are more doors, the existence of which we do not know, simply because they have no signage.

I finally reach the end of the long corridor; it seems to go on forever. Things are a lot calmer here, and I encounter no signs of any urgency for dispatch.

Harry approaches and calmly greets me. "Good morning, Rupert. Are you ready to start transition?"

"Yeah, Harry, but you don't seem to be in too much of a rush."

"Ah, you know me, Rupert. I take things in my stride, but you will notice that I get everything done all the same. Now follow me to stage one."

"No probs. Lead the way."

I enter, and a warm glow hugs me tight. Everything here is usually so white and bright that it is a shock to my eyes to see another colour. I am to stay in the stage one until my eyes adjust to a level safe enough to adapt to a less-bright environment. The furniture is also different; it is more "earthy", made of wood and fabrics, rather than metal, glass and plastic that we have become adjusted to living here.

"Make yourself comfortable, Rupert. I will come back in a few minutes to bring you to the Vortex."

"Thanks, Harry. See you then"

I choose to sit in a big, strong-looking arm chair. I put my head back, and my phone rings. "Hello?"

"Hi, Roo, what's going on? Are you okay?"

"I don't know, Syd. Maybe I am just paranoid after what we were all talking about last night, but Jayden met me in the dispatch entry in an awful panic to get me dispatched early. I am now in first stage of dispatch, and Harry isn't in any panic –but, you know Harry, he doesn't ever panic. What do you think?"

"I think you should just watch out. I don't think that you can trust Jayden. I will keep an ear out, and if I catch wind of anything, I will send you a message."

"Thanks, Syd. I appreciate you watching out for me, but all seems to be going smoothly here now. I better go, because Harry will be back soon."

"All right then, Roo. See ya."

Harry knocks on the door and enters. He brings me over to check that my eyes have adjusted.

"Well, your eyes are ready, Rupert. If the rest of you is ready, we may as well get you dispatched."

"Very cool sense of humour, Harry."

"Maybe for you, Rupert… but, when you have said it as many times as I have, it soon loses momentum."

"Oh, right. I thought that I was the first."

"Sorry to disappoint you, Rupert….Well, you didn't answer me. Are you ready to go?"

"Oh, yeah. Sorry, Harry. I suppose so. Yes, I am ready."

"Have you got everything with you? You know that I can't stop once I have started."

"I'm right to go, Harry."

"Right then. Follow me, young man."

We go through to vortex room, which is quite big. Right in the centre is the large oval-shaped vortex window. It is about 10 feet tall and 6 feet wide, and it has a washing-machine effect in the centre, as it swishes around and around—faster than you can imagine. Its sheer intensity never ceases to amaze me. Every time I witness the magnificent phenomenon that is the Vortex, I feel part of something bigger than big.

"Please take your position and focus on your destination. When you are ready, give me the thumbs up."

I take position, I focus, I give thumbs up, and I enter the Vortex.
"All right then, Rupert. Good luck and goodbye."

CHAPTER 3

Carrie

I can only describe the setting as picturesque. Green fields, farm animals grazing, the sun shining through the fluffy white clouds. In the distance I can see the outline of a castle. In front of me is a cottage, freshly painted white, with a bright-red front door. The cottage is very old, but someone must live here, as I can see smoke coming out of the chimney. It is quite like the old Irish cottage John Wayne and Maureen O'Hara emerged from during scenes of The Quiet Man.

Some activity catches my eye. A tall handsome fellow has just left the house; he walks down the adjoining field to what seems to be a building site. I must check this file to refresh my memory: yes, it says that they have applied to move to another country, so why are they building a house? All this seems somewhat complicated, but maybe that is the reason for my coming — to bring some clarity to the situation and put their lives back into perspective if they have lost their way. I will not know for sure until I observe some more.

A young woman carrying a small boy comes out of the house. I recognise her as Carrie. She also carries her handbag, and she seems flustered. She approaches the tall handsome fellow. I must assume, at this point, that he is her partner. He doesn't seem happy; I can hear him grumbling away but can't make out the words.

I hear her say, "Okay, I am off to playgroup. Is there anything that you want me to bring back?"

"Just my son in one piece, please. Oh, and sometime today. Thanks."

20

"Please don't be like that. I'm just going to playgroup...." She sighs. "Would you like me to bring you back something to eat today?"

"Don't worry about me. I will be okay. I will just work away here, building a future for us whilst you go out socialising. Did you ever stop to think that I might need to go somewhere?"

"Well, do you?"

"That's not the point! What if I needed to get something for the house?"

"But you know that I go to playgroup every Wednesday."

"How could I forget? You never know when to come back. I would die of starvation before you would think of coming home."

"I'd better go. See you later... if you need anything, call me," she says as she walks to the car, with her head lowered and her heart broken.

Carrie's aura is one of intense sadness, yet no tears will come, as she numbs herself to emotions so intense that they ripple through her, deflecting on those around her. I can only imagine how this type of home environment affects their young son. I do believe that she takes the boy to playgroup in order to get away from this destructive atmosphere for a bit, even if only once a week.

Her partner comes across as very harsh and hurtful, but he must have a reason for this spitefulness — maybe he is calling out for help and she is ignoring his cry, as she is so caught up in her own struggle. She must fight to survive each day as she struggles to overcome the post-traumatic stress that she still experiences. I do wonder how they have come to this unhappy, torturous place in their relationship; suddenly it all becomes clear why I am here. How can so much sadness exist in a place of such beauty? If only they would open their eyes and let the beauty that surrounds them enter into their lives, they would naturally feel more fulfilled.

Before I go any further, I must find out more. I open the box and look at the beautiful gems, taking out the one intended for Carrie. Her gem glows brightly as I look into its core to discover the secrets that lie in her and her partner's past. I see the cottage, with three people — two men and a woman — gathered in a cosy room warmed by a roaring fire.

They seem merry as they enjoy some alcohol. But, as time progresses, the two men start to aggravate each other. One is so drunk that he can barely stand up. An arm raises a bottle, and the drunken man falls to the floor. The other man continuously punches the fallen man in the head as he lies on the floor, unconscious. The attacker strengthens his blows by holding a little Buddha statue in his clenched fist. The woman is on the phone, frantically trying to get help. The man won't stop, and the beating has gone too far. All the while she is on the phone, the woman also tries to stop him; she also holds a crying baby in her arms. In a panic, she hits the man on the back numerous times. He bolts towards her, enraged, and pushes her across the room. She remains upright, sailing to a corner of the room, with her baby cuddled in her arms, thankfully unharmed.

She shouts, "Get out! Get out!"

He runs out the door and drives away. The man lies unconscious, bleeding from his ear; the woman kneels beside him, trying to wake him up, but he does not respond. The intense shock hits her like a strong right hook: this might be the last time that she sees her partner — the father of her child. So much time, love and energy invested into one person, and yet it could be all gone so quickly. The ambulance comes, and the drivers enter the cottage, seeing a young woman sitting on the floor. She cradles a crying baby in one arm whilst her free hand strokes the face of her unconscious partner, whose head she nestles in her lap.

She keeps repeating, "He tried to kill him; he tried to kill him...."

I see that the next few days take a toll. Her partner, discharged from hospital, lies in a dark room for days, trying to heal from the inflicted damage. At the same time, her own reaction kicks in, taking the form of post-traumatic shock. Her body shakes wildly if she talks about what happened, and a darkness has engulfed her thoughts. She realises that the attack has changed everything; she cannot fix things no matter how hard she tries. She has blamed herself for it all, as she invited the attacker – her own brother – into their home. She feels trapped between her love and loyalty to her partner and her love and loyalty to her family. Her family reacted to the incident by protecting her brother, justifying his actions in order to ensure that neither a convictions nor a revenge attack would result.

Yet this incident is not the only reason that Carrie now suffers from post-traumatic stress: it was merely the catalyst that pulled the trigger. Other elements have built up inside her, and these have grown out of control, attacking her soul far more than the attack itself ever could have done. She has had to give up her passion for learning about teaching drama and discovering herself, and this has left a void deep within her – even worse, she has felt that she has no one to talk to about any of it. Also, she has breastfed her son ever since he was born, and this causes heightened emotions. Add to all this her partner's depression and constant put-downs, all of which have certainly impacted her, and, as she does not deal with them, they have stored up inside her, grinding her down, eating away at her confidence and self-worth. The financial pressures that have resulted from her not working, yet still servicing debt in her attempt to not stress her partner further, as he would just become more depressed. It has been a juggling act for her, and no one can juggle forever. The attack was just one more ball, but it was one too many – and so all the balls came crashing down.

I see that Carrie's aura, once so vibrant with yellows and oranges, is now unclear and hazy – yet it is changing, and this indicates that she has started a spiritual journey of self-discovery. All people do not encounter such dramatic changes in their auras, but when such changes do happen, they turn people's lives upside down, as individuals can sink to levels of deep sadness, possibly even trauma. If only Carrie knew that at the other end of her journey of self-discovery she will find divine happiness – and that, no matter what happens, she will be so in tune with herself spiritually that she will be practically unbreakable.

I need to go back to another significant time in Carrie's past. Back to a time where I can see and judge if she and her partner are a couple that should be as one. The scene shifts to three years earlier.

The scenery is the same, but the cottage is not. It appears rather derelict; the inside looks as if birds have been nesting there for years, and the outside is wildly overgrown and worn. I see a for-sale sign. A black sports car pulls up, and a glamorous blonde steps out; she wears a very flattering shirt, trousers and high heels. Her long blonde locks are highly styled and well maintained, and they shine in the sun as they flow down her back. She smiles a bright, confident smile. It is Carrie, but I hardly recognise her. Her aura glows so intensely, it seems on fire; if only she knew that the world is her oyster and she has decided on this place. Why? Out of the driver's seat hops a tall, handsome man. He, too, has a vibrant aura, but Carrie's is so intense, it outshines his.

"What do you think, Tom? Can you do anything with it?" she asks.

"Well, I will have to take a look inside, but I thought that it would be a lot worse."

"I just love it! I think that we can make some money on it if you can do it up a little to make it liveable. I will get the grant for it, and then you can build…"

"All right, Carrie," he says as he puts his arms around her waist.

"Let us just take it one step at a time and see if we win the bidding war."

"Oh, so you mean that you think we should take a chance and do it?" she says very excitedly. She looks deep into his eyes, leaving him no option but to say yes. He just loves her with all his heart, and so he wants her to have anything that she wants.

"Yes, if you are sure.…"

"Oh, I'm sure, hon! Thank you!"

They passionately kiss, not unsettled at all by the curious neighbours who drive past.

"Can we at least look inside before I totally condemn myself, though?"

"Oh, yeah! Follow me—I think it has so much potential."

They push open the makeshift front door and enter the cottage.

The scene shifts to six months later. They are both at the cottage again. I sense that this place is a big part of their lives. The outside looks wonderful; Tom has cut away all the overgrown bramble and weeds, which are now in a pile of ashes in the adjoining field. He has painted the outside of the cottage a gleaming white, fixed the front door and painted it fire-engine red. Tom approaches the cottage whilst Carrie is inside, painting. The inside is liveable, once again. Tom has built a strong fireplace, using his own two hands, and the walls are brightly painted in whites and creams to give a sense of freshness and space. He comes into the house, puts his arms around her, and kisses her tenderly on the neck.

"I have to show you what I have found!" he says excitedly.

"What is it? Tell me, please...."

"No, I have to show you. Follow me."

They both go outside and walk around to the back of the cottage.

"Look, Carrie—it is a baby horseshoe! How lucky is that? It is a sign that we are going to be lucky here."

"Oh, Tom! How cute is that? We have to keep it. Hold it up right, or all the luck will fall out."

"We can put it alongside the big one that I found."

"The little one can be for baby," she says, placing her hands onto her lower abdomen.

"It sure can, hon. I cannot wait to meet the little mite!" He places his hands on hers, and they look lovingly into each other's eyes. They kiss deeply, totally in tune with one another. Two hearts beating as one.

"Right. Let's get back to work, or we won't be moved in before baby comes with all these distractions."

They walk around to the front of the house, stopping in the front garden to look at the home they are creating. He wraps his arms around her. Snuggling into his embrace, she says, "This is our first family home, Tom. I don't care if the cottage is old; we have made it our own."

"It sure is, perfect hon," he agrees. "If we want to get moved in, we had better get a move on!" He slaps her lightly on her bum. She giggles like a schoolgirl with a crush, smiling as she walks back towards the cottage.

Their little gem has tired itself, so it loses its glow and stops there. It is a lot to take in, and I will have to take a timeout to absorb this introduction; the situation is more complex than I thought. This cottage also seems to be significant, so I will have to investigate it further. It is so unfortunate that Carrie and Tom have lost their way, as they were truly happily in love. Their hearts that once beat as one now miss each other's beats entirely. They need to stop walking different paths and come together again.

I shall move on to observe my next assignment. I must focus on the destination, so I shall take a walk down the lane to absorb some of the naturally beautiful scenery that helps cleanse the mind. I have found that nature acts like a filter. When we allow it in, it gets rid of the entire mass of unwanted gunk that clogs up the mind, thus assisting pricelessly in making things seem so much clearer.

The stroll clears my mind, and I am now ready to move on.

CHAPTER 4

Tracy

I have not had to travel far. In fact, I do believe that Carrie and Tracy have met frequently; however, their friendship has not yet blossomed. Tracy lives in a small town, so her environment is not as picturesque Carrie's. I now stand in front of Tracy's home, which is a terrace house facing a cul-de-sac of older terraced houses. The front room has a large window, and I imagine this allows her family to observe many goings-on, keeping them in touch with the outside world. The initial vibe from this house is a significant one, emanating much grief and sadness. This home has a lot of death connected to it, and this has taken its toll on the family.

Tracy has received many gems, but only one gift so far; yet she has desired so many. I do not know why they have been held back, but I do recall her profile outlining a medical problem. I enter the house and see an old woman sitting on a chair in the kitchen, having a cup of tea and a bun. The kitchen is small, with a big table that dominates the floor space. I notice matching pine dresser that holds plates with a topiary-tree design. The cupboards are fresh and clean. The walls are painted in neutral colours, but, along the middle, topiary trees are stenciled all the way around. I have a feeling she likes a theme. A woman whom I recognise as Tracy is standing at the kitchen sink.

Through the bright-white net curtains, she watches her young son playing with his dog. Observing her lovingly gaze outside, I know that her only wish right now is to provide her son with a brother or sister.

Tracy's mother looks at her daughter, knowing what she is thinking.

"Don't worry, love," she says. "You will get another one someday."

"Someday, Mam? I can't wait until someday. I am almost forty, and Joey is getting older...."

"I know that, love. But stressing yourself out about it isn't going to do any good, is it?"

"But they said that at your age, Mam...."

"Women go through this all the time, love. I think that you need to focus on what you have."

"How can you say that when you know how much it all means to me?"

"But, love..."

"No, Mam! I have heard enough," she says. "Come on, Joey!" she calls out through the open window. "It's time to get ready for playgroup."

"Yeah...Coming, Mammy!" he calls back as he skips across the yard.

Tracy's sister enters the house, calling, "Hello! Good morning, all!"

She walks into the kitchen with a brazen fake smile on her face.

Observing her mother, who looks sad, she says, "What's wrong, Mam?"

"Nothing, love, it's just...oh, never mind."

So she calls out from the kitchen to the living room that adjoins it, "Tracy, what's wrong with Mam?"

Tracy replies with a shout. "What's wrong with Mam! Are you kidding me? You should ask what's wrong with me."

"I am lost here. Who is going to tell me what's going on?"

"Well, love…" Their mother starts to say, but then Tracy storms out of the living room and back to the kitchen.

"Mam has told me that I need to get on with things — I should stop thinking about having another baby, and I also should get over any miscarriages I have had because women have them all the time."

"Mam is right, Tracy; it has all gone on for too long. If your mother can't tell you the truth, who can? You're not helping yourself or Joey by acting like this. It is starting to be impossible to be in your company. Is it any wonder Rob can't wait to get out of here for any opportunity he finds?"

"Well, that's a lovely thing to hear coming from your own sister!" Tracy snaps back. "Come on, Joey. We're going." She storms out, with Joey in tow, and slams the front door behind her.

Wow! Tensions run high in this house, too. With heightened tensions come strong emotions — and, although it is hard to hear the truth, as it hurts, it is necessary for us to face the truth so we can move on. Through conflict comes change. Tracy wears her heart on her sleeve: if she is feeling down, everyone around her will know, and those who are closest to her will possibly feel down, too.

Tracy's aura is red and pink, which means that she is a person with no hidden agendas. She is not afraid to make her point of view heard, as people with a mostly red aura are usually quite direct. They readily move on from different hobbies, jobs, and the like, as they can get bored easily. I see that, for Tracy, this has resulted in her not having an outside interest; her main focus is her family. The slight pinkness in her aura shows that she is strong willed and expects high standards from others. She has very strong ideals and definite opinions about which morals and values are acceptable.

I do not know why this lady has been chosen to receive yet another gem. I do believe that it will tip her over the edge and cause some mental instability, as she has experienced each of the gems she already has received as a trauma. The support of her family seems to be dwindling, so she is likely to suffer more intensely the grief of any further loss.

I take out the box of gems, and I see that Tracy's is glowing. It needs to show me something, so I look into it intently.

It is the same house, but we are upstairs in what I can guess to be Tracy's mother's room, as I see a lot of flowers and lace around. There is a dressing table covered with a lace cloth, and numerous objects are on top of it: a jewellery box, talc, perfumes, prayers, and other things accumulated and treasured over the years, each one with its own memory. Tracy wears a nightgown with a pussycat on the front; it looks like a long light-green T-shirt. Her mother, lying on the floor, has obviously had a fall, and Tracy helps her back into bed, making sure that she is settled and comfortable. She reads her mam some verses from her favourite book of poems.

Kissing her on the head, she says, "Good night, Mam." Tracy gets up, switches off the bedside lamp, and walks to the door.

She doubles over; the pain has made her drop to the floor, and she crawls out into the corridor, where she calls for her hubby. He comes running out, shocked at the sight that he witnesses.

"I think it's the baby, Rob. Please help me. I don't want Mam to hear."

Bending down, he picks her up in his arms and carries her to bed.

"Is there anything I can get you before I call the doctor?"

When she says no, he runs downstairs and calls the after-hours doctor, who promises to call straight away.

"The doctor said to make you comfortable; he should be half an hour at most," Rob tells Tracy. "Here is a drink of water, love."

"I don't want a drink of water! I want this pain to stop...I want our baby to be okay."

Their son calls out from the other room; he appears to be about two years old. Rob goes to see to him.

"Why is Mammy crying, Daddy? Did she hurt her knee?"

"No, son. Mammy is just sad, but she will be okay. Sometimes it is good to cry if you are sad."

"I don't want Mammy to be sad, Daddy."

"I will make Mammy happy again, son. Don't you worry. You go back to sleep and have some cool superhero dreams."

"Okay, Daddy. Do you promise?"

"I promise, son. Good night."

"Good night, Daddy."

Rob goes out into the corridor, hears a knock on the door, and goes downstairs to answer it. He leads the doctor upstairs to the bedroom, where Tracy lies sobbing. Rob waits outside the door. After a few minutes, he hears her cry even more. He buries his face in his hands as if he is going to break down also, but he doesn't.

The doctor comes out into the corridor, closing the door behind him.

In a whisper, he tells Rob, "She is going to need to take it easy, and she will need a scan in a couple of days. It looks as though she has lost her pregnancy, and so she will need a lot of support. I have given her something to help her sleep tonight, and I would like her to visit me tomorrow."

"Yes, Doctor. Thanks for everything," Rob says.

"I'm sorry that I couldn't do more to help. I will see you tomorrow, and I will let myself out,"

31

"Okay. Good night, Doctor."

Rob opens the bedroom door, only to see the love of his life in so much emotional pain that he feels helpless to make better. They look at each other, and he rushes to her side. He puts his arms around her, holding her in his warm embrace all night long as she continues to sob.

It is now time to move on to another time. The gem brings me to the same house, but it must be a few years earlier. The shifts in time are not as clear as they were with Carrie and Tom.

I see Tracy and Rob, somewhat younger; they giggle and laugh, snuggling on the sofa. They nibble from a box of chocolates whilst watching a movie.

"Everyone is going to wonder why we are not out tonight."

"Don't worry, Tracy. We'll just tell them that we are saving."

"Yeah, I know, Rob. But we always go out on Friday night, so they are going to suspect that something is up."

"It's only for a few more weeks, and then it will be all done. We will be Mr and Mrs."

"I know. I can't wait! But our ones are not going to be impressed that they didn't get a big day out, you know."

"Ah. Well, sure isn't that why we haven't tied the knot yet? No, we are right to do it our way, Tracy. You even said yourself that you wouldn't feel right walking up the aisle without your dad. God bless his soul."

"I know you're right, and it is just for me and you, Rob. Just as it is we that have to live together for the rest of our lives—living as one, having lots of children... it's all so exciting! I never thought that I would feel this way, or I would have done it a lot sooner. Why didn't you ask me sooner, by the way?"

"Sure, you have always put me off by saying the things that you say, and with all of the things that have happened. Anyway, don't think of that now. It is happening, and I couldn't be happier," he says as he passionately kisses her on the lips.

Her sister walks into the room, all dressed up ready to go to the local pub.

"Are you sure that you guys aren't going to come out for a few? Mam is all settled, so no worries there."

"Nah, we're okay here. It'll do us good to have a few weeks out of the pub."

"You mean you're not going out next weekend, either? It's Dave's birthday; you have to come."

"Yeah, we'll see, sis. You guys have a great night."

"We will. You guys have a good, boring movie night."

"We will!" Tracy and Rob say together, looking deep into each other's eyes and giggling.

"You two are up to something. I just know it. It's not right to keep secrets in a family, you know."

"Yeah, we know. See ya, sis."

"See ya," her sister says reluctantly as she closes the living-room door.

"Oh, I can't wait to see her face when we get back and tell her! She will go crazy. Mind you, I don't like lying to Mam. Do you?"

"No, of course not, but look at what happened any time before. There has always been a death or misfortune, so I thought we were agreed that this is the best thing to do for everyone."

"Yeah, of course, it is best for all, especially now that this baby is coming."

The gem stops there. It seems as though this family has endured a lot over the years. I can see now why Tracy has a heavy heart. I feel that she would truly benefit from having a chakra clearing, as this can help anyone who may constantly experience bad luck. But, for Tracy, it will be especially beneficial, as chakra clearings help those who have difficulties moving on, or who are anxious, unhappy, confused or depressed.

To have come from such a place of love and joy — with both her and her potential hubby hoping to have a big family — to now, with all that joy and all those hopes dwindling, it is no wonder that Tracy is -so distraught. She has endured the pain of losing the things that she has worked so hard to get, and this has destroyed her emotionally.

Deep down, she may even hold her mam accountable for her first pregnancy loss, though she has never said anything — she just allows it to eat her up inside. Tracy would never, ever inflict such guilt onto her mother, no matter how harsh her words might be at times. All this has led to Tracy's being resentful, in a way; her focus cannot shift to anything else, and she cannot move on. Her urge to have a sibling for her son is so intense that it consumes each and every thought that she has, which results in her slowly isolating herself from friends and loved ones. She needs guidance to enable her to get back on the route to happiness. And that is why I have been sent.

CHAPTER 5

Bethany

I arrive in a city and stand outside a tall apartment block. Drawn to go in, I arrive at apartment number eight and enter. It is spacious, with windows all way around, framing a wonderful view of the city. I have always perceived man-made creations to be ugly, but, when visualised from this vantage point, I can only describe the view as breathtaking. Inside, the apartment reminds me of where I live: the white walls, the pristine white-leather sofas, the glass tabletops, and the metalwork — it all seems designed as if from heaven, looking down onto the earth. Whoever thought of this design is a very creative individual. A large white bookcase with hundreds of books dominates a section of the apartment, standing out from the rest of the furnishings.

The apartment is the site of a lot of activity; people seem to be rushing around organising things. Someone has a hairbrush in one hand and a styling iron in the other. Another person scurries about, setting up cameras in different locations. Someone else dictates everything, and he has everyone in a panic. Things need not be so chaotic.

I eventually locate a young woman whom I believe to be Bethany, but I can hardly see her, as so many people are around her — styling her hair, putting on her makeup, and dressing her — all at the same time. It all seems so unnecessary; if they each took a turn, it would be a lot easier. Is this her home? I wonder to myself.

Everyone rushes around that little bit faster, and then, in an instant, they all stop. It looks as if they are playing musical statues, and someone just turned off the music.

"Bethany, da-a-arling, would you like to follow me? I think that we will take our first picture here on your sofa. I'm thinking a relaxed, 'I love being at home' look." I think his French accent is fake, or at least highly exaggerated.

She lies down on the sofa and holds a pose, asking, "Like this?"

"Pe-e-e-erfect, sweetie. Just hold it there."

A last brush of powder dusts her already-perfect face, and a last pump of hairspray mists her long chocolate-brown locks. (I have always wondered why they do this; it is not as if one brush of powder and one mist of hairspray at the last second will make any difference.) Bethany doesn't move an inch; she is almost a statue.

"Well, is everyone ready? We want to get this shoot wrapped up in time, so we need to get into position. Bethany, darling, when do you think your handsome Hanson will get here?" Enquires the same man. His Frenchman look comes complete with beret, moustache, neckerchief and tight trousers. In short, he is a sight to behold.

"Oh, I don't know Claude. Did your people get in contact with him to confirm? He didn't mention it this morning."

Worriedly, he calls, "Justine, did we get a confirmation from Hanson's people for 10.00?"

She quickly answers, "Yes, we did, Boss."

"Well, can you call them again to find out what time he is expected?"

She quickly gets on the mobile to locate Hanson's whereabouts.

"His guys have said that he should be here, Boss. They will call him and are to get back to us ASAP."

"Thanks, Justine. Keep me updated,"

Her phone chimes again, and she answers it before the second ring.

"Yeah, great. Thanks for getting back to us."

She turns around to see everyone looking straight at her, waiting in anticipation to hear the outcome of the conversation.

"He's getting a sausage roll at the deli down the street; he will be here in five."

Trying to hide his anger and frustration, he shouts, "Okay, we will focus on our single shots first."

Just as Claude says this, Hanson strolls into the apartment, eating a sausage roll. He has a confident, casual way about him that can frustrate some; he appears to just take life in his stride, never succumbing to the constant fast-paced demands that everyone else here seems to exhibit. He is like a breath of fresh air—he's not the most handsome chap in the world, but he definitely has a "presence".

When Bethany sees him, her love for him glows from within. This sends Claude into a spin, and he calls for a five-minute break.

Bethany gets up from her pose, gliding across the floor with a little skip in her step. She stops at the spot where ten people hover around Hanson like bees around a hive. When he sees her coming, he shoos them away to make way for Bethany. He acts as if he hasn't seen her in a lifetime, yet he only left the apartment a few hours before.

"Beth, is everything okay?"

"Yes, hon. I'm all the better for seeing you," she says. Standing like a school girl with a crush, she twists her feet and looks straight into his deep-blue eyes.

"Come here," he says passionately, exuding confidence as he grabs her in a tight embrace. She practically disappears in his arms, she is so thin.

A few moments later, Claude starts a commotion, trying to get a photograph of this moment of tenderness.

This is so lovely to observe. I can see Bethany's gem start to glow, even in the wooden box, and I gaze into its core to discover more about her past. It brings me to a large family home, with the stately grandeur of an older style—a lot of rooms but not a lot of people to fill them. I see a man, a woman and a beautiful young girl. I believe this to be a young Bethany, possibly at age eleven. The man and woman, whom I take to be her mum and dad, seem to be having an argument whilst she looks on.

"No, Harry, she must go to the competition. If she doesn't win the state heat, she doesn't qualify for the national heat. She just must go! I am not letting her ruin her future just because she wants to go to her friend's twelfth birthday."

"You are exaggerating, Hil. There will always be lots more beauty competitions... sure, how many has she already won this year? It would be healthier for her to go to her friend's birthday, because that is what she wants to do...."

"It would be more beneficial to her future to go..."

"She needs to spend time with her friends."

"She sees her friends every day in school."

"Yes, school. How much of that has she missed because of comp—"

"I was wondering when you would bring that up."

"She needs an education, Hil; she is not going to be so young and beautiful forever."

"That's why she needs to make the most out of modeling now, so that she is set up for the future."

"No, Hil! You just want her to succeed because you didn't."

She slaps him hard across the cheek, her face red with anger.

"Just stop it, both of you!" shouts Bethany through her tears. She has been crying all along, and they didn't even notice—or maybe they just didn't care.

"I can't please both of you, so I am going to my room." Bethany storms off to her room, and no one follows. They just start bickering all over again; this time it's about who was responsible for upsetting her.

Bethany feels so alone and unloved. How sad it must have been for her to grow up in that type of environment. Parents always want the best for their children, but they tend to enforce their ideals rather than letting the children have room to discover their own ideals for themselves—thus, discovering themselves naturally.

The gem moves on a bit further. It seems to be a few years later; Bethany is about sixteen. They are still in the same house, and her mother is getting her bag ready. As her father walks in the front door, her mother holds out her hand for him to give her the car keys.

"We are away, Harry. Your dinner is in the oven. Come on, Beth, or we'll be late. We don't want that Josie to get chatting to the judges before it starts."

Her father doesn't even respond, he just hands over the keys, drops his bag, and takes off his coat.

Bethany kisses her dad on the cheek as she goes past him. "Goodbye, Dad."

He kisses her cheek, too. With a smile, he says, "Goodbye, love. Good luck tonight."

"Thanks, Dad." She shuts the door behind her.

How sad that things have deteriorated so much between her parents. All has certainly had an effect on her attitude towards relationships. I sense that she blames herself for the years of bickering and also for the years of silence.

The gem pulls me to another time. The setting this time is a nightclub; it seems to be a more upper-class establishment from what I can make out. One of the big men standing at the door approaches Bethany, saying,

"Follow me, miss." He leads her and her friends past a long queue of cold girls in short skirts, high heels and low-cut tops. They look at her with jealous hatred as she passes.

Once inside, the big man escorts her to the VIP area. It seems that only a selected few and their friends have access to this area, which has a private bar and its own waitresses, so VIP guests need not battle any crowds at the bar. The dance floor, situated in the centre of the room, has its own very well-renowned DJ.

Bethany has caught the eye of a young man across the room.

One of her friends says, "Look, Beth! Hanson Jones has been checking you out since you walked through the door."

"No, he hasn't," she answers shyly as she sneaks a quick peek.

"Yes, he has Beth! Wait until you see… he so has the hots for you."

Hanson watches her for a while. When he catches her eye, he smiles and she smiles back. He stands up, straightens his clothes, and shimmies across the empty floor to get her attention. He approaches her table, gets on his knees, and says, "Where have you been all my life, beautiful princess? Can I have this dance?"

Knowing who he is, she blushes with embarrassment at the scene he has made and the attention he is giving her.

Everyone in the room has stopped to stare at her, waiting to hear her answer; it was as if he had asked her to marry him. In the distant background of her pulsating brain, she hears the music change to a slower pace.

She answers, "Yes, I would love to. Thanks."

The relief is clearly apparent on the young man's face, as I do not think he ever had to wait as long for an answer before. He stands up, swoops her up into his arms, and twirls her around. She giggles, and he carries her to the dance floor, where he sets her on her feet as carefully as he would a porcelain doll. They dance all night long, holding each other close, but without saying a word – so comfortable are they with each other. Their hearts are beating as one right at this moment, and I can see that they would never want to separate.

The gem's light dwindles at this point, and I feel that I have gained enough insight into Bethany's past. I now stand and observe her aura: it is one of purples and some green, colours which further enhance her beauty. The purple has struck a chord, explaining the bookcase: people with purple auras are born to learn about a wide range of subjects, which tends to make them very knowledgeable and interesting. This is not a colour I would expect a model to have, but those with predominantly purple auras can be perceived as mysterious and secretive, which further explains the colour. The presence of green suggests that she prefers to have things thoroughly well thought out before acting upon them, indicating that she is not impulsive and doesn't like surprises much. Oh, this could be a problem — but I won't jump to conclusions just yet. It is now time to move on.

CHAPTER 6

Kath

I arrive in a busy town, with some definite hustle and bustle, but not with the unfriendliness I encountered in the previous city environment. I see people talking to one another other and waving as they drive past people they know. Life here has a slower pace, but seems to offer a more meaningful existence—but, hey, that's just my opinion. So many people work so hard, focusing on "bettering themselves" in order to be able to move on to somewhere else— usually a place that millions of others who already have "bettered themselves" have to moved, as well. Cities of "better" people imagine that this is so. However, I beg to differ. I believe that people "better themselves" from within, not by means of the qualifications they obtain and the jobs they secure.

I finally catch a glimpse of a woman I believe to be Kath. She has just parked her little red sports car in a reserved spot outside a fitness centre. She gets out of the car and walks very fast towards the centre's doors. She has a presence about her, and she looks very fit in her tight black yoga pants and crop top. I didn't expect her to live in such a small town, as her profile states that she often appears on TV and has her own line of fitness DVDs.

I enter the studio, where she stands in front of a group of around sixty men and women (mostly women). Posters of Kath line the walls, and she is talking the group through the steps of her newest DVD, giving them the opportunity to try some of the exercises with her before they commit to investing in her latest workout programme. She explains that this new DVD complements any previously launched DVDs that these people might have purchased.

42

"Hi, everyone! Thanks for coming today," she says. "Well, as you probably know, this is my home town, and I always love it when I get a chance to come back here to catch up with everyone. Unfortunately, I don't get to stay too long, as I just stop over on my promotional tours. This tour is for my newest DVD, which one of you lucky energisers will win today, simply by being here. So what are we waiting for? Let's get started!"

Exuding the motivational energy she began to create when she spoke to the audience, Kath walks over to a stereo bearing her logo, "Energiser", and she puts on some funky music to get a rhythm going.

"All right, energisers, let's get those energy levels heightened. We'll start with a warm-up, and then we'll progress to a higher energy-boosting level; just stay at your own pace, where you feel comfortable."

This goes on for ten minutes, and I have to admit she gets me energised, too — I even tried a few moves whilst observing from the sidelines. To be able to make others feel so good inside can only be a good thing; Kath is a good person for doing this. I can understand now why she has dedicated her life to helping others by introducing them to the world of exercise. I have to admit that, initially, I thought that she was selfish for just wanting to follow her career and accumulate wealth. But, during this short time of observing her, I have changed my opinion. I do believe that, for many years now, she has sacrificed her own selfish desires — which are to settle down and have children — just so that she can keep energising people, because this is what she is good at, and she genuinely wants to help others.

I decide to view her aura, as it will give me a clearer picture of Kath. Her aura is significantly blue, which is a very rare dominant aura colour. Many world leaders, in fact, have blue auras, as individuals with a mainly blue aura are very successful in engaging others. People with blue auras are born leaders who effectively communicate their beliefs, are very well organised, and successfully motivate others. This draws me to look deeper, and I discover a shadow, which indicates that a secret from the past follows Kath. I do wonder why her profile does not contain this information; she must have hidden this secret so deep within herself that she believes she has erased all traces of it from her mind. This I must investigate further.

Her gem starts to glow, right on cue. I gaze deep into the gem, observing that I am still in the same town, albeit some twenty-five years earlier. People are on the streets chatting with one another. Everyone seems to be going in the same direction, so I follow.

We all arrive at a big green field, which seems to be the site of a fair. I notice stalls set up to attract adults and kids alike – with candy floss, hot food, small toys, and such, all to make a quick profit on the one day of the year that the town comes together all in the same place.

The atmosphere is that of a feel-good, community day for the whole family. All sorts of competition games are on the agenda. The men line up to pull tug of war, which is a must to win, as bragging rights will belong to the winning teams and their supporters (wives and children) for a full year. The horn blows to start tug of war, and then the only sound heard is a mighty "heave ho!" Each team of men dig their feet into the muddy ground, pushing their legs as hard as they can in a desperate bid to secure a win for their team. I scan the field, observing other games, including the three-legged race, the egg-and spoon race, and the greasy pole – always a favourite, as each person tries to get to the top of the pole in order to obtain the large amount of cash dangling from the top.

I spot a girl whom I think is Kath. If my calculations are correct, she is around fifteen. I'm surprised to see that she is pleasingly plump, given how fit and slim she is now. Perhaps she has not yet outgrown her baby fat.

She and a handsome young lad are holding hands, giggling whilst they run around the big performance tent. He looks about, making sure that no one sees them hide behind it.

"I hope no one has seen us coming around here, James."

"Don't worry, Kath. I made sure no one saw us."

He goes to kiss her, but she pulls back.

"I thought you liked me, Kath."

"I do, James. It's just…"

"Just what? … Don't tell me that you're gonna get all fidgety on me."

"No. No, James, I promise I won't."

She lets him kiss her, and he puts his hand up her top. He always seems to push the boundaries with her. They do this for a few minutes, lying on the grass together, and then he sits up.

"Are you still up for me coming around to help you babysit your little cousin at your house tonight?" he asks her.

"Yeah, of course… if you still want to, that is."

"What time are your parents going out?"

"I heard them tell Uncle Harry that they would leave at seven, so come any time after that."

"Are you still up for… you know?"

"Erm, eeh…" she stammers.

"Ah, you're just unbelievable, Kath! I might just not bother coming around at all. You obviously don't like me. We've been going out for a whole five weeks now," he says, in a slightly raised but highly irritated tone of voice.

"I'm sorry, James. It's okay… I am just a bit nervous. You promise it won't hurt?"

He pulls her into his arms and hugs her. "I wouldn't hurt you, Kath. You're my beauty queen."

She smiles, feeling treasured in his warm embrace.

The gem moves on at this point. I have arrived at a two-storey country house, with wonderful gardens. The fragrance of wild roses fills the air with a perfume that one could never capture in a bottle, just cherish in memory. The house is at the edge of the town.

Inside the living room stand a man and a woman, both looking rather stressed. The woman is crying, and she sits down whilst the man begins to quickly pace the floor. Kath, wearing her school uniform, sits on a chair. She is crying, too.

"I'm sorry, Dad," she says. "I didn't mean for this to happen."

"Sorry? Did you hear that she said 'sorry'? The stupid girl doesn't know what she has done, does she?"

Her mother doesn't answer.

"You have always been such a good girl, Kath. You pass all of your exams, you study well, and everyone likes you. You could be anything that you want, but you go and throw it all away. I just can't believe it."

"I'm sorry, Dad."

"Who is the father? Who did you let take away your innocence?"

"I can't tell you, Dad. You are too mad."

"You're not going to tell me who it is that has ruined your life? Well, there is only one thing we can do."

At this point, to Kath's obvious relief, her mother speaks up. "We can't make any rash decisions, love. We must think this through."

"There is nothing to think about, love. We are good Catholic people, so we can't get it terminated. She is just going to have to go to the nuns."

46

"No, Jim. We can't send her away!"

"We have no choice, Sue. We cannot let anyone find out about this; our whole reputation that we have built up our whole lives will be destroyed in one instant. We will just tell everyone that she has gone to visit your sister."

"Please, Mum, don't let him send me to the nuns! I will stay in my room. I promise I won't go anywhere. Please don't let him send me away!"

"Do you think that I could live in the same house with you? Just watch as my daughter's tummy swells with a child that has no father? No way, miss! You are just going to have to leave, and that's the end of it! Now go to your room; your mother and I need to speak in private."

Kath goes to her room, where she cries all night and through the following day. It isn't long before the nuns from the local convent come to take her to a hideaway, where she will stay until she has her baby. The nuns will place the baby with a couple who cannot have children.

I am brought forward in time six months to a disturbing sight. A young woman is screaming and crying. She has only just given birth to a baby girl, and a nun is already taking the baby away.

"No! Don't take my baby! Give her back to me. I want to hold my baby."

She tries to get up to run after the nun who has taken her baby, but another nun restrains her. This doesn't take much effort, as is the girl is greatly fatigued after eighteen hard hours of labour.

One of the nuns says, "Hush now, it is for the best. What kind of life would you be able to offer a wee one? Sure, she doesn't even have a dad."
"I will love her!" the girl shouts hysterically.

The nurse gives her an injection, saying softly, "There now, you will feel better in a moment. Just relax."

The girl cries out, "She's my baby!" She breaks down in tears, and then she slowly drifts off into a deep sleep.

I now see Kath in a totally different light. How traumatic her life was at this point and how alone she must have felt! And then to return to her parent's home to act "happy family" again, so that people would just think that she was away at her auntie's for six months, must have made it even worse.
I really feel like I need to observe a positive, happy experience that she has had. Thankfully, the gem starts to glow, giving me the opportunity to do just that.

I seem to still be in the same house, although not in the same period of time. Kath looks a few years older. The atmosphere feels happier. Her mother is calling for Kath excitedly; she has an envelope in her hand, and she is holding it up to the light in a desperate attempt to view the contents.

"Katherine, come quickly! You have a letter from Mc Lloyds University. It must be about your application."

Kath comes running down the stairs. She seems to have lost a lot of the teenage plumpness that she had a few years before. She has been working out upstairs, I gather, noting the towel around her neck and the sweat on her brow.

"Thanks, Mum," she says as she takes the letter and turns to go back upstairs with it.

Her father steps out of the front room, saying,

"You can just bring that in here, young lady. We are a family. We all deserve to hear the outcome of your application."

She just gives him a look as she reluctantly enters the room. I get the impression that they have quite obviously not resolved their issues. I also sense that the reason she does not want to enter this room is that this is where her father made the decision to send her away.

Kath tears open the letter, reading it to herself but saying nothing.

The suspense is all too much for her mother, who finally asks, "Well, what does it say? Did you get the place?"

"Yes, Mum, I have been offered a scholarship, as I had the highest marks of all the applicants."

"Are you sure it is sports science that you want to study? You do know that with your grades you can study anything at all."

"Yes, sports science, it is. I'm sure of it. Exercise is my life, and I am going to help others benefit from it, too."

"It's a waste of a good brain, if you ask me."

"Ah, Jim, leave her. She is happy now," her mother says. "And she is going to university, so you should be happy, too."

"It's just such a pity, is all; she could have studied law or medicine or anything. That's all I'm saying."

Turning to Kath, her mother says, "Well, I am proud of you, love. You have achieved so much, and I hope that it all works out for you."

"Don't worry, Mum, it will work out for me. I will make sure of that. I am finally getting my opportunity to get out of this town, and I am not going to mess it up."

The gem stops there. It is all so much clearer now. I can see why Kath has invested so much of her life in exercise. With her aura, she was destined to be successful—and what a bonus to be successful at something that she is passionate about! I understand why she wanted

49

to move away from this place, as her father never forgave her for the teenage pregnancy. Although she has never expressed it, she will never forgive him for what she had to endure. By deciding to move on, Kath has made a sacrifice: by not taking any time out from her regime, she has not been able to meet anyone to start a family of her own. Maybe she doesn't want to, as she knows that her daughter is out in the world somewhere, and Kath feels empty because she doesn't know her—doesn't even know who she is.

This visit can only help make Kath face up to her unresolved issues and make decisions for her future.

CHAPTER 7

Siobhan

I am back in the city; it is a fast-paced street. People walk past each other as is they have turbo boosters attached to their ankles, leaving them incapable of stopping for a chat. Should any people stop, it would be at their own peril, as others would surely mow them down and trample them on the pavement. It is like a sea of heads, and the survival technique is to go with the flow — or pay the price. This sight of so many people doing the same thing, even though they each are totally individual in character, never ceases to amaze me.

A building draws me. I read its large sign, which has large gold letters: "Maximus Corporation". It is an old limestone building which stands out architecturally from the adjoining glass-paneled skyscrapers that dominate the skyline.

I stand outside for a moment to observe the woman whom I believe to be Siobhan amongst the crowd. Her appearance sets me back at first, and I try to remember what Boss said to me the night before dispatch.

I recall his words: "Remember the profile, Rupert, because what is inside is not the same."

Yes, of course. I know that it's what's inside that counts; I must catch a hold of myself.

Siobhan starts to head towards the door where I have positioned myself, and I repeat Boss's words in my mind: Remember the profile; what is inside is not the same.

A man sits on the pavement in front of the door. He holds a cup which he shakes, looking for some spare cash. She ignores him totally.

"Any spare change, lady?" he asks.

"Go get a job and a life, you sponger. People like you make me sick," she says, with venom in each word.

The man lowers his head and does not reply. Her words were very harsh, and they kicked him right in the pit of his stomach, when he was already feeling quite low. People like Siobhan should take more consideration for others' feelings; not everyone has a heart made of iron. What she said could be detrimental to the mental and emotional stability of this man.

Her immediate reaction towards this man assists me in overcoming my initial setback, and I am able to focus again.

I continue to follow her into the building as she thunders her way through the lobby towards the lift. People in her path stop whatever they are doing to greet her.

"Good morning, Miss Roe!" they each say. I hear it so many times that it reminds me of listening to a harmony.

She just storms past these people without even acknowledging them or their greetings. The guy at the lift door must be new, as he appears very nervous and looks towards the other staff for support.

They attempt to indicate what he should do by signing to him; but, apparently, it is too late.

In the midst of it all, Siobhan starts to speak quite suddenly, and the other staff put their hands over their faces. "Young man, are you not going to greet me? Why do you not have the lift waiting?" she demands. "I want to see your supervisor straight away. This is most inconvenient."

The tongue-tied young man cannot even answer her.

"You must be new; I do not want this to happen in future. Ever. Do you understand?"

The young man nods excessively to indicate his compliance.

Finally, he is able to speak. "Yes, Miss Roe, I understand. It won't happen again, Miss Roe."

"I certainly hope not."

She then enters the lift alone, even though a queue of people still wait in the lobby, all of them needing to get to work on various floors.

As the lift door closes, she says sarcastically, "Where do they get these imbeciles from? Do they just pick them up off the street?"

She arrives at the top floor, bursting out of the lift as soon as the doors open. Once again, all the people stop what they are doing to greet Siobhan as she storms past. A young woman runs to assist her with her bag and coat, which Siobhan practically throws at the girl.

Siobhan's office is on the opposite side of the building from the lift. Her walk across the floor is more like a stampede designed to ensure that everyone is aware of her presence. When she enters her office and closes the door behind her, everyone sighs in relief.

The young woman who took Siobhan's coat and bag follows her into her office. She hangs up Siobhan's coat, sets down her bag, and straightens out her desk.

Meanwhile, Siobhan continues to move about, never ceasing her frenetic pace. She walks back and forth whilst looking out of the massive Georgian-style window.

"That boy at the lift downstairs, Bea. I want him fired," Siobhan tells her assistant.

"But, Miss Roe, this is his first..." says Bea.

"I don't want to see him there tomorrow. Do you understand?"

"Yes, Miss Roe. Will that be all for now?"

"Where is my coffee?"

"It's coming right up, Miss Roe."

Cautiously backing away from Siobhan, Bea opens the door and goes out, closing the door noiselessly behind her.

Siobhan is in a league of her own. I am not at all surprised to see that this woman's aura is a fiery red. People with dominating red auras usually have a lot of stamina and physical energy. They can be spontaneous, and their presence will be dominant, no matter where they are. They easily get bored with others, so they tend to isolate themselves; also, the effort of making friendships is a pointless exercise in their eyes. If something holds their interest, success and wealth can prevail. They also are straightforward people with nothing to hide. I can honestly say that I have never witnessed an aura quite like this one. It is as though the fires of hell blaze around her. Red does not necessarily mean "bad" — in truth, no aura is bad — but when a person like Siobhan uses an inner anger to fuel her character, whilst expressing it so freely as to fail to consider the feelings of other people, it is a recipe for causing them emotional pain.

Siobhan is a well-renowned lawyer, which does not surprise me. This suits her character, as the law appeals to her; each case is different, and so her work holds her interest. Maybe she is bored now that she has made her way to the top of the ladder. I believe that she did enjoy climbing it, although I hate to imagine what terror she must have left in her wake.

Her gem starts to glow, and I look inside reluctantly, as I expect that what I am about to witness will not be pleasant.

I am in the same building, but it is a few years earlier. It looks like Siobhan's office, but it seems to have belonged to someone else at this time — the décor is different, and a framed photograph of a woman and child sits on the desk.

I see a woman who has her back to me. Her red hair cascades down her back in long waves. She and a man are in a very compromising position on his chair. She sits straddled across his lap, flirting very seductively. She stands up, lifting her leg in a way that makes her short skirt ride up her perfectly shaped thigh to reveal a suspender and lace-trimmed stocking.

She whispers, "My panties are crotchless. Would you like to take a look?"

He just sits there, as if in shock, and then he nods. He appears to be a lot older than she.

She sits up on his desk, tucking her foot under his chair and pulling it towards her. She places each foot on an arm of his chair, giving him a full view of her crotch.

Bubbles of sweat start to form on his head, and he mumbles, "Oh, gee... it's beautiful."

To which she replies, "Would you like to kiss it?"

He nods again, and so she pulls his head forward.

She tells him what to do as he sticks his head under her short skirt, and then she takes a quick peek at the clock when he can't see. I find this extremely odd.

Raising his head from under her skirt, he rises off the chair.

"I know this might be unprofessional of me to ask, especially as I am your mentor, but do you think that we could... you know... ?"

55

"Mr Baker, what are you implying?" she replies in a very innocent tone.

He backs down onto the chair and says, "Oh, I'm sorry! I didn't mean to..."

She takes another quick look at the clock and moves around the desk.

Suddenly, she lies back on the desk, opens her legs wide, and says, "Please just take me, Mr Baker! You don't know how long I have waited for this moment."

Wasting no time, he jumps up from his chair, all empowered, and confidently pulls her to the edge of the desk. He enters her, thrusting with all his might.

Just as he is about to climax, the door bursts open, and a woman stands in the doorway. It is the woman in the photo. Horrified, she stands frozen to the spot for a moment before she screams.

Quickly composing himself, he runs over to her.

"How could you? How could you?" she shouts.

"I'm sorry, love. I really am." He begs her to forgive him.

"I got a call to meet you here so that we could go for dinner. Did you want me to find out this way? Do you love this ...?" Looking Siobhan up and down, the woman finishes with, "This girl?"

"No, it only just happened this once. Someone has set me up, love."

Siobhan gets up and walks past them, brazenly saying, "Excuse me," so that they have to move out of her way as she leaves the room, closing the door behind her.

The gem moves on a bit in time. Siobhan is now fully dressed in a respectable suit, a total contrast to the seductive attire that she wore the night she seduced poor Mr Baker. She is in a conference room, the only woman amongst a small group of men in suits gathered around a very large table.

One of the men stands up, saying, "Thank you all for being here. As everyone knows, over the past few months Mr Baker has been suffering a nervous breakdown and will not be able to return to his position in this firm for some time. As the board, it is our job to appoint a new member to our team. I think we all have come to an agreement, Siobhan, that we would like to have you join Maximus Corporations as one of our top lawyers."

Siobhan acts all shocked at this announcement.

He continues, "The work that you have completed during your time with Mr Baker has shown that you are a very capable lawyer, and so we would be honoured if you would accept the position that we have just offered. Obviously, this is a big decision, and you may need to take some time to consider it...."

"No, no, not at all. I would love nothing more than to become a member of the team here at Maximus Corporations, and I would like to thank you all for thinking of me. I know that I could never fill the shoes of Mr Baker, but I promise that I will endeavour to do my best at all times."

The man who has been speaking is the head lawyer; I hear one of the other men call him Bill.

Bill says, "Welcome to Maximus Corporations, Siobhan."
Everyone stands up and claps, and then, one at a time, they all turn to shake her hand.

Has this woman no shame? First she ruins the man's life, and then she takes his job.

I need to look back into her childhood to see where all this vindictiveness stems from. Hopefully, I will find some answers there.

I look deep into the gem, and it brings me to a place that is already familiar to me. I realise it is the same town that Kath is from. It is a small world, indeed. A pub on the main street draws me; I notice the sign: "Roe's Bar". At the door stands a tall man, smoking a cigarette; people are beeping their horns and waving in their cars as they pass by.

A person shouts, "Hey, Roe, see ya tonight!"

He waves and answers, "For sure, Mac, see ya then!"

I enter the bar; the fusty smell—a mixture of alcohol and cigarette smoke that is enough to make anyone barf—assails me. Behind the bar is a woman with red hair just like Siobhan's, but this is many years earlier, so it can't be Siobhan. Perhaps it's her mum. The woman has her back to me, so I can't see her face. She seems to be arranging glasses. I go closer to the bar, and now I can see a little girl helping the woman. The child also has red hair, so I guessed right: it is her mum. I sense that this is Siobhan as a child; she appears to be around six.

She says, Mum, where will I put this one?"

"Let me see, darling. Oh, better not touch that one, pet. That is Daddy's special glass."

The little girl starts to panic, and she accidentally drops the glass as she passes it to her mother. It smashes into pieces on the floor.

I am taken back by this woman; her aura and her appearance are so strikingly like…

Forcing myself not to get lost in my own memories, I focus on the scene.

The man at the door runs towards the bar, enraged.

"What was that? Can you two do nothing without making a commotion?"

"It was just a glass, dear. Nothing to worry about," the woman tells him, winking at her little girl.

"At the rate you two are going, we'll have no glasses left! We are in business to make money, and you're not helping by smashing our profits on the floor around you."

"Calm down, Mike. It's not good for Siobhan to see you so cross."

"Cross, I have good reason to be cross. What is she doing in there, anyway? Come on, out you come! Get back upstairs. Do some reading, colouring, or some such thing."

"But, Daddy, I'm bored."

"You are a child. Go and find yourself something to do; just get out. We are trying to build a future for you here."

The little girl puts her head down and walks slowly out from behind the bar, where her mother is on her knees with a dustpan and brush, frantically trying to erase any evidence of what was actually smashed. She looks relieved as she empties it all into the bin.

"Wait a minute. Get back here, Siobhan!" her father says, suddenly.

Siobhan freezes on the spot, and so does her mum. Each has a look of horror on her face.

"Where is my glass trophy that I won for 'Publican of the year'?"

They don't answer, as fear seems to have taken control of their bodies.

"I mean it, Rosie. Where is it?"

She gulps. "It was just an accident, Mike...."

"I knew it! Everyone upstairs right now! Can I have nothing?

59

Get over here, you stupid girl. What happened? I need to get to the bottom of this."

Her mum quickly runs to lift Siobhan and carries her upstairs. Once there, her mum continues to hold Siobhan, cradling her in her arms to protect her.

"Put her down, Rosie! You can't protect her from the world; you know she has to face up to what she has done. Do you know how much that trophy means to me? You know I worked hard to get it."

"Of course we know, Mike. We helped you, remember?"

"For all you did. Now tell me what happened."

"Well we were… It wasn't her fault."

He grabs Siobhan by the arm and drags her out of the room. She is crying, her small body heaves in convulsions of fear.

"You are going to spend the rest of the day in your room until you learn not to touch things!" he roars. "I knew that I was never supposed have had girls. Give me a cub any day. You will never make anything of yourself, stupid girl."

"Leave her alone, Mike, she has done nothing wrong; I dropped the glass."

Dropping Siobhan on the floor, he storms back towards his wife.

"Well, you can just fix it, you clumsy bitch."

Grabbing her by the arm, he drags her downstairs to where she deposited the glass fragments into a bin liner.

"Mummy, I need you!" cries Siobhan as she creeps back downstairs.

"It's fine, love. Mummy will get you in a moment. Just go up to your room, and I will be with you soon."

"No, you don't! You get over here and see what happens to people who tell lies and then try to cover it up."

He makes her mum take it all out of the bin bag, piece by piece, with the sharp pieces of glass cutting her hands. It is very painful, but she does not let on because she does not want Siobhan to be upset. It has been awful enough to see her little girl watching her. Her mum is humiliated by what her husband has done to her, and Siobhan is horrified by what she has witnessed. Her mother sits all day with a tube of glue, sticking each little piece together, until she has almost the entire glass put back together.

When she finishes, he comes over to her. "Look at the set of that!" he says as he grabs it and smashes it into the bin.

"Now go sort yourself out, woman. We will be opening up soon."

The psychological trauma endured by this child throughout the years has obviously left its scars. She has obviously decided to not be the walkover her mother was. Siobhan loved her mother very much, and she knew that her mother did all in her power to protect her from her father's rages. She always wondered why her mother never left him, but she believes that her mother felt that she couldn't leave him – she feared losing her daughter so much that she endured all the agony for Siobhan's sake. Her father suppressed her mother so much that she became somewhat brainwashed into believing that
she was worthless and had nothing to offer her child. If only she had been confident enough to realise that her daughter only needed love and protection from her. Because of this childhood environment, the adult Siobhan decided to be the controller, not the controlled.

It always fascinates me to see how as the victims of physical or emotional abuse usually go on to become abusers themselves. I reckon it is a defence mechanism. If only they would decide to break the cycle of abuse, they would discover that they are far more powerful and in control by showing love and respect for others than by being abusive. Abusers choose not to control their behaviour, thereby knowingly inflicting pain on others — especially the people they love — and, when this happens, they are not in control and often do things that they later regret. Nevertheless, none of this takes away the abuse.

I see Siobhan in a new light, and I now understand the roots of her vindictiveness; however, I far from condone it. I understand why she has been chosen for a visit, as her head is so far up in her own personal cloud that she needs to be brought back to earth to deal with the emotions that she suppresses.

CHAPTER 8

Rupert

Of all of the initial observations I have carried out to date, the last one has affected me the most. I have realised that I, too, have issues that I have not dealt with. I knew that Siobhan was going to resemble my dearly beloved late wife, which did shock me when I first saw the photo in the file, but it wasn't until I witnessed Siobhan's mother's presence that my heart skipped a beat. Her tenderness and devotion to her daughter brought back a flood of treasured memories; I have to admit that I was not fully prepared to experience this. Her mother's aura was so warm, yet bright and angelic, just like my Josie's. Tears gather in my eyes now, and I feel that I must take time out to gather myself, as this has knocked me off track, big time.

It all brings me back to a beautiful time that we shared together. It is many years ago. Josie and I are on our honeymoon. Nowhere fancy, just the seaside a few towns away from our home town, but that doesn't matter— we don't intend on doing much sightseeing. We want a big family—boys and girls—it really doesn't matter as long as they are healthy. I know exactly the moment that we receive our gem.

We are in our little cheap beach house that we've rented for two full weeks - after looking forward to the trip for months—and we have not left the house for days. It has reached the stage where we may starve to death if we do not get out of bed soon. I can just imagine the headlines: "Honeymooners die of exhaustion and starvation!"

Have you ever been so happy at one moment in time that you never want it to end? Well, that's how Josie and I feel. We are so afraid of not achieving the same level of oneness again after we move that we just

stay wrapped in each other's embrace for days. Eventually, though, we have to give in and get up, lest we make headlines. That night, as we unite again, it is even more special than before. We made love many times before, but this time stands out, as we are completely in sync. Each thrust feels like heaven; we groan together,
and, eventually and reluctantly, we come together — we just don't want it to ever end. At that moment of total oneness, the lights flicker. We both feel the same shivers all over our bodies, and every one of our hairs stands on end in heightened sensation. It is the most magical experience that I have ever felt.

Three weeks later we discovered that we are expecting.

"It happened that night, Roo, I just know it. It was so magical… it had to be when it happened."

"I can't believe how perfect everything is, Josie; I need to pinch myself to check that I'm not dreaming."

"Roo, it is destiny. We are as one, and we will never be apart."

"I would die happy at this moment knowing that I have achieved the maximum point of tranquillity," I tell her.

I lift her up in my arms and swing her around. And then I carry her across the threshold of our two-bedroom cottage, which we fell in love with and were lucky enough to buy. It has roses in the garden that leave a lingering perfume all year long. (Whenever I smell roses, it brings me right back to that time.)

I will always treasure this moment. So much so that I have it tattooed on my brain for everyone to see, as I am proud to have been lucky enough to have intimately shared my life with the woman I will treasure forever. I will never feel that love again, and it wouldn't be fair to get involved with anyone, as I know this beforehand.

It's hard to explain how the effects of the emotional shattering that we experienced a few weeks later turned it all upside down. The roller coaster of life caught up with us; a few weeks before, we were on the highest point of the ride of life, and then we crashed straight to the bottom. Quite simply, for us, the ride just stopped.

We discover that Josie has cancer in her womb; abnormal cells appeared in a smear test that she'd had just before we got married. It's like being shot in the stomach. All we see are doctors and more doctors. They all advise us to terminate the pregnancy, as this is the only way that Josie will have any chance of survival. Of course I know that she will never agree to do that, as she is very in tune with herself and her spirituality. I remember the conversation that we had about it.

"No way, Roo. I cannot kill our baby. Our child has come to us for a reason, during the most magical moment in our lives, and I will never destroy that."

"But then you will not survive the cancer, Josie. You heard what the doctors have said."

"Of course I hear them, Roo. But God has sent us this test for a reason, and we have got to trust him."

"Josie, I can't live without you. If we just do nothing, you and the baby will die. I can't live with that."

"We don't know that for sure, Roo."

She sits upright in her hospital bed, puts her arms around me, and kisses me so tenderly that my heart melts. I know in that moment that I must do as she wishes. As hard as it would be for me to terminate our pregnancy, Josie could never live with knowing that she got rid of what would probably be our only chance to have a child of our own. I know this.

As the next few months progress, Josie's health deteriorates rapidly. It all seems so unfair — we were so happy, and then it was just taken from us in an instant. As she grows weaker physically, I grow weaker mentally and emotionally; but, no matter how much physical pain she

must endure, she never wavers in her spiritual beliefs. She prays a lot during this time—not for herself, but for our baby growing inside her, and also for me, so that I will have the strength to carry on. This I know because I often lie in the armchair at night, letting on that I am asleep so I can listen to her words of strength. I often wonder, How can this woman be so selfless? She is the one who suffers
intense pain, yet she prays only for others. This shows me first-hand her essence, and I understand the wise saying: "Our outer glow comes directly from our inner essence."

My life now consists of going home to sleep, getting up, going to the hospital, and then going home again. This consumes my life; all I live for is to go watch the life drain out of my wife's body. The once-rosy cheeks that flushed with shyness at times are now pale; her long, shiny auburn hair that flowed gently down over her shoulders is now dry and lifeless, tied back from her face to reveal cheekbones in a gaunt face that once was soft and beautiful. The one thing that has not changed is her eyes—they are every bit as green, and the love and warmth that they have always held and projected onto me every time we are together still shines forth.

Each day she gets a little weaker, yet each day she is thankful for still having the strength to hold onto her life—as the longer she can do this, the better chance our baby has of surviving. Her faith becomes stronger, whilst my resentment towards having to endure such intense sadness also grows stronger. Why can I not have it all? My beautiful, healthy wife carrying our beautiful, healthy children—I would give anything to just have this. A lot of men take this for granted, yet I would give anything to be in their shoes instead of mine.

I, too, try to pray: "Dear Lord, please don't take my wife from me. We are as one; if you take her, you may as well take me, for my life has ended also. Please don't leave me on this earth to suffer a life without her, as it will be no life worth living at all."

But no matter how hard I pray, she never seems to get better. Each day she seems to get a little worse. At least she is still here with me, I often think. She does not allow the nurses to give her the full recommended dose of pain relief, as she believes that it will affect our baby growing inside her. Each day, too, the baby grows stronger inside her, slowly draining a little more life from her already-weak body. Yet Josie often looks down and smiles at our little bump. She does not say much, as the pain will not allow her to, but when she smiles down on our child, she doesn't have to talk — I know exactly what she is thinking at these moments, which is that it is all worth it if she can give our child life.

She is a very strong woman, so in touch with herself and her spirituality that she is also strong in her mind. Even though she is pale because of her illness, she still has a glow around her. (Later I will learn that this was her aura.) It is a white glow, visible to one and all. People with white auras are angelic, highly spiritually evolved, and close to God.

Suddenly I hear Josie's voice; she has not been able to speak for a week. "Roo, you know I love you, don't you?"

"Of course I do Josie, and you know how much I love you, too."

"Even as much as you loved me that special night at the beach house?"

"Yes, of course, Josie. I would give anything for us to be back there right now. Those are moments that I will treasure forever."

"Let's pretend that we are there, Roo. Will you hold me?"

I sit up on the bed beside her and hold her in my arms. I start to tell her about the sounds of the waves rushing up the sand towards us as we lie together, listening. I tell her about the birds that swoop constantly into the sea to catch some food for lunch. I describe the smell of the ocean; it's so pure and refreshing that it revitalises our bodies with every deep breath that we take. I tell her how close we are in the unity of us; we are as one, two hearts beating together, never to be apart. She turns to me and smiles. She puts her hand on mine, and, with all the strength she can muster, she drags it towards our little bump. I feel it move and kick, so full of life; I understand in that moment that she feels alive through this child. We just lie together in the peace and tranquility of the moment, and then, suddenly, she leaves me.

Monitors start beeping, and doctors and nurses surround the bed, rushing me out the door in their desperate bid to resuscitate my wife who lies lifeless on the bed. This goes on frantically for a few minutes, and it does not was appear to be successful, as I hear someone shout,

"Notify theatre that we are on our way; we have to get this baby out now!"

It is all just a blur to me; I have known that this would happen someday, but I had not prepared myself for the emotions that it would involve. I do believe that, as a survival technique, my body simply freezes. As a result, I have an out-of-body experience. I watch as a glow leaves Josie's body, realising at that moment that God has called her to leave this world. I understand, as she is so special, he wants her to be with him — I was just so lucky to have had the wonderful time with her that I did.

When I come back to my body, I hear one of the nurses talking to me.

"Rupert, would you like to come this way?" she asks.

I follow, as attendants push the trolley with my wife's resuscitated body to theatre to enable her to release our child into the world. I wait and wait to hear a cry, but it never comes.

At last, the doctor comes out of the theatre and says, "I'm sorry, Rupert, but there were some complications…"

At this point, I just run; I don't want to hear what he is going to say. I run out of the hospital and into the street. I just run and run, not knowing where I am going, just wanting to be with my wife and child, who have just disappeared from my life in an instant. I come to a high bridge, and I just jump. As I fall, I hear screams at first; and then, nothing.

I just cannot go on without them; the pain is too much to bear. Right after I jump, I begin my search for Josie and our child.

I don't reach the gates of heaven, as I am not worthy because of the suicide. Instead, I am introduced to Boss. He explains the rules: I was not granted access to heaven because I took my own life; but I am a good soul inside, and so I have the opportunity to complete my journey to divine spirituality, which will allow me to enter heaven— and I know my wife and child will wait for me there....

And so that is why I do what I do, this is why I am on this journey. I have received the opportunity to earn eternal happiness through helping others start on or progress along their own spiritual journeys of self-discovery, which will enable them to evolve to a spiritual level so that they are closer to God and divine happiness.

I have come to see that the contrasting differences in my life during those vital six months defined my very existence on this planet, and, for that moment in time, it was all too much for me to endure. It was a mixture of my fragile state of mind at that time and the opportunity that presented itself to me, which offered me the chance to end the pain right there and then. One could call it circumstance or fate; I haven't yet decided which it was.

When I reflect now on what I did then, I know that I was not thinking rationally. If I had been, I would never have even thought of taking my own life. If I had of stayed on earth and endured the pain of my losses would I have travelled on a voyage of self-discovery naturally? I don't know, and I suppose I never will know. I also will never know if I would have been more spiritually evolved when my life was naturally ready to end. Would I have gained instant access to eternal happiness? I don't know the answers to any of these questions, and, again, I suppose I never will know. But, hey, at least I have this opportunity, and I am grabbing it with both hands .I did the wrong thing; I played God by taking my own life. I am just lucky to know that the journey I am taking is now focused on the right track, straight back into the loving arms of my Josie and our child.

69

CHAPTER 9

Home Influences

Now that I have had some time to evaluate my initial observations of each assignment I can find a few connections and comparisons between them. What has drawn my attention, in particular, is the influence of the home environment—either the home where each now lives or the home from which each has come from. Each woman seems to have a connection with an old house, and with every old house comes history.

Many people don't realise that when they buy or move into a house that has been previously occupied, they are bringing their energies and the spirits that follow them into that home, which already holds the energies of past occupants. Depending on the history of each individual house, this may never be a problem; however, I find, on most occasions, that it is necessary to spiritually cleanse the inside and outside of the new home to avoid upsetting any previously established karma which may cause problems when introduced to changes. The people in the home may never know of what is happening in the darkness, but the negative energies projected will directly affect them, as this is unavoidable.

I will go back and study the energies of each significant residence in each of the individual cases. I first arrive at Carrie's old cottage home. Outside the aura of the home is quite aggressively red; this is not good at all, as the home should be full of natural colours which blend in with the natural environment in order for the home to remain tranquil in its surroundings. Carrie and Tom both are away.

I enter the cottage, only to discover the same aggressively red tone inside. The negative energies meet me at the door, almost pushing me away. Whatever inhabits this home does not want company.

"Who is here?" I ask.

There is no answer, which confirms my suspicion that the energies are not welcoming. A fiery-red glow is all that I see. For this couple, it is like living in the belly of a beast; as long as they reside here whilst not spiritually cleansing the house, they are only going to attract an abundance of negative things, because this house is negative to the core. They will never have any good luck living here. They must move on as soon as possible, or conduct a very intense cleansing, which may or may not work in this instance.

It does however assist me in obtaining a clearer picture as to how things have gone so wrong for this couple ever since they moved there. I remember back to what I first observed and then what the gem revealed to me: early on, they were so in tune with each other, their two hearts beating the same one beat, but now they are completely the opposite, where he will say anything to hurt her, and she is numb to feelings and expression—and it is all because the two years that they have lived here have taken a toll on them, as the run of bad luck has continued without end.

If only they could see it themselves; listen to their subconscious minds or just simply know when enough is enough, instead of enduring the suffering. They need to take control of the situation themselves and move on—or maybe that is exactly what they have done, and it is why they hope to move to the other side of the world. It is just a waiting game for them now. A lot will change for them when they move. The energy in their house doesn't like them, but why?

I move on to Tracy. She lives in a terrace town house facing a cul-de-sac of older town houses. Upon looking at the energies projected from the house, I notice that, out of all twelve houses in that terrace block, Tracy's house stands out because of the gloomy dull colour that it gives off. It even intrudes itself on the neighbouring properties, therefore affecting the positive flow of energy that should otherwise flow. With this type of energy colour, people often discover illness on their doorstep. Sadness and loss will also be quite prominent in the history of such homes.

I enter the house; this I do in a different way than when I am completing an observation of a person. I scan the home inside and detect the same energies that I saw exuding the dull colour from outside. These energies bolt around the house, hitting walls, doors, ceilings and windows. If a window is open and one of the bolts escapes, the target it hits will have misfortune. For example, if a bolt hits a car, it may break down; if it hits a person, he or she may become ill. I can only imagine what effect this has had, and continues to have, on this family, each and every day. The family, however, will be more immune to the energies' detrimental effects. These energies will also affect visitors to the house.

"Hello! Is anyone there?" I call.

"Yes, me," says a dreary voice.

I follow the sound of the voice, and I see the spirit of a man sitting on the bottom step. His expression is forlorn, and he holds his face in his hands.

"Why have you not moved on?" I enquire.

"Do you really want to know?"

"Yes, please, tell me. Do you know why I am here?"

"No, not really, but I am sure that you have been sent to deliver something bad; I have seen it all over the years."

"I have come to give Tracy an opportunity to change things."

"Well, we'll see." he replies.

"You were going to tell me why you are still here," I remind him.

"When we first moved here, we were so excited to have secured a home for ourselves. But since we moved in we have had nothing but bad luck. I got sick and died, leaving my wife to take care of four wee ones all on her own.

"Are there any other spirits here?"

"Not that I have ever met, but when I first became a spirit, I saw that there was a reddish haze inside the house that I had never seen before — that is, I had not seen it when I was alive. It has now turned quite grey and dull."

"Do you not feel that grey is better than red?"

"Oh, yes! That's why I am still here, you see, to make sure that my family is okay."

"The red haze was a composite of leftover energies from previous tenants. When you and your family moved in, these energies clashed with the peaceful harmony of your energies. As you were the main protector of the family, you must have absorbed all of that energy flow, which resulted in your early departure from life. There is no more of that energy present now, only the dull grey energy that you project, but this causes sadness and misfortune for your family, although not as aggressively as the red did."

"I didn't realise that at all. But my wife won't be here for long, so I may as well wait for her."

"The waiting room at the gates of heaven will present itself to you; if you move on, you can wait for your wife there."

"I didn't know that," he says, brightening. "That sounds fine; see you, then."

In a flash, he disappears, taking with him the grey dull energy that he unknowingly released and infected so many with. It has already begun to look brighter around here, and I catch a glimpse of yellow energy glowing inside. The people in this house will notice a dramatic change in their luck, for the better. This is an example of the instant, dramatic effects that result from having your home spiritually cleansed. I now know that I would go through a cleansing if I had it to do over again, but not a lot of people know about these types of cleansings, even though they surely must feel the negative energies draining them and making them ill.

I feel myself subconsciously called back to Carrie's house. The energies projected are the same, but when I enter the cottage, they are toned down slightly. A spirit of an old man reveals itself to me.

"I'm sorry about before, but you can't imagine what I have had to witness here since they all moved in! You know, they're not even married and they are living together; 'living in sin' is what we called that in my day."

"Is that why you decided not to move on?"

"I have lived here all my life — and my entire afterlife up to now — and very happily, I might add. That is, until these intruding sinners came along and destroyed everything. Do you think that it is easy for me to watch this? Well, let me tell you, it's not. This is my family home; I grew up here, and then when I got married, I raised my family here. It all seems so dirty since they moved in. This is my home."

"But to cause them such deep traumas and sadness; do they deserve that?"

"I have to get them out! You don't understand."

"If I promise that things will change to be more in line with your standards, will you agree to tone down your aggressive energies and consider moving on?"

"I will never move on, as I belong here for eternity, but I may consider easing my anger."

"Well, that's all I can ask, then. I must go now."

I leave him to it, for he is a prime example of a spirit that refuses to move on. Such spirits devote themselves to a property, and guarding it means more to them than moving on to eternity. I have tried to encourage him to move on, but he refuses, so this cottage will need a strong spiritual cleansing, which can only be conducted by a messenger of God.

However, I am pleased with the groundbreaking progress that I have made here, and now I must move on to Bethany's apartment.

It may look new and it may be filled with the most contemporary accessories, but the building is drenched in history. It is always harder to see a true energy ray when dealing with a multi-occupant building, as each apartment or flat will have its own history. It is worth remembering that your neighbour's energy can have a positive or negative knock-on effect on your own residence.

Bethany's apartment is on a corner block, and she is on the top floor, so at least she does not have to worry about the energies from above or to the right of her apartment. However, seven apartments are below hers, and, as the energies always rise upwards, her apartment may be at risk of being invaded by other negative energies.

From outside I look up towards the sky, using my peripheral vision to absorb the energies projected from number eight apartment. The energy ray is like a rainbow; I see so many colours, some more significant than others. This is a concern, and so I must enter her apartment in order to see what is going to greet me. I arrive at the door, surprised to find that all seems calm. I enter, but inside it is no different: all is tranquil, with no sign of the chaotic, multi-coloured aura that I witnessed outside. Maybe I am losing my powers of reading energies; I must get my peripheral vision checked again.

On further inspection, I notice that lavender seems to be used as the number-one fragrance in the home. This is a relaxing scent which can also be used in the process of keeping a home spiritually cleansed. I see crystals hanging in different areas of the apartment, and these deflect negative energies.

I decide to check out the broom cupboard, just to be sure. When I open it, I see that what I suspected is true. There is a sea-salt floor wash present, along with a traditional broom. The sea-salt floor wash is used to mark the floor area as the domain of the practitioner. The broom is used to sweep all the spiritual dust and dirt from the home by brushing from the back of the home to the front door. Bethany is obviously in the know about how to keep her home spiritually cleansed, as it is a miracle that it has not been overrun with negative energies from the evidence that I witnessed from outside. I know that I have no concerns about a negative living environment with her. I have to admit, though, that I am curious as to why she is so conscious of this process. Have negative energies affected her before? I feel that I need to visit her past residence, as indicators lead me to suspect a concern.

With this in mind, I now decide to use Bethany's gem to check out the energies that surrounded her as a child. Her childhood home draws me once again. I believe that I have discovered the link between these five women. I am beginning to understanding that the energies that each one of them has been exposed to, or still is exposed to, within these residences in the past or the present has had, or is still having, an impact on the energies that have surrounded them up to this point in their lives.

As I approach Bethany's family home, the energies surrounding the grand house look familiar to me. As I recall, they are the same colours that surrounded Bethany's apartment block in the city. All the colours of the rainbow beam from the walls, indicating a confusion of energies. A cocktail of colours has built up over the hundreds of years that this stately home has been standing. As each new family took residence, the new energies joined the uncleansed energies that were there before. It is a cycle that would be great if all energies projected were positive, but it seems to be the negative ones that like to hang about the longest and, they have the biggest knock-on effect for the new inhabitants.

As I enter, I see a woman in a maid's uniform polishing a long wooden banister; I smell a woody, fresh scent that I remember distinctly from my past. I look into her cleaning bucket, but I do not see lavender or sea-salt wash, and she doesn't use a broom, so I conclude that she is not doing a spiritual cleansing.

The energies in this house are confusing for me, as I do believe that different energies flow in each of the rooms. I hear a lot voices echoing through the corridors, although nobody is visible; I feel that numerous spirits call this place home, but they don't want to make themselves known to me, as they must sense that I am a messenger of some sort. I do see their energies everywhere; by using my peripheral vision, I can see many glowing and gravitating orbs, which float freely all around.

I go to Bethany's room, which in the middle of the house, indicating that all of it affects her. As I watch her sitting on her bed reading a book, I realise that she has sat upright quite quickly. I do believe that she has sensed my presence. Her head moves as though she is scanning from one end of the room to the other. I am shocked to realise that she is using her peripheral vision to see me. I quickly depart the room.

Bethany is very connected spiritually both to her own being and that of everything in her environment, so the energies around her will have had more of an impact on her than the average person, as she can see them herself. I never cease to be amazed by this young lady; not only is she very intelligent and knowledgeable, she is also so in tune with herself and so aware of the spiritual energies surrounding her. She must have been so scared here when she was a child, as, with her senses, she would have heard and seen all that I have, and on a constant basis. I can only imagine how it would have been for her, especially at night. (I have always believed that everything seems so much worse in the night-time.) Her mother's main focus was on enhancing her daughter's modelling career, her father worked most of the time, and she never had any siblings—she would probably not have shared her fears with anyone. Such a lonely isolated childhood she had. I decide to move on now, as I feel that I have witnessed enough.

Kath's childhood residence now draws me. I know that it was an old two-storey homestead on the edge of a small town, so I am sure some unresolved energies still reside there.

As I evaluate from outside, I do not initially perceive anything of concern. The house has character and charm, standing tall amongst the still taller trees that surround it. These trees obviously protect the home and provide its source of oxygen.

I decide to enter anyway, because once I start an energy evaluation, I like to follow through so that all of the boxes are ticked. As I enter, the first thing to happen catches me totally off guard, and I leap about 10 feet in the air. A big fat hairy cat makes a leap for me, meowing wildly whilst it sails through the air. It could be mistaken for a young tiger, with its stripy fur and aggressive nature, but it is a well-known fact that cats are very sensitive to spiritual presences; in fact, they are the natural alternative to spiritual cleansings.

I am about to leave when I hear a timid voice call, "Hello, deary, can I help you?"

I turn around to see a little old grey-haired woman sitting in a rocking chair in a corner. The cat now sits beside her, purring as she gently strokes it.

"Oh, hello! My name is Rupert. I am a visitor, and I was just hoping to check the energies in this house."

"Oh, I see. Why would that be, dear?"

"I am hoping to help Kath find direction in her life, and I wanted to check out her childhood energy influences to see if they have a link to some issues that she has had."

"Well, I am Kath's gran, and I look after her just fine, deary."

"I am glad to hear that, Mrs…"

"Mrs Young. And, as you can see, Felix here helps me out in keeping the bad energies away."

"I see that, yes, and what a great job he does, too. I am sorry to have intruded."

"Nice to see a friendly face, dear. Are you sure that you won't stay for a cup of tea?"

"Thank you for the offer, Mrs Young, but I think that I will be on my way."

So Kath has also had an influence with the spirits when she was young, albeit a very positive guardian spirit. I can't see too much getting past her gran and Felix. Kath had a traumatic experience, though, when her father forced her to go to the convent, and her gran wouldn't have been able to protect her there. Given its history, I would expect to encounter numerous conflicting energies there.

I discover that I am at the building where Siobhan works. This must mean that she doesn't spend much time, if any, at home. As it is an old and public building, I expect that I will not see any specific colours to determine the energy influences which are being potentially absorbed. I channel in my auric sight and discover that the building has two significant colours projecting from it; each colour projects from different sides of the building, as if it were divided in two. One half is yellow, which is bright and fun, confident and positive; the other half is a reddish-orange, which signifies that the focus there is channelled on success and the desire to have the power to control others. Somehow I do believe that this is Siobhan's side of I go in and up to the top floor, where I enter the room that I believe is her office. Yep, it's her office, for sure — the energy flow is strong, whooshing past me as I open the door, flowing out into the corridor like a river that has burst its banks to affect the day of everyone it encounters. This room has been residence to many a power-hungry control freak throughout its history. She works

79

long hours, spending most of her time in this room when she is not in court, and so it all has relevance, as it affects her aura.

I also want to quickly evaluate the energies that she grew up with in the pub. I have my suspicions as to what they are, but I want to check before it is time for release, and that is coming very quickly, indeed.

Standing outside, I can see that the energies are really negative — greys, browns and some reds. A pub is often thought of as a hub for fun and communication, but, actually, in this instance, it is a cauldron of depression and negativity which can be detrimental to those residing and visiting; add alcohol to the mix, and it can be a recipe for disaster. I believe there have been many such disasters here. This would be a very dark place for a child to grow up in; I would compare it to living in a deep dark dungeon.

It is obvious that the meanness within Siobhan stems from here. The controlling and power-seeking negative thoughts — which are the only kind of thoughts that she knows – will only attract other negative things into her life. She leaves a trail of destruction behind her, as she lives her life as if she were a tornado, destroying everything in her path.

It has been interesting to discover how the current and past energies have influenced each of their characters. I feel that I have witnessed enough to allow the gems to be released.

CHAPTER 10

Releasing the Gems

If only they knew how close each of their gems has been to the other and how much they have discovered. This is the part of my job that I love; this is a magical moment that I never get tired of viewing — it's kind of like the way you can watch a really great movie a hundred times and never get sick of it. Well, that's just my opinion; not everyone will feel the same.

Back to the gems. I never know which one will release first, as I do not have the insight into when any of the women will undertake the dutiful deed, but the gems will enlighten me when it is time.

SIOBHAN

I immediately see one of the gems glowing, so I know it is time. I check to see whose gem it is and discover that it is Siobhan who is ready to receive. I am back at her office — my goodness, does she do everything here? I have yet not experienced her home, but I suppose that these high-flyers think of work as home.

I can see her. She has let her hair down and has a few extra buttons opened on her shirt to reveal her bosom. A dashing young man in his early twenties is with her. He is tall, with a lean frame, black hair and blue eyes. They are very close, indeed. She has a very seductive look in her eye, and he is a very keen and willing participant.

"Check the door, Will; we don't want to get nearly caught again."

He runs to lock the door whilst she clears her desk with one swoop of her arm. (This desk has been a prop for a lot of action over the years, it seems.) Rushing back, he pulls her into an embrace and holds her tight.

"Oh, Siobhan, you are so hot! Can't I just take you now?"

"No, you cheeky devil! You will have to earn your reward. I wouldn't be much of a mentor if I were to let you away with doing no groundwork, now would I?"

He gets stuck right in her bosom by burying his head in between her breasts. Using his teeth, he proceeds to open the few buttons on her shirt that are still closed.

She pushes him away. "Do your act, Will. Entertain me."

He quickly obliges, backing off into the middle of the floor and humming a tune that resembles a striptease song. He sways to and fro, smiling at her.

From her compromising position on the desk, she giggles; it is good to see her laugh. And then she shouts, "Get them off!"

"My pleasure, madam" he answers, quickly shedding his suit with disregard on the floor. Moving closer, he stands in front of her, wearing nothing but his bright smile.

"Come on, you eejit—take me!"

He quickly positions himself, and I get ready.

I hold out the gem in the palm of my hand ;it glows with such intensity. The lights start to flicker with the power of the energy that the gem contains. It lifts up off my palm and hovers in mid-air. In the next instant it zooms across the room, with a light so brilliant that it hurts my eyes. The gem meets its target as it enters Siobhan's body with a jolt. She sits upright.

"What the hell was that?" she says accusingly.

"I didn't do anything wrong!" he says defensively.

"Well, just don't do that again Will. It wasn't funny."

She has obviously felt the intensity. The gem is now at work.

BETHANY

On we move as another gem starts to glow. It is Bethany's, and I find myself at a little café on her street. She is sitting with Hanson, and they gaze deeply into each other's eyes.

"Beth, you know that I love you, right?

"I love you, too, Hanson...."

"No, please, let me finish....We are always under a lot of pressure with the media and all sorts of things, and it is hard living our lives in the spotlight.... But, darling, I don't think that I would ever be able to live my life without you, and I was wondering if..."

"What, Hanson? Please say it."

"I was wondering if you will come to Paris next week with me whilst I film Born Leader."

Bethany seems a little disappointed, as I think that she expected him to ask something which would require a little more commitment than hopping on a plane to Paris.

"Yes, of course I will go to Paris with you, Hanson. It is also hard for me to be away from you."

"How fantastic, Beth! You fill me with so much joy.... I do love that top that you are wearing this morning. Is it new?" He beams a smile and winks at her. "I have to admit it would look better on our bedroom floor....What do you say? When do you have to be at the studio?"

"Not for an hour... but I thought that you had to..."

He grabs her by the hand, and she hurries to her feet. They walk from the café to their building, still holding hands, and he eagerly pulls her up the stairs to their apartment. Actually, they both are quite eager; it is as though this is their first embrace.

It doesn't take long for the gem to lift off my palm and enter her body. They are so close that he feels the intensity also.

Holding her tight, he says, "Oh, Beth! Did I hurt you? Are you okay?"

"No, you didn't hurt me. I just felt something strange, like a fuzzy glowing feeling entering me; it's hard to explain."

"I felt it, too," he says. "I still feel a bit strange. Maybe we should lie here for a while to recover...we obviously are not well enough to move yet, darling."

And it is as if their fast-paced world has just stopped rushing around them. Without a care in the world, they lie together in each other's arms. His love and passion for her fill him, and this warms her heart and soul. She feels so lucky to have met him because she knows that he loves her for who she is inside, not just what she looks like on the cover of a magazine — in fact, if he had his way, she wouldn't need to model, as he would far prefer to take care of her. This gem is in a good place.

TRACY

The next gem also takes no time in glowing, and I am happy to see it is Tracy's. I arrive at a hotel. Tracy and Rob sit at a table, about to have a meal.

"Five years married. Can you believe it has gone in so fast?"

"I know, Tracy. We surely have had our ups and downs since then."

"Yeah, but do you remember the shock of it all when we told our ones what we had done?"

"It was priceless, but at least we have the intimate memories of our wedding that we always wanted."

"You're right, Rob. Now why don't we focus on tonight and making a few more memories for us to chat about next year?"

"I'm up for that! Do you want another vodka and tonic?"

"Ah, go on, then — it's only once a year."

They indulge in a few more drinks and have their dinner.

"Why don't we just go home, love? I would rather be at home snuggled on the couch with you than stay here much longer. I don't want you to be too drunk for memory making."

"Yeah, come on, Tracy. Let's get the bill and go."

On their way out, they bump into some old friends who persuade them to stay for one more drink, which of course leads to another, and so on. An hour and a half later, Tracy stands up, a bit unsteady, and convinces Rob to follow her, as she promises to buy him a portion of curry chips and a battered sausage in the café. He follows her out the door, and they hold each other up as they walk down the street, singing quite loudly and out of tune.

Some of the people who live on the street poke out of their windows, shouting, "Would you two keep your mouths shut? There are some decent people trying to get some sleep!"

They both just giggle, and, with a white-paper parcel of fish and chips to share instead of curry and battered sausages, they quietly make their way home, knowing that they will be the talk of mass if they upset many more people.

They arrive home and can't seem to get the key into the door; it is like a comedy act, as they are under the impression that the keyhole is moving, not their hands. Eventually, they make it inside, finish the fish and chips, and go upstairs to bed. (Gee, this has been the longest wait I have ever had to release a gem, and I may be missing an opportunity to release others, given the length of time these two have taken.!)

Finally, they are in bed, and the deed is done and over in a few short minutes. They do not experience the intensity to the same extent as the others, probably because they are numb as a result of their intoxicated state. In the morning, they may not even remember that the event took place — but they will know soon enough.

The gem is in place and ready to help bring more hope to their lives.

KATH

Kath's gem is the next one to start glowing. The setting where I arrive is strange, to say the least — not at all what I was expecting, but there you have a prime example of how expectations are sometimes presumptuous, and so they can be shattered in an instant.

We seem to be in a ballroom; a disco ball in the centre of the room reflects sparkles of light all around. About fifty people, all of whom seem to be in their late thirties or early forties, stand around talking to one another; most hold glasses of punch in their hands. I overhear a conversation.

"Oh, Frank, how you have changed! And to think that I gave you up to date James, but, thankfully, that was before he did the dirty deed with you-know-who. Did you hear that she is a celebrity fitness instructor? Apparently, she replied to the reunion committee and said that she will be attending. I think it's terrible that she never has had kids. She must be..."

"Can I stop you there, Francine? I think I see Carol calling me. Nice to see that you have not changed one bit in all of these years. Take care now."

"Oh, okay. Righto. I might see you again later," she says as she slurps a big mouthful of punch which catches her breath, and she starts spluttering.

Frank smiles a big fake smile. Under his breath he says, "Not if I can help it, you won't."

I then see a big scuffle of people make their way towards the door, and I quickly realise that they are approaching Kath; even Francine is making her way there.

I catch a glimpse of Kath, who stands out from the crowd. She has a special glow that simply outshines everyone else's. This is what we mean when we say that someone just "lights up the room".

Kath makes sure that she chats and is friendly with each and every person, leaving each one of them feeling fulfilled, connected to her, and at ease in her company. She spots James at the bar; he is on his own and looks over in her direction, giving her a cautious smile.

Currently she stands listening to Francine waffle on about how much she loves Kath's new exercise DVD.

"I lost six pounds in just one week! You know, Kath, I wouldn't have believed it possible for it to happen so easily, as you know I have four children now....Oh, I hope that I didn't make you uncomfortable talking about kids.... But, as I said, I just told my friend Margaret about how good the DVD is, and she is going to buy it, too.... So I am conjuring up some sales for you; maybe it would be a good idea if I did an ad for you...."

"Maybe we could chat about this again, Francine; it has been great chatting after all these years, but I must just go over..." Kath quickly makes her exit before Francine realises what she is doing.

Karen Weaver

Kath makes her way over to the bar to where James is standing.

Leaning up against the bar and drinking a pint, he remains unaware that she has appeared beside him until she suddenly speaks, asking, "Would you like a drink?"

"Gee, Kath, don't do that! You made me jump just then..."

"Sorry, James. Well, how have you been?"

"Ah, you know, same old: got married, got divorced, usual malarkey these days. You've been doing well for yourself, from what I hear."

"Yeah, not bad. Life has been good to me since..."

"Oh, so you left me here to pay the price, then!" he replies sarcastically.

"Don't be like that, James. You know it would never have worked between us—especially after all that happened—my dad just wouldn't have allowed it. I couldn't let him know it was you; he would have killed you, you know that."

"Yeah, I guess, but it has not been easy, I can tell you. Now did you ask if I wanted a drink?"

"Is it the same again?"

"Why not?"

"Excuse me, barman, can I have a pint of lager, a vodka tonic, and two shots of tequila?"

"For old times' sake?" James asks, curious.

"For old times' sake," Kath replies, and they both knock them back, trying to catch their breath afterwards.

At this point, most of the room is focused on them.

They happily chat for the rest of the evening, so relaxed in each other's company.

"You know, I wasn't going to come here this evening, Kath."

"No, neither was I, James. But I was curious as to how things turned out for you."'

"Yeah, well, I was kind of hoping that you would be here, too. It's nice to see that we still get on so well. I don't know if you feel the sparks trying to ignite, but I do… or maybe it is just the tequila!"

"Oh, James, you crack me up sometimes…." she replies merrily.

He grins.

"Listen, James, I have had enough of this place and of my every move being watched. Do you fancy walking me back to my hotel? If you like, you could come in for a drink… I have a minibar," she adds meaningfully.

"Love to. I'll just get our coats. Shall I?"

"That would be great…. You go on; I will catch up with you."

As she walks past Francine, Kath overhears her say to one of the other women, very judgementally, "Well, she hasn't wasted any time getting reacquainted. Has she?"

At this point, Kath has had enough, and she approaches the woman. "Francine, about your offer to appear in one of my TV commercials. I must let you know that until you add another twenty pounds to the six pounds that you say you have already lost… well, I couldn't even consider it, as we have levels of fitness standards to maintain…. I do hope that you enjoy the rest of the evening as much as I am going to enjoy the rest of mine." And then she walks away confidently, satisfied that she didn't do what she had always done before, which was walk away, say nothing, and let others talk about her.

Francine is left with her mouth wide open, unable to speak. "I bet that's the first time she has been speechless since birth," says another one of the guests.

As Kath and James arrive at the hotel, things progress very quickly. Obviously, a lot of passion still exists between these two; it has been suppressed for so long, and is about to be released in one big expression. It starts in the lift. It is just the two of them, and as they look at each other, they cannot contain it any longer. The school-kid emotions come flooding out, and they passionately kiss, leaning up against the wall. (What is it about lifts that arouse people? I have often wondered about this. It must be the confinement of them.) They quickly have to straighten themselves up when they hear, ping! The doors shoot open, and an elderly gentleman gets in, looking at them strangely, as though he has sensed the atmosphere.

They finally reach her room door, and she struggles with the key in the lock.

"Give it 'ere," James says, taking control of the situation before he explodes with anticipation.

He gets the door open, and they rush in, take of their clothes, and embrace immediately. I get the gem out just in time for its release.

They feel its intensity straight away, and its magical bonding powers keep them in each other's arms all night; holding each other tight, they just do not want it to end. I, too, remember that feeling.

Their lives are now going to change.

CARRIE

I have to admit that I am surprised that my last gem to release is Carrie's. I did expect hers to be one of the first to release, as she lives with her partner; I expected that they would have "regular practice", so to speak. Nevertheless, as I have not been summoned yet, I will have to go investigate.

The little cottage is in darkness, and so I enter, only to discover that the sleeping arrangements are not as they should be. She is sleeping on a makeshift bed in the living room with their son, and he lies alone in a big bed, unable to sleep—probably wondering how it all came to this, I'll bet.

Their relationship has deteriorated more than I had anticipated, so I must intervene. I have a small crystal, which, when released ensures that those in receipt fall in love for a time. This happens by means of the crystal's energy, which instils only positive thoughts and memories in the recipients; this should ensure that they end up in a loving embrace. I usually would not take this action; but, this is an extreme circumstance. I feel that, because so much negativity and depression surrounds this couple, they need some special assistance. I sense that if only the negative energy would vanish—or be eliminated—Carrie and Tom would be happy with each other again.

I release the crystal, leaving it to work its wonders....

The next day I am delighted to see that the final gem—Carrie's— has started to glow.

I begin anew. The scent of fresh flowers meets me at the door of the cottage when I arrive. Carrie and Tom are sitting in the living room. The atmosphere is calm and loving. A fire blazes, enhancing the warm mood. They are having a drink; she has a bottle of rosé wine, and he has some cans of lager. The television is switched off for a change, and they are talking—laughing and joking together, as natural as can be, talking about things that they used to get up to and the risks they took.

"Do you remember the time that we went to that Shania Twain concert?"

"Yeah, you wore those leather pants, and all the girls were looking at you."

"We never did make it to the concert, did we? We were having so much fun in that pub! I cannot for the life of me remember the name of it, can you?"

"We did get to the concert, Carrie. Sure, didn't I buy a Pink T-shirt?"

"Are you sure, Tom? A Pink T-shirt at a Shania Twain concert?"

"Sure, I'm sure; I wore it to the Pink concert that we went to after that."

"Oh, yeah, that's right, you did. I don't remember much about the whole day, but I do remember leaving with all the crowds."

"Yeah, and then we couldn't find the car, and with us supposed to sleep in it that night..."

"We went around in circles, and you were so peed off because I was so slow and giggling because I thought that it was funny."

"You were so slow because the heel had come off your boot, and you were trying to walk like you had an invisible heel."

"I loved those boots, too; but they made such a noise when I walked because I needed new caps."

"You don't have to tell me! Everyone could hear you coming a mile off. I was glad when the heel finally came off."

"You should have said something if I embarrassed you."

"Would it have made a difference if I had?"

"Nah, you're right... probably not. Do you remember that there were a lot of people sleeping in their cars in that field that night? Sure, weren't we invited to join in a game of football at half two in the morning?"

"Yeah, those were the days, weren't they... ?"

"Mmm."

They both seem to be thinking back, and then, in no time, they are in a passionate embrace on the floor in front of the warm glow of the blazing open fire.

I prepare the gem for release. I hold out my hand; it glows brightly, lifts off my hand, and zooms like lightning towards them.

"Wow! That was like dynamite, Tom."

"You're too kind. Did I ever tell you just how beautiful you are?"

"Not recently, no."

"Well, I am sorry, hon. I won't leave it as long the next time."

She smiles.

He kisses her tenderly and says, "Now let's have another drink and do it again."

As I leave, they are in each other's arms, reminiscing. I know that I made the right decision to intervene, as I could tell that they still "had it," they just needed help finding it again. I believe that they have made the first step to recovery; it will all turn out beautifully for them.

I have now released all the gems. I do feel quite lonely without them, as they have been with me for a while, assisting me with my observations. Now I must go it alone.

Karen Weaver

I wonder now, as I often have in the past: do the women feel it? Do they feel connected to something — to some power — in some way? Do they feel that something special has taken place? It always seems to me that they do, but I wonder if I am sensing it because I know what will happen. Perhaps this will always be a mystery....

CHAPTER 11

Discovery

My messaging connector starts to vibrate, which is very strange, as I usually am the first to initiate contact. I check the connector to read the message:

"Roo, problem with gems — do not release! Syd."

This has never happened before; the problem must be severe, indeed! I message back immediately:

"Syd, release complete; what is problem? Roo."

I cannot even imagine what has happened — maybe one or some of the gems were not ready, or maybe some change of plan as to who would receive the gems occurred. I could speculate all day, but that would be to no purpose. It would just be like me to run around in circles trying to catch my tail. I tell myself to just wait for Syd's reply.

Finally, I receive Syd's reply:

"One gem was gift. Jayden swap. C u soon at Vortex."

I am shocked. I knew that something was amiss at dispatch — Jayden was being unusually helpful and seemed stressed for no apparent reason, but to go to the extent of messing with the gems so that I would get into trouble and lose my job because of negligence… that is just too much. He has stooped to a lower level than I ever imagined that he would. Syd was right to warn me to be cautious about him; it must have been her woman's intuition. I should never have dismissed her concerns so quickly. Oh, boy... this is a potential disaster! This could have quite a negative effect on the recipients, as well as the gift that they receive, as the gift was neither given nor received as intended.

I message Syd back to let her know that I am on my way:

"C u soon."

I immediately make my way to the Vortex, and Syd arrives at the same time.

We both go through the Vortex.

"Roo, am I glad to see you!" Syd says. "You wouldn't believe what has been going on since you dispatched."

"It all sounds as though it has been somewhat crazy."

"You could say that."

"Come on, Syd, fill me in! There are so many things swimming around in my head, and I don't know what could possibly have happened."

"Well, remember I told you to be careful about Jayden..."

"Yes, yes—don't rub it in!"

"Well, I just have to say 'I told you so'. Sorry, Roo, but I had to get that out of the way first."

"Syd, please..."

"Oh, okay. Well, when you messaged me from dispatch, I smelt a rat; it just didn't seem right, and so I got in contact with Jonnie to see what he thought. He thought the same way I did, and so we put on our detective hats and started to investigate, it was a bit impossible at the beginning, as Jayden never seems to leave his spot! Finally, Mother Nature called; he went for a toilet break, which gave Jonnie and me time to check the gems and gifts. We found one extra gem glowing, as if in desperation of being left behind, and so we knew to expect that one of the gifts missing...."

"The son of a bitch! He has stooped to the lowest level of all! These poor innocent gems and gifts are too precious for him to use as weapons in his game."

Syd continues, "Right, Roo, the consequences are too high; heads will roll when Boss finds out; he'll go crazy. So Jonnie and I decided to check the dispatch records. Sure enough, there was your signature on a dispatch release form for four gems and one gift to be released. You can imagine what a story Jayden had concocted to cover his ass."

"This is going to end in disaster, Syd—I can just feel it. If only I had of known about all this before I released them."

"I know, Roo. It would all be so much easier, but there is nothing we can do about that now. We had just better focus on limiting the damage."

"You're right, Syd. Thanks for going to such lengths to help me; this could just ruin any chances that I have of making it into heaven, and then I would never see Josie again.... I just couldn't deal with that."

"I know, Roo," Syd says softly. "And that Jayden is just thinking of his own selfish desires, not even considering the consequences that his actions could have on others. So many people can, and will, be affected by this one problem!"

"Well, there is not much we can do until we discover whose gem doesn't return."

"I know. That is why I brought us some heavenly delights to keep us going in the meantime."

"Syd, you are so perfect! You know, if ever I was in need of a heavenly delight, it is now, for sure."

We sit on the top of a high hill covered in the greenest grass. In silence, we devour two delights each, whilst we look through the Vortex, watching the world flash quickly past us.

"You know, Syd, you never told me the story about how you ended up in the waiting zone."

"You never asked, Roo. It's not something that you want to think about every day, is it?"

"No, not really, I suppose…. But, I do want to know, anyway. Please tell me why you have to wait to enter heaven."

"Well, it is simple and straightforward, really. I was living my life happily, working away as a support worker for a mental-health organisation. It was a job I loved; challenging but also very rewarding. I was working towards a future with my then-fiancé, Simon. We hoped to get married and have children as soon as possible."

"That doesn't make sense, Syd. Why would you be kept from heaven? You sound as though you gave so much to others and lead a good, respectable life."

"Yeah, I know, Roo. But hear me out, will you? You asked me to tell you, remember? Anyway, as I was saying, I'd reached a point in my life where I was so happy and I was planning my future as best I could. That day…you know, the day it happened… I had got up feeling particularly happy, and I told Si how much I loved him. We had been very close that morning, and Si wanted to have a duvet day because he had an unexpected day off. It was freezing cold outside, and I no more wanted to get out of that bed than he did. After pushing it for as long as I could, I eventually made a bolt out of the bed. I told Si, 'Sorry, hon, I gotta go in… I can't let them down; they will be short-staffed, and it will kill me all day to think that.' 'Ah, Syd, it wouldn't kill you to just take one day off… right then, I'll make you a deal… meet me for lunch at Mauritio's… deal?' 'It's a deal,' I promised. I kissed him, and then I left. Are you sure that you really want to hear this, Roo?"

"Syd, I have wanted to ask you ever since you and I met. I just thought that you didn't want to share your story, unlike me — I wear my heart on my sleeve, and everyone knows what my story is."

"Right then, Roo. Well, when I was leaving work at lunchtime to meet Si, one of the members jumped up out of his seat, gave me a hug, and told me to take care. It sent shivers down my spine, but I promised him that I would be careful, and so he finally let me go."

"That was a strange thing for him to do."

"I know it was, but he must have sensed something. Anyway, I left and started on my five-minute walk to the café strip where I was to meet Si. I stopped at a pedestrian crossing; the wee man was red, so I waited. I could see the café, and Si was waiting outside in the alfresco area. He saw me, too, and he waved. Just at that moment, an elderly gentleman came charging past me and straight onto the road.

My immediate reaction was to stop him, so I stepped onto the road to pull him back. I pulled him to safety, and then all I could hear was a loud horn and Si screaming my name; as I turned to see what was wrong, the big lorry hit me. I still remember the initial contact.

The pain, the shock, the realisation — they all rolled into one in that instant. After that, the rest was a very surreal experience; I started to lift up into the sky, leaving my barely recognisable body behind. As I continued lifting, I remember seeing Si running as fast as his legs would carry him. He knelt at my side, and I tried everything in my power to lower back down into my lifeless body — but, no matter how hard I tried, I could not return. Instead, I just went higher and higher. I remember thinking, Why could I not have been allowed to stay until I told Si how much I loved him?... you know like what happens in the movies and stuff."

I nod. "Wow, Syd, how very sad... but you must be so proud of yourself, though, as you are a hero."

"I suppose I should be, Roo, but I am not. It was reckless of me to have intervened in fate."

"What do you mean? I don't understand."

"Let me put it like this. The elderly gentleman I saved was eighty- six; it was his time to move on from this world, and this was how it was planned for him… this was his 'calling', so to speak. Sure, after he witnessed what had occurred from his stupidity, he had a heart attack and died on the pavement beside me. He was going to die, anyway; but, because I intervened, I was also taken when I shouldn't have been. When I arrived at the gates of heaven, there was no place reserved for me; actually, my place was reserved for when I would be eighty-two. I would have had a great life… if only I had of not played the superhero! Now I will miss out on all the things that I planned – marrying Si, having kids, and even being a granny, for that matter."

"So, why did you end up in the waiting zone? Why did they not just send you back if it was not your time to die?"

"Well, I asked Boss the same thing when I first met him. He explained that people like me – I mean, people who die before getting to live their lives to the full – provide the very gifts that we in the waiting zone work to deliver. That is why we do the gem test first, because the gifts are truly that – each one is a 'gift' – they are special and not to be given to just anyone. They are gifts that have to be earned, as what they produce are special children with big hearts and minds, who will grow into people willing to help others without question; but, to their advantage, they also have a built-in awareness control which enables them to foresee danger so that they will never ever come to any harm until it is their time to move on."

"Wow, Syd! How did I not know all of this?"

"Well, I suppose you never asked Boss, did you, Roo?"

"No, I suppose I didn't. I also arrived here because I shouldn't have died when I did. I wonder, has the gift I produced ever been used? I suppose that is something that I will never discover."

We both sit in silence for a few moments, each engaged in our own deep thoughts.

"How many years do you have left to wait, Syd?"

"Thirty-eight years, Roo. And then I can move on."

"Well, I hope Si will be there waiting for you."

"He won't be waiting for me, Roo."

"How do you know that, Syd? He might be...."

"He got on with his life, Roo. He met someone else, and they've had five children together. He has a big family, and I am just a distant memory for him. I often dream about what my life would have been like had it not ended so early. I know that I would have what his wife has now: plenty of children and love. But I also know that I have to move on, too, as it would drive me crazy to think about it too much."

"Well, Syd, if I enter heaven before you, I will wait at the gates for you to enter."

"That's very kind of you, Roo. I really appreciate that you would do that for me."

She leans over and gives me a kiss on the cheek, and I felt a spark in my tummy that I haven't felt in a long time. We both look deep into each other's eyes, naturally entering each other's souls to see what we each can find there. It is a very intensely intimate experience.

This kind of shakes me up, as I feel that I am being unfaithful to Josie. I speak to break the connection between us. "Well, anyway, Syd, what do you suggest we do about this Jayden? He has gone too far, and he cannot get away with it."

Syd looks at me for a moment before she answers. "Yes. Well, I have a plan."

"You certainly do come prepared, Syd, I'll give you that—no hanging about where you are concerned."

"You have to be in this game, Roo. Sure, look at what Jayden did and how he expects to get away with it! Anyway, my plan is simple: we have discovered it here, and so we can manage the situation. The way we deal with it all depends on who has received the gift. What do you think?"

"That's exactly what I was thinking, Syd… see, great minds think alike! How about this: we do a quick rundown now of what we think initially, and if they react as expected to the news that they are expecting, we will decide if they should be allowed to keep the gift. And then we can contact Boss to fill him in."

"Oh, boy… he isn't going to be happy."

"No, of course he isn't, but once we explain what Jayden did—and how we have been trying to sort it out with as little upheaval as possible—I am sure that he will understand."

"Yeah, I suppose so… and, hopefully, he will sort that Jayden out, too."

"Right… let's see who got the first gem. Oh, yes, it was Siobhan; she conceived it with some young law student that she is mentoring. I do not think that a child has first priorities in her future plans; but, hey, the gems are supposed to stop the recipients in their tracks and make them think. Siobhan could surprise us, but I don't feel that she is ready for a child; the process has not begun for her… not yet, anyway."

"Yeah, I agree with you. Let's see now, Roo, who is next?"

"Bethany got the next gem. She is such a gorgeous girl, on the inside as well as on the outside. She is quite young, and I feel that she is hoping that her actor boyfriend will ask her to marry him. She has been through a high-pressure childhood, with her mum being so pushy and all... treating her as if she were a little display doll. It will be interesting to see how she reacts to her news."

"Tracy was next, wasn't she? I would so love for her to be the one who has received the true gift, because I don't think that she will deal very well with another loss. Life can be so cruel sometimes."

"Yeah, Tracy has had it hard, and it would be great for us if it was her, as I know it would be easier to go to Boss knowing it was Tracy who received the true gift... as if a miracle occurred. This is a plausible explanation, I think."

"Yes, of course, Roo... it's very plausible. Wasn't Kath next? Wow! She went through a time of it during her teens, didn't she? But she's still a good person. It is a pity she never found love and settled down before now, but maybe her insecurities stemming from her baby being taken away meant that she was always afraid to take the chance of it happening again."

I nod. "Last but not least was Carrie. I was surprised that I needed to intervene with a crystal to instigate enough of a connection for them to get to a place where they would share their love for one another. I don't feel that it would be a good time just yet for a new baby to enter into their lives, as Carrie still needs a helping hand to guide her towards her full emotional and spiritual restoration—that violent incident shocked her to her very core, and she needs to emerge from shock survival mode in order to be ready for another child. Her body and mind have protected themselves effectively by going into shock survival mode — and, luckily, she understood what was going on, listened to her body, and took her recovery one day at a time.

But it is now time for her to move forward in her spiritual journey of self-discovery so that she can reach a better place of positivity, peace and forgiveness within; this will ultimately bring her to a place of spiritual happiness for the rest of her life… and beyond. I know I keep saying it, but, if only she knew now how happy she is going to be in her future."

"I know exactly what you mean, Roo. Sometimes when we feel that we have gone as low as we ever possibly can, it is actually a good thing, as we all have the power to rise from that dark and depressing place, and when we do, we are always wiser and more aware of true happiness as a result of having embarked on our own private voyage of self-discovery. We emerge more in tune with ourselves and more in control of our reactions. We are able to look at life from a totally different perspective than before, and that can only be a good thing."

We stayed on the hill all night long, gazing at the stars, not saying a word. Syd and I know each other so well that we can do this often; we do not need words because we know each other's thoughts. We work so well together; Boss knew exactly what he was doing when he teamed us up: she looks out for me, and I look out for her — that's why I promised her that I would wait for her at the gates if my gift is planted first. Because Syd and I have stuck together through thick and thin over the last thirty-four years, if it were the case that I had no one waiting for me, I would want Syd to wait for me at the gates, too. However, that will not happen, because when my gift is planted, I will enter the gates to live eternally in divine happiness with my Josie and our child.

CHAPTER 12

Positive Results

Well, we have used our time-travelling capabilities to accelerate six weeks into the future. I didn't like using this feature when I first started this job, but I soon realised just how valuable an asset it is.

Syd has decided to stick with me so that we can assess the situation together. To be honest, I am quite glad to have her moral support. I would do exactly the same for her, and I think she knows that—I certainly hope she does.

Back to the task at hand. The process of deciding which three of the five women should receive the gift is sometimes hard; we must thoroughly assess, as we are dealing with people's future happiness. In a sense, we are playing God, as we determine the outcome, thereby quite possibly changing the fate of these women and their families.

So, with a fresh, clear, revitalised mind, I will now embark on the duty of observing the reactions.

TRACY

I decide to visit Tracy first. It has been six weeks since I released her gem, so she should be feeling some changes already. When I arrive, I see that she is still in bed. Rob has just come into the bedroom holding a tray.

"Thanks, love, but I am not hungry."

"You have to keep your strength up."

"I need to get up, Rob. It's not good for Joey to see me just lying about. Anyway, you have to go to work."

"Don't worry about Joey, love. I am going to take him for a walk to the park; and, as for work, I have taken the rest of the week off."

"Yes, but..."

"Yes, but nothing.... I was due some holidays, anyway, so I am at your service."

She starts to cry, and he runs to her side.

"Hey, what's wrong? You should be happy, love."

"Yes, I know.... But, what if it happens again, Rob? I don't think that I could stand it."

"If it happens again, it just wasn't meant to be, love. It would mean something was wrong, and so it would be for the best, as its quality of life would not be the best."

"Thanks for being my rock, Rob. This should be a joyously happy time for us, and I am ruining it by being like this.... But I can't help how I feel."

"Listen, love, some things are out of our control. We just need to deal with them the best we can and try to get on with things, but it does no harm to be cautious, either."

Giving her a kiss on the forehead, he gets up to leave the room. He stops in the doorway, turns towards her, and says, "Now make sure that you get some rest, love. I will be back in an hour or so. Do you want anything before I go?"

"I am okay; make sure that Joey doesn't try to run away."

Tracy is obviously nervous about the prospect of miscarrying; if she does, it will hit her the hardest, I believe, as she wants this baby so much. Still, everything happens for a reason—and the outcome of that is for the greater good of the person and the people closest to that person.

CARRIE

I move on to visit Carrie. She is inside the cottage; the windows are very small, and she does not have a light on, so the visibility is not great. Tom has just gone out the door, and she has rushed to the bedroom, where she looks in the side pocket of a large bag. I can see that she has pulled out a pregnancy test that seems to have been in the bag a while. She checks on her son; he is having a nap and looks very peaceful. She strokes his face lovingly with her finger, and then she goes to the toilet to conduct the test.

When she comes out, she looks quite pale. She is shaking a little as she holds the stick up to the light. Opening the front door, she sticks her head out and calls Tom back to the house.

"What's up? You look like you have just seen a ghost."

"Here, take a look at this, will you… ?"

She hands him the stick, and he looks at it, not comprehending.

"What is it?"

"It's a pregnancy test, Tom. It says that I'm pregnant."

"Oh, but that's good… right?" he asks her cautiously as an inner glow starts to beam from his very core.

"Well, I don't know, Tom.… I was gonna ask you the same thing."

"I am happy about it… if you are."

"Yeah, I think that I am. I just never thought about us having another one. Have you?"

"To be honest, yes, I have. I would love another child, but I wasn't sure that you wanted to, Carrie."

"I might just pop into the chemist to get another test… just to be sure. Can you stay here with Max? He is still asleep."

"Yeah, sure. Go on ahead, darling."

He gives her a loving kiss as she goes out the door. He saw that she was shaking from the shock of it all. It was an "I am so happy that we are having another child" kind of kiss. I wait to continue my observations.

Carrie returns a half an hour later, still shaking, and completes a second test, which is also positive. When she shows Tom the results, he smiles with deep joy — he wouldn't care if the whole world fell in around him. From his spot in a chair, he pulls her down onto his knee and hugs her. She beams him a smile, looking as though she could not be happier about anything than feeling his warmth again. They just sit there in each other's arms until Max wakes.

Carrie knows that it will all be okay. Things seem to be coming together here; the gem is doing its job well. I am relieved that my intervention with the crystal seems to have turned out for the best.

BETHANY

I go to the city next, visiting Bethany's apartment first. I go in to discover that she is in the bathroom, with her head in the toilet bowl. She is heaving her stomach out poor, thing.

"Are you okay, Beth?"

"I'll be out in a minute; I'm not feeling…uugh!"

"Can I get you anything? Do you want me to call your agent?"
She cleans herself up and comes out of the bathroom.

"Sorry, hun, I just couldn't stop it. I must have eaten something dodgy last night."

"But, Beth, we both had the same things to eat, and I feel fine. I think you had better make an appointment with the doc."

"I don't have time to do that today. I will try to get in tomorrow."

"If you don't call, I will! You cannot go another day like this — you will waste away on me."

"Okay. I will ring before I leave; I promise."

"And you will let me know what he says straight away, won't you?"

"Yes, of course I will. I don't want you worrying any longer than necessary."

He kisses her on the cheek and rushes out the door. Sure enough, she rings the doctors to see if they have any cancellations; they have an 11.30, which she books. She texts Hanson to let him know.

She arrives at the doctor's office, where the usual scurries of people approach her, asking for pictures and autographs. Luckily, she is called almost immediately.

"Hello, Bethany. How can I help you today?"

"Well, it's just that I haven't been feeling very well lately, Doctor.

I was wondering if I have caught a bug or something."

"How long have you been feeling unwell?"

"I wasn't feeling too well yesterday, but it's worse today. I have been getting sick all morning, and Hanson made me promise to come see you."

"Would you be able to do a sample of urine?"

"Oh, yes, I suppose that I could."

"Good. Take this for the sample. The toilet is the second door on your left; just come back here when you're done."

She takes the little plastic bottle from his hand, goes to the toilet, and completes the task. Once back in the room, she takes her seat again. The doctor conducts the necessary urine tests, and then he sits down at his desk, facing her.

"Bethany, have you ever considered that you might be pregnant?"

"Well, no, Doctor. We always use protection. I couldn't afford to... oh... you mean... ?"

"Yes, my dear, it seems that you are pregnant. How do you feel about that?"

"Erm... I don't really know... I have never thought about it before.... This is a bit of a shock, to tell you the truth, Doctor."

"I can understand that, dear. Take a few minutes to let it absorb, if you like. Do you think that Hanson will be pleased?"
"Oh, yes, Hanson... I don't know... we are not even married or anything... we hadn't really talked about starting a family, if I am to be honest."

"Is there anyone that you can go talk to about this at the moment? Would you like me to call Hanson to come pick you up?"

"No, no... I will be okay. I will just go home and wait for him; it will give me a chance to think."

"Are you sure? Because I can ask one of the nurses to make you a nice cup of tea, and you can have a little chat with her...."

"Thanks very much, Doctor, but I think that it will be fine. Goodbye, Doctor."

"Goodbye, Beth You know where we are if you need us."

She politely leaves the room.

She goes home and sits by the window, just staring at the city below. Her mobile rings constantly with calls from Hanson and her agent (actually, her mum). Yet she doesn't even flinch at the sounds; she just stares ahead and rocks slowly, back and forth, in a desperate attempt to comfort herself.

Hanson rushes into the apartment to see her sitting in the dark; she doesn't even move an inch after his dramatic burst into the room like an all-time superhero. He switches on a light and runs straight over to her.

"Beth, what is it? What is wrong, my princess? I have been so worried all day!"

She still doesn't answer; it is as if she doesn't even know.

"Beth, come on... you're killing me, here. Please! Was it something the doc said? Are you very ill? Please, Beth, just tell me, and then I can help."

"He said... he said that I am pregnant. I'm sorry, Hanson! I didn't mean for it to happen...."

He picks her up in his arms, as though he were carrying her over the threshold.

"Oh, Beth! That is wonderful news! You'll just have to marry me now."

Those words seem to bring her back to life.

Karen Weaver

"What did you just say?" she asks.

He sets her on her feet, ever so gently.

"Just stand there a minute, Beth… don't move."

He rushes off, coming back to her side just as quickly, and then he gets down on one knee.

"Bethany Georgina Moore, will you please do me the honour of becoming my wife?"

Lovingly, he gazes up into her eyes, opening a little black velvet box that he has clutched in his hand. The diamond ring he reveals is like no other I have seen; a real sparkler, for sure.

"Yes, Hanson Murdoch Jones, I would love to be your wife."

He kisses her tummy, stands up, and then picks her up again, swinging her around joyfully. Suddenly, he stops, saying, "Oh, sorry, Beth! I shouldn't have done that… are you okay?"

"I'm fine. Do it again!"

So he does, and then he carries her to their oversized sofa, where he sits down, cradling her in his arms and kissing her tenderly.

"Thank you for making me the happiest man on earth."

"You're very welcome. I have to admit that I am kind of chuffed myself. I didn't know that you wanted kids."

"I have been planning to ask you to marry me for a while now — that's why I had the ring at the ready — but the 'right moment' just never seemed to arise. We were both too busy… working all the time. I would love nothing more than to slow life down and have some children with you. You will be a wonderful mum."

Those are the words that she has needed to hear. The reason for her shock was that she has resisted bringing a child into the world, not wanting to make any little one as miserable as her mum made her.

"You do know that there is going to be a lot of publicity about this, Hanson. Let's not tell anyone about the baby yet. I would like to save something for us to treasure without those reporters making judgements about us, and I don't want my mum to know yet, either. You know what she is like; she will try to control everything — I just couldn't stand it."

"You really have to start standing up to her, Beth. You are your own person, and she does not own you. I think that you should sack her as your agent."

"I know you're right, Hanson, and I will do it. But we have more important things to deal with right now."

She puts her hand on her tummy, and he puts his hand on top of hers. They just gaze into each other's eyes without saying another word.

Well I think that the gem has made dramatic progress here. It is strange how her first reaction was that being pregnant was a bad thing. I believe that her mother has instilled a lot of her own beliefs into this young woman, not allowing her to make decisions or have her own views when she was younger, and, instead, forcing her to comply with whatever her mum thought was best. But I think that Bethany has begun to realise that she can make decisions on her own and no longer needs to be under her mum's control. She is going to be a mum herself now, and that has made her stronger; she has more to think about than just herself, and there is no way in the world that she is going to let her mum dictate what she does with her child — in fact, she probably will not allow her mum to have anything to do with the baby at all.

I will leave Bethany at this point, as I do believe that the gem has done its job. Bethany has covered a lot of ground; her life is moving quickly now, and it is in the direction she chooses and feels comfortable with.

KATH

Kath, too, is about to discover her news. She is in a gymnasium doing a fitness class with her energisers. She isn't feeling so well, and the class notices that she doesn't seem to have her usual motivational energy. She stops for a moment to gather herself together, as she is feeling quite dizzy.

"I am so sorry about this; I have come over all dizzy," she apologises to the class. "I do believe that I will need a moment to compose myself."

One of the other women rushes beside Kath, handing her a bottle of water.

"Thank you..." Kath manages to say, but, before she can say more, she passes out.

After she faints, someone calls an ambulance. The paramedics bring her around; in the distance, she sees her energisers looking on, concerned, and so she tries to get up.

"Sorry, lovey," one of the paramedics says. "I need you to lie here until we find out what is wrong."

"But I am feeling fine now, thanks... really, I promise."

"I am sure you are, lovey, but you didn't faint for no reason, and it is my job to discover what the reason is. Your blood pressure is a bit high; have you been under any stress lately?"

"No, nothing out of the ordinary."

"Well, there must be a reason for you fainting like that. Have you been eating properly? How have you been feeling generally?"

"Now that you mention it, I have been feeling a little extra tired. And I'm off my food, as the prospect of eating, especially first thing in the morning, makes me feel quite nauseated."

"Is there any chance that you are pregnant?"

This question takes her by surprise, drawing her straight back to her teen years — she remembers the school nurse asking her the exact same question.

"No, I am definitely not pregnant. There would be no chance... no chance at all."

The paramedic, immediately picking up on Kath's defensiveness, replies, "Oh, right. Okay. Standard question."

"Can I go now?"

"I am sorry, lovey, but you won't be able to go anywhere for a while. I am going to have to bring you in for some tests, so that we can eliminate some of the worst-case scenarios."

So they bring her out on a stretcher to the ambulance. Kath finds it all a very embarrassing experience, further enhanced further by the large number of photographers waiting outside to get shots for the media.

In hospital, they do some blood tests, and Kath needs to wait for the results before they will discharge her.

She lies in hospital bed in a little private room, reading a magazine. She looks up when she hears the door open and shut, and, to her surprise, it's James. She can hardly believe it, but there he is, holding a bunch of flowers that he obviously bought in a garage along the way.

"How did you know I was here?" she asks him. Her tone sounds accusing, but she doesn't mean for it to.

He takes it in stride. "Well, I heard on the radio that you had collapsed in one of your classes. I was worried, so I rushed over. They only let me in because I said I was your husband."

She melts a bit and then giggles. "You didn't... did you?"

He grins. "Are you okay, Kath?"

"They don't know what's wrong yet, but they are waiting for test results to come so they can give me the all clear to go."

Just at that, the doctor comes into the room. "Kath, we have the results of your tests. I am glad to tell you that we know what is wrong with you."

He looks over at James as if he expects him to leave.

"Don't worry about him, Doctor. I will be telling him whatever is

wrong, anyway. Well what is it?"

"Well, Kath if you are sure.... It seems that you are pregnant."

"I am... what? That can't be possible, Doctor. Are you sure you haven't made a mistake?"

"Sure, I'm sure. We will just check your vitals, and then you will be free to go."

Kath just sits in a daze.

"Kath, are you feeling okay? You seem a bit... well... shocked."

"Of course I'm shocked, James! You can't tell me that you planned this to happen to us... again."
"No, of course I didn't plan it! But you can't compare it to the last time, Kath. We were only kids, and your parents took over. It can be different this time, Kath, we can do this. We can do it together."

116

"But I have my career to think of, James."

"You're just looking for excuses now. It happened, and we are going to have to work it out together."

"I need to think things through, James. Do you mind giving me a lift home?"

So she is not alone this time; if things had been different twenty-two years ago, I do believe that these two could have made it work, even as young as they were at the time. If they'd had the support of their families, instead of the intervention that took place, which ruined so many lives, I do think Kath and James could have worked it out. I will be interested to see how this progresses.

SIOBHAN

I visit Siobhan last. I have been good, as I have purposefully stopped myself from making any judgements as to how she will react to her news. I can only pray that she has not received the gift, because I feel that that would be the worst-possible result at this time — but there I go again, being judgemental....

Today, as she storms through the building, it is not hard to see that she is not her usual self. Her hair is not brushed, and her makeup is incomplete. Her usual welcoming committee are taken aback, barely able to get out the usual, "Good Morning, Miss Roe" — so shocked are they by the sight of her unkempt appearance at such an early hour. However, they are relieved to avoid the torrent of abuse that usually flies their way whilst they just try to get on with their jobs.

As she reaches her office thirty minutes late, her assistant is keen to help her, clearly concerned by the disturbing sight that confronts her.
"Miss Roe, is everything okay? You look terrible."

"I know, Bea. I feel terrible, and I have to be in the high court in an hour."

"What can I do to help? Do you want a coffee?"

"Erm, no I had better not. A glass of ice water would be good, thanks."

Bea is not used to her boss talking civilly to her, but she is keen to help, and so she doesn't wonder about it too much.

"I have a friend down the street who is a hairdresser, Miss Roe. Would you like me to ask her to call up here?"

"My hair... oh, yes, my hair... it must look a dreadful sight... yes, would you, Bea? That would be great."

So Bea goes off to get a glass of water and to phone her friend.

When she returns, Siobhan tells her, "Hold my calls, Bea, and I don't want to see anyone today, either. Okay?"

"No one at all? Are you sure, Miss Roe?"

"Yes, Bea. No one. I am quite sure."

"Okay, Miss Roe, just call me if you need anything."
Bea quickly leaves the room to call her friend on the bottom floor; who informs her that Siobhan's condition has turned out to be the topic of the day at Maximus Corporations.

The buzzer goes on Siobhan's telephone.

"Miss Roe, Will is here, and he says that he needs to see you urgently...."

"Let him in, Bea," Siobhan says quickly, before Bea can question why she's changed her mind about having no visitors.

Will enters her office, which is quite dark; she has the blind tightly closed and no lights are on.

"What's going on, Siobhan? The whole building is talking about you! They are saying that you are having some sort of breakdown.... Gee, you really don't look well. Are you sick?"

"Well, you could say that, Will. I just have a few things that I need to sort out. Do you mind just giving me some space to do that?"

"I will, Siobhan, if you explain what's going on."

"Why? So that you can go and share it all with your comrades on the bottom floor? I don't think so."

"Siobhan, you know that I would never talk about us! What we do is between us—just you and me—and whatever anyone else says is just speculation.... You know that, right?"

"No, I don't know that, Will, but what I do know is that I have a lot of sorting out to do, and you are not helping by pushing me at the moment."

"I take it tonight is cancelled, then?"

"Oh, just get out, Will! Is that all you think about?"

She pushes him out the door, watching him shrug his shoulders at Bea on the way past. She knows that she could never share her news with him, as he is just her plaything. He is not in it for the long haul; he is just trying to sleep his way to the top—just like she did.

She closes the door, goes back to her desk, sits in her chair, and sighs. With her head in the palms of her hands, she says, "Dear Lord, why me? Why now? I don't think that I am ready; how will I make a good mum?"

And then she cries. This is not a reaction that I expected from her. Ever since she learned her news, her attitude has completely changed. I feel potential here, as she seems to have dramatically taken her head out of the clouds and come back down to earth. The fact that she is not conscious of her appearance indicates that she is having an inner conflict; she is dealing with issues that she has kept covered up for a long time. With conflict comes change, and the first thing that has changed is the tough-guy act that she puts so much effort into portraying. Now she has exposed herself as not being so totally in control – not nearly as tough as she wants others to think she is – and I believe that, over time, she will discover that she receives a better response from others when she is just herself.

Different people react differently to the news that they are going to have a "new addition"; some reactions are physical, and some are psychological. All these changes are necessary in order to prepare a woman to be more resilient during her pregnancy. My advice to women is simple: Listen to yourself. If you need to be sick, get sick; if you need to cry, go ahead and cry; if you are doing too much, your body will respond by shutting itself down for a time, and you may faint. The body truly is a wonderful thing.

CHAPTER 13

Summoned

Syd has viewed all that I just have amongst the five different women, and now she and I need to assess our observations. We have decided to go back to our hilltop spot and have a picnic. We set it up, and it looks picture-perfect—complete with a checked picnic blanket and a wicker basket. She really knows how to do things, does Syd. I have always admired her for the efforts that she takes; over the years, she has really gone out of her way to put on some great bashes.

We don't celebrate birthdays in the waiting zone, as none of us age here; we stay the same age that we were when we arrived. We measure time by the number of years of service that we have completed. Obviously, the older you are when you enter, the shorter period of time you will have to remain in the waiting zone, as you have arrived closer to the time for your intended entrance into heaven. Syd's and my lives were cut short unnecessarily, and so we both have longer to wait. In short, our gifts are not yet ready to return back to the world.

I remember when I arrived in the waiting zone. Of course, I was in a state of confusion as I searched for my Josie, desperate to be reunited with her and our newborn. I was convinced that the physical pain I felt deep within because of losing them would never be relieved until the three of us were reunited. However, since that time whilst doing my job in the waiting zone, I have discovered that time is a great healer.

And not just time. Syd has helped me tremendously, too. From the time I arrived, she has always been there for me: she let me talk, and she just listened; she was my shoulder to cry on when the realisation hit me that things could never be the same again; she helped me come to terms with the changes that had consumed my life as it was. We have been close friends ever since, and I have come to see that it is as if we were destined to meet. I hold our friendship so dear to my heart, and I know that, without Syd, my stay in the waiting zone would have been more of a challenge.

Over the past thirty-four years, Syd has always gone out of her way for me. Each year on the anniversary of the day that I entered the waiting zone, she has thrown a "surprise party" for me. She goes to such lengths and puts forth such effort every year to disguise the fact that she is organising a party — and I go to such lengths and put forth such effort every year to pretend that I don't know what is going on. It is quite comical, really, and such fun, too, now that I really think about it, which I haven't over the years. We are like one of those old married couples, so content when we are with each other, and there is nothing that we don't know about each other — now that Syd has told me the story of how she entered the waiting zone. I have just realised that we have been practically inseparable for the past thirty-four years — gee that's sure is a long time when I compare it with years spent in the world. Syd and I truly are the closest of friends. Why am I just now realising all this?

I now see her in a totally different light. I watch as she sets up the picnic with such attention to detail; any party organiser would be proud to do as well. Everything that she does, she does with style and class; she truly is wonderful, and I realise that I have only just recognised that....

Syd and I are inseparable at times, comrades in our quest to give the true gifts to those worthy of receiving them. We have always made great decisions together, as our minds think alike, even though our characters are ever so different.

Syd's message connector beeps, and she shoots right up like a lightning bolt. In that instant it happens — what I have dreaded ever since Syd told me about Jayden's trickery.

"Uh-oh."

"What? What is it, Syd?"

"Boss is looking for me, and for you, too, I believe."

Just as she says that, my connector beeps, too. "You have one new message from Boss," it tells me. I open it:

"Need you to come back to base ASAP."

"Yeah, I just got summoned, too. Will we go together?"

"Sure, Roo, we may as well... what have we got to lose? At least we can support each other."

"Good idea, Syd. But what about our picnic?"

"And what do we tell Boss when we arrive in the zone late, Roo?

'Sorry we're late, Boss, we were just finishing off our picnic lunch first.'" Syd pulls a face.

She's right, as usual. I shrug. "Well, when you put it like that, Syd... I think we had better get a move on."

So to the Vortex we go straight away; I definitely didn't expect to be back here so soon. We knock on the door to Boss's office, and it suddenly opens itself. Syd and I look at each other, and then we nervously walk in and approach the desk, which looks the same as ever — very large and white, and very tidy, indeed.

The grand white-leather swivel chair is facing the wall. All of a sudden, the chair swings around to reveal Boss, sitting with his legs crossed and his hands together.

"Well? Have you anything that you need to fill me in on?" he asks.

Syd and I look at each other, swivelling our eyes in a strange motion, which, if it could talk, would say, "you tell him", and then in response, "no, you tell him".

I eventually speak, as I know that Syd would never give in to the swivelling-eye thing. Besides, she is the one helping me, so I need to step up.

"I am sorry, Boss. I have only just discovered the problem myself. Syd messaged me just after I had released the gems."

"What problem is this?"

"The reason why you summoned us, Boss… is it because a gift has been released?"

"Yes, it is, Rupert. I know all about it. Jayden visited me to inform me that you had taken a gift."

"But, I didn't just take it, Boss! He tricked me," I say, feeling well within my rights to defend myself.

"Listen, Rupert. I have known about this all along; I do get alerted every time a gift is released. I have checked the records, and so I know that the gift was released before you entered dispatch. I also understand that Jayden has been creating a few problems for you lately."

"Yes, well, I know that he wants my job, Boss. He has made it quite clear that he wants to be the Visitor, but I don't think that he has the qualities." I say boldly.

Syd finally pipes up in my defence. "Yeah, Boss, it is not Roo's fault."

"Ah, thanks, Syd. You really jumped to my defence there—better late than never." I say in a low voice. After all she's done for me, I suppose I could have suppressed the sarcasm, but I really am in quite a state.

"Yes, thank you, Sydney. I do know that; I take it all into account. Would you please wait outside for a few moments whilst I talk to Rupert?"

"Of course, Boss," she says. Before she leaves the room, she turns back toward me and whispers in my ear. "I'm just outside, Roo, call if you need me."

I certainly do not know what to expect. Boss usually likes an audience when he gives us a drilling.

"Rupert, you know how the waiting zone works: we are here until our gifts are released; the release of our gifts is our 'ticket' to the gates of heaven, so to speak."

"Yes, Boss, I understand that clearly," I say, not indicating that I really did not see the full picture until my recent talk with Syd. "I have been waiting thirty-four years to earn that right so that I can be reunited with my wife and child."

"Well, I must inform you that it was your gift that has been released, which means that, after this assignment, you will be free to enter heaven."

This has taken me aback quite severely, and I fall into the seat behind me.

"Are you sure that it is mine, Boss?"

"Yes, Rupert, I am sure. One of the women is carrying your gift."

"I just can't believe it.... I have waited so long for this moment, and yet it is all quite surreal.... I don't know how I feel. Do you know who has received the gift?"

"Now, Rupert, you know that I cannot tell you that, even if I wanted to. You will find out soon enough."

"Okay, fair enough, Boss. Can I go absorb it all?"

"Yes, surely. But, before you go, I want to share something with you."

He leans forward in the chair, resting his hands on the desk. I observe a warm expression on his face that I have never seen before.

"Rupert, as you already know, I have been the Boss here since you arrived. I actually started the position of Boss many years before you came. I entered the waiting zone under circumstances similar to your own; I, too, was assigned the role of Visitor."

"You were once a Visitor, Boss?" I ask, utterly surprised.

"Yes, Rupert, I was. That may be hard for you to imagine, but, like yourself, I took my role very seriously — in fact, I see some of myself in you.... But, anyway, I must finish my story. When my time to enter heaven came, I arrived at the gates only to discover that nobody was there to meet me. My wife had not passed on, and it was probably quite a number of years before she was going to do so. I was alone, and I missed the waiting zone and the life that I had built up here. I was given the opportunity to return as the Boss because the previous Boss had seen potential in me, and he felt it was the right time for him to move on to heaven as the arrival time of his loved ones drew nearer. Do you understand what I am saying, Rupert?"

"Yes, Boss, that is a very touching story. I don't want to be rude, but I don't know what it has to do with me."

"That's fine, Rupert. I just wanted to share that with you, is all. You are free to go, and I hope that you and Sydney have a lovely picnic."

"Oh, yes. So you know just about everything, right?"

"Right," says Boss, smiling.

I just smile back, realising that Boss has known every single thing that I have done over the past thirty-four years—and not just everything that I have done, but everything that everyone else has done, too. Gee, I can't wait to tell Syd! ...

As I exit the office, Syd comes rushing towards me.

Throwing her arms around me, she exclaims, "Please tell me that you are not going to be sacked as Visitor, Roo! Tell me that Jayden is not going to take your place—I just simply couldn't bear it."

"No, Syd, nothing of the sort. Where did you get that idea from? You have been thinking worst-case scenarios again, haven't you?"

"Well, it just prepares me for the worst-possible outcome, and it works for me. So what did he say?"

"Oh, Syd, I am so excited! Boss told me that my gift has been released. This is my last assignment as the Visitor—how great is that?"

Syd releases me from the embrace she has me held in. I see that her face has just dropped, and all the blood has drained out of it. I watch as she absorbs the realisation that I will be leaving.

"Oh, Syd, I'm sorry. I didn't realise... I was just so wrapped up in my own joy, I didn't even consider that you might be upset.... Are you okay?"

"I'm fine, Roo. I just didn't expect you to say it, that's all.... I thought you and I would be here working together longer. But I am just being silly." She beams me a smile. "So you are finally going to be reunited with Josie—how excited are you?!"

I grin. "Well, Boss said for us to have a lovely picnic. Do you fancy picking up where we left off before we were summoned?"

"Sure, why not."

I fill her in on what I recently learned about Boss's omniscience as we head back through dispatch.

Jayden is still there, which I find strange; somehow, I didn't expect him to be there. I thought that Boss knew what Jayden had done. Boss did say he was aware of the circumstances.... That was a serious offence, and Jayden certainly should not still be in a position where he has control over the gifts; they are just too precious for him to be messing about with them!

A realisation suddenly hits me: How did Jayden know which gift was mine to plant?

As I pass Jayden's desk, he looks up at me. I stare at him coldly, just to let him know that I know what he did. It doesn't seem to bother him, though, as he just smiles and goes on with his work. It is strange that he didn't give a comment, but I shrug it off—maybe he has decided to mend his ways. One can only hope....

Anyway, I am not going to let Jayden ruin the happiness that I feel right now, knowing my reunion with Josie and our child is so close at hand; nor am I going to waste any time I have left to spend with Syd... I shall miss my dear friend sorely.

CHAPTER 14

Attaining the Gems

This is the part of my job that I do not enjoy. But, alas, it must be done in order for my assignment to be complete. It is by observing each woman at this point that I get a true picture of the depth of her desire to have a child. For some reason, it is even harder than usual this time. I wish Syd were here to observe with me, but she has had to go back to the waiting zone. We have arranged to meet up there later to discuss my observations of the five women.

I reflect that perhaps it is more difficult because this is my last assignment; I will enter heaven before long. I am ecstatic at the thought of eternal happiness with Josie and our child. But I cannot allow my mind to wander—I must focus on the task at hand, complete my assignment, and then be on my way....Forcing my mind back to the five women I must observe, I think about what I have learned during my time as Visitor.

Life sometimes grants wisdom in mysterious ways: to enable us to reach the tranquility of the destination, we must endure some pain on the journey—but, ultimately, the pain is worth enduring, as most people will agree at the end. To appreciate the true wealth in life, such as the gift of life, we sometimes need to be brought back from a place that values materialistic gain over the gift of life. This process of balancing values takes time to complete, and the amount of time varies from person to person. However, people who have experienced the process and achieved true balance always feel happier within, more satisfied with life, and more comfortable in their own skin. This voyage of self-discovery grounds people, cementing each brick of their lives together, so that they are able to build secure and stable lives. As they have now built the foundations which will enable all their succeeding bricks to stand tall, proud and secure amongst the ones already in place. Those people who take the time to build sturdy foundations will discover that they are more secure and better able to withstand the "surprises" of life, such as when an earth-shattering moment occurs. They will discover that their life's structure will not fall to the ground; it may sway and be shaken, but it will still be secure after the dramatic event.

When the gem comes, it is like an earthquake for those whom it visits, shaking them right to the core; but, if they have secure life foundations, they will be stronger when the effects of the personal trauma have stopped rippling through their every thought. However, some people are built of steel, and they may not feel any ripples at all—this is unfortunate, as they will miss out on the grounding natural realities that come with life.

I prepare myself to call the gems. I stand on the highest point of the tallest mountain, and I open the box which sends out a signal that summons the precious gems back to where they belong. The signal is so intense that it causes lights to flicker all over the world. I see the first gem racing towards me: it is as bright as the sun and as beautiful as only a gem can be; it shines brightly in the sky, radiating all the colours of the rainbow as it speeds along. Should you ever see a rainbow when there has been no rain, you will know that a gem is returning home.

One by one, they all return, each one creating a spectacular scene as it zooms through the fluffy white clouds until it reaches the destination of its sanctuary: the treasure box. The speed at which each one comes is so fast, its journey is but a blur of colour; and then, just as quickly, each one stops and hovers above its allocated spot. Five were released, but only four have returned, and so I know for sure that a gift has been released… just as Boss assured me. This time is different from any other time, as I know that the gift released was my own. I am tempted to peek in order to see which of the five women has received my gift, but I know that I am not yet ready to discover that. It might affect me and any judgements that I make during the last stage.

I will complete my assignment in the standard manner, by observing each of the five women for the last time. The main objective is to see how they deal with the loss and how deeply they desire to have a child, as I already started to explain. This is important because the gifts that we distribute from the waiting zone are priceless: children born from gifts are special and will exceed any expectations because of their knowledge and self-awareness. The high value that they place on life will be so strong that their positivity will spill onto others who have the pleasure of their company; their aura is white, which represents an angelically spiritual person who also incorporates the good qualities from each of the other aura colours.

The courier comes to pick up the gems. I meet him at the entrance to the Vortex. He is tall and does not have much meat on his bones. He has brown hair which looks as though his mother licked her hand and patted it down. He always wears a brown uniform: a pair of trousers (which are way too tight, and someone should inform him about that); a jacket that cuts off at the waist, and that has breast pockets and a zip that he never fails to have zipped up halfway, revealing a beige shirt that opens at the collar.

"Hi, Rupert. I believe you're leaving us," he says in greeting.

"News sure travels fast in the zone, Jake."

"You know how it goes — once it's in the system, everyone knows about it. What's this I hear about a missing gem?"

"Yeah, there are only four gems to collect because one was a gift, and we all know that gifts don't return unless they are terminated."

"Wow! You're having a ball down here on this assignment, aren't ya?"

"Well, you know me, Jake... I like to keep things interesting."

"Okay, mate, I'll let ya get back to it. I'll probably see you at your leaving party."

"What leaving party?"

"Ah, don't let on you don't know. Sure, hasn't Syd organised a party for you every year since you came? Do you think she is going to miss an opportunity to organise your leaving party? Either she has a thing about parties, or she is really crazy about you....I know which one I would put my bets on, you lucky guy!"

"Come on, Jake. Syd and I are just good friends."

"Yeah, yeah. I've heard that one before."

I wave him off. "Great... See ya, Jake."

"Okay... See ya, buddy," he says, taking the treasure box.

There is nothing that Jake likes more than a bit of gossip! He is the courier, after all. He is so suited to his job, as he not only delivers and collects goods, but also spreads good and bad news.

Can a man and a woman not simply just have a friendship? In some people's eyes it is not possible, as they believe that the laws of attraction will intervene at some point—because, obviously, some attraction must exist in order to enable friends of the opposite sex to spend so much time together. I do acknowledge this, but I still say it is possible for a man and a woman to "just be friends". Syd and I have been friends—good friends—for thirty-four years, we hardly ever fight, and we have never been intimate—well, apart from one kiss, but that was nothing....

TRACY

I must now put all that out of my head and focus on completing my assignment. This is the penultimate moment, and I need to focus all my powers of concentration on each of to the five women so that I can conduct an honest final observation.

Checking my list, I see that I will visit Tracy first. This poor woman and her family have been through the mill, and now I have just added to it.

I enter her home to see her in tears, desperately pressing the numbers in the telephone handset. Her son, Joey, is in the living room, watching Tom and Jerry cartoons. She puts the phone to her ear, sits down, and buries her face in her free hand.

"Rob... it's happened again... can you please come home?"

"Yes, I will be there straight away," he tells her.

Ten minutes later, he rushes through the front door, peeking into the living room to see if Tracy is there but finding Joey, instead.

"Mammy is sad again, Daddy. Will you fix her?"

Giving his son a kiss and hug, Rob exits the living room and heads towards the kitchen, where he discovers Tracy sitting at the table. She is crying, with her head nestled in her arms.

He sits beside her. "Oh, love... did you make an appointment with the doctor?"

"What's the point, Rob? He won't do anything. We've been here before. Why does it keep happening to us? What have we ever done wrong? I can't do this anymore, Rob—my heart is breaking... I can't handle it. I can't think straight anymore... it's just not right."

"I am going to call the doctor, and I will go with you. And we are not leaving until we get some answers."

He calls the doctor and gets an appointment straight away.

Tracy straightens herself up, asks her mam to keep an eye on Joey, and leaves with Rob for the doctor's office. After a long wait, they are called in.

"Hello, Tracy and Rob. What can I do for you today?"

"Doctor, Tracy has just lost again, and we want you to refer us as soon as possible for tests to find out what is wrong. It should not be this hard to have a baby. We have a healthy child already."

"I am sorry to hear that news. I understand your frustr —"

"No, Doctor, please don't give us the spiel," Rob interrupts. "We just want a referral."

"It is not that easy, Rob. At Tracy's age, it is not uncommon…"

"I don't want to hear that, Doctor. I am sorry, but we are not leaving here without a referral."

"Okay, Rob. I will refer you so that an investigation can take place…."

He types on his computer keyboard, waits a moment, and then takes a printout from the printer tray. Handing the paper to Rob, he says, "Here, take this with you to the early pregnancy clinic today, and they will get the ball rolling. That's all I can do. Tracy, do you need some tablets to help you cope with the stress?"

"No, thank you, Doctor. I just need some answers… like Rob said."

"Okay. I will be in contact when I receive some results from the clinic."

I have thought about the benefits for her to encounter another gem, and I have concluded that she has received it because her profile states that she has a medical condition. I do not have the power to cure, but I do have the power to instigate action. Hopefully, by encountering yet another loss, Tracy will now have the reasoning behind a plea to her doctor to conduct an investigation. She will discover that she has a problem, and that will help her deal psychologically with the fact that she was lucky to have received the miracle gift that is her young son, Joey. I have made a note of her desire to have a child. It is a pity that she was not the person who received the true gift, as she would have been an ideal candidate for the miracle that was released unknowingly….

134

CARRIE

I must move on now to Carrie. It looks as though she is getting ready to go to out. She is glowing with happiness, so I am holding out hopes that maybe she has received the gift. I follow them to a family gathering, where they have shared their news with some of the family members. They don't stay long, as they must ensure that they get their little Max home at a reasonable time. When they get back to the cottage, they all just go to bed straight away.

The next morning, Carrie is up first. I see that she is a little concerned about something. When she comes out of the bathroom, I see that she is as white as a sheet. She rushes to the bedroom.

"Tom, there's something wrong."

"Eh... err... what?" he says as he tries to wake up so that he can comprehend what she has just said.

"I said that there is something wrong. There is some blood." She is shaking as she explains.

He jumps straight out of bed and coaxes her back in. She gets into the bed, afraid to move, as it might make matters worse.

"What can I do? Please tell me what I can do to help, Carrie."

"I suppose I had better ring the doctor, so will you bring me my mobile?"

He goes out and comes back with her bag, setting it down gently beside her. They look lost; neither one knows what to do.

"Will you get Max some breakfast?"

"Sure thing. Can I get you something? You will need to keep your strength up."

"I really don't feel like anything… but I suppose you're right, I must… maybe a cup of tea and a piece of toast. Thanks."

He leaves the room, and she looks in her bag, trying to locate her mobile. She lifts out what looks like a card; it has a picture of an old woman on it. Carrie looks at it for a moment, and then she kisses it and holds it close to her heart.

"Granny, if you can help, please don't let me lose this baby. Please, please, please."

And then she starts to mumble, as if she is praying. Tears trickle from the sides of her closed eyelids. I will leave for now and call back later.

* * * * *

When I return, Carrie is still in bed. A woman who looks quite similar to her, but with different hair, is sitting beside her on the bed. She gives her a long caring hug.

"Well, what did they say in hospital?"

"They said that it is still there… but I may lose it, as I am still bleeding."

"How are you feeling?"

"A little confused and sad… I so want this baby, Sis! I didn't know that I did when I first found out, but I know now… I want another child so much. I just want the bleeding to stop."

"Has it gotten any better?"

"No. It's worse. I know that it is going to happen—it is just a matter of when."

"Oh, I am so sorry, Carrie! I feel so useless. I wish there was something I could do."

"So do I, but all I can do is pray that it will all turn out wonderful in the end."

I leave them as they hug again, as only sisters can. I will leave now and come back in the morning.

* * * * *

When I return the following morning, I first assume that it was a sleepless night here. Carrie's eyes are red, and she is no longer in bed. She is sitting in the living room, and Tom sits beside her, holding her hand supportively.

Two older people are at the door; they knock and walk inside. I sense that they are family, maybe through Carrie's grief there has been a reunion of hearts.

"Hello, it's only us," the woman calls out, walking over and giving Carrie a hug.

"So how are you feeling, love?"

"I'm not too bad, Mum; I just feel a little crappy, but I suppose I will for a while."

"Don't worry, love… you will have another child."

"I know, Mum, but that won't bring this one back, will it?"

Her father sits down beside her on the sofa and puts his hand around her shoulder; it looks quite awkward, but she seems to have found a deep comfort from it.

"Don't worry, love… it will be fine in the end," he says, and then he pulls her head onto his shoulder, as if she were his little girl again.

She closes her eyes for a moment as she drifts back to the sanctuary that was her father's embrace when she was a little girl. She has always loved her dad so much; he always protected her. She wants him to protect her from the pain and emptiness she is now feeling, and for those few moments he has done so.

The gem is doing its work here. For so long, Carrie has been filled with emptiness, unable to feel any emotion. Now she has the power to cry, the power to feel pain, and, most importantly, the power to move on. She built a wall around herself for protection, without realising that, although it kept out sadness, it also kept out joy. It has been so long since she experienced any joy. That will all change now that she has made the decision to move on.

But before I move on I feel compelled to observe another interaction. This one is in a totally different setting; it seems to be a local playgroup. I see Carrie and Tracy standing beside each other as their two boys play trucks together.

"Yeah, he just proposed. It was totally unexpected, but I was so happy; we have been through a bit of a rough time of it lately, but this has made the atmosphere in our home feel so much brighter."

"Well, congratulations."

"Thanks, Tracy"

"A rough time... what happened?"

"Oh... we had a miscarriage, and I took it rather bad; but, we are going to keep trying. He has been so strong for me."

"I, too, recently had a miscarriage... it is tough."

"Yeah, and people don't understand just how hard it is unless they have had one themselves."

"You're right, Carrie. Hey, do you fancy meeting up for a cuppa some day?"

"I would love to."

"What about tomorrow? Our boys can have a play at my house, and I will get some nice buns to make us feel better."

"That sounds great, Tracy. I will look forward to that."

How wonderful these two will be a great support for each other now — and their personalities complement each other, so they will make great friends.

Now I must move on, but I am so glad that I stayed on to witness this.

BETHANY

I will now visit Bethany to observe how she has progressed since experiencing the shock of the discovery that she is pregnant — followed so quickly by the shock of Hanson's proposal. She's had to absorb so many big changes in such short space of time.

When I arrive at the apartment, paramedics rush past me, pushing a stretcher that holds an apparently unconscious and definitely very pale Bethany.

Across the stretcher, one paramedic shouts to the other, "Tell ER to be ready. We will be there in ten minutes!"

"What's going on? Is she going to be okay? Does this often happen after a miscarriage?" asks Hanson, panicked.

"I'm sorry, sir, but she has lost a lot of blood. Do you happen to know your fiancée's blood group?"

"No, I am sorry... I don't. But her mum is her agent, and she should know."

"Can you call her? It is vitally important that we know. If her mum doesn't know, ask her what her and her father's blood groups are. We can work it out from there."

139

"Okay. I will ring on the way to hospital."

Whilst in the ambulance, Hanson calls Beth's mum.

"Hi, Hil. We have an emergency here, but I need you to keep it cool. Just tell me what Beth's blood group is.... Well, if you can't be sure of what hers is, you need to tell me yours and Harry's so that they don't have to do tests to find out..... Okay, Hil, thanks. We are on our way to hospital now.... What do you mean, 'Wait, I shouldn't have said that'?... Oh, okay. I'll see you then.... Bye."

The paramedic looks at Hanson, waiting for the information to be shared.

"She doesn't know for sure, but she thinks that Beth is AB- negative; her mum is O-positive, and her dad is A-positive."

"She must have it wrong, because those blood groups would never match," the paramedic tells Hanson. "We will have to conduct our own tests."

"AB-negative is a rare blood group, and so we may need her mother or father to donate blood, as supplies are always low," the other paramedic says. "Will you call her mum back? Ask her or her husband—whichever one of them is blood group AB-negative also—and tell them to get to hospital ASAP. Their daughter's life depends on it."

Struggling to remain calm, Hanson phones Hil again.

"Hil, the paramedics say that whether it is you or Harry that is the same blood group as Beth, you need to get to hospital quickly... what?... please tell me you're joking.... I can't tell Beth, Hil; she is
lying here in front of me unconscious.... Okay, see you there. Bye."

He turns to the paramedic, whose expression turns to concern as
he watches the colour drain from Hanson's face.

"Are you feeling okay, son? You don't look so good," the paramedic says.

"Let's just say that I have just had a bit of a shocking revelation. I don't think that Beth's mum and dad can be of much help with the blood, she says that Beth is definitely AB-negative."

The paramedic doesn't press for an explanation. He just says, "That's good to know, son. I will tell them that information, as anything is better than nothing at all."

I did not expect such a drama to be unfolding when I arrived. I will revisit later to see how things have developed.

* * * * *

I arrive back at hospital the next morning, delighted to see Bethany sitting in bed, propped up by numerous, plump, white pillows. Some colour has come back in her cheeks, but she is crying.

She speaks quite angrily to her mother. "I was adopted? And you never told me? Did you never stop to think that I have a right to know—it does, after all, affect me. What right did you think you had—do you think you still have—to keep this information from me all of my life? Is it any wonder I never felt loved like a daughter should feel loved, or that I never felt a part of the family? I have always been your dress-up doll—a pretty plaything for you to showcase and get to win contests with. That's all I ever was to you... all I ever will be...."

"No, Beth it wasn't like that. Your father and I have always loved you as much as we would have loved our own child."

"What was it like, then? Please enlighten me."

"I think that you need to focus on getting better first, and then we will talk about it. You need some time to recover from your ordeal, and then you will be thinking more clearly."

"Well, if you are not going to tell me anything, you may as well leave, because I really don't want you around me at the moment."

"I understand, love... you know where I am if you need me."

Hil gets up and leaves the room.

Hanson stands up, sits beside Bethany on the bed, and gives her a loving hug.

"Are you sure that you still want to marry someone who doesn't even know who she is?"

"I am determined to marry you as soon as possible, especially if it will help you feel that you do have an identity."

"Will you please promise me something, Han?"

"Of course... anything."

"Promise me that we will never lie to our children and that we will always be honest with each other — forever."

He squeezes her tight and says, "I promise that I will never be untruthful to you or our children, Beth. I love you too much to hurt you."

"I will also need some help finding my real parents, Han. Will you help me?"
"We will find them, Beth. Sure, you need your dad to walk you down the aisle."

The gem has surely been hard at work here. The gem's departure has instigated both realisations and revelations. Bethany has realised that she does want children, after all; she is automatically seeing her future with children in it now. The revelation that she was adopted as a baby has been the biggest shock of all to her, but it seems to have provided her with the missing piece to the puzzle of her life — the piece that she has always felt was missing. This would not have come to light for goodness knows how long if it had not been for the unfortunate event that was her need for urgent medical attention and blood. To top it all off, the gem's arrival gave Hanson the opportunity to propose, which he had been waiting to do for some time. I feel that a long and happy life together lies in store for this couple.

SIOBHAN

I will move on to Siobhan now. I feel as though she is calling me, and so I must answer. When I arrive, what I witness shocks me: the last time I saw her, she was quite rough and ready, as the shock of the real possibility of a child entering her life had begun to sink in. For the first time, I have not arrived at her workplace, which I find strange, as it is a midweek day.

Instead, I am at her home: a two-storey town house, not the type of property that I would have visualised as Siobhan's residence. I go inside to discover that she is not alone. Another woman must live there, too.

Siobhan has a different glow about her. Her aura no longer is an angry, fiery red, it has calmed down tremendously, and it is a little hazy,
which indicates that she is undergoing a personal transformation.
She has her hair down, but this time it looks healthy and shiny, and the red locks fall down over her shoulders. She is not wearing her military-style suit, either; a very flattering dress, bursting with colour, completes her bright new look.

She is making tea in the kitchen, and she carries a tray through to the back of the house, going outside to a high, raised deck section.
Walking over to a table and chairs, she sets the tray on the table.

"Mum!" she calls. "Tea is ready."

"I am coming, love," her mum calls back.

They both get comfortable, sitting with their feet up on the two spare chairs.

"This is really nice and peaceful, isn't it Mum?"

"It is just perfect, love, and these éclairs are just yum."

They sit in a contented silence for a few moments.

"So, Mr Maximus didn't mind your taking some leave, then?"

"No, he didn't, actually. I explained the situation, told him that I was taking a year off, and he understood. He has decided to take Will on for that year. Will has great potential, just like I had at his age, and it will be a great experience for him."

"When is your scan, love?"

"I have one booked for next week. I am so excited, Mum! Just look at me—to think that just a few months ago I was a very bitter person who felt nothing but frustration with others. Now, as I look back, I cringe at how I acted and how I treated people at work."

"You weren't such a joy to be around at home, either, love. You were very cross—just like your dad was."

"I know, and I am sorry, Mum. Things are going to be different now. I am going to be a mum; and, even better still, I am going to be a good mum."

"You'll be a great mum, and I will always be here to help."

"I know, and I am grateful for that. You know, I have been meaning to ask you something. Will you be the godmother? I think of you as the baby's guardian angel."

Her mum smiles with delight. "I would be honoured, love, and I promise that I will be a great godmother."

"I have one more thing to tell you, Mum."

"Oh, yes? What's that, love?"

"We're moving."

This comes as a big surprise to her mum.

"Moving? Where are we moving to? I hope it is not one of those high-rise apartment blocks. You know I would not make it up the stairs if the lift was ever broken."

"No, Mum it is not an apartment. It is a bigger house on the outskirts of the city; it has green grass and a big backyard where this little one can play," she pats her tummy affectionately. "It is just perfect, Mum... you are going to love it. There is a flower garden for you to take care of, too."

"Oh, love, it sounds absolutely perfect! I will be ever so happy to spend time in a garden, filling the house with such beautiful colours and scents from that flowers that I will grow from seedlings."

"It is going to be wonderful, Mum. This little gift has come to me at this time in my life for a reason: to change how I once was and to focus on the future, not just for myself but for all of us."

"I am so happy to hear that, love, because I felt so sad watching you self-destruct just like your dad did; he was his own worst enemy, you know. I have one thing to ask you—and I hope that you don't mind my being so direct—but, who is the baby's father?"

"Well, Mum, let's just say that he is in the know, but he chooses not to be part of it, as he is focusing on forwarding his own career right now."

Wow—what a shocker! Her life now has purpose and meaning. I must admit that when I first realised that a gift had been released, Siobhan was the one person I hoped would not receive it. I judged her by the

145

way she treated others, and I realise that by doing so, I was as judgemental as she was. It hurts to admit that, but I must, because it is true. I should have realised that her aggressive behaviour had to stem from a missing link in her life. Now, after what I have just observed, I am comfortable and happy knowing that Siobhan is carrying my gift. She is strong in mind, and she knows what she wants for her child. The support that she will also receive from her mum's warm and caring nature will help the child grow up with strong foundations for a good life. That's the best that we can ever hope to give our children.

I am getting all emotional, and I feel connected to Siobhan and her mum. I suppose that is because I know that it is my gift which Siobhan has received. Nevertheless, my observations here are complete, and I cannot wait to share my discovery with Syd. I know that she will be so pleased for me.

CHAPTER 15

The Final Observation

This now means that Kath has also received a gem, and so it will be interesting to observe how she is progressing on her journey of transition. As soon as I arrive at the location, I home in on her essence. She is back in hospital again, but James is with her. It seems that they are spending a lot of time together, so at least she is not alone. Isolation at a time of personal trauma can lead to internal combustion, as we feel the emotions more intensely when we have no one to share them with. Hence, the saying: "A problem shared is a problem halved."

I hear Kath say, "Why are we never to share a child, James? Is this some type of sign to let us know that we should not be together?"

"Oh, Kath, please don't think like that! I think that the whole ordeal has brought us closer together; I feel more determined to make things work for us, and I hope that you do, too."

"You are right, there. My first reaction when I found out that we were expecting was, 'Oh, no, not again… this man must have super sperm!'… but that was only because it wasn't exactly how I had planned it would happen."

"Let's look at it like this, then: now we have the opportunity to plan it."

"James, I so want us to have a child together… maybe it will be third-time lucky. What do you reckon?"

147

"I love you, Kath. I missed you so much when we were forcibly separated all those years ago, even though we were only children. But, that's just it: we were children. We didn't have a say, and we couldn't have made a go of it on our own. Now, all these years later, we can! I want us to really make a go of things. I know that this is a sad time for us — it is hard to lose a pregnancy, let's not let it be in vain. We are in control here, and we can turn this negative into a positive. I want to spend the rest of my life with you, Kath. Will you marry me?"

"Are you serious, James?"

"I have never been more serious about anything in my life, Kath. You are the woman for me, and I don't want to lose you again."

"Yes, James, I will marry you."

They hug and kiss — a long, passionate and very loving kiss.

"When are you going to be allowed to get out of here?"

"I am not sure yet, but I can't see any reason why they might want me to stay. It's not like they can do very much for me now…. Why do you ask?"

"Well, we have a ring to buy."

"Oh, right… I will call the nurse now."

They smile at each other.

I will leave them now. Well, what a turn-up for the books this is! I think that the gem has certainly moved things along nicely, here. It seems that these two are supposed to be together, through destiny – maybe as teenagers they just met too soon. The gem has given them the opportunity to get close enough emotionally to realise that they can trust each other.

My final observation is now complete, and so it is time to return to the waiting zone. However, I find myself drawn back to Kath's house, although I don't know why. I have completed all the observations, which means my assignment is complete; still I sense that it is not time to leave yet, as I have something more to witness.

I allow the energy to draw me, and, a short time later, I arrive at Kath's house. Kath and James enter the house, and she carries a little bag that has what looks like a ring box in it. They rush into the living room.

"Let me do this right, Kath."

Taking the bag from her grasp, James gets down on one knee.

"What are you doing, James? Don't be silly!" she says, giggling with delight.

"I can't have you saying that I didn't do this properly, now can I?"

He takes the box from the bag and opens it, revealing a dazzling diamond ring.

"Katherine Johnston, will you do me the honour of becoming my wife?"

"James Justin Joyce, it would be my absolute pleasure — and it's about time, too, I must add."

He stands up, pulls her up into his arms, lifts her off her feet, and swings her around.

The telephone rings, and she says, "I think that I had probably better get that."

"Ah, do you have to?"

"Yes, it might be important."

She doesn't make it in time. It rings off, and the answering machine starts. Kath's recorded voice fills the room: "Hello, you have reached the messaging bank for Kath Johnston. Please leave a message after the beep."

"Oh, don't you just hate hearing your own voice on those bloody machines? It is just so embarrassing!" says Kath as a flush glows on her cheeks.

A man's voice leaves a message: "Hello, Kath Johnston. You probably won't know me, but my name is Hanson Jones, and I am the fiancé of Bethany Moore. I don't know if you know Beth, but she is a model.... Anyway, that has nothing to do with why I have called... it's a little awkward, you see... I won't say it on a machine, so could you call me as soon as you can? My number is —"

In the meantime, Kath has run to the telephone, and she picks up the handset, interrupting Hanson's message.

"Hello, Hanson. This is Kath, here; you don't need to leave a message.... Yes, that is correct.... Is this for real? You are not joking me... ? Yes, of course I do.... Will you tell her that I will have someone else for her to meet also... ? Yes, thank you for calling, Hanson, I am indebted to you for the rest of my life...."

She hangs up the phone, laughing and crying at the same time, and she starts dancing around the room, unable to hide her excitement.

"Are you going to ever tell me just what is going on, Kath?"

Kath stops dancing. In between her tears and laughter, she begins to explain the message to James.

"Do you know Hanson Jones? He is an actor."

"Yes I think so. Why?"

"Well, he is about to become your son-in-law."

"What are you talking about, woman? Have you gone completely mad? Did they give you too many pain killers in the hospital?"

"No, silly! It has all come back to us, James, can't you see? We have trusted our love for each other, and it has turned full circle to bring us magnificent joy. The call was about our daughter – the one who was taken away from us. She never knew that she was adopted until just recently. She had a miscarriage, needed a blood transfusion, and the truth came out. Her fiancé retraced records and found a link with the name Katherine Johnston, so he has been ringing all the Katherine Johnston's he could find. Luckily, he found me – I mean us! Do you understand what I am telling you, James? We have got our little girl back; she was lost, and now she is found – my lovely little princess who was stolen from my body in the harshest way imaginable has come back to me! Now I can be a proper mum for her at a time when she needs a mum to love her, and when I need a child to love. Thank you, whatever divine intervention that has made this happen Thank you, from the bottom of my heart."

James drops onto the chair, speechless, as he allows it all to sink in.

"Oh, and, by the way, she is getting married next month, so you may get the tux out – she will probably need you to give her away... James, are you okay?"

"Just nip me Kath. I have to be dreaming.... How one day can go from being complete and utter devastation to complete and utter joy so quickly? I am going to need time to let it sink in."

"You don't have time for it to sink in, James. Come on... we're going out."

"Where are we going?"

"We are going to meet her."

"What... already? Can't it wait until we're ready?"

151

Karen Weaver

"Wait?! Are you kidding me? I have waited twenty-two years to hold her in my arms—do you think that I am going to wait one minute longer?! Are you coming?"

"Yes, of course, I am."

Grabbing both their coats, he follows her out the door.

My work here is done; they have finally found each other. It is amazing how, when something in life is destined for you, it won't pass you by twice. It may take a while if it misses you the first time, but it will always come back—and when it does, it will be even bigger and better than the first time.

CHAPTER 16

Back in the Zone

I can't wait to catch up with Syd! She will be so interested in finding out who I believe should receive the gift, as she is a real believer in children being born to parents who will love and protect them as much as possible. This belief stems from Syd's having witnessed bad parenting when she was young, she has often recounted to me the horror that was her childhood; as a result, she understands the detrimental impact that this can have on children and their life foundations. I so appreciate Syd's values, especially when it comes to the final decision at the team meeting. The gift of life is the most precious gift of all, and it should never be given to those who don't appreciate it, as they will only pass those negative values on to their children, who will then pass them on to their children, and so on—and the knock-on effect is drastic. That is why, here in the waiting zone, we try our best to eliminate the possibility of that happening; when we do our jobs well, we are able to control some of the reciprocators of the gift of life.

I go straight to Syd's quarters. She does not answer, so I ring again. No, she is definitely not there. I was supposed to be back sooner, but I got so caught up in things that I didn't even think of messaging Syd to let her know I would be delayed. Oh, goodness! I do know all too well how she always thinks of the worst-case scenario.

How inconsiderate am I? I will have to make it up to her somehow. I had better contact her now and hope that she will meet with me. I send her a message:

"Syd, I am back. Can we meet? Sorry I didn't message sooner! Roo."

I head back to my own quarters to wait for Syd to message back. I wait a while but still receive no reply, so I go off in search of Syd, as it is not like her to give the cold shoulder for long — she likes to get things sorted out straight away. As I leave my quarters, I cross the corridor to ring her bell again; still no reply. I send the message again, and I hear a receptor beeping in her flat; either she is there and not letting me in, or she has gone out and forgot to take her message connector.

I decide to go in search of her, as that is the only way I will find out what is going on. The first person I bump into along the way is Jonnie.

"Ah, Jonnie... thank goodness! How are you?"

"I'm good, mate. How did your assignment go?"

"Interestingly. Have you seen Syd around?"

"Not since this morning. Gee, she hasn't been the same since she got back from meeting you. What did you do to her, Roo? I could hardly talk to her without her biting my head off for no reason whatsoever."

"I didn't do anything, Jonnie. We had a great time together."

"Would it have anything to do with you leaving us, do you think?"

"Erm... I haven't really considered how Syd feels about my leaving. Thanks for the wake-up call, buddy."

"You're welcome, mate! Don't forget — meeting tomorrow morning. 9.00!" Jonnie shouts after me, as I have already turned around, quickly moving along the corridor back to Syd's quarters.

"Cheers, Jonnie! I'll see you there," I call back over my shoulder. Ah, Syd! How selfish am I? I'm some friend. When I arrive back at her door, I knock continuously.

"Open up, Syd! I know you're in there, and I am not leaving until you talk to me!... I mean it, Syd — I can do this all night, but then we will just be wasting more time...."

The door unlocks, and I let myself in. Syd doesn't look happy, and her eyes are bloodshot, which means that either she was on the alco pops again, or she has been crying. I presume the latter.

"Syd, I am so going to miss you. Thirty-four years..."

"Please don't, Roo; I just need some time alone. I always knew that you would go before me, but I can't believe it is happening right now."

"You know that I will be waiting for you, and your time will be along soon, too... just you wait and see."

"What am I supposed to do until then, Roo? I don't think that I can bear being hooked up with a new partner. Did you hear that Jayden is supposed to be the one allocated as Visitor once you're gone?"

"You have to be kidding me! Boss can't; sure wasn't it Jayden who sabotaged the gems in the first place.... But, hey, let's not get into all that now."

"When are you scheduled to leave?"

"As far as I know, it is set for the day after tomorrow."

"I must focus. I have to get a grip; enough of this feeling sorry for myself. My best friend is about to go forth to once again hold the woman he loves in his arms; and, this time, it will be for all eternity. So I must give him a send-off to remember."

"Ah, Syd, please... really, you don't have to do that. I just want to spend as much time as possible with you before I leave."

"And you will, because you can help me organise it."

155

"Oh, okay. And I suppose I don't have a say in this, do I?"

"No."

"Are you sure we were never married, Syd?"

"Ha-ha! You would be so lucky. Anyway, I have decided that you are right now going to pop down to Dave's to get an obscene amount of heavenly delights, whilst I put together two fluffy-dream large espressos, and then we are going to sit down for the rest of the evening and have a laugh and a giggle like we always do, and then you will fill me in on everything that happened in the final observation. How does that sound to you?"

"As always, Syd, that sounds perfect. You have read my mind, as usual."

"That's just one of my many talents, you know."

"Oh, yes, I know that... don't you worry."

I leave for Dave's, coming back after a bit, carrying a whole tray of delights. I am sure that anyone who saw me on my way back must have wondered what I was doing with an entire tray, but these cakes are just so good – and, oh boy, am I going to miss them when I leave. I wonder if they deliver to heaven....

I spend the whole evening at Syd's. We sit, snuggled on the cosy couch, reminiscing about all the things we've done together over the past thirty-four years. We just laugh and relax all evening – and well into the early hours of the morning, when, at some point, we fall asleep in each other's arms. I wake at 7.30, which is very late, as I have a lot of organising to complete before the meeting at 9.00. I slip out of Syd's grasp, stretching my body, as I am rather stiff after being in that cramped position for some time.

I take a moment to just look at Syd before I leave. She lies in peaceful beauty on the couch, her golden locks spread out everywhere.

"You are beautiful, and I am going to miss you so much," I whisper, bending down and kissing her tenderly on the forehead.

Turning away abruptly, I leave her quarters.

CHAPTER 17

Final Meeting

As I approach the boardroom, I sense a change in the atmosphere. No one is standing outside the door in a military fashion. They are all already in the boardroom, sitting comfortably in the fluffy white chairs that just swallow you up as though they were clouds or marshmallows, not chairs at all. Everyone seems to be in a good mood, chatting and laughing and joking with one another.

I enter, and, although they must struggle to get out of the chairs, eventually, they all stand up and clap as I take my seat. I am kind of embarrassed but also honoured.

The Boss enters the room. Everyone is quiet once again; I am in awe of his sense of presence, which I could never equal.

"Good morning, everyone."

"Good morning, Boss."

"As everyone has probably heard by now, a long-standing member of the team has earned his right to enter the gates of heaven. Congratulations, Rupert."

Everyone starts to clap.

"Well done, Rupert!" a few of the guys shout.

Boss continues, "So, Rupert, we would like to say that we wish you all the best for your eternity — may it be all that you have ever wanted it to be."

"Thanks, Boss."

"However, we must put that aside for the moment and focus on the job in hand. You have had a busy time on this assignment. Please fill us all in now, so that we will be able reach our final decisions as to who we consider worthy of receiving the gifts."

I take a quick glance at Syd, who is looking at me in a strange but caring way.

"Yes, of course, Boss. I will start with Carrie. When I first started observing, she was in a disturbing state. She was living day by day, just trying to survive. The relationship between her and her partner was deteriorating rapidly, as he tried to get an emotional reaction from her by being mean and she just deflected it; this was so destructive for their relationship. I had to release a crystal just to get them close enough to have the opportunity to release the gem. I completed an energy check on their home, only to discover a hostile energy field. He was not happy that they were not married — and not even thinking of marriage — and so he continuously projected negative energies throughout the house. I tried to cleanse the home, but the negativity was just so strongly rooted that I couldn't shift it. When the gem was released and the discovery was made, it brought Carrie and Tom together; they believed that their bad luck had changed. She took the loss very badly, and she realised just how much she wanted another child. She also recognised how supportive her partner had been throughout the experience, and so, when he proposed, she said yes. They are now able to deflect any negative energies. Plus, because they will soon be married, the negative energy force should stop his release, and their luck will now change for the better. I believe that the gem has done its work here, and that this couple are ready to have another child."

"Right. Very good… so who's next?"

"Yes, next... (I rustle through the file; I never remember the order of my observations). That would be... Tracy. When I first observed Tracy, I noticed that a very sombre energy was always present everywhere around her. Everything seemed so dull and negative. The past losses affected her badly, and she feels the mental and emotional strain. All she can think about is the past; she can't focus on the future, or even the present. She has always had a lot of losses to deal with: her father passed on when she was young, and he has been a spirit in the house ever since—in fact, he is the one projecting the dull, negative energy force. I explained to him how he could move on, and, as soon as he did so, the energy flow changed colour immediately—it was amazing how much brighter things seemed...instantly. Anyway, during the flashbacks, I learned about a past loss, and I was also brought back a few years prior to a happier time for her, when she was planning to elope with her then-fiancé, who is now her husband, Rob. Because of this gem, I believe that she will get some medical answers as to why she is having so many issues keeping a pregnancy—her profile indicates a medical condition. These answers will help her to move forward and deal with her emotions, so that she can appreciate what she has and not focus on what she doesn't have.

In the words of Oprah Winfrey, 'Be thankful for what you have; you'll end up having more. If you concentrate on what you don't have, you will never ever have enough.' I don't believe that we can intervene when it is a medical issue, and I have wondered why a gem was sent to her again, but I do believe that it is because she needs closure; she needs a medical professional to spell it out for her, letting her know how lucky she has been to have had her first child. This final gem has given the push, enabling that to happen, when up to now, she had lost all hope."

"Interesting observation, Rupert... go on, please," says Boss.

"Next was Bethany—such a young thing... only twenty-two, but so in love with her partner. She has had a tough life, as her mum pushed her so hard to be successful in a modelling career that she didn't have a childhood at all. During the flashbacks, I witnessed just how intense this pressure was, and how her mum pushed her dad away from the situation. Beth and her fiancé are perfect for each other; he just worships her, and she feels so lucky to have his unconditional love and support. At first, she thought that she did not want to have a baby, but I believe that was only because of her own mother's behaviour. But, as time and events progressed—and, especially after she discovered her partner's desire to settle down and have children... not to mention his surprise proposal - her perspective on her surprise pregnancy changed. However, when the gem returned, complications resulted; she needed blood, which led to her discovering that her parents were not her real parents—she had been adopted as an infant, but never knew—and this freed her from the shackles of blind loyalty to her mother, whom Beth never felt really loved her as a daughter.

"Things have dramatically progressed, as it turns out that Beth is linked to Kath, who is the next recipient of the gem that I have to report on. Kath had a horrific teen experience: when she was fifteen, she fell for a cocky lad called James. She ended up pregnant, and her parents sent her to a convent where she endured six months of sadness, only for it to end in horror as her child was snatched from her as soon as she was born. Kath never married, but she did become very successful in the fitness field. She attended a school reunion, where she and James saw each other again for the first time since the trauma. They hit it off straight away, and he was the instigator of the release of the gem. The news of her expecting drew them together.

When the gem left her body, she was devastated, but he helped her though it... and even proposed! That same day, Bethany's fiancé tracked Kath down to let her know that she is Bethany's real mum—which also means that James is her real dad—and so they all arranged to meet. The gem's main purpose was actually to reunite these two women, as their opportunity for a lifetime of happiness together was stolen from them. Those who take it upon themselves to play God with others' lives should have consequences to pay themselves. Mind you, Kath's father lost the love of his daughter because of his actions; at least Kath now has the chance to redeem her love for her child.

They both can now move on to the next stages of their lives together, and it is my opinion that they are both ideal candidates to receive a gift. And why not make it a fairy tale come true? Let them share their pregnancies together, as there would be no stronger way for them to seal their bond."

"That is a Hollywood blockbuster all in itself, Rupert. It fairly pulls at the heartstrings," Boss says. "Who was last?"

"Yes, that was Siobhan. After first observing her, I was so shocked that she was even considered for receipt of a gem, never mind a gift. I was shown a seductive young woman, with no moral standards, who would do anything at all to get what she wanted. She was ruthless when it came to talking to others, showing no regard or consideration for their feelings whatsoever; her tongue was like a lightning bolt, firing insults with no hesitation, showing no concept of consequence. It was all very disturbing to watch. I went back to her childhood, only to discover that her father was a brutally harsh man, humiliating both her and her mother at any opportunity. It was plain to see that her mother was a broken woman, but I never got to see her face, as her head was always down, and her hair covered any part of her face that might have been visible. The poor woman must have had no self-confidence left! This man was the energy vampire, and she was his victim.

Siobhan shocked me on the final observation, however; when I arrived, I discovered that she had made a total transformation from a vixen to a woman of substance. I was shocked to discover that she was the recipient of my gift, and, even with my discovery of her metamorphosis, an initial horror overcame my thoughts. But, I soon realised that it was the best thing that had ever happened to her, and it has now transformed her into an ideal candidate for a gift."

"So, considering all these facts, Rupert, whom do you nominate as the three women that you would like us to vote for?" asks Boss.

"Siobhan has already received a gift, so she is no longer in the running. Out of the four women left, I wish I could send each of them a gift, but, as only three gifts are available, I would send the first gift to Carrie, as she is so ready. I would send the second gift to Bethany, and the third to Kath. I would love to send a gift to Tracy, and, initially, I hoped that she had received the miracle that was the release of my gift; but, on further consideration, I believe that she is not yet ready, as she needs to get the medical investigation out of the way first."

"Thank you for your detailed analysis, Rupert," Boss says. Turning to the group, he instructs, "In light of what you all have just heard, I want you to write down your nominations. When you are finished, send them to the top table for counting."

This process takes about twenty minutes, which I suppose is not bad, really… but it is rather boring.

At last, Boss announces, "The nominations have been counted, and I can now tell you who will receive a gift, and in what order: Bethany will be the first to receive a gift; Kath will be second; and… Carrie will be third…. I am sure that we all would hope that someday Tracy will be in a position to receive a gift."

Everyone agrees.

"Now that all of the formalities are out of the way, as Rupert is leaving us tomorrow, we can't let him go without a bit of a send-off."

As he says this, Boss turns toward the boardroom door.

The door opens, and a giant heavenly delight cake is wheeled in. I can't believe my eyes, and my poor stomach is screaming, 'no more', as I overdosed on the sugary delights last night at Syd's.

Everyone cheers as Boss says, "Let the party begin!"

CHAPTER 18

Entering the Gates

So it is finally here. The day that I have been waiting on for thirty-four years has finally arrived. The day has come when I finally get to hold my dearly beloved Josie in my arms once again. The gates of heaven will open wide for me today as I receive the right to enter. I have finally been forgiven for the sin I made all those years ago. I have earned eternal happiness, and the feeling is overwhelming.

Mind you, the feeling of nausea is quite overwhelming, too, as I really did overdo it on the heavenly delight last night. The party was great, and it was such a wonderful "surprise". Syd really went out of her way to make my last night in the zone a memorable one. I had the opportunity to hang with everyone that I have gotten to know over the time I have been here, and I value that so much… I am almost sad to leave, as this has been my "little heaven" for so long.

I must start getting ready for dispatch; although I do not need to take anything with me, I have still to mentally prepare myself to leave, as my desire is not to leave. Of course, I want eternal happiness with Josie and our child, but I also love the zone and all my friends here—especially Syd. The only thing that I will bring with me is a gift from Syd—it is a gold chain and pendant that she gave me last night when we said our final goodbye. The pendant bears two engravings: "Special Friend" on the front; and, on the back, "Your memory is engraved in my heart forever—Syd". She wouldn't let me open it last night whilst she was there; but, when I got back to my quarters, I opened it, and then I just sat and looked at it. It sums it all up: I now realise that she has strong feelings for me, but I am not in the position to consider my feelings for her — other than the deep feeling of friendship — and so I don't.

It is time for me to make my way to dispatch. I exit my quarters and close the door, turning around to see Syd's door. I stare at it for a moment; the desire to knock on the door and embrace her is overwhelming… but I can't do that, and so I shake that thought right out of my head.

I start walking down the corridor. Just as I reach the stairs, I hear a voice call out from behind me.

"Roo! Hold on a moment."

I turn around to see Syd running as fast as she can down the corridor. She is wearing her polka-dot pyjamas and her cow slippers that moo when you squeeze the toes. She makes me laugh, and my heart warms at this vision of utter silliness.

When she finally reaches me, she says all defensively, "What are you laughing at? Here I am, making an effort to say goodbye, and you are laughing at me!"

"Oh, Syd, just be quiet."

Pulling her towards me, I give her the strongest, warmest, most caring hug that I have ever given anyone. She stays there, just so content to be in my arms.

"I am going to miss you so much, Syd… I can only hope that it won't be long before you finally join me."

"Roo, it is too long already."

She pushes herself away from me and holds onto my lapel.

Karen Weaver

"And, anyway, you are finally going to be reunited with the love of your life. You have waited for this day for a lifetime, so I will not hold you back—I just wanted to say that I hope it all goes as you have dreamt it would for as long as I have known you."

"Thanks, Syd.... I am going to miss you so much.... I had better go."

I do something now that is the hardest thing that I have ever had to do. Ever. I turn around and walk away; my stomach wrenches.

I arrive in dispatch, and who is the first person that I bump into? Jayden—of course!

"Well, well, Rupert. You are finally moving on."

"Hello, Jayden. I thought that you no longer worked here."

"It is my last day," he beams proudly.

"Have you any advice for me, seeing as I will be slipping into your shoes? Maybe you can fill me in on how to get close to Syd...."

He enrages me, and I make a go for him; Jonnie, who happens to arrive just in time, is the only thing that saves Jayden.

"Don't you listen to him, Roo, he's just trying to rise you.... I will be taking care of Syd when you go, so don't worry about him."

I give Jayden a stare that speaks volumes, and he smugly smirks back. Oh, he does rise me; it kills me to think that he is going to be the person who takes over my job as Visitor—he has no values and so much to learn.

"So, Roo, I am gonna miss you, mate!" Jonnie says. "The place isn't gonna be the same without you."

"Thanks for saying that Jonnie... and for coming to see me off."

"What are mates for?"

"You will keep an eye on Syd for me, won't you?"

"I promise I will. Listen, I better get back, mate. I wish you all the best… you never know, I might see you in heaven someday."

We give each other a man hug, and I set off down the long corridor to the dispatch lounge.

Harry, ever his calm self, is on duty again. I have yet to meet a person as relaxed about life as he is. It is a calming experience just to interact with him.

"Hello, Rupert. You back again so soon?"

"Yeah, Harry. I am on my final journey to the gates of heaven."

"Well, good for you, buddy! I am so glad for you… you have waited a long time for this to come along."

"You're right, there, Harry."

"What's up? You don't seem to be as chuffed as I would have expected you to be."

"Oh, it's nothing. It's just… ah, I am being silly. I am just a bit nervous, is all. To wait so long for something to come… and then, when it does finally happen, it is a bit surreal, and I don't know what to expect."

"It will be whatever you think it to be, Rupert. You have the power to control your thoughts: if you want it to be wonderful, it will be — but, if you have already decided that it is not, it won't be. The mind is a powerful device, you know."

"Oh, I know Harry; you seem to have it sussed, though. What's your secret?"

"Now that would be telling, wouldn't it?"

We go through the usual protocol before I reach the Vortex. As I stand there, ready to dispatch for the very last time, I have an overwhelming feeling of nervous excitement at the prospect of my reunion with Josie – and I start to wonder if things could ever be as they once were. Have I not been realistic towards the situation, and have I romanticised that it will be more than it actually is going to be... more than it ever possibly could be... ? I will never know unless I go and find out. So I give the thumbs up to Harry, and I enter the Vortex.

When travelling in the Vortex, I am more aware of myself and my past, which the Vortex picks up on; as a result, snapshots from my memory start to flash around me. It is all quite startling, to be honest, as I see images of Josie as she was on our honeymoon, laughing and happy; and then I see images of her in hospital, followed by images of me jumping off the bridge. Finally, I see images of Syd and some of the things we did together. The whole journey through the Vortex consisted of what I can only describe as a movie of my life up to now.

It certainly has been an eye-opener. When I finally arrive at the gates of heaven, I need to take a few moments to compose myself.

Wow! I have always known that it would be a spectacular entrance, and I am not disappointed. Even so, I could never have imagined such magnificence. God must really know what he wants when it comes to making a statement. The gates, constructed of the goldest gold that I have ever seen, rise higher than I can view. A constant gleam shines from them, projecting angelic rays everywhere. It is utterly mesmerising, and I can see why people passing on from earth are drawn towards the light; it must act as a beacon, guiding them to paradise.

I check that I have my pass ready, as I am next in the queue to enter. I see what I can only describe as a heavenly ticket box, and I watch as the people ahead of me hand their passes in and receive stamps on their hand as if they were about to enter a concert. It is my turn, and I submit my pass, receiving the stamp, which doesn't dye my hand... it just sort of glows there like a tiny neon sign. It's very strange. As I follow the queue towards the gates, I get the first view of people waiting for their loved ones to enter. The feeling amongst the crowd is one of mixed emotions — anticipation, nervousness, excitement at the prospect of reunion with lost loved ones; yet, on the other hand, sadness for the ones that they have left behind. I, too, feel this way, even though I have come from a different place. These similar feelings unite us all.

I keep watching to see the familiar beautiful face that stole my heart all those years ago. I watch through the crowds for her auburn hair that swept down over her shoulders. I am almost at the gates, but I still have not gotten a glimpse of her.

The gateman, sensing my anticipation, comments "Have you not spotted anyone waiting yet?"

To which I reply, "No. I expected my wife to be waiting with our child, but I cannot see her yet."

"Well, just you keep to the left at all times, do you here? That is the way to your eternal destiny."

"Oh... okay... Thanks."

It doesn't make any sense to me, but I take it on-board, as you never know what information may come in handy.

I enter through the gates to see a place of divine beauty. It is everything I have ever imagined... and more; it even outshines any picture that I have ever created in my colourful, imaginative mind. I am awestruck, gobsmacked with utter amazement. I find myself just standing there, whilst people rush past me into the arms of their loved ones. I snap out of my daydream. Once again, I scan the crowd, peering at everyone in my view, straining to find what I have always imagined this moment would be: Josie waiting for me, holding our baby in her arms; as she catches sight of me, she runs into my arms, longing for my warm embrace... and she clings to me, never wanting me to let her go, ever again. This is what I have imagined for the last thirty-four years, but she is nowhere in sight… no sign of her at all. I have a strange feeling that something isn't right. This is not supposed to be the way it ends for me — I just know it.…

Someone taps me on the back, and my heart skips a beat. I turn around, only to discover Tracy's father standing there, with Tracy's mother at his side.

"Thank you for helping me to pass on, young man," he says.

"You are very welcome."

"This is my wife, and we are finally together again."

"Hello, nice to meet you," I say.

"Nice to meet you, too," she replies.

"We had better be off now… you take care."

"Thank you… I will."

I suddenly realise that, as Tracy's mother has passed on, she will now have the power to send Tracy a miracle gift, so I call out to them.

"Sorry! Hold on a moment… I must let you know that you can send your gift to Tracy to enable her to have the second child that she has always wanted."

"Really? I would so love to be able to do that!" her mother says.

"The poor love has been devastated by the news that she is not capable of carrying another child, and if I can send her one… oh, it would mean so much. Thank you for taking the time to tell me, son."

"You're very welcome.… I wish you both eternal happiness."

They smile and walk on.

I look around, but I do not have a clue which way to go. I look up to see two signs pointing to two different paths. One sign says, "Eternal Happiness", and it points to the path on the right. I so want to walk down this path, but I feel compelled to check out the other sign; first, because the gateman said to "stay to the path on the left", but also because I don't want to head down the path to eternal happiness without Josie and our child. The other sign says, "The Waiting Zone". Now I am really confused! I have just come from the waiting zone, but I reason that this must be a sort of waiting room that coincidentally has the same name. I start to walk along the path towards reception.

Who is the first person I meet? None other than Boss.

"I don't mean to be rude, Boss, but I thought that I would not be seeing you for a while."

"Rupert, I am glad that you found your way. You got the directions okay from the gateman, then."

"Yeah, I suppose. What's going on, Boss? My head is spinning. I need some answers."

"All right, you have been through enough, Rupert. I have those answers for you."

"Great! Why am I back here with you, then? Please tell me that."

"I am glad that you have asked me that first.... Can I ask you to follow me to the office?"

I follow him, and we both take a seat—not at opposite sides of his desk, though; we sit on the sofa in the corner of his office, as if we are about to have a sociable chat.

"Now, Rupert, I must ask you to be prepared for a shock, as what I am going to tell you... well, let's just say that you will not be expecting to hear what I am about to say."

"I'm tougher than you think, Boss, so please just get on with it. Anything that you say cannot be worse than the thoughts that are entering my head right now."

"Okay, then. Josie is not here to meet you."

"What? Why?"

"She did not die. She had complications, but she did not die—you just did not hang around long enough to find out what happened."

"What about the baby? Where is the baby?"

"The baby survived, too. She also had complications, but they stuck together and got through it."

"I am sorry.... I don't understand.... Why did I not know this before now? Why have I been in the waiting zone all this time, living in the hope of being reunited with them, thinking that they were here all along, just waiting on me... when they weren't. You must have known, Boss; you should have told me."

"It was not my place to tell you, Rupert. They are living their life on earth as they are meant to. I can't control that, but I can influence it slightly."

"What do you mean?"

"I suppose I have to tell you," Boss pauses. "Rupert, this is going to put your life in a whole different perspective, I must warn you of that. Now you must think about this carefully. Do you want me to tell you something that will change you forever?"

"I must know, Boss! I have been living a lie for long enough—what I must have done to my poor Josie! She needed me, and I just left her on her own with our child. I had the one thing that I have always wanted, and I threw it away in a moment of insanity. Why did I not just stay with them? They needed me—why did I not stay?"

"You must try to control your thoughts, Rupert; they will run wild if you don't try to control them. There is nothing you can change about it now. Things have moved on, and you must deal with these new revelations when your body tells you that it is ready."

"You're right, of course, Boss.... No need to panic; all will be well.... Please go on."

"Well, I have to tell you that you have met them since."

This I cannot comprehend.

"Siobhan is your daughter, Rupert. That is why I arranged for her to receive your gift, as she was taking the wrong path, mowing people over as she sped along the road of life, caring only about herself and achieving power. She had so much hatred inside her; but, when your gift entered her body, it was as though you gave her some part of you that she had not received at birth. Suddenly, she began to see things more positively... she began to value life and care about people."

"Siobhan... ? But I saw her... I watched as she... excuse me, Boss."

I run to the private toilet in Boss's office, where I vomit uncontrollably. The flashbacks of some of the seedy acts I witnessed her perform flood through my mind; it was such a gut-wrenching thing to discover that Siobhan is my daughter. I always knew that she was some father's daughter, but I thought that Mike was her father, and she'd turned out the way she did because of that.... That bastard! What he did to my daughter... ! I need to get sick again.... I should have been there for her.... I clean myself up quickly, as I must get back out to the Boss.

"Now let me get this straight, Boss: Siobhan is my daughter, but what about Rosie? Who is she?"

"Rosie is Josie, Rupert. She was never the same after her illness, and then when she discovered that you had... well... you know... let's just say that she didn't deal with it very well. Her unwavering belief and faith was never the same. She ended up marrying Mike Roe in an attempt to get a father figure for Siobhan. She very rarely showed her face, as she lost a lot of her confidence, and that is why you didn't recognise her. She also changed her name to Rosie, because Mike didn't like the name Josie. I can understand how you wouldn't have guessed. But, as you can see now, Josie and Siobhan are very happy, and it is because of the gift that you have sent them. Their lives have turned around for the better, and your gift will bring them so much joy... for the rest of eternity."

"Yes... and I can wait here for them until then."

"Well, it is not as simple as that Rupert. They have now lived thirty-four years without you: Siobhan doesn't even know who you are; Josie will find love again, and she will be very happy—and he is the one who will wait for her at the gates of heaven. It is entirely your decision, but I am offering you the opportunity to take a chance and wait here—or to return to the waiting zone."

"Whoa! Back to the waiting zone...? I never thought that I would be doing that...!"

"Listen, Rupert... I have something else to share with you."

"I don't know if I can take any more, Boss."

"I must confess that I have not been fully straight up with you.... The fact that your gift was released was not a mistake or a sabotage mission planned by Jayden; I ordered him to do it, and I told him to be quiet about it...."

"What...? But, why, Boss?"

"I am sorry, Rupert, but if you're going to keep interrupting, I won't get to tell you everything."

"Oh, right... okay.... sorry."

"I have been the Boss of the waiting zone for more years than I care to remember. Well, it so happens that I would like to move on now. I would finally like to take the path to eternal happiness. My wife is due to pass on shortly, and I would like to be the one who meets her at the gate."

"With all due respect, Boss, can I ask what this has to do with me?"

"Rupert, I would like you to become the Boss of the waiting zone. I have watched you for many years, as I always knew that I would need a successor someday. And you are the ideal candidate."

"Me—Boss of the waiting zone?"

"Yes, why not? You will then have full control of your own destiny. If it doesn't work out, you can do what I am doing: allocate someone else to take your place, and then you can enter heaven again, as you have earned the right to do. It is your call, Rupert. I will leave it with you, as you have a lot to absorb at once."

"It is a lot for me to take in, Boss, you sure are right, there.... Can I be quite honest with you? I am rather relieved by this turn of events, as I think that this may end up being the best outcome for me. Can I go back to the zone straight away?"

"Yes, of course, Rupert. But, before you do, I just want to share a few words of advice, if I may."

"Yeah, please do, Boss! I am in need of some positive inspiration at the moment."

"It is a simple sentiment, Rupert, but I believe in it: 'Regrets are a waste of time; they are the past, now crippling you in the present. It is up to you whether you let them follow you into the future.'"

"Wow! Those words are powerful, Boss."

"Yes, they are Rupert. Before you go back to the waiting zone, have you considered my offer? I must add that Sydney would be able to join you in the penthouse quarters as your forever-united-for-all eternity partner."

"Syd... ? What... ? I am so confused right now, Boss... can I think it all over and get back to you? I must go."

"Yes, I understand. Of course, Rupert, take your time. I shall prepare the Vortex."

CHAPTER 19

Happily Ever After

I arrive back in dispatch, much to Harry's shock. I have never seen him so shaken up. Actually, I have never seen him shaken up; as I've already mentioned, he is always completely calm.

"What's going on, Rupert? Did I not send you right?"

"No, Harry, nothing like that. I am just back, is all."

"I will never understand you, lad! Here I thought that you'd waited all these years to get to heaven—and what do you do? You turn right around and come back...!"

"Yes, Harry. And it looks like it will be for eternity. Sorry—I must dash. See you later."

I run off down the hall, nearly giving Jayden a heart attack as I walked past dispatch. I run as fast as my legs will carry me.

Everyone is stopping what they are doing, as they wonder why I am back. I suspect they still feel the after-effects of the night before.

I finally reach Syd's quarters, and I continuously bang on the door—rather loudly, I might add, to make certain she hears. She comes storming out, ready to give the person banging on her a door quite a mouthful. However, as soon as she sees that it is just me, her whole attitude changes. She beams me a bright smile, wrapping her arms tightly around me, as if to say that she is never going to let me go again.

"What are you still doing here, Roo? I thought that you left hours ago."

"I did… I'm back."

"Don't be silly! You can't come back…."

"Oh, Sydney, my dearest… apparently, I can… and I have."

Her head shoots up, and her eyes narrow as she peers into my face. "What's going on, Rupert?"

"Can I come in and tell you?"

We go in to her lounge. Yes, sure enough, Cupid is pointing in my direction, as usual. But, this time, I don't mind; I want his arrow to strike — in fact, I do believe it struck a long time ago.

"Boss wants me to take over his job, which means I would remain in the waiting zone for all eternity. I will have my eternal happiness right here, Syd."

Syd gazes at me for a moment. "This doesn't make sense, Roo! What about Josie?"

"Brace yourself, Syd: Josie never died; neither did our baby…." I pause for a moment to let that part sink in, and then I tell her the rest.

"Syd… Siobhan is my daughter, and Rosie is Josie."

"Hold on a minute, Roo… I can't keep up. I just need to get this right in my head. There was no one waiting for you at the gate, so you decided to come back to me as your second choice, is that it?" She moves away, and I see tears in her eyes.

"No, Syd, it is not like that at all! Do you not understand? For years, I have suppressed my true feelings for you; I felt that my loyalty had to be towards my wife and child. I believed that I had to remain in the waiting zone to earn eternal happiness because I had taken my own life, but that they would be waiting for me when I earned my right to enter heaven. I believed that the three of us would spend eternity together — that my destined eternal happiness was with Josie and our child. Now I know that this has not been the case, and it never was. I am free of the shackles of my loyalty to them, as I realize that they are fine without me. My earthly destiny with them is closed, through the power of my gift's release to Siobhan. Now I am free to love you for eternity, and that is what my eternal destiny has been all along. I promise that I will do all in my power to ensure that we have eternal happiness, Syd — will you marry me?"

"Yes, Roo, I will marry you!"

Epilogue

So we did exactly that. I contacted Boss to accept his job, and so he was able to move on to his eternal happiness. On the same day as my inauguration as Boss of the waiting zone, I married Syd. It was the best day ever. She has always been my soul mate — we have been destined to be together for all eternity. I can see clearly now that this is why we were such good friends for so long. Syd and I just "get each other"; we always have and always will. Now, after thirty-four years of friendship, we join together as one to share eternity; we don't need to go to heaven to have eternal happiness — we have it right here..... As I watch her walk up the aisle, wearing the most beautiful, sparkling- white dress that I have ever seen, I know that this is it: the final piece of my jigsaw is in place; I am now complete.

As Syd has decided to stay in the waiting zone with me as my wife for all eternity, she has signed away her desire to enter heaven, thus giving me the power over her gift. Just as the Boss decided the destination of where my gift should end up, I as the new Boss, have control of this miracle. I decide to keep Syd's gift right here for us.

Our little miracle will bring wonderment to our lives, lasting for all eternity. I can't wait to see Syd's face when she discovers it! She has always craved children, and to think that she has given herself this treasured gift — for, she alone supplied the gift, and I have just navigated it in the right direction, as I now have the power to do so.

Syd's and my time of eternal happiness commences, and the next chapter now begins for each of us — and for the two of us together, and for the precious one that we will have....

About the Author

Karen Weaver currently resides in Perth, Western Australia, with her husband and five children, after emigrating from Ireland in September 2008. She now regularly writes articles for buildingbeautifulbonds.com, and can be contacted there or via her facebook page.

Her children are the most important things in her life. Writing comes a very close second, and she is currently working on her next novel.

She came from Ireland—a place of magical beauty—and she now resides in Australia—a place of inspiration and opportunity; these two special but very different places, together, give her the passion and determination necessary to incorporate positive writing in her life daily.

Karen successfully completed a diploma in humanities, which instilled in her a desire for learning new things; this, combined with the experience of a miscarriage, led her to write this book, in order to give hope and a degree of understanding to women who suffer such pain.

This book's opening quote continues to inspire Karen daily, and so she chose to use it in closing, as well:

*"From all negative situations is the potential
for a positive outcome."*

KAREN WEAVER

View more writing by Karen at *buildingbeautifulbonds.com*

5 STAR REVIEW OF The Visitor

Reviewed by Brenda Ballard for Readers' Favorite

Five women, each with their own tribulation, walk through life with their dreams that mean everything to them. The Visitor comes to make changes, to provide each a gem that, if things go well, will be the pivotal point that they yearn for.

The plot twists and the enticement of what the next page may unfold will leave the reader with chores still to be done and dinner uncooked. It is that impossible to put the book down! I loved the uniqueness of the plot; I have never read a story like this before. The author is very skilled at pulling the reader in and does not disappoint. She is a descriptive writer who manages to make the lucky reader feel as though they are right there in the story. Being the mom of four, it is clear that Karen Weaver surely has a lot of opportunity to utilize her fantastic imagination but she doesn't stop at the family: she shares her gift with the world. I went back and re-read a couple of parts just because I enjoyed them so much. I cannot say that I do that often (if at all) normally. The author's name is one that I will look for now and then, just to see what else she has written. While I am really not the groupie type, I will definitely follow this woman's work! I highly recommend "The Visitor" to readers who enjoy this genre. It is that great!

Award finalist 2012

Readers' Messages to the Author

"This one experience really seemed to lack any positive side; although everyone around assured you 'it happened for a reason', which might have soothed your logic mind, somehow your heart still yearned for a deeper kind of understanding.

The Visitor gave me the answer my heart longed for.

My own experience with miscarriage now has a whole new meaning which I am able to positively accept and embrace.

The deeper sense of understanding that I have gained from reading this fantastic book, lovingly created from another woman's similar personal experience, relates not only to miscarriage itself but also to many circumstances that I have experienced — and will go on to experience in my life. Thank you for the insights shared, Karen."

With love from
Donna Di Lallo

"The Visitor is captivating, humorous and heart-rending. Weaver translates beautifully a topic traditionally shrouded in silence. It is a true privilege to partake in her spiritual journey.
McDermott is the true gift'!"

Sascha Brooks

THE SECOND BOOK IN

THE ENLIGHTENMENT SERIES

The Wish Giver

"The true magic is when it all comes together"

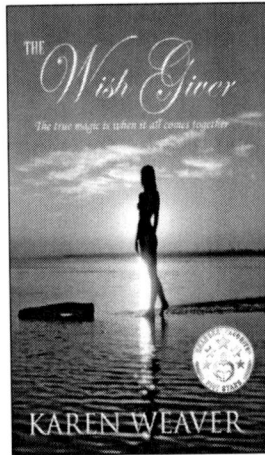

5 star reviewed by Readers' Favorite

Join Syd on her mission as The Wish Giver. This journey is sure to be packed full of adventure, emotion and magic for all those involved.

Who will be chosen to receive the gift of a wish?

What will they have to sacrifice to receive it?

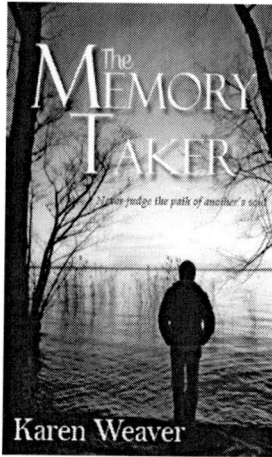

Lightning Source UK Ltd.
Milton Keynes UK
UKOW04f1931240315

248455UK00001B/6/P

HUNTED

Book 2 of the Hybrid series

Nick Stead

To

Lauren

On our first con at
Birmingham - Arrooo!

N. Stead

A Wild Wolf Publication

WILD
WOLF
PUBLISHING

Published by Wild Wolf Publishing in 2017
Copyright © 2016 Nick Stead

ISBN: 978-1-907954-61-0
Also available in E-Book

www.wildwolfpublishing.com

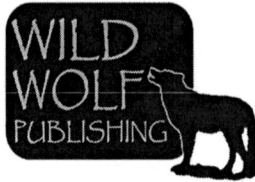

2

As always, for my amazing family for their continued support and belief in me, especially my Mum, my sister Amanda, and my Auntie Debbie for always being there for me at local events.

And for my friends for all their support, with special thanks to my beta readers Hannah, Clare and Charlie for the great feedback to help make Hunted the best read possible. Special thanks also goes to Lauren and Francine for their help with the Hunted trailer and especially Tom (aka White) for not only driving all the way up from Wales to let me chase him in wolf form across the moors, but also acting as chauffer for the day and dealing with numerous aches and pains from filming.

I would also like to thank my fellow writers and friends at Huddersfield Author's Circle once again for their support and feedback, and helping me to continue to grow as a writer.

And a big thanks to the team at Wild Wolf for all their hard work in putting my work out there for fans to enjoy.

Nick

Prologue

Light creeps across the woodland floor as a new day dawns, painting a grisly scene amidst the natural beauty of the bed of autumn leaves – your final resting place. Blood seems so bright in the early morning sun, ruined flesh glistening wetly. Flies crawl across pale skin, feeding and laying their eggs in every suitable crevice available to them. The insects venture inside your ears and your mouth, and those gaping holes of blood and gore where once your eyes resided, before fangs obliterated them.

Reduced to no more than this lump of mutilated flesh and bone, no one will recognise you for who you were, not by sight alone. Your limbs lay sprawled, one arm bitten off at the elbow, ripped tendons, ligaments and flesh hanging from the bloody stump like gruesome rags. Chalky white bone, streaked with red, lies bare in places where chunks of meat have been ripped away, and your torso is completely torn open, leaving nothing but an empty cavity, many of your vital organs gone, others strewn around and half eaten. And around that bloodied mask that was once your face, brains lie like a ghastly halo, where they oozed out from the puncture marks in your skull.

Somewhere nearby a chilling howl sounds from a bloodied muzzle, turning to a human cry of anguish. You might have been dragged through the black veil of death, but it seems there is more for you than darkness on the other side after all. Your presence lingers on in this earthly plane, still aware of the world but powerless to do anything to help shape it.

Those loathsome scavengers feasting on the decay suddenly buzz away, fear overriding hunger. Birds singing to the early morning fall silent, and rodents seek refuge in the undergrowth. They know better than to linger in the presence of the unnatural beast invading their habitat, instincts saving them where thoughts failed you.

And here I stand over your mortal remains, your blood staining my bare flesh. Underneath the blood and dirt my skin remains as flawless and unmarred as the day I was born, despite everything my body's been through over the years. And yet for all the healing capabilities of my curse, I still carry the scars, invisible to the naked eye but they mark me nevertheless. And just as scarred flesh from old physical wounds can still throb years later, so too do I feel the ache of these mental wounds, all the more potent whenever I must walk alone. So why take your life when my heart yearns so greatly for companionship? I began my tale out of the need to share the burden of this pain I carry, the weight of all the deaths surrounding me that still hangs over me even now. Killing you only added to the weight of my burden, undoing any relief I might have found in the telling.

I could blame the hunger of course, or the call of the moon robbing me of my senses. But to do so would be a lie. In truth I'm no more than a killer, a monster born of humanity but also driven by a wolf's hunger for raw flesh. Most people don't know what it is to truly dwell in the darkness, but that has been my reality for some time now. The darkness at the heart of the human side to my nature has ruled me for so long, I don't think I could pull myself back out, even if I was willing to try. And to drag others into the darkness has become all I know. So it was back then, early in my lycanthropy, and so it is now.

Did you pity me when you first heard how my life was ripped from me by this curse, I wonder? Did you feel sorry for this poor, wretched creature, condemned to prey on those around him, before I crushed that pity, along with all your other thoughts and feelings, your very life. And does it now bring you pleasure to hear of my suffering? I've proven myself to be the monster beyond a doubt now, after all. Perhaps I've earned your hatred. That is, if there is anything left of you to hate. Are you truly still with me now, or am I merely imagining this presence I sense? No matter. I promised to continue my tale after the full moon, so continue it I shall. If it brings you some form of enjoyment to hear of my pain then it's the least I can do in return for the life I stole from you to fuel my own cursed existence. And if you are no more than another product of my guilty conscience, perhaps voicing some more of the pain I carry will bring some relief again, no matter how temporary. You may not really be here this time, there may be no one listening, but I want to continue.

Very well then. We began in the year 2003, on my final day as a human, though I struggled through my last year of high school in an attempt to carry on in the remnants of my life before the curse. Now we go back to where I left off in 2004, just after I'd chosen to leave the human world behind, when a new struggle was only just beginning.

Chapter One – A Harsh Reality

Blood pooled at my feet, seeping into the soil, the last remnants of life from my latest kill. He fell to the ground and another human took his place. The sounds of battle filled the night, gunfire ringing in my ears, the heavy thud of sword through bone, and the wet, tearing sounds of flesh being ripped apart.

Corpses littered the battlefield, some rising as zombies, others never to rise again. Zombies – they were everywhere. Moving through the battle in a cascade of maggots, each in various stages of decay. The new dead walked almost like humans. The older ones limped, their muscles stiff and almost useless. Some were reduced to skeletons, Lady Sarah's power the only thing binding the bones together. Some had died in the last world war, their legs long since blown off. They dragged themselves along with their hands. Some groaned. Others were silent, their vocal cords rotted away years ago. Few of them were whole, but they didn't need much to kill. One of them even had a head missing, but it seemed to be doing well enough without it. They pulled their victims apart. Some of them tore through flesh and bone with their teeth. And they were literally unstoppable. Bullets tore holes in them, blades hacked them to pieces, and still they carried on their relentless attacks. Most of them didn't even bleed. The freshly dead did, but there was no clotting, no healing, not like the living. Of all the undead, they were the closest to being truly dead.

Another human came at me with a sword. Clawed hands shredded his skin and blood poured, my fur soaked with it. Then a zombie crawled towards me, dragging its useless legs behind it because the nerves had been torn out at the base of the spine. A short length of intestine trailed behind it, the rest having been cut away after it had served its purpose as rope to bind her. It was a woman once, barely recognisable now. The face was a bloody mask, nose broken, ears missing, eyes long gone, save for the remnants of jelly like substance clinging to her cheeks. The flesh around the jaws had been completely torn off, giving her a permanent skeletal grin. There wasn't an inch of her body that had been left untouched.

Other zombies lurched towards me. I suddenly found myself surrounded. But something was wrong, we were supposed to be on the same side. The zombie of the tortured woman latched onto my leg and bit down hard enough to draw blood. A scream tore from my throat as a second zombie sunk its teeth into my shoulder. I tried to fight them off but it was no use, they were too strong for me. I tore at the zombie on my shoulder with human hands, trying to pry its jaws off me. But that wasn't right either, I didn't remember transforming back to human...

A werewolf loomed over me, blood on its jaws and death in its eyes. I was no longer one of the undead, just a human again, body frail with mortality. The zombies ripped me apart in seconds. Like piranhas, they stripped me to the bone. A last dying scream tore from my throat, death drawing nearer. And then came the sound of real enemies somewhere on the edge of consciousness, beyond the nightmare, and I fought my way back to the waking world.

Lady Sarah was already alert beside me, her senses focussed on the group of Slayers creeping towards us. They were stealthy for humans but for all their training and technology, it was no match for our supernatural sight, hearing and smell. It had been only three nights since the battle in my hometown, in which we'd defeated the force there. I hadn't expected them to send more so quickly, or for them to find us so soon after leaving the area, but no matter how they'd located us, the fact remained we had become the hunted.

Of all the deaths I'd caused in that fight, only one weighed on my conscience. For the blood ties and the bonds of family are difficult to break, and on some level I supposed I had loved my Dad, though such emotions had been hard to find in my heart towards the end, once my rage had broken free and the anger had consumed me. To say I grieved for him would not be entirely accurate but in the aftermath of the battle, once my rage had subsided, there were the stirrings of guilt such as I had not felt in months. What troubled my conscience the most was the thought of the destruction I had wrought on the lives of my Mum and my sister, Amy. In losing both me and my father that night their world had surely been left in ruins, by my own hand. It pained me to think of the heartbreak I must have caused them, whenever I was given the chance to dwell on it.

I rose beside the vampire, stiff and aching from sleeping on the hard floor. She relied on me to watch over her during the daylight hours when she was at her most vulnerable, and I had been allowed a few hours of rest while she watched over me in return. But sleep had not been easy since the curse of my lycanthropy had awoken nightly horrors to plague me every time I closed my eyes, and sleeping rough had only added to my problems with insomnia. I was not adjusting well to the new way of life somewhere between the world of man and nature, neither of which we could ever belong to. Nothing had been the same since I'd been bitten roughly a year ago, and day by day I'd slowly lost my humanity until I knew I could live among humans no more. The battle had brought with it the final realisation that I had to leave my old life behind and move on, or risk hurting my remaining loved ones. But that was proving to be more of a challenge than I'd expected, as it had been all I'd known prior to this new, harsh lifestyle I'd suddenly found myself in. After years of living in the world of modern human comforts, it was something of a shock to the system to be without all that which most people take for granted.

As well as missing the comfort of my bed, I found myself longing for a shower more than my teenage, human self would ever have anticipated. There had been no time to wash since the battle and my body was covered in dried blood and filth, as well as my own grease and sweat. And while I had become accustomed to living with hunger when I'd been captured and starved by the Slayers, it was already becoming a constant sensation which only added to my discomfort. Lady Sarah had promised to teach me how to survive in the shadows, and the first lesson had been to hunt only small prey which would attract less attention, or to scavenge when possible. But this meant I'd not been permitted to eat my fill since before the battle and such small morsels as rabbits and birds could only ever take the edge off the hunger. I needed far more meat to satiate it and as I turned my attention to the Slayers, I watched them ravenously. I also felt a sense of hatred, still blaming them in part for bringing my human life to an end, and I let it awaken my anger, constantly smouldering within the darkest recesses of my very being. A growl rumbled deep in my throat and I bared my teeth as I readied myself to fight.

"No, Nick," Lady Sarah whispered.

"Why? There's only a handful of them," I said.

"No, we must choose our fights carefully if we are to win this war."

I ignored her and let the transformation take hold, wanting to revel in the destructive power of my lupine body once more. I hungered but it was no longer the mere craving for human flesh that drove me. No, I thirsted for blood and hungered for death, for slaughter. I had developed a need to kill, born of the rage and bloodlust awoken by the curse, all the more potent for the waxing moon overhead which would soon reach its fullest. In fighting the Slayers I could indulge my dark desires, but it was more than that. I embraced my rage because it kept the guilt and the pain at bay, and I felt I needed to lose myself in the bloodlust to avoid falling back into the dark pit of despair and depression I'd been in for the winter months following my friend Fiona's death.

"Foolish boy!" Lady Sarah hissed. "Do you not recognise the spellcaster from three nights past? It is a fight we cannot win."

"Don't treat me like some mortal kid anymore," I snarled, but suddenly my skin felt as if it was burning with the memory of the witch I'd faced in battle who had nearly ended my life, if Lady Sarah hadn't been there to save me. Much as I hated to admit it, she was right. The spellcasters could easily have been the end of the army we'd gathered for that fight, and between their power and the guns we would face from the mortal Slayers, the two of us alone couldn't hope to defeat them.

"There is no shame in tactical retreat," she said in a gentler tone in an attempt to soothe me, aware that arguing could cost us our lives.

"Tactical retreat," I snorted. "Call it what you want, it's still running."

But I let my anger burn back down to the embers deep within, though I didn't reverse the few changes that had already begun, intending to take the transformation all the way to my faster wolf form.

"There's no time," Lady Sarah said. "We have to go, now!"

I had no choice but to run with the vampire in human form, unable to keep the transformation up whilst moving. It was too painful and too awkward to run on shifting flesh and bone.

Even in human form, I was still faster than any mortal, though I would have had no hope of keeping pace with the vampire if she'd run at full sprint. She let me set the pace and ran effortlessly beside me, graceful and agile as only we paranormal predators could be. Within minutes we had covered enough of a distance to be safely out of range of the group of would-be hunters – the mortals and their guns at any rate. I still had much to learn about the supernatural world I'd been dragged into and I could only guess at the rules of witchcraft. Were there any limitations on spells over a distance? If it was as easy as chanting an incantation to strike down enemies from anywhere on the planet then they would have surely killed us already, so I had to assume there was some kind of a range on witchcraft as well, but what that range was perhaps only the witches and warlocks themselves knew. From the look of determination on Lady Sarah's face, it seemed she didn't plan on stopping until we'd put a few hundred miles between us and the spellcaster, so I had to assume the warlock's power was still a threat over quite some distance. It seemed we would need to spend the remainder of the night on the run, if we were to rest safely through the daylight hours.

"Wait," I growled, coming to a stop and scenting the air. "Don't you smell that?"

"Fire," the vampire hissed.

"Over there," I pointed. The unmistakable scent of smoke was thick and unpleasant to my sensitive nose, and as we watched, the faint glow of flames could be seen creeping through the darkness. "Coincidence?"

"We can't take that chance. If it is the work of witchcraft it could be our undoing. Come, this way."

"Wait," I repeated. "There's another group of Slayers closing in. It's a trap; they want us to keep running so they can catch us between the fire and their guns."

"Then we must keep going towards the flames and hope we can outrun the blaze before it spreads too far round."

"Fuck that, we need to fight our way out!"

"If we stand and fight we will die," she argued.

"And since when has running into a trap ever been a good idea? If we keep going they'll kill us. If we fight we have a chance to escape, and at least if we do die we can take some of them down with us. What are you so afraid of?"

"I fear nothing," she hissed. "But I have not survived all these centuries by being reckless."

"Fine, you keep running," I snarled. "I'm staying to face them."

Without waiting for any further response from the vampire, I let my anger rise once more, my blood boiling as it coursed through my veins. There was a savage joy as the feral power of my lupine nature surged through my body, all vestiges of the human weaknesses falling prey to the might of the predatory wolfish features taking hold. But there was no time to take it all the way to wolf form, so I chose to fight in the hybrid form I'd first been trapped in by mistake one cold December night, but had since grown to enjoy.

Where not so long ago there'd been horror at the agonising sensation of my body becoming monstrous, I now embraced the painful feeling of my face stretching out into a muzzle, teeth blunt and pathetic growing into natural weapons to rip and tear the flesh from my enemies. The sound of the approaching Slayers was suddenly sharper as my ears became pointed and slithered up to the top of my head, as did their scent to my superior canine nose. The smell of the smoke was almost unbearable and somewhere within my mind I felt the wolf's instinctive response to flee. But my rage was stronger than the animal fear the fire invoked in the lupine half of my mind, and as ever my bloodlust rose with it, bringing the overwhelming need to hunt and kill. My hunger also intensified and with an excited howl I bounded forward to meet the Slayers in battle once more, running on

11

all fours despite my body remaining mostly humanoid. As well as my lupine head, my spine had also elongated to form a tail and my hands were now clawed, and I'd let my fur burst forth from my skin, forming my pelt which resembled that of a natural timber wolf. But that was as far as I took the change for the coming battle. There was as much fun to be had in fighting in this hybrid form as there was when fully wolf, and it meant I could swipe with my clawed hands like a cat as well as savaging with my fangs.

The Slayers were quick to react once I leapt into view, opening fire in an attempt to stop me before I could get close enough to kill any of them. Two came dangerously close to hitting their mark, one bullet nicking my ear and the other thudding into my chest, just missing my heart. The pain was enough to rival that of the transformation, my ear stinging and gushing blood, my chest throbbing. I let it fuel the rage and kept going, not even slowing when another bullet passed clean through my left bicep or when a fourth grazed my right shoulder blade. Then I was on the first of the humans and all he could do was scream as his gun clicked empty, my fangs ripping his throat out in a spray of blood and gore. I left him dying and turned to face a woman just as she was about to shoot through my skull. At point blank range I would never have stood a chance if she'd succeeded in squeezing off the shot. But I was too fast for her, ducking so quickly she couldn't track my movement with the gun and grabbing her leg with my bloodied muzzle.

Fresh blood oozed out as my jaws clamped down, staining my fangs and matting my fur. I lost myself in the bloodlust, the world reduced to a red haze that centred round the frantically beating heart of my prey and the blood pumping from her ruined calf where I savaged the flesh with wild abandon. I was only vaguely aware of more bullets flying through the darkness as I pulled the woman's leg out from under her, causing her to fall heavily on her back. With a whimper she tried to pull herself backwards and away from my bestial fury but I was on her once more, digging my claws into her chest and ripping it open, greedily burying my snout into the feast I'd unlocked within.

The heart was the choicest of the organs I'd laid bare, and it brought a sense of primal ecstasy to feel it beating between my fangs, my tongue bathed in her blood, so rich and juicy. With a jerk of my head I ripped it free of its tubes, more blood splattering my body and the earth around us, and gushing into the cavity I'd created in the woman's chest. I felt a dark pleasure as the organ grew still in my mouth, another life ended, and gulped my prize down. My hunger wanted more flesh but the bloodlust overrode it, causing me to rise from my latest victim and take another. It was only then I realised Lady Sarah had entered the fray, which was probably the only reason I was still alive. I'd been so intent on my kill, the other Slayers could've easily put a bullet in my brain while I tore into her soft flesh. But the vampire had kept them busy, the gunfire aimed in her direction while I'd been so lost in my bloodlust to take any notice.

I ripped a second woman apart while Lady Sarah kept the rest engaged, rising again to see one of the Slayers stood apart from the rest. He was older than most of their recruits I'd come across, grizzled and scarred like a soldier who'd seen too much of battle, his eyes the cold grey of winter skies. It seemed he too believed in 'tactical retreat', but there was no sense of panic like most other Slayers I'd encountered in the past when I'd driven them to flee. He merely backed away slowly, keeping his gun trained on me but saving his bullets. I snarled and took a step forward, meaning to end his life as brutally as the other three I'd killed, but Lady Sarah had just dispatched the last of her opponents and she grabbed my arm to pull me back.

Roaring angrily I turned to her, but her own anger had awoken and much as I hated to admit it, I was no match for a vampire. For all the power the curse granted me, it was still not the equal of the vampiric power Lady Sarah wielded.

"Control yourself!" she hissed. "The other group are catching up. If we give the warlock chance to reel off an incantation we're both doomed. Let him go."

I roared again but did as I was told, turning my attention back to the body that lay at my feet and crouching back over my kill. There was still plenty of meat to be had, and as I wolfed down a couple more mouthfuls, the bloodlust and the rage began to drain back into the abyss where once my soul had been, before the curse had robbed me of it. My anger and my need to kill seemed to be all that were left to me, poor replacements though they were, and it was only when I embraced them did I feel truly alive.

"Nick, there is no time! Take your full wolf form now, before they draw any closer, but hurry. We must make haste before the warlock has chance to ensnare either of us in a spell."

Feeding seemed like a much more valuable use of the time we had, but without my rage to fuel me I became aware of the pain from the bullet wounds I'd sustained when I'd initially charged into battle. I'd been bleeding heavily and I suddenly felt the weakness brought on by loss of blood. Hungry as I was, the transformation would heal the damage and it would allow us to cover more ground once I'd recovered my strength and could run swifter as a full wolf. Feeding would have to wait.

As I let the change take hold once more, I felt my strength returning as the wounds closed, the bullet that had lodged in my chest being forced out by the newly formed flesh. It fell to the ground with a metallic clatter, no more than a small lump of bloodied metal, yet if it had hit me just another inch to the left and successfully passed through my heart it would have been the end of me. Maybe I was growing too reckless, but that thought brought me no shame – indulging the bloodlust had felt too good.

The initial feeling of strength faded as the transformation completed, only to be replaced by a wave of weariness and renewed hunger. I wrestled with my instincts, the scent of all the fresh meat almost overpowering, but it was only the vampire's presence that kept me in check. I knew she intended to teach me greater self-control over the coming months, as soon as we succeeded in losing the Slayers for any considerable length of time, but until then I had to struggle with the hunger and the bloodlust as best I could. Had I been on my own I would probably have given into it once more, but as it was I didn't want to anger Lady Sarah any further, knowing I needed her if I wanted to survive, annoying though she could be.

Beside me the vampire also took her own wolf form, although the transformation was so very different from my own. Where my kind are cursed and the change is a brutal, painful affair, Lady Sarah (and presumably other vampires who possessed the same ability) made it graceful, like shadows melding together. It was too quick for a mortal eye to follow – one form simply merged into the other, and in the blink of an eye a beautiful she wolf stood before me, holding the old fashioned black dress in her jaws which was the only thing I'd ever seen her wear. My transformation was always smoother when I willed it, rather than being forced into one form or the other by the rise and fall of the full moon, but it was still awkward when compared with the shapeshift Lady Sarah could perform. And then minutes later we slunk away, moving more swiftly and silently than any natural predator. I ignored the hunger and the weariness as best I could, pushing my lupine body to its limits in a bid to put as much distance between ourselves and the group of Slayers as we could in the time left before dawn.

Chapter Two – New Challenges

Around two hours before daybreak, we began to search for somewhere to shelter through the day. We'd reached a city sprawl, the heart of which lay nearby. The fields had given way to endless rows of houses and buildings, and we'd been forced to skulk in the shadows, moving much slower than I knew Lady Sarah would have liked.

At the speeds we could move we made hard targets to hit. If we'd have kept running flat out we could potentially have passed through the urban area unharmed, even if we had crossed paths with any more Slayers. But if we were to find somewhere safe to spend the daylight hours we would have to slow eventually, and the last thing we wanted was to alert any Slayers in this new area to our presence, having only just lost the group we'd been running from. So proceeding slowly and cautiously was the safer option in our current surroundings, as painful as it may be.

This was the closest we'd been to civilisation since leaving my hometown, Lady Sarah insisting we keep to rural areas for the first few nights where we were less likely to encounter Slayers. Or that had been the plan, prior to that night when it seemed they'd been actively hunting us.

As we crept through the streets, the vampire taught me to be careful when choosing where to go whenever the need arose to enter a human settlement, as the nearest might not always be the safest. A small town or village might have less Slayers patrolling the streets, but if we were to visit somewhere too small we could potentially be detected quicker. Larger towns and cities offered more places to hide, as long as we were careful of security cameras. And if we ever needed to pass as human, a city that had a lot of strangers passing through and was large enough that people barely knew their neighbours was the safest place for hiding in plain sight.

Most of her lessons so far had just been common sense, but I would never have thought about these things had I been on my own. In fact if it weren't for Lady Sarah, I would probably have given in to the desire for human comforts and found a room to stay in, stealing the money and new clothes from the corpses of my victims. I wouldn't have lasted two minutes without the vampire's guidance, whether I wanted to admit it or not.

We turned away from the city centre. With our superior senses it was easy to determine where to find the nearest run down area, which should offer numerous choices for shelter. It didn't take us long to slink over there, at which point Lady Sarah changed back to her human form and dressed, though I remained a wolf for the time being to conserve energy.

We wandered the unfamiliar streets, looking for somewhere safe to rest. The vampire had no coffin of her own and was forced to take refuge wherever she could – anywhere that offered shelter from the sun's rays. Though she was used to it, having been forced to move around a lot in all her centuries upon this earth, while I was still adjusting.

As predicted, there were many abandoned buildings in this old industrial estate we'd come to. Lady Sarah caught a small stray dog as we walked. She drained it of blood and tossed me the carcass when she was done. Catching it in my jaws, I carried it with me till we found an old shop which the vampire deemed perfect for our needs.

Its windows and doors were boarded up but Lady Sarah ripped the wooden planks away with ease. I thought for a minute I would somehow have to board up the doorway again, but fortunately there was a basement which was likely used for storage back in the day, and the door into it was still intact. There was no way the sun's light could penetrate down there.

Lady Sarah glanced around and nodded to herself, apparently satisfied.

"This will do," she said. "You should change back; you're less likely to lose control in your human form. There should be enough meat on that dog to support another transformation, then you will have to make do till tomorrow night. It's not safe for you to hunt anything else."

I didn't like taking orders but I knew transforming back made sense, especially as spending too much time in wolf form meant risking what little humanity I had left, even if it was a form more suited to this new lifestyle. But I wasn't going to accept her instruction not to hunt without argument.

"Don't hunt?" I growled, once I was human again. "What if they set another trap for us tomorrow night – how am I meant to carry on running and fighting if I can't feed?"

"If they locate us here we will find a way to deal with it when the time comes, but there is no sense advertising our presence and inviting trouble when we may yet go unnoticed."

Even though I knew her argument made sense, I was far from happy. "And what will you do in two night's time when the moon turns full? You can't expect me not to answer its call to hunt."

16

"We will find a way to manage the full moon as safely as possible, but until it completely robs you of your control you must fight the hunger. Our survival depends on it."

Fuming, I sat down on the hard, cold stone floor, wincing at the discomfort of it. The vampire settled down beside me, positioning herself so that no direct sunlight would fall on her if the door opened for any reason during the day, and instantly fell into a deep sleep.

I ate the dog carcass with little enthusiasm, already tired of living off the vampire's kills, which were far from appetising once she'd drained them of blood. It did little to ease the hunger ravaging my insides, a sensation that was only going to worsen the longer I went without feeding. My mouth and throat were also dry from running for so long without being allowed to stop to drink. The vampire didn't need any fluid other than blood, but my body was still living and I needed some fresh water to keep everything functional. Thirst plagued me, almost as powerfully as my other urges.

I resigned myself to a long day filled with discomfort, shivering in the early morning chill which only added to my woes. The cool air was much more noticeable on my bare skin in the absence of the fur which had covered me most of the night, but I didn't even have the human luxury of clothes to wear in place of my lupine pelt. I hugged my knees and tried not to think of the greater hardship I'd face during the winter months.

I don't know how long I sat like that in the gloom of the cellar. My eyes roamed round the dusty room, taking in the cobwebs hanging overhead and the cracks in the walls, like cracks in reality. Too little time had passed for boredom to truly set in, but during the daylight hours when I had only my tortured mind for company was when my thoughts strayed to what Mum and Amy must surely be going through. My imagination threatened to conjure up images of them grieving for Dad and praying for me to come home, but such dark musings were of help to no one. I was forced to remind myself I'd left because they were better off without me, and it was better they went through a period of grieving before being allowed to carry on with their mortal lives than to suffer the consequences of being in my cursed presence.

So close to the full moon, my thoughts suddenly became dominated by hunting and killing once I'd pushed my family to the back of my consciousness, especially with the hunger roaring in my stomach. I could feel the waxing power of that ghostly orb as it drove me to stand and pace round the room, and I longed to answer its call. I was aware of the wolf pacing just as restlessly inside my skull, his eagerness just as strong as my own, but as our two personalities brushed against each other, I also felt his wariness to give into his predatory urges and hunt the human prey we craved. His survival instinct was far stronger than mine had ever been, but given the moon's hold over us and the power of the hunger itself, I knew from experience we would probably have no option but to obey.

As I paced, my gaze settled on one of the many spiders occupying the empty building, no doubt enjoying the peace granted by the lack of human inhabitants, free to explore without fear of meeting a sticky end. I prowled towards the biggest one, the arachnid suddenly springing to life as I drew near and racing towards the crack from whence it first came. But it was no match for my supernatural speed, and with my bare hand I caught it in my fist and squeezed till I felt the small frame crush between my fingers. So small a life seemed insignificant in the vastness of our universe, a mere speck amongst bigger souls burning more brightly. Did that make killing such small, primitive life forms right? Maybe not, and its death brought me no pleasure. But that didn't stop me ending the lives of the other spiders stupid enough not to have fled the instant I'd first entered the cellar with Lady Sarah.

After I ran out of spiders to kill, I licked the remains from my hands and resumed my pacing, tempted to leave the sleeping vampire and go in search of prey. But the moon wasn't quite full enough to rule me yet, and as much as I longed to lose myself in the savage joy of more bloodshed, I knew venturing out of the temporary shelter was a bad idea. So instead I focussed on finding more creatures to kill in the room which was beginning to feel more and more like a cage, hoping for something more satisfying than spiders.

My senses were sharper than when I'd been mortal, even in human form, and I listened intently for the tell-tale signs of any life nearby. A rush of excitement ran through me when I picked up two faint heartbeats, the bloodlust rising once more. But my excitement soon faded when I realised the prey I'd detected were no more than rats cowering within the walls, terrified of the unnatural predators they sensed in their midst. I still tore at the entrance to their nest until the crack was wide enough to get my hands in and catch one, ignoring the pain from sharp teeth biting into my flesh, but such small prey was really no more than a snack and it was only marginally better than the dried dog meat. The second rat had found another bolt hole and was beyond my reach, so I resumed my pacing, feeling thirstier for the salty blood which had spilled down my throat from the small body.

I started to become on edge as the hours dragged by, feeling like the next encounter with the Slayers was imminent. I half wanted them to attack again so I could indulge my need to slaughter and to feed on their flesh, even if it cost me my life. At least if I went down fighting it would put an end to this new misery I'd found myself in.

The outside world grew more inviting the longer I felt trapped in the old cellar and again I entertained the thought of exploring the city, where fresh water and prey would be plentiful. And I might have been reckless enough to venture out, if I hadn't been naked and covered in dried blood. Clothes just weren't practical when I was having to shift between forms so regularly and sometimes at a moment's notice, as had been the case the night before. Even if I'd had access to any clothes that day, there was nowhere to wash in the immediate vicinity. Of course I could have transformed back to my wolf form to hunt, but with my energy already drained from the number of recent transformations without being allowed to feed long enough to completely replenish it, and with the hunger so powerful as a result, I didn't want to risk another change unless I had to. There was no guarantee I'd be able to find enough meat to make the change worthwhile and as reckless as I had become, I hadn't completely lost my ability to reason.

Footsteps sounded from that human world I longed to roam and I tensed, adrenalin pumping through my system as I readied myself for another attack. It seemed the Slayers had found us, and I had no choice but to fight, hungry and weary as I was. The moment they came through the door there would be nowhere to run, an oversight on Lady Sarah's part perhaps, but I don't think she'd expected them to find us again so quickly.

My rage blazed up and I gladly opened myself to it, relying on that fury to give me the strength to face my enemies once more. With barely a conscious thought, my teeth and nails lengthened into fangs and claws, but I had enough sense not to allow the transformation to go any further. If I tried to take it too far I wouldn't have the energy for a fight, and it may well be the death of me. I would have to hope the supernatural speed and strength I possessed even in my human form would be enough, without tapping any further into the greater strength of my lupine nature.

Time seemed to slow as I crouched there, my heart pounding with the anticipation of more combat. Yet the minutes dragged on and still no one entered the abandoned building. Then the footsteps grew quieter as the humans walked past. The Slayers hadn't found us after all, or at least not yet. But that wasn't to say it hadn't been a group of them I'd heard outside so I didn't let myself relax, nor did I reverse the changes, in case I had need of my own natural weapons.

The anger still roared through me, the presence of potential Slayers a reminder of the very reason I was being forced to endure such discomfort. Even in a world without them where I'd been bitten and turned, maybe leaving my family behind might still have been inevitable to protect them from my predatory side. But if it weren't for the Slayers I wouldn't be forced to cower in the shadows like a lowly prey animal. Humanity were supposed to be my prey, their lives mine to crush just as I had with the spiders, their flesh mine to feed on. They were only mortal after all, so what did it matter if I was the one to rip their lives from them? No matter how great an imprint they left on the world or how intensely their souls burned in life, that light would eventually be extinguished one way or another. Their mortal end was inevitable, so why should I not be the one to end it for them? Why couldn't I be allowed the freedom to kill them as easily as the spiders, especially when the world was crawling with a greater population than the earth could sustain. It was so tempting, but only the thought that, unlike the spiders, human prey could fight back, kept me from bursting through the old building and falling on the first person I came across. The danger they posed to even so great a predator as a werewolf or a vampire was enough to keep my anger in check, just enough to prevent me from doing anything stupid, but the rage wouldn't drain away with the possible threat posed by the group of humans I'd heard in the area.

All was quiet again outside but still I remained tense and wrestling with my dark desires, until finally life, for want of a better word, breathed through Lady Sarah's corpse with the advance of dusk, and the vampire rose beside me.

"More Slayers?" she asked worriedly, quick to notice I'd readied myself for a fight.

"There were humans nearby," I growled. "But they passed here a while ago."

"Let us hope they were civilians then. Come, we need to search for somewhere suitable for the full moon."

We were both wary as we left the darkness of the basement behind us and emerged onto the streets. All was quiet and we were able to slip away unnoticed, the adrenalin and rage that had been flooding my system finally beginning to fade in the absence of any enemies. Another wave of weariness crashed over me and it was only with an effort of will that I was able to keep moving, until the moon broke free of the clouds, bringing a much needed rush of energy. It was almost full, the wolf stirring within my subconscious once more, again feeling its call. I felt my eyes change from their usual human greenish brown to lupine amber, and it took another effort of will to suppress my desire to hunt. I would have loved to have given into the bloodlust once again and run free through the city, ripping and tearing the unsuspecting humans until the streets ran red with their blood. But the vampire would never allow it, so I had no choice but to keep running beside her.

Once we'd passed through the urban area, Lady Sarah led us back into the countryside, searching for shelter isolated enough from civilisation for the full moon. She knew she was no match for the power the moon would have over me and thus wouldn't be able to keep me from killing, so she planned to spend the next three nights as far from the human world as possible.

It was another long night spent running over great distances, but finally we found a large stretch of woodland with an old abandoned building set in a clearing between the trees. The area appeared to have been used as a campsite once, but given the state of neglect the place had been left in, it seemed the site was no longer in use. Lady Sarah was not about to take any chances based on appearances alone, however. She had us search the grounds for any hint of recent human activity in the area, but there were no fresh scents of people passing through there.

We did come across a large pond, murky and uninviting, but thirst drove me to my knees at the water's edge, my body's need for liquid overruling any misgivings my brain might have had. Lady Sarah waited impatiently as I lowered my head to drink, my reflection just visible, faint and ghostly. I paused to study the image of myself, the face of the human boy I'd been still physically the same, yet no trace remained of who I once was beneath the dried gore staining my skin. So little time had passed since the curse had robbed me of my humanity, but already it felt like a lifetime ago. Memories of the happier times with my family and friends seemingly belonged in a past life, as if it had never been truly me, or not the current incarnation of me. Maybe it had only ever been the dream of a monster who wished for a human life, and now there was only the cruel reality of the present and the knowledge that this was for eternity. The past would become increasingly like a distant dream.

I might have stayed there for the rest of the night, transfixed by my own reflection, but my thirst soon broke the spell. The stagnant water tasted terrible though I lapped it up anyway, grateful for the soothing effect of the liquid washing over my dry mouth and down my parched throat. Behind me I was aware of the vampire growing restless, no doubt feeling we'd lingered too long when there were still things to do before the sunrise drove her to hide inside another makeshift shelter, and I was forced to rise before I could drink my fill. At least I'd be able to come back for more later in the day, which would mean one less discomfort to cope with while I watched over Lady Sarah.

We also found a rabbit warren. By that point the vampire had deemed the area acceptable for our current needs, for which I was relieved. I welcomed the chance to rest, exhaustion suddenly taking over as the moon retreated behind the clouds once more. But first we fed on the family cowering inside their burrows, though there was not nearly enough blood and flesh to satiate either of our hungers. I'd caught the scent of deer as we'd searched the grounds but the trail was a few days old and they weren't likely to come back to the area while we were there. The meagre meal the rabbits offered would have to do for that night, though such small prey would not satisfy when the moon rose again as full. If Lady Sarah had plans to help me manage it without endangering us both she didn't let on, but I suspected it would be the hardest trial I'd face in that first week of struggling to adapt to this tough new lifestyle.

Once we'd eaten, I was permitted a couple of hours sleep before the new day dawned. Lady Sarah sought shelter in the old building which was little more than a converted barn. There was a large storage cupboard no doubt once filled with supplies for groups staying on the site, but now empty, save for more spiders that had taken up residence there as nature slowly reclaimed the area in man's absence. The cupboard was just big enough for the vampire to climb into for the day and she did so without complaint. Such a cramped space was far from ideal for her, but no doubt she had been forced to make use of far worse shelters in the past.

Safe from the sun's deadly rays, the vampire spoke to me through the wooden doors before entering the death like sleep of her kind.

"Try not to give into the change too early tonight," she said. "All being well, I will be with you when it happens, but if you let it come too soon I might not awake in time. The last thing we need is for you to run off alone."

Her counsel was as good as ever but I still wanted to rebel against her. I'd only survived so long in my hometown because the Slayers there had wanted to use me to gather an army of undead for them to massacre and bring us that bit closer to extinction. And if they'd succeeded in killing me in that battle it may well have been the extinction of my race, since Lady Sarah believed I was the last werewolf alive. I don't think they'd expected us to find enough strength to defeat them, believing us to be but a shadow of the great predators we once were, reduced to skulking in the shadows and scavenging on what we could. If I indulged in the greater bloodlust the moon awoke in me and hunted freely, I was much more likely to be discovered by our enemies, and it seemed they would no longer suffer me to live, as evidenced by the trap we'd almost been caught in the night before. Yet I wanted nothing more than to run rampant, answering the moon's call to hunt and gorging myself on the flesh of the human prey I craved until I was so full I could eat no more.

I tried to settle down to keep watch while the vampire was vulnerable through the day, but I was far too restless to stay still. I could feel the coming of the full moon that evening, and though the exertion of fighting and fleeing, coupled with too little sleep, had begun to take its toll on me only hours ago, I felt charged with energy once more. My lupine instincts were as strong as ever, urging me to hunt. I paced back and forth in the old building as I struggled to keep control, but since the human part of me wanted to hunt just as badly as the wolf, that was one fight I was never going to win. I soon found myself stalking through the woods, intending to find more rabbits to prey on or perhaps some birds, even though it was humans I truly desired.

I prowled between the trees, trying to tread as lightly as possible, though my lupine half was still a far better hunter than I was. I could move with some of that animal grace and agility wolves possessed, but there was still some human clumsiness as my bare feet crunched over ferns and other plant-life. Unless I surrendered control of my mind completely to the wolf, I was never going to move quietly enough to catch any birds. Even with my supernatural speed, they took flight too quickly for me to grab them. And I was having no luck finding any other prey, unable to sense any more rabbits or rodents to kill. It must have been late morning when finally I was forced to return to the old building, aware I shouldn't leave the vampire alone too long in her corpse like state.

Tiredness crept over me once more and I settled down miserably on the hard floor, cold and hungry as ever. But exhaustion soon got the better of me and I dozed off into a light sleep.

The snap of a twig brought me back to the waking world with a jolt, my instincts recognising it as a potential threat and making me instantly alert. So close to the full moon, I had the usual sense of wanting to swivel my ears towards the sound, but I was still in human form and knew I had to remain so until that night. The hunger would be powerful enough without another transformation prior to the unavoidable one the moon would bring, and since the vampire was probably going to make me try to fight it, there was no sense in making a nigh on impossible task even tougher.

I listened closely to my surroundings and seconds later picked up the sound of another footfall. Though I still hadn't fully mastered my enhanced senses, I knew the smell of humans well enough by that point and I had to assume they were more Slayers. I vaguely wondered how they'd found us again so quickly, but such thoughts were soon lost in the chaos of my rising bloodlust. I could feel the wolfish part of my mind strong as ever in response to the lunar cycle and for once we both wanted the same thing – to tear into the soft flesh of human prey and enjoy a bloody feast that would satisfy both the hunger and my need to kill.

I could spare the energy to grow fangs and claws once again, and with a feral smile I got to my feet as quietly as I could manage. There would be no Lady Sarah to hold me back this time, and surely she couldn't argue with the need to fight in this instance. She was vulnerable through the day and it had fallen to me to protect her. Fleeing was not an option so I had to make a stand and defend her sleeping, corpse like form. And my need to kill and to feed would not be denied so close to nightfall. It was a fight I wanted, and I welcomed the oncoming bloodshed, summoning forth my rage once more as I prepared to face the foolish mortals who dared test me yet again.

My anger was quick to respond to my summons. I felt it stir and claw its way up out of the darkness it resided in, a separate beast to my lupine side – one born solely of the human in me. That anger was everything. It was the fire smouldering in the dark pit of my being, blazing up into a raging inferno whenever it was fed and given rise to consume and control me. It was the tidal wave that rose up and crashed back down, flooding my body with fury. It was the storm that sparked into life, its thunder rumbling as my rage awoke like a sleeping giant, flashes of lightning streaking within the dark emptiness where once there had been a living soul.

I gave voice to that anger in a primal roar, before charging to meet my enemies once again. No longer attempting to be stealthy, my feet crashed over the dead leaves and twigs littering the ground, the sound of my own heartbeat loud in my ears as the anger and adrenalin coursed through my veins. I judged this latest group of Slayers to be roughly a mile away, but it only took me around a minute to reach them, running at full sprint.

The humans had frozen, perhaps at the sound of my roar, wondering which form they were going to encounter me in. I crashed into the first one, smashing his head into a large tree root and cracking open his skull like an eggshell, shards of bone and brain matter exploding over the ground from the impact. Moving far too fast for the mere mortals to follow, I rose from the corpse and slashed another one of the men. My claws were long and sharp enough to rip through his clothes and into the wall of his stomach, shredding the muscle to expose his guts. A loop of intestine slipped through one of the claw marks like the coil of a snake, or a huge slug emerging from the hole, so slick with blood it appeared slimy in the autumn sun. He stumbled back in shock, hands pressed against the wounds to try and keep his organs in place. Disabled by the pain, he was no longer a threat so I left him for the time being and lashed out at a third, this time raking my claws across her throat. Blood spurted from her jugular vein and she too fell, death quick to take her.

I turned to the last two in the group, utterly confident in my power. So few of them. When would they learn to stop underestimating me, especially with the moon giving me even greater strength? Clearly they'd thought I'd be an easy kill with no Lady Sarah to save me if I lost myself so completely in the bloodlust as I had in the last fight, but I would not make that same mistake again. Still, if they wanted to believe such a small group could kill me who was I to argue? All they'd achieve would be to send more lambs to the slaughter, and I was all too happy to oblige in that.

My eyes had turned lupine again but I didn't try to wrestle the wolf back into our subconscious this time, though I didn't grant him complete control yet either. He would have his fun during the night but this was my prey, and I would enjoy killing the last of them and eating my fill.

I felt invincible as I rushed the last two Slayers left standing, but suddenly the glare of the bright autumn sun was in my eyes, blinding me. In my arrogance I'd failed to notice they'd manoeuvred themselves so it was behind them, and I was forced to slow, squinting as I tried to keep track of their movements. I heard gunshots but I'd already anticipated it and darted to the side, the bullets thudding into the trunk of a tree just behind where I'd been standing. I didn't give the men chance to fire again, grabbing the nearest and throwing him against the same tree the bullets had lodged in. He fell to the ground screaming in agony from numerous broken bones, including an open fracture in his upper arm where the jagged edge of the bone had pierced the skin. Like the other survivor I'd left alive for the time being, he was too lost in the world of pain I'd thrown him into to be a threat, leaving me free to take my time with my final victim.

I pounced on him, his gun flying from his hand as he landed on his back, just out of reach. The man reached for a knife even though he knew he was finished, but I caught his arm as he attempted to slash at me and twisted until I heard the snap of another broken bone. He screamed and dropped the blade, and finally I gave myself completely over to the bloodlust, savaging him with tooth and claw like the beast I truly was, and gulping down chunks of bloody flesh.

Once I'd eaten my fill I went back to the man lying broken and bloody at the base of the tree he'd collided with. The pain had proven too much for him and he'd slipped into unconsciousness, but the new pain of my fangs sliding into the exposed muscle of his fractured arm brought him back with a cry of agony. I ripped the meat from his broken bones until he took his last laboured breath, rising from him as death claimed him.

I stood there panting, feeling the anger drain away now my dark needs had finally been satisfied, my eyes turning human again and the sharp predatory points of my teeth and nails receding into bluntness once more. With the retreat of my rage, only emptiness remained in its place, despite the moon rise being only a few hours away. Beads of red liquid rolled down my body as if I'd just bathed, but rather than cleansing, the blood only dried and added to the layer of filth which already caked my bare skin. A chill breeze passed through the woods, ruffling my hair and stirring the bodies littered around me in some poor imitation of life.

I'd ripped the cheek off one of the men I'd savaged, the bloody tatters of torn flesh waving in the wind across bare jaw bones grinning morbidly. The breeze was strong enough to cause ripples across the pools of blood surrounding the remains, as if there was still some life in the liquid, despite the dead hearts that it had come from, which would pump it no more. Then the wind died down again and all was still. No scavengers descended on the grisly feast I'd left for them, no living thing daring to come close to the unnatural predator in their midst. All was still, save for the one human I'd left alive.

The man whose stomach I'd ripped open sat propped against another tree, grunting and shivering in pain, his hands still pressed to his belly to hold his guts in place. My hunger for killing now satiated for the time being, I decided I should keep him alive long enough for the vampire to wake and have her fill of the human prey she too must surely be craving. But his ripped shirt was soaked with blood and I knew he'd never last that long if I left his wounds open.

"Don't die on me," I growled. "I need you to hold on till dusk."

The Slayer was conscious enough to fix his eyes on me, making his hatred for my race plain to see, but he didn't answer.

I turned away from him to search the bodies of his comrades. The smell of smoke was heavy on two of the men and sure enough in one of their pockets I found cigarettes and a lighter. Taking the lighter, I then retrieved one of their knives and held the blade to the small flame. Then I stalked back over to the Slayer, roughly pulling his hands away from his wounds and pinning him down. He realised what I was about to do and tried to struggle, his eyes wide, but I was too strong for him.

Before I could tend to the gashes my claws had made, there came the crackle of a walkie-talkie and the voice on the other end asked "What's your status? Report."

"Tell them it's all clear," I said.

"You're going to kill me anyway, so why should I obey you?"

"Tell them it's all clear," I repeated, digging my fingers into his wounds. "Or I'll make your last hours agony."

Whatever training the Slayers put their forces through evidently didn't include withstanding torture, because my captive couldn't take the pressure on the damaged nerves already sparking and throbbing with pain for more than a few seconds. Once I withdrew my fingers he did as instructed, grunting "All clear, targets had already moved on some time before dawn."

"Roger that, return to base," came the reply.

"Tell them you've picked up our trail and you're in pursuit."

The man co-operated a second time.

"Roger that," the voice on the other end responded. "If you don't find them before dusk, abort the mission till we send back up."

"Good," I said, satisfied that would buy us enough time before they sent any more hunting parties out to try and take us unawares.

With that taken care of, I went back to delaying the man's death long enough for the vampire to make a meal of him. I reheated the knife before pushing the guts slipping through his wounds back into his abdomen and pressing the blade to the torn flesh, cauterising each one like I'd seen in some of the movies I'd watched as a human. The woodland rang with the man's screams until he passed out from the pain. The world was still and quiet once more, but again my thoughts threatened to turn to the emotional pain my family were likely still going through, so I heated the knife a third time and pressed it to his cheek. He awoke with another scream.

"Since I need you alive you might as well keep me company for the rest of the day," I told him.

27

"I have nothing to say to you, monster. You might as well kill me now; I won't be your chew toy."

"Maybe you should have thought of that before you came here."

"I won't deal with monsters," he said stubbornly.

"Monsters? I suppose that's what I am now, but only because your kind turned me into one."

"Your curse did that."

"Oh the curse changed me, sure, it made me a killer. But humans pushed me over the edge. All that violence and aggression that came from the curse only grew at the hands of your kind. The bullies at school, you Slayers, even my own father, you all had your part to play in making me the monster I am today. You all fed my rage until it took over."

"You could have fought the curse. You didn't have to give in to your hunger or your rage. Look at what you've done, look at all this carnage you've caused, and tell me you deserve life. They were good men; they didn't deserve to die like this, savaged by some mindless beast."

"So you think I should fight my nature, rather than embracing it? Maybe I would have kept on fighting, but you people calling yourselves Demon Slayers didn't exactly give me much choice. You've made it a game of kill or be killed, so here we are. And if you really think fighting the hunger is so easy, if you think you could do better, maybe you should become one of us. You might not have the wolf blood for me to make you a werewolf, but I could let the vampire turn you."

"I'd rather die than be one of you."

"So noble. So righteous. And yet you people are just as monstrous as we are. How many innocent lives have you taken in your quest to wipe us out? How many fellow humans have died simply because they got in the way, while you wage this war with us in the shadows? Perhaps not you personally, but one of my closest friends was taken by your people purely to get at me. She would have died at the hands of you Slayers if I hadn't got to her when I did. My friend, a human who knows nothing of this war. Why should you people be allowed to murder and go unpunished, and we undead be killed for the lives we take to survive?"

He had no answer to that.

"I wonder how you found us so quick," I said, changing the subject. "It's only been days since I left my home and I didn't think we'd left any of you alive in the area to follow us. But a group of you tried to catch us unawares the other night, and then today, even though I'm pretty sure we weren't seen entering this old campsite, your group

28

attacked. Can your pet spellcasters track us, I wonder? But surely if it was through their magic then there would be another witch or warlock with your group, and I sense no other humans nearby. So how did you find us?"

"I have nothing to say to you," he repeated.

I stayed by him for the rest of the day, though I could get nothing more out of him without resorting to more torture, which I didn't want to do in case it proved too much of a strain on his body and killed him before the vampire could feed. Clouds began to amass in the sky overhead, obscuring the sun and making it difficult to judge the time, but eventually I sensed the onset of dusk after what felt like several long hours. As the sun set those clouds turned red, as if there'd been so much bloodshed that afternoon, it had been absorbed and the sky was now heavy with it.

The moon wasn't visible behind such thick cloud cover, but I could sense it up there and I felt the wolf's yearning to run free. As much as I wanted to obey the moon's call and let the transformation take hold, I knew I should wait for the vampire to appear. She'd have no trouble finding me and the human with her superior senses so I remained standing guard by my captive. I didn't have to wait long.

"Good, you're still human," Lady Sarah said as she stalked over. "And you've been busy, I see."

At first she sounded relieved she'd reached me in time, no doubt believing she'd been too late to find me before the transformation when she'd awoken and I'd not been in the building with her. But there was disapproval and a hint of anger in her second observation, and defensively I replied "They attacked first. If I hadn't engaged them they'd have found and killed you, so what was I supposed to do?"

"You were lucky there was no spellcaster with this group. We can't afford to move from here until after your full moon, but as soon as it's passed we will have to flee this place."

"I took care of it," I growled, giving her a quick run through of what had happened while she slept. "And I left this one alive for you to feed on. You could show me some gratitude."

"Forgive me, Nick, I just worry you underestimate our enemies. When the time comes we will make a stand again, but until then we can't afford for you to throw yourself into every little skirmish they send our way. You did make the right move today though, and I do thank you for thinking of me."

My anger threatened to engulf me once more, despite her apology, so I merely nodded. But while we'd argued the Slayer had also been busy. Blood spilled from his mouth where he'd bitten through his

29

own tongue, fearing we would question him some more. He might have been able to refuse me, but he'd known he would be at the vampire's mercy if she used her hypnotic powers to place him under her spell. It was a drastic move and one I'd not expected after he'd been unable to deal with the pain I'd inflicted on him earlier. Short of getting him to write in the dirt, we weren't getting any answers out of him. And he knew as well as we did that there wasn't time for that when the full moon could break through the clouds at any minute, which would bring on the transformation whether I was ready for it or not.

"Clever human," Lady Sarah hissed, but since he was no longer useful as anything other than prey she wasted no more time, feeding so long and deeply that he was nothing but a dried husk when she'd finished. Even though the vampire was so wary of taking human prey and engaging our enemies in combat, the pleasure and satisfaction the human blood gave her was plain to see. "I must thank you again, Nick. Now, if you can just hold on to your human form for as long as the moon remains hidden behind the clouds, it will be safer for both of us."

But my attention was already turned to the sky where there was a brighter patch amidst the blackness where the moon hung overhead. No sooner had she spoken than the pale orb slid into view, bathing us in its ghostly light. My eyes became lupine once more, my voice already growing wolfish as I growled "Too late."

Chapter Three – Lost in the Rage

The moon called and I obeyed. I felt the usual pain in my stomach and the feverish symptoms of my flesh burning, my blood boiling, a primal fire blazing through me in response to my lunar master. And to think I had once fought this, not so long ago. Yet now I embraced my true nature, revelling in the power of the transformation itself, so much more potent for the full moon overhead.

My skin itched as fur sprouted. A deep ache ran through my entire skeleton and muscles throbbed as bone and flesh stretched out or shortened as necessary to take on the anatomical shape of the wolf. I welcomed that pain, crouched on all fours and giving myself fully to the transformation, no longer struggling to retain my humanity. As intense as the pain was, I could feel my body growing stronger for the changes it endured and it gave rise to a savage joy once more.

The transformation completed, all physical traces of my humanity lost to my lupine side, and with an excited howl I answered the moon and the call to the hunt as the wolf seized control.

"Nick?"

My howl tailed off and I was about to bound off into the night, but I paused on hearing my name.

"Remember what's at stake," Lady Sarah growled at me in the wolven tongue. "It's too dangerous to run wild with the Slayers on our trail. Fight it, Nick. Fight it if you want to live to see the morning."

I boldly locked gazes with the vampire. Though I didn't share the human's recklessness, the need to hunt awoken by the moon and the hunger from the transformation were overwhelmingly strong. And the human part of my mind was much stronger than it used to be and remained closer to the surface than in the early days of the curse, when it had been forced deep into our subconscious whenever I took control. The human now shared in my predatory desires and my bloodlust had only grown stronger as a result. That, coupled with the human's rage, made my hunting instincts that much harder to resist. My survival instinct had always been much greater than my human half's, but it was lost in the chaos of my mind that night, as were the vampire's words. I'd once considered her my alpha, but the moon was my true alpha, and its call was greater than any leadership the vampire could offer. I snarled in response to her.

Lady Sarah must have realised she wasn't going to get through to me because her form shifted and a she wolf stood before me, snarling in return. The next thing I knew she was on me, trying to wrestle me into submission. But in my current state of madness brought on by the full moon and the human's rage and eagerness for the

31

kill, I was so desperate for the thrill of the hunt and to spill fresh blood that I fought against her with everything I had. We grappled with each other, twisting and snapping until finally she succeeded in clamping her jaws round my snout, muzzling me like natural wolves. Still I writhed in her grip, desperately trying to break free, her fangs carving deep gouges into my muzzle the more I struggled against her. The pain only drove me into more of a frenzy and blood was running freely down my snout, but the vampire held me firm until I was eventually forced to submit.

Lady Sarah didn't release the pressure on my muzzle immediately after I ceased fighting her, but as the moments dragged on and I remained still and seemingly docile she finally let me go. I lay panting, readying myself for a renewed assault, but when I looked up she was stood over me in human form once more. One of the Slayers the human had killed earlier had carried a sword, which the vampire had retrieved from the corpse.

"I'm sorry, Nick," she said, and before I could make any move to stop her she drove the long blade through the muscle of my upper left hind leg, stabbing clean through my flesh and deep into the soil until it was buried to the hilt, pinning me to the ground.

I yelped with the pain but after the initial shock it only served to drive me into even more of a frenzy. I twisted to try and pull the sword out but I couldn't get a grip on the hilt with my jaws, so instead I started to scrabble at the ground with my front paws, trying to pull myself free. But the more I thrashed around, the more fresh blood leaked from the wound and the greater the pain became. Even in my crazed state the pain became too much, and eventually it forced me into submission once more. I gazed up at the moon, whining pitifully.

"Eat," Lady Sarah said, placing one of the human corpses in front of me. "I suppose we were lucky they attacked you earlier, since now it means you can still feed and keep up your energy for the duration of the full moon."

I snarled at her but I was too ravenous to refuse the meat, as unappealing as it was now rigor mortis had set in. So I attacked the corpse and devoured chunks of cold, stiff flesh until it was reduced to little more than a bloody skeleton. I continued to gnaw the bones, the hunger for flesh satiated at least, but still the desire to hunt tormented me. Since I was unable to satisfy that desire, I was left with little choice but to settle down for the remainder of the night and rest. With sunrise the transformation would heal the wound in my leg, but until then I was stuck, and I could only dream of my freedom.

Lady Sarah watched over me while I slept but the Slayers weren't foolish enough to send another hunting party after us that night. With the coming of dawn she fled back to the darkness of the old store cupboard, leaving me to transform back whilst still pinned down by the sword. As my limbs shifted the flesh tried to knit back together where the blade had pierced it, but with the sword still in my leg the tissue was forced to fuse around the metal, which only buried it more securely in the muscle. I retreated into our subconscious, leaving the human to deal with removing it and the intense pain that would no doubt cause...

Even though the wound in my leg had tried to close around the sword, I was acutely aware of it as I regained control. The full moon had always been a blackout period for me in the past, as had the other occasions where the wolf had taken over, but since I'd started to embrace my lupine side I'd learnt to lurk near the surface of our consciousness as the wolf had always been able to do. And that had granted me some awareness of what the wolf had been up to, even if it was only a few snatches of memory of the night's events. But it was clear enough who had stabbed the blade through my thigh.

With human hands I was able to grip the hilt of the sword and pull it out, a roar that was equal parts pain and rage tearing through me as the blade slid free. Removing it caused fresh damage to the tissue and my blood flowed freely from the hole it left in my leg, until I used the cell regenerative power of the transformation to heal it.

The wound closed up as if it had never been, my flesh unmarked and as flawless as ever. The drying blood on my skin was the only proof of it that remained, that and the anger blazing through me, which was currently directed solely at she who was responsible for causing me such pain. The vampire; not only had she dared deny me the hunt on the night that belonged to me, to my kind, but she'd also caused me torment and pain. It was her fault I'd had to endure the agony of the blade through my flesh. It didn't matter that she'd felt she was acting in my best interests, she'd caused me pain and the pain had fed my rage, giving it rise once more. And as always my anger brought with it my bloodlust, and the only clear thought burning through my fevered mind was the need for revenge on the one who'd hurt me.

I stormed through the woods, my rage so powerful that I barely even noticed the hunger from the transformation back to human. It wasn't long before I found myself stood in front of the cupboard she was using as shelter, and I stood there seething. I wanted to throw the doors open and drag her into the sun's deadly rays, where she would burn for what she'd done to me. I reached for the door handles, my hands shaking with fury. Then came the voice.

"Are you really so lost that you would kill the only friend you have left?"

There was something familiar about that female voice but I couldn't place it. Out of the corner of my eye I could see a humanoid figure, but when I spun round, my anger now directed at this person who would dare interfere with my vengeance, there was no one there.

With another roar I charged back out of the building, now intent on hunting whoever had just interrupted me. The vampire would wait – after all, she was confined to the darkness through the day so it wasn't like she could escape me.

I crashed through the woods trying to find the girl, but there was no sight or sound of her anywhere and I could detect no fresh scents, human or otherwise, amidst the woodlands smell of trees and vegetation. Had there been room in my head for rational thought I might have considered the possibility I was hallucinating again, but I was too lost in the rage.

My hunt took me to the edge of the woodland where a narrow road twisted through the countryside, a capillary connecting the extremities of man's territory to the main cities that formed the heart of their world. I came to a stop at the treeline, listening intently. If my ears had still been lupine they would have been cocked in the direction of the distant sounds of civilisation carried to me on the wind. I was so tempted to carry on to the freedom that awaited me outside of those woods, away from the vampire and the restraints she insisted on placing on me. The anger pulsing through my veins still screamed for blood, but the blood of the humans I could hear in the distance would just as easily satisfy as the mystery girl I'd been hunting for. I just needed to kill someone.

"Nick, you're talking about murder," came a new voice, shocked and fearful, but one I instantly recognised.

"Fuck off, Amy," I growled, turning to face this latest hallucination.

"Oh well that's nice when we've not seen each other all week, dickhead!" she replied with her usual teenage attitude, but before I could respond she calmed again and sadness crept into her voice. "Why did you leave us, Nick?"

"Well what else was I supposed to do? Stay and risk you getting hurt whenever I lose control?"

"You broke my heart, you know," said another voice, the image of Mum appearing beside my sister, her eyes red from crying.

"What more do you want from me?" I roared. "I left to protect you all. Do you think I want to be stuck out here in the middle of nowhere, cold and hungry and alone all day, with nothing to do?"

"You abandoned us, Nick," Amy said. "You left us in a town taken over by monsters. How can you think we're any safer without you?"

The images began to change, my treacherous mind showing me Mum's corpse, dried and bearing the two fang wounds in her neck that marked it as an unmistakeable vampire kill, while Amy grew paler and her canines lengthened. The thought of either fate befalling my family was too much, the existence as an undead the last thing I wanted for either of them after it had brought me so much misery. It set my rage bubbling up to new heights, fury coursing through my veins and making my blood boil. Or maybe that was just the onset of the transformation again, my eyes turning amber and blazing with such anger that I imagined they looked like flames burning in my skull. I struggled to hold my form, a part of me all too eager to give into the change and run towards the human world I could hear in the distance, but some small part of me knew it would be a mistake to change again so early in the day. I needed my energy for later under the full moon, and even if I ran towards civilisation there was still no guarantee I'd successfully make a kill. Not with the threat the Slayers posed. Plus I still needed to eat after the change back to human that morning, and another transformation before I fed would only weaken me.

I was still struggling when the hunger chose to make itself heard again as if to reinforce what little rationality was holding me back, and it ravaged my insides with renewed force. It freed me of the hallucinations conjured by my tormented mind, for the time being at least, powerful enough as it always was during the full moon. The hunger wouldn't wait any longer, and the remaining corpses of the Slayers were beckoning.

Reluctantly I turned away from the road, back into the gloom of the woods, returning to the scene of the skirmish with the Slayers the previous day. Only one of the decaying bodies was still whole. The man whose skull I'd bashed in remained otherwise untouched, wide, dim eyes staring sightlessly as I crouched over him. With teeth that I allowed to grow into fangs once more, I bit into what should have been the soft flesh of his belly, but still in the grip of rigor mortis the muscles were cold and hard, and far from appetising. I was hungry enough to force down my fill, the anger slowly draining away while I ate, until I felt that emptiness inside me once again.

In the aftermath of my rage there came another wave of weariness. The long days and nights spent raging and fighting had finally taken their toll, and I gave into the exhaustion, falling into a deep sleep which not even the nightmares could disturb me from. Only with the rise of the full moon did I stir, to answer its call again.

That night passed much like the previous one, though Lady Sarah didn't even give me chance to try and fight the moon's call as she had before. She drove the sword through my leg before the transformation had even had chance to fully complete, pinning me down again before I could run off and find fresh meat. There was still plenty of rotting meat left on the corpses of the Slayers and I was forced to make do, though I hungered for the warm flesh of a fresh kill.

I changed back the next morning to find the blade piercing my thigh a second time. Overcome with rage again, I spent more long hours chasing phantoms in the woods, until the hunger grew too strong and I was forced to strip the dead of yet more of the decaying flesh still clinging to their bones. But I was unable to sleep for long that afternoon, feeling more restless as the night of the third and final full moon that month approached. The wolf had been denied the thrill of the hunt for two nights running, and I could feel him pacing restlessly inside my skull. Lady Sarah might have found a way to restrain me, but I would be all the more frenzied after the rage she'd already caused which had gone unsatisfied. She would have her work cut out for her if she wanted to keep me from killing a third night running.

As if she'd read my mind, the vampire appeared beside me that evening with sword in hand. I snarled at her defiantly as I felt the change begin, but my attention turned to the sound of a car on the road that bordered the woods. There hadn't been many cars passing by while we'd been in the area, but this one was of interest because I could hear it slowing, and then come to a complete stop.

"I'm sorry Nick, but if you won't listen to reason there's not much else I can do," Lady Sarah was saying.

"No," I growled, and stumbled away in the direction of the car I'd heard. When there came the sounds of a car door opening and closing and a human walking towards the treeline, I recognised the person's presence for the opportunity it presented.

The vampire stalked after me, watching me closely and waiting for the right moment to tether me in place once more. As I fell to all fours she raised the blade that would form a makeshift restraint for the third night running, but there came the snap of twigs as the human ventured into the woods, and she paused to listen, trying to determine if it was a threat. While she was distracted I struggled back upright and continued to stagger away, driven by my determination to reach the human we could hear at the edge of the woods. Moving was agony as the full moon overhead drove the transformation onwards but I forced myself to keep going, before the vampire had another chance to pin me down.

My femurs were shortening as my limbs changed to become more suited to running on all fours, and I was forced to my hands and knees. Still I pushed myself to keep crawling, until the pain became too much and I lay defeated, waiting for the transformation to finish. The wolf fought for control of our mind in answer to the moon, and reluctantly I surrendered it to him, beaten into submission by the ghostly light of our tormentor.

The scent of the human male in the woods came to me like a summons and I prowled closer, mouth watering in anticipation of the feast I would soon make of him. Whether he was a Slayer or a civilian didn't matter: he was a human and they served but one purpose, as prey to my unnatural hunger.

I crouched between the trees, readying myself for the hunt. Hungry as I was, I wanted to enjoy the thrill of the chase after being denied for the last two nights, but one crazed thought spilled from the human half of my mind with a sense of urgency. The scent of prey had caused me to briefly forget the vampire, and as I became aware of her drawing closer the need to escape took over. The chase I desired would have to wait; this human offered a chance to get away from Lady Sarah, and I couldn't afford to lose myself in either the hunger or the bloodlust if I was going to take advantage of that.

It seemed the man wasn't another Slayer who'd come hunting us after all; he'd stopped on that quiet stretch of road to urinate and merely happened to be caught in the wrong place at the wrong time. He looked around nervously while he went about his business, as if he could sense my presence nearby. But to his eyes there would only have been shadows between the trees, cast by the brightness of the full moon. He couldn't have guessed what lurked in those shadows, and when seconds later I was upon him it was already too late – his fate was sealed.

I pounced on the human, knocking him to the ground, and shredded through clothes and skin with my fangs until his blood gushed from mortal wounds. But I didn't kill him, nor did I begin to feed. The vampire stalked towards me and I rose from the human triumphant, knowing the fresh blood would also be a temptation for her, and one I felt certain she wouldn't be able to resist. She'd not fed since the first night of the full moon, and her hunger must surely have grown powerful enough to rival my own in that time.

I didn't wait to see what Lady Sarah would do, turning and bounding off into the night, in search of more prey. But when the man's screams came to an abrupt halt, I knew the vampire had given in to her own lust for blood, just as I'd hoped, and that left me free to hunt as I'd been longing to do for the last two nights.

Once free of the woods, I loped across the road and over a stretch of open fields. Some of those fields were occupied by livestock, the animals going wild with panic as I passed through. But as ever it was human prey I hungered for, and though the terrified sheep and cattle called to my predatory instincts, I fought the urge to slaughter them in favour of the human meat I craved.

My patience was rewarded when I eventually came upon a large farmhouse, on the grounds of what humans would probably call a petting zoo. There were more livestock in fields like those I'd already crossed, but I also sensed barns full of smaller animals like rabbits and guinea pigs. Yet the house held the most interesting prey and I padded over to it, looking for a way in. It was an old building which had already stood the test of time, still standing as strong as ever in the present. With my supernatural strength I could probably break through the door or a window to get at the fresh meat locked within, but I had another idea. Luring my prey out would be easier and more satisfying for my bloodlust, which was only growing more powerful the longer I went without a kill. So I turned back to the barns where the prey animals cowered, finally giving in to the internal chaos raging in my skull.

If I'd been rational I would have wanted no part in such slaughter as the human longed for, not when it was such a waste of so much precious life. But the human's fury was too powerful and the moon's call too strong, and the bloodlust crashed over me like a tsunami, flooding my mind with the overwhelming need to spill fresh blood. I sent up a crazed howl to the lunar master calling to this madness within me, before throwing myself at the door to the nearest barn. It was padlocked but the humans obviously never really expected any trouble in so sparsely a populated area, as there was little else in the way of security. The wooden door splintered under the force of my body crashing against it, and I was able to rip my way through to the massacre awaiting within.

The mesh of hutches offered little resistance to my powerful jaws, and I tore my way through cage after cage until each and every one of the little bodies lay in bloody ruins. Next I raided a barn housing several goats and sheep, and a third containing rare breeds of pig, leaving none alive. It wasn't until I started on the carnage of the donkeys in the fourth building that finally I heard one of the humans coming to investigate, roused from sleep by the animal screams of pain and terror.

"For fuck's sake, that fox better not have got into the chickens again," I heard a man's voice say. I hadn't yet touched the nearby chicken coop, but the panic had spread to the birds nevertheless and they added their clucking to the chorus of terrified prey.

"Don't go," came a female voice. "It sounds bad out there; what if it's not just a fox? Please Jack, just call the police and let's wait for them."

"I'm not waiting for that bunch of incompetent local fools to show up. All the animals will be dead by the time they get here! Whatever's out there, I'll take care of it myself."

Moments later the man emerged from the safety and comfort of his home. I listened to him approaching, crouched between scattered donkey limbs and entrails, in a pool of blood. I could see the light from a torch sweeping across the grisly scene I had left for him, and I heard him breathe the words "Oh my God."

Whatever he'd been expecting to find, it clearly hadn't prepared him for the evidence of the brutal, savage end I'd brought to his animals. He seemed to be in a

38

state of shock as he stumbled through the bloodbath I'd left him, until finally his torch shone through the wreckage of the door to the barn where I waited, illuminating my bloodied form. I must have looked all the more fearsome for the gore matting my fur, revealing me for the monster my human half had made me.

The torch was blindingly bright, but I could just make out the man's form silhouetted in the doorway. It angered me beyond all reason to see he had a gun, stoking the fires of my hate for human hunters, even though he had every right to defend his family from the predator that had attacked them. The man recovered enough from the sight of me to raise his rifle, and I snarled in response, eyes blazing with fury. I could sense his panic as he hurried to squeeze off a shot, the bullet thudding harmlessly into a lump of donkey meat, and then I was on him before he could fire again. But I didn't kill him immediately, instead ripping off chunks of his flesh and eating him alive. The night rang with his screams, bringing his wife out to investigate as I knew they would. Only when I heard her running towards us did I silence the man forever, the torch he'd dropped acting like a beacon.

"Jack?" she shouted, her voice high with alarm and the fear digging its claws deeper into her heart, evolving into terror. "Jack!"

I continued to feed on the earthly remains of the man the woman had called Jack, until his wife drew close enough to see us clearly.

"No," she whispered in shock, trying to deny what her own eyes were telling her. But then I rose from the corpse, growling threateningly, and her fear took over once more. Primal instincts kicked in, instincts dulled over the years by mankind distancing themselves from nature, but they were there, deep in the human psyche, and they only had one response to the threat of a predator. She ran, and with an excited howl I gave chase, as I'd been longing to do.

Where my prey was clumsy and stumbled in the dark, my body might as well have been one with the land, my paws gripping the earth with more surety than any human footwear, my limbs moving with an effortless grace. I felt more alive than I had in months, full of energy in the moon's light, and powered by all the lives I'd taken over the last hour. My prey's only hope would have been to hide, but I raced ahead of her as she ran for the house and barred the open doorway, forcing her to seek cover elsewhere.

The woman soon realised there was nowhere for her to hide on the farm, so she fled down the dirt track leading up to it, no doubt praying that if she could just reach the road, there might be help there. I didn't let her get that far, closing the distance between us and snapping at her heels, bringing her crashing down. She screamed and tried to rise, but I heard a car in the distance and knew I had to end this game, or risk losing the kill.

Grabbing her ankle in my jaws, I dragged her back towards the barns I'd already turned into slaughterhouses, where I was free to ravage her flesh without being disturbed. Blood welled up as my fangs raked her skin, bloody rivulets becoming gushing streams and spraying fountains, muscle exposed, wet and glistening in the moonlight. Her bones showed through in some of the deeper wounds, and I soon tore my way through to the rich organs that provided the greatest sustenance. She died screaming alongside the carcass of her husband, and surrounded by pieces of the animals that had been her life, before I'd snatched it so cruelly from her in my bloody jaws. If it hadn't been for the curse and the human in me I would never have killed so many, instead taking only what I needed to survive. With the hunger and the bloodlust satisfied I felt a sense of regret for wasting so many lives unnecessarily, but it was too late to take back the blood I'd spilled. I felt a fresh wave of anger and hatred towards the human part of my mind, and I spent the remainder of the night curled up in the driest of the four barns, wishing I could be free of my own humanity as well as the taint their wretched kind had brought on the land, until finally I drifted off to sleep.

My dreams were troubled but I didn't wake until sunrise, when the transformation took hold once more and the bright, early light of day revealed me for the monster I truly was.

The wolf fought to remain in control out of hatred for me, but the sunlight called me back and I overpowered him before I'd even returned to human form. The scent of the massacres I'd committed in the night was overpowering, and perhaps that was the reason the transformation came to a halt for the first time on a morning after a full moon since I'd been bitten. I had the form of a hybrid wolf man once again. I could have allowed the change to resume until I was fully human, but I found I didn't want to, the smell of so much death renewing my bloodlust until I felt the need to take yet more lives.

I felt jealous of my lupine half as I took in the scene of his moon crazed slaughter. There was blood everywhere, bright and lurid in the morning light. Animal limbs and entrails lay scattered around in each of the barns, a bloody jigsaw that even an expert in biology would have had trouble piecing back together. But there was little left of the two human corpses, which the wolf had clearly gorged himself upon. It seemed I'd made an utter ruin of the two lives I'd taken that night, not even leaving the legacy of the petting zoo for their family to continue on in their name. Yet it seemed the horror I'd visited on the family was not quite over, for the sound of a car approaching reached my ears, new victims driving unwittingly to their doom. I retreated into the gloom of one of the barns, waiting for the humans to come to me. I knew Lady Sarah would not have approved if she'd been with me, but that thought only made me all the more eager for the kill. I would indulge my bloodlust again that morning, and there was nothing she could do to stop me.

Chapter Four – Out of Control

The car parked up in front of the old farmhouse and I heard a family of three climb out. They couldn't see the damage I'd caused to the animal's housing and the front door to the house was closed; it had been the back door my two victims had run out of in the night. And the wind was blowing in the wrong direction to carry the smell of the carnage to their weak human noses. The family weren't yet aware that anything was amiss.

"Mummy," the little boy said excitedly. "Can I go see the animals, please Mummy?"

"Go on then, while we unpack," the woman answered him. She'd barely finished her sentence before her son set off running towards the barns, the pitter-patter of little feet sounding loud and clear in my lupine ears.

"Not for too long, Elliot!" his father called after him. "Your Aunt Sally and Uncle Jack will want to see you too!"

A low growl drew the little boy to me as he raced towards the damaged enclosures. He slowed as he came to the barns, trying to decide where the sound had come from, but I heard him approaching the one I hid in. Too young and innocent to realise something was very wrong, he probably thought his aunt and uncle had added a new dog to their menagerie. Moments later he was stepping into the gore that now decorated the interior of the barn, his nose wrinkled as if to fend off the foul stench assaulting it. The child stared in shock at the grisly sight that met his eyes, his gaze locking on the dead eyes of a severed sheep head.

"Timmy?" he said, his eyes filling with tears and his lip quivering. Then I growled a second time and he looked up from the carnage to see the monster lurking in the shadows, and he screamed as I pounced on my prey.

The sound was painfully shrill and high pitched to my sensitive ears, but it cut off once I wrapped my jaws round his throat, sinking my fangs in and ripping the flesh free. I watched the life drain from those young eyes, so full of life and excitement only moments ago, bright as blue summer skies. Death crept over those bright orbs like a shroud, dulling that spark of life until they were completely empty as they stared sightlessly up at the beast that had dragged them into darkness.

"Elliot?" his mother cried from the front of the property, where they'd still been unpacking the car and wondering why there was no answer after knocking on the door.

I heard his parents rushing to the scream of their son, but I'd cut it off before they could pinpoint his location and they split up, frantically checking the barns for their little boy. Not yet giving myself completely over to the bloodlust, I retreated back into the gloom, waiting once more.

It was the mother who was the first to come upon the scene of any parent's worst nightmare. Overcome with grief, she fell to her knees beside the small body lying there in a pool of its own blood, cradling the empty shell of her beloved son.

"Oh God Elliot, please no, come back to me, come back to mummy," she sobbed hysterically, rocking back and forth.

I watched my prey coldly from the shadows, as utterly devoid of any sense of empathy for the woman as the corpse she held in her arms, no matter how disturbing others might have found the sight of her grief, or how moving the depth of her love had clearly been for her child. Besides, they would be reunited in death soon enough.

The boy's father heard his wife's anguished cries and hurried over, already fearing the worst after seeing the evidence of some wild animal's attack on the farm. He must have also found the bodies of the aunt and uncle they'd brought their little boy to see on that fated visit, as he'd armed himself with the rifle Jack had carried during the night.

The father squeezed his wife's shoulder, but when he glanced over to the back of the barn where I crouched and our eyes met, through the tears I could see a rage that mirrored my own. Here I was, the monster who had taken their little boy from them, their son's blood still wet on the jaws that had ripped the life from him, and the mere sight of me gave rise to the man's need for revenge. He must have felt so powerful and righteous as he raised the rifle and sighted down the barrel, ready to kill me with so simple an action as the squeeze of a trigger. A life for a life, and could I really blame him for wanting that kind of justice? Yet in the grip of my own anger I saw only another human with a gun, intent on slaying any beast that posed a threat to human life which they so arrogantly considered more sacred than the life of any other creature. I responded with a challenging roar, and charged towards him.

Still distraught over the loss of her son, the mother hadn't noticed what was going on around her, and the thundering shot of the rifle made her jump all the more because she hadn't been expecting it. She screamed when she saw me and scrambled to her feet, carrying Elliot's corpse in her arms as she fled, leaving her husband to battle it out with me.

The rifle proved to be as little use for this man as it had been for Jack during the night. He was far from a master marksman and his aim was not true, though he did land a lucky shot in my shoulder. If I'd been a mortal creature he might have succeeded in bringing me down, but without the skill required to put a bullet in my heart or brain he would never even be allowed the comfort of vengeance. Unfortunately for him, he didn't realise the rifle wouldn't stop me until it was too late.

I crashed into the man, throwing us both to the stone floor, and pinned him down while I ripped into his torso, stringy flesh like wet rags tearing away so easily from the ribcage in my fearsome jaws. Bones snapped like twigs and organs ripped from the tubes chaining them in place, until only a hollow cavity remained. It took only minutes for me to rip my prey apart, which hadn't given his wife much time to get away.

Just as I rose from the carcass, I heard the sound of a car door and I snarled with a fresh wave of fury. On foot I'd have run her down easily, but if she'd given up on her husband and had enough wits left about her to make her escape by car, she may well succeed in escaping the same fate that had met the rest of her family.

I burst from the barn and bounded towards the car to find the woman carefully lying the body of her son across the backseat. Either she was unable to face the reality that her little boy was really gone or she didn't want me to feed on the body, but whatever her reason for taking the corpse, she was determined not to leave it. Even though it had meant spending a portion of the precious time her husband's death had bought her, she wouldn't leave her son's remains for the monster to ravage any further.

The woman just managed to climb into the car before I closed in, desperately rifling through the contents of her handbag in search of the key. But I threw myself at the car door before she could find it and start the engine, denting the metal and smashing the window. She screamed and scrambled across to the passenger side, climbing back out seemingly with the intention of running for the house. I leapt onto the roof and back down on the other side of the car, landing just in front of her. Unlike my lupine half I wasn't interested in the thrill of the chase, only the savage ecstasy of the kill once I'd given myself completely to the bloodlust, and the feel of frail mortal bodies ripping and tearing in my hands and jaws. So I grabbed the woman by her throat, my bestial face twisted into a feral snarl. She wriggled in my grasp but the mere strength of a human was no match for me as I threw her body down onto the car bonnet, denting more of the metal shell and breaking her bones with the impact. My prey was too damaged to make another run for it when I released my grip on her throat, only to plunge my clawed hands into the soft flesh of her belly, ripping open a hole to bury my snout in and eat her alive like I had with her husband. Intestines hung like a string of sausages between my teeth, but there was more appetising flesh and viscera to be had, so I dropped them and went in search of tastier organs.

The woman died screaming as I drew out her liver, which I bit in two. Half of it fell to the ground, where it quivered like a slippery lump of jelly. I ripped my way through her torso, as much to feed the bloodlust as my hunger for flesh, until only a bloody mess remained of what had once been a human being. Only when the bloodlust was satisfied and my mind cleared of the red haze did I rise from my meal, suddenly aware of the amount of noise my victims and I myself had made. Though the area was sparsely populated, I felt I should check no other humans had heard and come to investigate. So I abandoned my kills to search the premises, but it seemed I was alone, with only the dead for company. I returned to my freshest kills and ate my fill of what was left, before slinking back into one of the barns to rest while I had the chance, making the most of the relatively warm shelter. I knew I should probably try to find Lady Sarah, but it would be riskier to run around in daylight when there was more chance of me being seen and hunted by the Slayers, so I decided I'd wait till nightfall. Besides, she would already be hiding somewhere from both the sun and humanity, which would make finding her harder.

I settled down amidst the carnage both myself and the wolf had made, quickly slipping into a light sleep. Not even the nightmares troubled me that day, and I lay there for the remainder of the daylight hours.

It was already dark when I awoke, still in my hybrid form, to find someone stood over me. I growled in alarm, wondering how they'd managed to sneak in quiet enough so as not to wake me, but then I realised it was Lady Sarah and let myself relax.

"You are out of control," she hissed, gesturing angrily to the bloodbath I'd created.

Her anger ignited my own as if a flame reached out between us, catching the glowing embers that burned deep inside me and setting them alight once more.

"Well what else am I supposed to do with my time?" I snarled. "I can't be human anymore and there's no wolf packs to run with in this country. So what else is there, other than embracing my true, murderous nature?"

"I had hoped it would not have to come to this," she said, ignoring my question and grabbing my head, forcing me to look into her eyes.

"No!" I growled, realising she intended to use her hypnotic power to put me under her spell. I started to struggle, but it was too late. The anger blazing through me suddenly felt to be far away, as if it belonged to someone else, and in its place there was only adoration for this beautiful goddess I had the fortune to look upon. When she spoke, her voice sounded to be the kindest and warmest I'd ever heard, and there was no question of whether I would do what she wanted. In that moment, I felt I would do anything to please her.

"No more killing without my permission, except in self-defence. Do you understand?"

I nodded in response.

"Good," she said, and released me from her spell.

But I was aware of what she'd done and as soon as my mind cleared, the rage crashed back over me and I roared "You have no right to do this!"

"You left me no choice," she replied, all traces of her own anger hidden from me as she turned to walk off into the night. The show of calmness she now presented angered me even more. I wanted a fight and she wouldn't even grant me that.

"Killing is all I have left. Don't do this!" I shouted after her, but she didn't even turn to look back at me. I roared and lashed out at the walls of the barn, carving deep gashes into the stone, but still the vampire continued to walk away. "I swear I'll fucking kill you for this! You can't keep these mental chains on me forever, and when I break free I'm killing you first Sarah. Do you hear me? I'm coming for you first!"

Not even dropping her medieval title in a deliberate show of disrespect could bring her anger back to the surface, and she was suddenly so far ahead that she would soon be out of sight. I considered leaving her then, but I knew she'd only find me again and use more hypnosis to bind me to her. I had little choice but to run after her, though I refused to speak to her again that night. I would find a way to break free of her spell, and I would continue to indulge my bloodlust until the day a human succeeded in killing me. I was determined of it.

We found another abandoned building to shelter in through the day, in another rural area. Childish as it was, I wouldn't eat any of the dried meat Lady Sarah had offered me in the night, consequently leaving my stomach aching with hunger once more. The vampire had advised me to return to human form and I'd done so only because I didn't want her to use her power on me again to force me to obey her. But my body craved more meat to replenish the energy spent on the transformation and all I could think of was the need to hunt, and just as strongly, driven by the rage, the need to kill.

I prowled the fields outside the empty house Lady Sarah had chosen to hide away in, searching for more prey. My hunt took me to another stretch of woodland, where I found and caught a pheasant, and I gave myself to the bloodlust once more. Yet when I raised the plump, feathery body to my mouth, it was as if an invisible barrier surrounded the bird, preventing my fangs from biting down into the warm flesh. I growled with frustration and tried again, but no matter how strong the urge to rip the animal apart or how fiercely I tried to obey that urge, I couldn't break through the vampire's spell and end its life. My jaws began to ache from straining against the mental muzzle Lady Sarah had placed on me and I was just about to admit defeat, when it occurred to me that the restraint had been placed on me as a human, not the wolf. With a rush of excitement I surrendered control to him, thinking if this worked, then perhaps through him the spell would be completely broken and I'd be just as free to kill as the wolf once again.

As much as I'd grown to loathe my human half, I co-operated with it since I too shared in the hunger currently assaulting our body. My stomach screamed for food so badly it was almost sickening, and the pheasant I held was too good a snack to resist.

My eyes had turned lupine and my canines had already lengthened into fangs, but my body was otherwise human. Ordinarily I'd have taken the transformation to my full wolf form but I knew it would only leave me hungrier to do so, and now the full moon had passed I wasn't gripped by the same lunar frenzy which had robbed me of my reason and any sense of caution I may otherwise have possessed. I wouldn't waste energy on a mere whim, my instinct to survive too strong for me to throw my life away so recklessly.

I raised the pheasant still clutched in my hands to my jaws once more, but just as the human had found, it was as if there was an invisible force preventing me from biting down. I knew it would prove just as useless for me to try and fight it as it had for the human, so I retreated back into our subconscious, not wanting to remain in control of my body while necessity forced me to stay in human form. I was content to wait for the next full moon, when my time would come again.

The wolf retreated, leaving me still clutching the living pheasant I longed to tear into. Rage answered my defeat but since I was unable to take it out on my prey, I released the terrified animal still struggling in my grasp and instead clawed at myself in the grip of a new kind of madness. I scratched long bloody furrows in my scalp as if I could somehow break Lady Sarah's chains with my physical strength, since the strength of my mind had failed me. And as ever the pain only drew me into more of a frenzy, until blood splattered the surrounding trees. Yet there was no joy to be had in spilling my own blood and my rage soared to new heights. The morning rang with my roars of fury. I was a tormented creature, bound by invisible chains. If any were there to see I wonder if they would have felt sorry for me, or would you all take pleasure in my suffering? Perhaps I deserved this new torment I was being made to endure, but such thoughts didn't make it any easier to bear.

Some part of me was vaguely aware that this behaviour was more likely to attract the attention of the Slayers, but since Lady Sarah's power would allow for me to kill in self-defence, I wanted them to find me. I bellowed as loudly as I could but the land remained still and empty around me, and eventually my anger died down again.

I returned to the empty house, beaten and still hungry, and sat sullenly on the cold floor. After a while I slipped into more troubled sleep.

Back in the woods, I stalked after new prey, a deer this time. Shadows lengthened as the daylight began to fail, my hunger stronger than ever after enduring a full day without being able to feed. It had grown so powerful that this time I felt sure it would break the vampire's spell, and eagerly I pushed on in pursuit of my prey, threads of saliva dripping from my jaws in anticipation of the meal soon to come.

The snap of a twig was enough to spook the deer and it bolted. I gave chase, weaving in and out of tree trunks and leaping over a fallen log, closing in on my prey. The deer pushed itself to the limit of its physical abilities, but it was only mortal and I was soon upon it, pouncing and sending us both crashing to the ground. I closed my jaws round its throat and felt a sense of triumph when my fangs slid into the soft flesh, blood spilling into my mouth. But something was wrong, a sudden agony stabbing through my gums.

I drew my head back, blood now gushing from my mouth, and to my horror I felt my teeth coming loose. I bent over, spitting out blood and teeth, until my gums were bare, rendering me powerless to feed once again, and all I could do was scream in frustration and pain.

I was still screaming from this latest nightmare as I fought my way back to consciousness. It seemed Lady Sarah's power over my mind had even affected the nightmares, since this was a new one I'd not experienced before.

Dusk had fallen but the vampire had yet to rise. I stalked outside, seething once again, and glared up at the waning moon, feeling I had but one hope of breaking Lady Sarah's hold over me. Her power clearly wasn't enough to override the call of the full moon, or she'd have used her hypnotic abilities to keep the wolf from running wild instead of resorting to such brutal means as a blade through my leg. That meant when the moon next rose as full, I could indulge in my bloodlust once more. But since it had just been full, I now had a whole month to wait before I could slaughter freely, and the thought of that was enough to keep me fuming for the rest of the night.

I knew I was being childish again, but when the vampire awoke I still wouldn't speak to her, though I was too hungry to resist the meat she offered me that night – a deer she killed and fed on first, leaving me with another unappetising dry carcass. Even the nightmare I'd had couldn't keep me from eating my fill, and I tore through it as if I'd been starving for months.

By the time I'd finished my meal Lady Sarah was anxious to move on, and we spent more long hours running across the countryside until the approach of dawn forced us to stop and seek new shelter once more.

The next week or so passed much the same, though my rage gradually began to die down until, unable to feed it and the bloodlust it was tied to, it finally burnt itself out. Only emptiness remained and my faint glimmer of hope that was the moon, though as it continued to wane to no more than a slither of light in the sky I became utterly dejected, feeling I couldn't last the two weeks (or just over) till it grew full once more.

That rage had defined me for so many weeks that I suddenly felt lost without it. I thought I could feel a few embers burning faintly deep inside me, so maybe I wasn't entirely empty yet, but a part of me wondered if it would be completely gone by the time the full moon came. I could only hope the moon would rekindle it as it continued to wax and call to my lycanthropy once again, because if it didn't I would be left completely dead inside, and I didn't think I could face an eternity existing with this gaping chasm that had opened up inside me. I'd thought in giving into the rage and the bloodlust I'd embraced that inner darkness at the heart of mankind, but what if this was the true darkness, where no emotions, no life burned within? And in the absence of any spark of life, what reason was there for the empty husk I was becoming to continue to exist? I tried to stoke my dying rage with thoughts that this latest torment was all Lady Sarah's doing, since it was her power preventing me from killing which had led to my anger draining away, but even that couldn't call it back.

Lady Sarah sensed the change in me and decided to risk a few nights in the same place so she could teach me more to help me survive. I could tell what she really wanted to teach me was some self-control to help make the full moons easier, but she knew it was too early to attempt that when I'd only just calmed down from my last fit of rage.

By the new moon I felt a sense of despair creeping in. I gazed up at the night sky, feeling the burning remnants of my anger might as well be as far off as the stars glimmering faintly overhead. I wished I could reach out to the moon and drag it back into position to make it full again. I was only vaguely paying attention to what Lady Sarah was saying, finding her lessons almost as dull as those I'd endured at school in my human life.

"Now, should the need ever arise to return to the human world, there is more you need to know if you are to pass undetected for any length of time among them," she said. "Since the Slayers actively patrol the streets on a night, the daylight hours are the safest for you to enter a settlement. Crowds offer the chance to blend in and make it harder for the Slayers to attack, since they don't want the world at large to know of their existence. Some of them will also hesitate to shoot through human shields, but there are those who don't care about the number of casualties if it means bringing our races that bit closer to extinction, as you are well aware.

"You would need to acquire more clothes to pass for human of course, and if you need to visit a place more than once you should try to change your appearance as much as possible each time. Modern technology makes it easier for the Slayers to track us than ever before and you should be mindful of cameras, as well as prying human eyes. If you can't hide in a crowd then avoid built up areas where there's likely to be more cameras, and try to keep your face hidden as much as possible. In wolf form you need to be even more careful and keep to the shadows and alleyways. Civilians might mistake you for a stray dog, but after all the media reports of a 'rogue wolf' on the loose they may well attack, and the Slayers will be quick to recognise you if a large canid is spotted in an area."

"Okay," I murmured, still gazing up at the night sky.

"I can see your attention is elsewhere tonight so we will leave it there I suppose, but the sooner you learn all this the better. If we ever get separated or if you run into trouble in the daylight hours when I'm unable to help, you need to know these things to give you the best chance to survive in our world."

I gave a non-committal response and the vampire went to hunt for another luckless animal to sustain us both.

Another week passed but I had yet to feel any change, despite the waxing moon.

"You can make stitches from a few natural materials if the need arises in the wild," Lady Sarah was saying as part of my latest lesson, demonstrating the use of tendons from her latest kill as thread and a makeshift needle she'd fashioned out of wood.

"Why do I even need to know this?" I snapped. The night sky was completely black, the moon hidden behind storm clouds massing overhead. But I could feel it up there, growing fuller, and at long last my anger burned stronger again from within my inner darkness. "The transformation heals wounds for me; I don't need stitches."

"And what if you're bleeding out from a wound and too low on energy to heal the damage before it kills you?" Lady Sarah responded with a surge of her own anger, as if the two were linked again, flames leaping between us to set each of us ablaze with fury. "I am trying to help you, if you would stop behaving like a spoilt child and focus on your own survival."

"What's the point in surviving if all we're going to do is run and hide?" I snarled. "It's been weeks now since our battle with the Slayers and we've done nothing constructive. Time's slipping away from us and still nothing changes. They continue to pick us off one by one – they've already tried to take me and you out, and how many others have they successfully killed while we've been on the run? Why do we not fight? We came out victorious once already. Why are we not pressing the assault on their other bases? We could make another stand, instead of fleeing and allowing the Slayers to carry on weakening us."

"You are not ready for all out warfare!" Lady Sarah snapped back, unable to keep her anger in check this time. It seemed she didn't like me questioning her judgement. "You may have taken the role of leader when we fought in your hometown, but you are still very young, Nick. You know nothing of true war. We won a small victory and gained some time for those of us in that area, nothing more. The Slayers will be back. Yes, we could continue to assault their other bases but they will be ready for us in future, and we cannot hope to prevail if they're ready to mass against us!"

"Then we should be striking them down before they can gather their forces," I argued.

"Ah, if it were that simple! If we were to engage them in open warfare we would die. It would be genocide. We might have all the advantages in a fair fight, but you should know as well as anyone that humanity does not fight fair. They hide behind their machines, and even we cannot withstand some of this modern technology.

"I may have limited knowledge about the modern world, but I have seen some of their more recent instruments of destruction at play. I've lived through wars that they've waged against each other and I've seen the advances in their machinery. I've seen them develop bombs and other such weapons, and if it is we who are caught in the crosshairs I am not so arrogant as to believe we would somehow escape.

"And they would resort to such destructive measures. If they felt we had declared open warfare, are you really so stupid as to think they would continue to fight in secret from the rest of the world? No, they would use their influence amongst their governments to unite the world against us. They've already proven they will permit a few sacrifices to save the many – they would stop at nothing to smash whatever forces we could gather. This might not be the view held by all, but madness breeds madness, and eventually the doubters to their cause would come to think the same way.

"So no, we have not gone on the offensive following our one small victory. I repeat, it would be genocide."

"Well I won't just cower in the shadows until they find me," I snarled. "We were made for more than this! We were made to fight and to kill, and to inspire fear in mankind. I won't spend eternity running from my prey. It is they who should run screaming from me, and tonight I will make them scream."

"Fine, go out there and get yourself killed if that's what you really want! I will not stop you," the vampire hissed.

"No, you won't," I growled and ran off before she could do anything, though I think she was too angry that night to use her powers to keep me from going off alone.

I slowed only when Lady Sarah was beyond the reach of my senses. I could no longer hear her dead lungs inhaling and exhaling out of habit rather than necessity, her breaths coming more rapidly as she fought to control her own anger. There was no sight of her in the blackness of the countryside, nor any scent of vampire – another smell

I'd grown to recognise since spending so much time with her over the last month. Then the first rumble of thunder began like the growl of some mighty beast overhead, as if my rage had grown so powerful that even the elements felt it and responded in kind.

Lightning rent the blackness, a fissure in the sky through which it seemed the downpour started from. The rain was cold on my skin, a chill made worse by the wind driving it, but my anger burned so fiercely I barely noticed. Another streak of lightning revealed the water, so pure and clear around me, to be mixing with the dried blood still covering my body. Tainted by the horrific acts I'd committed over the last few weeks, the raindrops ran red across my skin, the rainfall growing heavier as if in response, in an attempt to cleanse my evil from the land. I roared in defiance and was answered by another rumble of thunder, swiftly followed by a further flash of lightning.

As British storms went, this one was impressive. It was easy to see why such an awe-inspiring, natural phenomenon had been mistaken for the work of gods in times long past. And who was to say it hadn't been caused by some divine being? Lady Sarah had told me demons existed, so that suggested the possibility of some kind of heavenly creatures as well. Was it mere rainfall pelting my body or did the heavens weep for the poor souls I had brutally ripped from their mortal lives and sent unwillingly to whatever awaited them in death? Was the storm truly a sign that I'd angered whatever God or gods might be up there, watching this unnatural thing invading the world they reigned over from above? I had let such thoughts trouble me before, but that night they only fed the fires of my rage. If any kind of gods existed they had let me fall victim to my lycanthropy, and they had forsaken me in my hour of need, back when I wanted to keep myself from killing. I owed them nothing, least of all any faith or respect. So I roared in defiance again and let the transformation take hold until my true nature of wolf and man hybrid was revealed once more. Then I turned my attention back to the earth.

Risen up on the fires of my rage, my bloodlust had re-awoken, and the need to kill was overpowering. I was desperate to taste fresh blood on my tongue, feel it spilling out of my mouth and down my chin, the warmth of it trickling down my body. I wanted to feel bones crush in my jaws and flesh tear in my hands, to hear living hearts beat their last and see eyes full of life dimming as I plunged them into the blackness of death. I wanted to kill again, and there was only one way I could overcome Lady Sarah's hold over me before the rise of the next full moon. I was able to remember the words she'd spoken to me whilst I was under her hypnotic power, the words I was forced to adhere to no matter how greatly I wanted to rebel.

"No more killing without my permission, except in self-defence," she'd said. That left me but one choice. I had to find more Slayers to fight and by engaging them, I could kill again.

"Slayers!" I roared into the night. "I know you're out there."

My only reply came from another rumble of thunder overhead.

"I'm on my own now; no Lady Sarah to fight by my side. So what are you waiting for? Come get me, you bastards!"

The night remained frustratingly free of human activity, leaving me to fall into another fit of rage driven madness. But as the anger began to die down enough for my thoughts to clear, an idea came to me. It was insanely reckless, but at least if it cost me my life I would go down in a blaze of glory. I found that thought strangely appealing, and more preferable to an eternity of running and hiding, dead inside except at the time of the full moon – which seemed to be the fate awaiting me if I returned to Lady Sarah.

The storm had passed and there was a hint of light creeping into the blackness overhead, signalling the approach of dawn. I took the transformation fully to wolf form since I still didn't have the means to make myself presentable enough to enter the human world, then headed in the direction of the nearest town. If the Slayers were too cowardly to face me I would have to take the fight to them, and it was in search of my enemies I now went. One way or another I would satisfy my bloodlust, even if it cost me my life.

Chapter Five – Looking for a Fight

I shivered in the early morning chill, still wet after being out in the storm which allowed the cold past the defences of my fur coat and free to harry my skin as if it was still bare. It hadn't been a problem till I'd paused in my hunt for the Slayers, but the hunger brought on by the transformation was becoming unbearable and the roadkill I'd found was too tempting to resist.

The mess of fur and flesh had been a living fox until recently. It was a fresh kill, the meat still slightly warm. As roadkill went it wasn't too bad a meal and there was just enough to keep the hunger at bay, though my appetite was far from sated. But the thought that I would soon feast on the flesh of my enemies kept me going, and once I'd eaten what I could from the remains I pressed on, careful to keep to the side streets and remain out of sight of prying eyes for the time being. I didn't want to be discovered too soon so I tried to follow the advice Lady Sarah had given me on avoiding detection, which I grudgingly admitted to myself was proving useful after all.

I searched the streets for any hint of Slayers still out on patrol in the early morning quiet before the human world awoke, but the town seemed deserted. Despite the ease with which the Slayers had found me before, they didn't seem to be aware I was somewhere in the area. I had to assume their nightly patrols had already returned to their everyday lives with the onset of dawn, since the other undead races were no longer a threat now it was daylight, or at least I assumed that was the case. As far as I knew I was the only one of us free to attack during the day. And it seemed likely the Slayers would keep their guard up if they knew I was nearby, probably patrolling for longer than usual, but if they thought I was elsewhere in the country they had no need to stay out after dawn.

Somewhere within the town a church bell tolled the hour – seven o' clock, which meant the streets would soon be busy with people rushing to work and to school, unless it was a weekend but I had no way of knowing that. The days of the week no longer held any meaning for me so I hadn't even bothered to try and keep track since leaving the human world behind. But the people of this town were still bound by their routines of education and employment and, assuming it was a weekday, the early morning rush was about to begin. So I was forced to retreat back into the surrounding countryside and find somewhere to rest and nurse my simmering anger, determined as I was not to let it completely burn out again, until nightfall when I could resume the hunt.

I returned to the town that night, only to find the streets almost as quiet as they had been that morning. There were a few people walking dogs or heading out for a drink, but no Slayers as far as I could tell. None of them seemed to be carrying any weapons or to possess that alertness of their surroundings that would have suggested they knew the true nature of the dangers the darkness held. I wandered the streets right up until dawn again, pausing in my search only to scavenge more roadkill, but the town remained utterly devoid of any Slayer activity. That should have signalled to me that something was wrong and that perhaps the wisest course would've been to abort this reckless mission I'd committed myself to, yet my stubbornness didn't want to listen to caution. The longer the Slayers hid from me like cowards, the more set I became on finding the force they had in that particular area and engaging them in combat, which was the only way to get around Lady Sarah's power so I could kill as I was so desperate to do. But I had enough sense to leave the town again during the daylight hours and changed back to human form, resting and waiting for nightfall once more.

After two more nights of unsuccessful hunting, I decided it was time to change tack. If I couldn't find any Slayers to follow to the place I had in mind to turn into the next abattoir, I'd just have to find it myself.

I remained in human form that night, already feeling the rising hunger from shifting forms so often without being able to eat my fill each time. I didn't think I'd need to venture into the town itself, or at least not into any of the populated parts. The building I was looking for was bound to be in another derelict area or hidden in the rural outskirts, though I could rule out the fields where I'd been spending my days as there'd been no evidence of any humans nearby whilst I'd rested there.

It took most of the night but I finally found a large building that looked like it might have once been used as a factory. It was isolated enough from the nearby town to make it a likely candidate for the place I was searching for, and as I watched from the shadows I saw two humans guarding the perimeter. They were both armed with guns, so it was probably safe to assume they were Slayers.

I wanted nothing more than to charge in and fight the two guards right there and then, but reluctantly I drew back. If I waited one more day and returned at nightfall there would likely be more of them for me to slaughter, and it was another bloodbath I was craving. So I forced myself to retreat back to the fields on the other side of the town which had proven safe enough for the days I'd spent in the area, though I didn't even attempt to sleep. The moon would also rise as full that next night, and with the promise of bloodshed so close at hand, I could only pace restlessly, impatient for the day to pass and night to fall once more.

With dusk approaching, I wasted no time in slinking back to the old factory building. I wanted to indulge my bloodlust before the full moon appeared and gave my wolfish half the power to take over, and I was as eager as ever for a kill after being forced to wait by Lady Sarah's hypnotic spell. But her hold over me was about to be broken, and once I'd whet my appetite on the Slayers my lupine half would be free to turn his insatiable hunger on the town, and there would be no one to stop me.

Once the building was in sight, I paused to give in to the transformation fighting to take hold, though I only let it go to the halfway point between boy and wolf again. Then, when I had the hybrid form I was beginning to favour more than either full human or full wolf, I boldly walked out of the shadows and stalked over to the old factory. There was no evidence of any guards that night which again should have raised alarm bells, but I was too drunk on the feeling of power brought on by the lunar cycle. So it was that I stepped so recklessly inside the Slayers' base, as if I was truly unstoppable and had nothing to fear from their mortal weapons. But they had known I was in the area all along, and they'd been preparing for my arrival. I'd walked right into their trap.

Chapter Six – Burnt Out

This base I'd found was much smaller than the one I'd briefly been imprisoned in a couple of months ago, and judging from a quick glimpse of my surroundings they seemed to be using the space for training new recruits. But there was nothing new or inexperienced about the thirty or so humans surrounding me, their faces set with expressions of grim determination. They thought they had the numbers to kill me but they knew some of them would die, even if they succeeded.

Already overcome with rage, there was no room for fear in my heart. I pictured myself as some mighty warrior about to single-handedly take down my enemies, hailed a hero by my fellow undead. I eyed the men opposite me, baring my fangs in a feral snarl. They seemed to be waiting for me to make the first move so I obliged, challenging them with a roar of fury and charging forwards into the first spray of bullets. Yet in opening fire they had unwittingly sealed their doom.

I can't explain how it is I'm still alive to tell you this tale now. I can't explain how I survived walking into that place and facing so many of them and their guns. No matter how good a shot or how many times each Slayer fired at me, somehow none of them could find their mark. It was as if I had a guardian angel watching over me, and yet no angel would have had a hand in such bloody slaughter as took place that night.

Through the spray of bullets I ran into what should have been certain death, but without that killing shot through my heart or my brain I proved unstoppable, barely feeling the pain of what wounds I did sustain. Once more my reality narrowed down to the beating of my enemies' hearts and the blood waiting to be spilled from each fleshy container. And how satisfying it was to spill that blood with tooth and claw, after being made to wait an entire month to lose myself in this savage joy once again.

As I tore the first of my victims apart, guns began to click empty. The Slayers nearest me drew their swords, whilst those on the other side of the room reloaded. One woman was especially quick to unsheathe her blade, and she brought it down in an arc that should have cleaved my skull in two. But I sensed the movement and turned, catching her sword arm in a clawed hand and ripping it from the socket with a wet sucking noise. She fell to her knees, screaming and clutching at her shoulder as if to stem the pain and the blood flow. I tossed the severed limb aside and turned to the next of my victims, reducing his throat to a red fountain in a vicious swipe.

One woman lost her nerve and began to flee, but I pounced on her before she could escape the building and bit into her lower back, flesh ripping beneath my teeth until I'd exposed a section of her spine. And like a dog at play, I worried the bone, shaking my head from side to side while she spasmed uncontrollably beneath me. She was utterly helpless to defend herself as I grew more frenzied, until the bone snapped and came free in my jaws, and she grew still.

I felt like a god to hold their lives in my hands, and to crush that life so easily in my great jaws until it faded into nothingness. What hope did these mere mortals have against the might of a god? Their guns had failed them, their blades too slow in their human hands. Men liked to think they had conquered the Earth, their technology making them untouchable to the beasts they'd once been prey to. But without that technology they were weak and for all their intelligence, it wouldn't save them from the great predator in their midst. I felt invincible as I tore my way through flesh and bone, ripping life after life from their frail bodies in a fierce display of my feral power.

More of the humans lost their nerve once I'd killed enough of them to even the odds and they too tried to flee, but I was sure to leave none alive. I ran down each of the cowards, pouncing on them and dealing out more brutal deaths. The shrill screams of my victims rang through the night, prayers which only empowered my god-like state and fuelled this primal joy born of killing and savagery. Even if there'd been room in my heart for mercy, I was too far lost in my bloodlust to spare any of them.

The last of them made it as far as his car before I was on him, digging my claws into the flesh of his back. He screamed in agony as I tore out another length of spine, this time bringing part of the ribcage away with it. The bloody bone looked almost like an alien creature in the darkness, the broken ribs like legs splayed out either side. I might have found some dark amusement in that but my prey wasn't yet dead, so I tossed the bone aside and lowered my snout to the gaping wound in his back. Hunger took over and I began to feed, only for the light of the full moon to touch me for the first time that night, forcing the transformation to resume. The wolf's time had come.

The frenzy I'd felt during the previous full moon was as nothing compared to the rage driven madness upon me that month. I shifted fully into wolf form atop the dying man pinned beneath my paws and savaged him until his carcass was nothing more than a mess of ragged flesh and shattered bones, unrecognisable as human. I have no clear memory of what happened after that, so lost as I was in the red haze clouding my mind. I know only that I turned my wrath on the nearby town, mauling and killing until the streets ran red with blood.

Not even the sunrise could stop me – my human half had given itself so completely to the bloodthirsty nature of the curse that I remained in wolf form. For three glorious nights and days I terrorised the human world, running free and wild as I was born to do. If humanity made an attempt to fight back I have no memory of it, but it's possible I encountered more Slayers in that time, as well as those ignorant of my true nature, believing me to be nothing more than a mortal wolf. But if there were any would-be heroes, they surely died with the rest of their people. Countless victims fell to my rage, until finally the moon's power began to wane and my bloodlust with it. Exhaustion took its place, crashing over me in an icy wave that left my entire body trembling from fatigue, and flooding my muscles with a deep ache. I collapsed beside the corpse of my last victim for the month, panting heavily until my eyelids locked into place and a deep sleep claimed me.

I awoke to find my body had shifted back to human form. I didn't know how long I'd lain there but my eyes still felt heavy and it was an effort to force them open. There was someone stood over me and as I began to come round I realised it was Lady Sarah.

"You came back," I said tiredly, feeling weak and drained in the absence of the fury that had powered me for so many days. I couldn't even feel any anger burning deep down in the dark pit of my being, but I was too tired to worry that it might have already burnt out for another month.

"Yes, I came back, infuriating though you can be. Now you seem to be in a more reasonable mood, I hope you can see that all I have done has been to help you. My methods might seem harsh but I am only trying to keep you alive."

"But why?"

"I realise you are struggling to adapt so I will give you another chance. And besides, where else am I going to find a pet werewolf? You're a rare breed these days."

I stared at her for a moment and then started to laugh. There was no real humour to it but I laughed anyway. To hear Lady Sarah making a joke had been the last thing I'd expected, even if it was a bad one, and I suddenly felt a connection to her that hadn't been there before.

She wanted to renew her hold over me to keep me from indulging in any more mindless slaughter that might get either of us killed, and I accepted the mental chains without struggling that time. She was right, in the absence of the rage I couldn't deny that she had

59

only ever tried to help me and even I could see that constantly leaving a trail of bodies in our wake would only lead more waves of Slayers to us. Besides, I didn't have the energy to fight.

The vampire kept watch while I ate from the remains of the victim I'd collapsed beside, but I was forced to abandon my meal when the wind carried to us the scent of more humans. It seemed the Slayers had found their courage once more and were back on our trail, and even if Lady Sarah had been willing to face them, I was in no fit state for another fight. I barely had the energy to run, even after feeding, but I pushed my body to its limits as we took off into the night once again.

Over the next three weeks the Slayers continued to harry us almost non-stop, forcing us to flee from place to place each night. Whenever we were permitted a brief reprieve Lady Sarah tried to give me more space for fear of re-awakening my rage, though she needn't have worried. I couldn't feel any hint of the anger that had driven me for so many months, not even when the moon began to wax towards full again. I continued to dream of my next kill and losing myself in the bloodlust so I could feel alive once more, but until I was permitted another fight or to hunt it seemed I would remain dead inside. And there didn't seem to be much chance of any more skirmishes with the Slayers anytime soon, since Lady Sarah had taken extra precautions to keep me out of trouble while she slept during the day. She'd tightened the hypnotic lead she kept on me so that I was forced to stay close by to her unless instructed otherwise, and she had us entering more derelict areas where we could make the most of old cellars in relative safety from an attack. She felt the risk of entering the human world to find these places was outweighed by the benefit of such shelters – namely that the Slayers couldn't send too large a group in broad daylight without attracting unwanted attention from the public. And knowing that, they were less likely to attack after the devastation I'd already caused to their other hunting parties they'd sent during the day. They'd learnt the hard way that they needed numbers if they were to take us down, which forced them to bide their time until the opportunity to strike with a larger force presented itself.

In the week leading up to the next full moon we were fortunate enough to seemingly have lost the Slayers again for the time being, though I had to wonder if they were planning something. They had to know that we would be forced to return to our rural haunts where the vampire had more chance of keeping me under control, and that could be exactly the kind of opportunity our enemies were waiting for. Regardless, Lady Sarah led me back out into the country, though there was a fairly sizeable town closer than she would have liked. A main road ran through its centre and presumably connected its people to neighbouring towns and the nearest cities, but mostly the roadways were made up of a network of narrow country roads twisting through the surrounding countryside, with a small patch of woodland, for want of a better word, bordering one of those roads. It was really too small to be considered a proper wood or forest, and it offered shelter for only the smallest of animals who would usually make their home there, though it seemed deer had passed through the area recently.

We found a barn which looked to have been out of use for some years, and far enough from any other buildings to avoid detection by the locals. It was virtually empty, save for a length of rope and a few old, seemingly forgotten tools leant against one of the walls, left to rust. The one thing it lacked was shelter from the sun which would soon rise, but Lady Sarah looked around and nodded.

"This will do," she said.

"Really? Where are you going to hide from the sun in here?"

"In the ground," she answered. "But if we are to spend the week here I insist on the comfort of a coffin. Can I trust you to bring me one while I hunt? That graveyard we passed on the outskirts of the town ought to be safe enough, if you can slip in and out unseen. Just don't do anything so stupid as to steal from a funeral home."

"I know, I know. It'll draw too much attention to us," I growled. "I'll see what I can find in the graveyard."

"Thank you. Then I grant you permission to leave my side to find a coffin. Fresh meat will be waiting for you upon your return."

Expecting more of her leftovers, I merely nodded unenthusiastically and slunk away. I made it to the graveyard without incident and checked there was no one around, Slayer or otherwise, before digging up a coffin. Wrenching the lid open, I wrinkled my nose slightly the smell, the corpse inside in too advanced a state of decay to be considered in any way appetising, even to the wolf. There was little flesh beneath the withered skin, stretched so tightly over the bones that it looked like the skeleton within could burst out at any moment. But as ghoulish as it appeared, it was just a corpse, limp and lifeless as I tipped it out of the coffin and back into the grave, which I filled in again to hide any evidence that it had been tampered with. That done, I hefted the large box up onto my shoulders and struggled back to the barn. The weight of the coffin wasn't a problem with my supernatural strength, but it was awkward to carry without any help and I had to pause a couple of times to shift my grip on it. I just hoped it was the right size for the vampire after the effort I'd put in to get it back to her.

As I neared the barn, I heard Lady Sarah talking to someone else in there. I put the coffin down as gently and quietly as I could on the grass outside and sat on top of it, listening curiously.

"If this happened last full moon, why am I only just hearing about it now?" came Lady Sarah's voice.

"You underestimate your evasive skills," a male voice answered. "It's not just our enemies who've had a hard time finding you."

"They've been finding us too quickly, so how is it that you took nearly an entire month?" she retorted.

"It matters not. I am here now and I advise you to return with me."

"I will not leave his side," she said stubbornly.

"Do you truly trust the wolf that much?" the male voice asked incredulously.

"Yes," Lady Sarah answered him.

There was a pause before the other voice spoke again, as if she'd taken him by surprise and he needed a moment to recover. "Even so, you must know that staying with him could potentially be dangerous for you."

"I do not believe he is the one behind this. I will not," she said with conviction.

"Whether he is the one responsible or not, you know he could still be found guilty. And if he is indeed ruled guilty we may not be able to protect you. Don't let the wolf drag you down with him."

"I will not leave his side," she repeated.

"So you would choose an animal over your own people?" the male voice hissed.

"I hope it will not come to that. I thank you for coming to warn me and I will consider our next move. But you should go now; we don't have long before the dawn."

"Very well. But you know it is only a matter of time before he summons the two of you and you will have no option but to answer. Do not be a fool and try to run – it will only end badly for the both of you."

"I am well aware how this works," she hissed.

"Forgive me, I am merely concerned you are letting your fondness for your pet cloud your judgement. Tread carefully, Lady Sarah. Until the next time."

I'd already guessed the male voice belonged to another vampire and sure enough he strode out of the barn, pausing to give me a look of utter disdain before he took off into the dwindling shadows, fleeing the sun's first rays creeping over the land. I watched him go, a part of me hoping he wouldn't make it to shelter in time. I didn't know what the conversation I'd heard had been all about but it was clear he was one of the vampires who had no love for my kind. Lady Sarah had warned me that there were still plenty of them out there who remembered a time when our races were at war, before the rise of the Slayers forced us to ally against the threat of extinction they posed. It seemed he still held a grudge for events long past.

"Nick?" Lady Sarah called. "The sun is almost up, hurry!"

I'd almost forgotten she still needed the coffin and it was growing too light outside the barn for her to come out and retrieve it herself. One corner of the barn still offered enough shadows for her to stand in without burning and I took the coffin over to her, placing it down for her to test. It would have been too late to fetch another if she didn't fit the one I'd brought but we could have buried her in the ground without one if it had come to it, less comfortable though it would have been for her. But as it happened I'd chosen a good size for Lady Sarah, even if it was purely by luck.

The barn was really no more than a large shed made from wood and we were easily able to rip the floorboards up and dig down into the earth beneath. The coffin alone would have provided enough shelter from the sun, but if the Slayers attacked again and I couldn't fight them off, burying the coffin added an extra layer of security for the vampire. There was always the chance they might not find her if I could cover the hole over well enough, and perhaps they'd assume we'd split up again if they couldn't find any evidence of her sleeping nearby.

"What was that all about?" I asked as I helped her dig.

"Nothing you need concern yourself with."

"Yeah right, I heard him talking about a wolf and we both know that could only have been me he was referring to. Even if we found more surviving werewolves out there, I'm the only wolf companion you've got."

"It is merely vampire business. If there is a need for you to know more I will tell you, but for now you are better off staying clear of it."

"How can it be 'merely vampire business' if it involves me somehow?"

"Leave it, Nick. I will say no more on the matter and besides, even if I could talk to you about this we are out of time this night. I left your meat in the corner over there, but bury my coffin before you eat please. We seem to have lost the Slayers again for now but it is better to remain cautious."

Reluctantly I filled in the hole once she'd closed the coffin lid and placed the floorboards back over the patch of earth. I did my best to ensure the spot where she was buried wouldn't be noticeable at a glance and then stalked over to investigate the kill she'd left me. I was pleasantly surprised to find the carcass of a small deer which she didn't seem to have drained of any blood, and I ripped into it hungrily, the most appetising meal I'd had since the last full moon. As I ate, I thought over the conversation I'd heard between the two vampires. What was this thing that had happened, and why would they think I was responsible? Were they simply blaming me out of the prejudice many of them held, or was there more to it than that? The more I puzzled over it, the more questions I had. Then a thought occurred to me – what if my reckless actions had provoked the Slayers into more aggressive action? Could it be that it was not just me and Lady Sarah they'd been hunting so actively, but all of the undead in general? And if that was the case, perhaps they'd even succeeded in killing some of us. It was the only thing I could think of that could be considered my fault.

My thoughts turned to killing again. I hadn't been feeling the need to kill since the last full moon, but I wanted to. I wanted to reawaken my bloodlust and let it rise up to fill the gaping chasm of the emptiness within, and since my anger had deserted me it seemed killing was the only way to do that. Yet no matter how badly I wanted to hunt down more prey, Lady Sarah's power wouldn't allow it, and so my thoughts turned to all those I'd left behind with my human life. Images of the pain those closest to me must be feeling passed unbidden in my mind. I didn't want to dwell on what my friends and family must be going through, wondering if I was alive and there was a chance I'd return or if my body was lying in a ditch somewhere. But with little else to do I couldn't seem to help myself, despite the homesickness such thoughts began to stir, which only made the emptiness worse. That dark chasm only seemed to gape wider with the sense of loss creeping over me, and when night fell again I was grateful for the distraction the vampire offered, even if she insisted on giving me more lessons in survival.

We hunted together, Lady Sarah making the kills, and I quenched my thirst in another pond, but when the time came to bury her again for the day she said "You may hunt for yourself today but only small animals and you are not to go anywhere near the human world. Understood?"

I nodded and helped hide her again, wasting no time in going off to hunt once she was safely back in the ground.

The nearby town was just coming alive when I first set out and if it hadn't been for Lady Sarah's hold over me, I might have given in to the temptation to fall upon the hapless mortals and slaughter them to my heart's content. As it was, the small animals she'd given me permission to kill would have to suffice for that day.

I prowled the fields in wolf form and soon caught a rabbit, but this wasn't how I had been picturing it. The simple act of killing my prey hadn't brought the pleasure I expected, nor the bloodlust that had ruled me so completely before it had waned with the moon. I'd thought the simple act of killing my prey would cause it to rise back up and bring me that bloodthirsty joy again, thought that was all that had been missing since my last kill. Yet the thrill at the sight of blood jetting out from an artery punctured by my fangs wasn't there. The desire to rip the carcass apart until limbs and organs lay scattered around me in a bloody circle remained quiet.

And without it what was there? Nothing. In its absence there was nothing but the emptiness, akin to how I'd begun to feel before the rage and hatred filled the void. Without that fire burning it seemed the joy of hunting down prey now lay solely with my wolfish half. The knowledge was of little comfort. Without the bloodlust what did I have to live for? Survival was far from a trial for a supernatural predator such as myself – not without the threat of the Slayers at any rate and they had yet to find us in this latest area we'd temporarily claimed as our own. When no prey existed that could escape my jaws what was there to enjoy from the simple pleasures of life? Without the struggle for survival experienced by most animals that left room for boredom, just like a caged animal or humans with little to do all day. Unlike humans I couldn't indulge in any of their hobbies to pass the time, and I had no human captors to provide me with enrichment like many caged animals (the lucky ones at least). What meaning did life hold for me now, then? Without any hobbies or kindred spirits to share this existence with, there was nothing but this growing emptiness inside, and these thoughts were doing little to help with that chasm re-opening in my soul.

Though she had been my constant companion for the last two months, Lady Sarah was still very much a stranger to me in many ways. Perhaps I would have to make a more concerted effort to get to know her, cold and distant as she often seemed. Yes, I'd try talking to her when darkness fell and see if I could get her to open up to me, share some stories from her past maybe. Or maybe she could give me some insight into how she managed with her eternal existence whenever she wasn't hunting, fighting or fleeing, or putting me through more of her damn lessons.

I looked back down at the dead rabbit and sighed in reluctant acceptance of the fact there was no fun to be had in my kill, and surrendered myself to the wolf so I might escape the troubling thoughts that had plagued me the previous day.

I stripped the small carcass of the flesh from its bones and gnawed on them for a while, but the rabbit was barely a snack which merely took the edge off my hunger, doing little to appease it. I really wanted to hunt something larger and more filling but I knew the risk was too high, so I buried the remains to hide my kill from any prying eyes and went in search of more prey.

The human may be having trouble adjusting to life on the fringes of humanity, but I was content to be closer to the natural world, if not quite a part of it. I belonged out in the wilderness, and truth be told I was glad to be living further out from man's festering heart, ever spreading their pollution outwards and smothering nature in the thick smog they wreathed their settlements in.

Yet despite my pleasure at no longer living among them, a part of me was drawn towards the nearby town and the hunting grounds that lay therein, though Lady Sarah's power kept me from wandering too close. The curse caused me to hunger for human flesh above all else, the one thing that truly set me apart from other wolves. Or at least it had been before the human half of me started to spread its poisonous nature into our lupine half, and had since given me a bloodlust that was not my own, one I despised but could not fight, so intertwined with my unnatural hunger as it was. The human seemed to think it was beginning to accept my nature and in doing so we were becoming one, yet it still did not understand the sanctity of life and the predator's place in the world, just like the rest of its wretched species. And until it learnt to respect our prey and only to hunt and kill in the name of survival, I wanted nothing to do with my other half.

My sensitive ears picked up the flapping of a bird's wings and I scented the air, struggling to pick up the bird's scent through my bloodied muzzle. I heard the bird's talons grip a nearby tree branch and pinpointed its location. Upon investigation it turned out to be a crow, which I also killed and ate. The fields around me grew quiet after that, the mortal animals knowing better than to venture from their dens when a werewolf stalked the lands. I headed off back towards the barn, since there was nothing else to hunt.

One of Lady Sarah's recent lessons had been on evading any would-be hunters and covering my tracks, so I doubled back on myself a few times before finally going back to our current shelter. Once inside I settled down to rest for the day, keeping an ear cocked for sounds of any potential threats.

My hunger was far from satisfied but I was still weary from the vast distances we'd had to cover over the past three weeks to keep ahead of the Slayers, and finally lose them. Exhaustion took over and I let myself doze off into a light sleep. The human would reassert itself while we lay unconscious, but I could bide my time. In the first few months of my awakening I'd struggled for control whenever the human did something to give me a strong enough grip, like when it let anger take hold, or hunger, or when the smell of blood called me forth. And once it learned the true nature of the werewolf, the truth of our hunger for human flesh, it had fought to keep me locked deep down in our subconscious. But much had changed since then and with this new sense of despair creeping over my human half, I knew I would be given more free rein between full moons, especially if there was no longer any pleasure in hunting for that other side to me. Though I still despised the human's nature, I knew to continue to fight each other was a pointless waste of energy. Neither of us could remain in control indefinitely, and our survival was more important than my distaste for humanity and that part of my being. I knew I'd have chance to hunt and explore our current surroundings soon enough, so I was content to surrender to the human for now. The full moon was close and I hoped Lady Sarah would give me more freedom this time, as long as I didn't become consumed by rage again. My time would soon come.

I awoke to the sound of knocking coming from somewhere beneath my paws, still in wolf form. The vampire was ready to rise for the night but she needed me to dig down to her coffin, otherwise she would have had to damage it to free herself.

"Come, there is much more you need to learn," she said as I returned to human form. "It is about time we worked on your self-control."

She'd noticed the absence of my rage and seemed to think it was time to risk coaching me to control my hunger for human prey, despite the moon nearing almost full, but the idea filled me with little enthusiasm. I didn't feel like putting myself through something so taxing when I was still feeling dismayed over my bloodlust seemingly deserting me.

In order for me to learn to resist my instincts, I knew Lady Sarah would have to put me in the way of temptation, so she could then teach me the self-control she had already learnt centuries ago. I had once considered myself to be slave to the hunger that plagued me after each transformation, especially at full moon, and I knew what it would cost me to attempt to resist it. I didn't think I could face the torment I'd have to put myself through, not with the despair I was currently feeling after the kill earlier had failed to fill the emptiness inside once more. And there was also the possibility that even that temptation, which had for a time filled me with anticipation and excitement at the prospect of the kill, would also prove to be empty and meaningless to my human mind. If that proved to be the case my existence would truly have lost all meaning, and I didn't want to face that possibility anytime soon.

I was about to protest but my feelings must have already shown. "You need these skills, Nick, and we must make use of whatever time we are given for me to teach you."

"Can't we hang on, just till the full moon's over with for another month?" I replied. "Those three nights will be exhausting enough as it is."

"Do you think the Slayers will wait for you to rest? You are no longer in the human world. You cannot afford days off; you must continue to push yourself if you wish to survive. It is precisely because of the full moon I would rather work on your self-control now. We have done well to lose the Slayers again for the time being, and it is imperative we remain hidden for as long as possible."

"But if I can't control the hunger, surely putting temptation in my way is only going to make me more frenzied during the full moon again. It's only a few more nights, then I'll work hard to master my instincts in time for the next one, I promise."

She was quiet for a few minutes, probably debating with herself the wisdom of waiting. "Very well. I need to feed, then we will see if you can concentrate on something easier. You may hunt as well, if you wish."

"Wait, don't go yet," I said. She paused and turned back to look at me. "I was hoping we could spend some time together beyond simply hunting and teaching me new skills. It's been over a year since we met but I feel like I still barely know you."

"I need to feed and I would do so alone tonight. You know it is not in the nature of vampires to live and hunt in groups: we value our solitude. I will return in time to give you another lesson before daybreak, if you are willing, but until then I wish to be alone."

Before I could argue she was gone, moving so fast it was as if she'd vanished into the night. She might have been able to take a wolf's form, but there was nothing in her nature that was wolfish, or particularly human for that matter. I was determined to learn more about her and how she coped with an eternity of living as an outsider, but I knew better than to attempt to follow her that same night. With little else to do, I hunted more of the field's inhabitants to satisfy the hunger from the transformation back to human form, though the act of killing them remained just as unsatisfactory, then returned to the barn to catch up on more sleep while I waited for Lady Sarah to return. Once she did so I tried to focus on the latest skill she decided to teach me. There'd been a noticeable drop in temperature over the last few nights so she deemed it time I learnt how to make a fire, which took me a while to get the hang of, especially as my mind kept wandering miserably back to my unsatisfactory kills. But I picked it up just before the new day dawned, grey and overcast like my mood.

The next few nights passed in much the same way, until the full moon was upon us again. It was a clear night and I barely had time to dig down to free Lady Sarah before the transformation took hold.

Without my rage, I was much more aware of the pain of the full moon transformation that night. I'd long since developed a higher pain threshold so it didn't have me screaming in agony like it would've done just a year earlier, but it still had me on my knees, digging lengthening nails into the dirt and gritting sharpening teeth. Blood boiled and sweat rolled down my grimy body, despite the chill of the autumn air. My guts felt like they were being moved, stretched and even squeezed by some invisible, sadistic surgeon. Some bones stretched outwards while others ground down to a shorter length. Fur erupted down the length of my body, and a tail grew from the base of my spine. The change complete, the wolf took control. I couldn't have fought him even if I wanted to, but given my current emotional state it had become a welcome reprieve whenever my wolfish half ruled us. I gave myself completely to the full moon madness once more, silently praying it would leave me feeling alive again when the sun rose.

I was much calmer that night than I had been through my last two full moons, but I still hungered for human flesh. The vampire watched me warily, ready to intervene if I showed any sign of becoming frenzied again. Once it became clear I wasn't completely out of control this time, she decided the easiest way to manage my hunger was to allow me to hunt more animals under her watchful eye. I wasn't entirely content, even with the deer I tracked down and killed, but at least I was allowed the freedom to run beneath my lunar master and answer its call with more blood. And at least I had fresh meat to feed the hunger, unlike the nights I'd been forced to feed on cold, rotting flesh.

This full moon was fairly uneventful. The human's rage hadn't rekindled as it had hoped, meaning I retained my ability to reason and didn't give in to the temptation to attempt slipping away from Lady Sarah and taking human prey. Though the bloodlust did return on the third night, rising up when I made my first kill and completely lost myself in the moon's embrace, causing me to savage another deer I'd found much more violently than the previous two nights. But the vampire was prepared for the sudden return of my bloodthirsty fury, and when I rose from my kill to bound off into the darkness in search of more, she wrestled me into submission in wolf form, muzzling me again until it passed.

Those three nights were far from perfect, but with the vampire's help we managed that month's full moon as safely as possible and successfully avoided any further encounters with the Slayers. So it was that Lady Sarah decided to risk staying in the area for some time, which meant she could focus on trying to teach me better self-control in the face of the hunger and the bloodlust, and even the full moon itself. My next trial was about to begin.

Chapter Seven – Growing Emptiness

My struggle to adjust to life outside of the human world wasn't getting any easier in the days after the full moon. My rage still seemed to be lost to me, as if I'd only ever had a finite amount of fuel to keep that fire burning and I'd used it all up during the previous month's full moon. In its absence, Lady Sarah hadn't felt the need to reapply the mental lead she'd been keeping me on, trusting that I would have enough sense not to do anything stupid now anger wasn't clouding my mind.

I still felt like my life held no meaning without that need to kill and the savage joy of the bloodlust I'd come to rely on, but the vampire wasn't any more forthcoming about her past or any current interests she might have. I still had no idea what she did besides feeding and giving me lessons in survival, and I couldn't even begin to guess at her innermost thoughts and feelings. So whenever Lady Sarah wasn't teaching me anything, I spent most of my time alone with my own thoughts, which might not have been entirely healthy at that point but what else did I have to do?

I kept thinking about the way I'd grown to enjoy mindless acts of violence, and what had been missing with my latest kills. Maybe the problem was the size of the prey. Could they be simply too small to reawaken my bloodlust? It might sound like a foolish idea now but such were the thoughts running through the last vestiges of my old human self. As a species are we not obsessed with bigger and better, and finding the next best thing? I started to wonder if larger prey could really prove to be more satisfactory. Entertaining the thought gave me something to focus on besides the growing emptiness inside, at least. But I tried to resist the temptation at first, since Lady Sarah had only just given me my freedom back. I didn't want to spend the rest of my existence under her spell because I'd given her too many reasons not to trust me.

I tried to talk to the vampire again about how she managed eternity without turning to killing to keep boredom at bay, still hoping she could help me find something to give my life new purpose.

"I still feel like I barely know you," I said to her as she stalked out of the darkness towards me. "Maybe we could chat for a bit before whatever you have planned for tonight's lesson?"

"There is little to know," Lady Sarah replied, wiping a trickle of crimson liquid from her chin – she'd just been to feed on another luckless animal.

"Well what do you do on a night after you've fed?" I asked. "Surely you must have needs besides the hunger that binds us. You say you left the human world behind long ago. Don't you ever indulge in human activities once in a while? Or do you prefer to be amongst nature? You must do something with the eternal life you've been given, besides eat and sleep."

"Once I have fed I am content to observe from the shadows," she said, which seemed rather cryptic to me.

"Who are you, Lady Sarah? You're more than just a predator. We all are, even if all traces of our humanity are gone. What do you do all night while you're alone?" I pressed her, not content with her vague answer.

"I cast off my humanity long ago and you would do well to do the same," she replied, suddenly sounding quite sullen. The topic was clearly not open for debate and she remained shrouded in mystery for the time being. I don't know why I hadn't thought about it more before. Since I'd been bitten she'd acted as my teacher, giving me insight and knowledge into the new world I'd been plunged into. She continued to teach me the new set of rules for survival and for that I would always be grateful. But it was hard to think of her as my friend when I still, even after all that time alone with her since fleeing my human life, didn't really know anything about her. And I suddenly felt I really needed a friend.

I'd come to realise I couldn't live amongst humans any longer after the battle against the Slayers, but shreds of my humanity remained, even if it was in tatters. Not to mention wolves are pack animals, and both halves of my being longed for company. She may be a solitary hunter but I realised I was growing lonely again, and she couldn't really fill that void while she remained so distant.

"I'm trying as best I can," I argued. "But it's not as easy as I imagined when I first decided I had to leave my old life behind. There was no room for boredom when we were constantly on the move and don't get me wrong, I'm glad we've been given this opportunity to settle down for some time, but I'm bored now and I need more than just sleeping and hunting. There's got to be something more than this."

"Then perhaps it is time we worked on your self-control; that should be suitably challenging to break up the tedium of staying in one place. The sooner you learn to survive undetected by humans the better, as I may not always be here to help you. And the key to that is controlling your instincts to hunt human prey, for a trail of human corpses will always bring the Slayers quicker than any other hint of your presence in an area. It would help if you could learn to truly accept who you are. You must embrace the wolf in you. He is a part of you, and without making peace with him you can never hope to truly master your own desires. As a whole you could be so much more powerful, and it would allow you greater control over your urges, no matter whether they are born of human or wolf. It is natural for the two to exist as separate identities when the lycanthropy first takes hold, but you must embrace him if you are to survive," said Lady Sarah.

"Just because I'm beginning to accept what I am doesn't mean I'm ready to become one with the wolf," I answered.

"How can you truly accept who you are if you're not willing to fully embrace your other half by becoming one with him?" she argued. "And if you were as accepting as you seem to think you now are, you would have said who and not what. Surely you don't still consider us to be monsters?"

"No, I realise now the undead are predators just like any other carnivorous species, and how can I continue to be horrified by our choice of prey when I've taken so many human lives myself, without the wolf driving me to kill them? It's our actions that make us monstrous, and after everything I've done these last few months I guess I have become one of the monsters. But it's not the thought of taking yet more human lives if I fully accept my lupine half. I guess you could say I'm still evolving. Most guys my age would just be going through the natural process of growing up and settling into a mature mindset but no, I have it more complicated. If I attempt to merge the two halves of my mind what effect is it going to have on my mental state, in addition to all the emotional changes still going on and the struggle to adjust to this new lifestyle?"

"You're new lifestyle would not be a problem for your lupine half, yet still you insist on suppressing him the majority of the time. Whether you wish to admit it or not, you need him to survive."

"Well I don't think he wants to join with me either. He only sees the darker side of humanity and he wants nothing to do with them. He might not be a true wolf but he wants to stay as close to one as he can, and he'd quite happily suppress me for the rest of our life if he could. Just as I would have suppressed him when I first learned he'd been killing people each month, and not animals like I'd originally thought. I don't think either of us is ready to make peace with each other yet so for now this is the way it needs to be."

"At least try to listen to each other then, if nothing else. Allow your wolf half more control, gain his trust," she instructed. I could tell she wasn't particularly happy with the way this conversation had gone, and sure enough she added "You may feel you need more time, but time is one thing we do not have. The longer you continue to live with a divide between your two halves, the longer you endanger yourself. You're much more vulnerable this way."

"Yeah, I'll try," I said, somewhat unconvincingly. "Forget the self-control lessons for now anyway; I'm still not quite ready after the madness of the full moon. There's got to be something you can share with me about your past, maybe some tale to keep me going? I mean, you lived in the age of heroes and magic and great battles for God's sake, the time when legends were born!"

"Yes, it's curious that, with all of mankind's advances, they should still be so interested in ages past. Mankind continues to seek out new truths yet science can only reveal to them so much. With each new truth their minds become closed to other wonders that have no place in their science. Truths long since forgotten now allude them, and so they continue to look to the past for all that which was once so much more than mere myth and legend."

"So tell me about life back then. Were dragons and wizards real? What about King Arthur and Merlin and the Knights of the Round Table?"

"You already know that there is magic in the world, so yes there were wizards and other types of magicians. But I know not whether dragons were ever more than legend. I have certainly never seen one. As for King Arthur and Merlin, they were before my time," she answered. "Now if you insist on waiting another night before we work on your self-control, I would be alone again. I have nothing more to teach you at present."

The void seemed to grow noticeably bigger as befriending her was beginning to seem hopeless. I let her go off alone, watching dejectedly as the shadows swallowed her up once more, as mysterious and distant as ever.

My loneliness only grew with the coming of dawn, when the vampire retreated back into her coffin beneath the soil. Feeling dejected after another failed attempt at getting closer to her, I wandered the fields, wrestling with the temptation to visit the nearby town. As dangerous as it would be to return to the human world, the need for companionship only served to make such places more inviting. But I knew it was too risky so I forced myself to turn away from the town and trudged towards the patch of trees. With nothing better to do, I decided I may as well hunt for more small prey to keep me going, though I didn't feel particularly hungry with the depression creeping back over me. But I knew I should make the most of these opportunities to eat and keep up my strength, especially with winter approaching, when natural prey would become scarce.

Rustling in the undergrowth alerted me to the presence of more wildlife for me to feed on and as I drew within range of the animal's hearing, I began to tread more carefully, prowling like the predator I was, even in human form. Yet in spite of my best efforts to move as stealthily as possible, I still lacked the skills my lupine half instinctively possessed. Something crunched beneath my feet and the rabbit shot off towards its burrow, which it was too close to for me to reach it in time. I considered digging down to grab it when there came the noise of grass being trampled from behind. Someone was following me! And I'd been too intent on my prey to notice.

I spun round to face the human who I was sure would be one of the Slayers, my nails and canines elongating with barely a conscious thought, my eyes turning amber. I bared my fangs in a warning snarl and readied myself to pounce, wishing there was time to take the transformation further. It seemed my theory about the need for larger victims to make for a satisfactory kill was about to be put to the test.

But for a supposed enemy, the guy was acting very strangely. There was no hatred burning in the dark eyes like I'd encountered before with members of the Slayers. No, those eyes seemed transfixed by my inhuman nature as they gazed into mine, a look of awe on a face only a few years older than my own as he breathed "So it is true."

"Do I know you?" I growled.

"Nope, but I've heard of you. I didn't believe the tales until I saw you for myself though."

Panic shot through me on hearing those words. "Tales? What tales?"

"Some say the rogue wolf of Yorkshire isn't an escaped wolf at all, but a monster of myth and legend. You've got the attention of paranormal investigators all over the world. Some are sceptical of course, but a few of them are planning werewolf hunts next full moon in the hopes of catching a glimpse of you. I wasn't on the hunt for anything but as I was driving along I spotted you in the fields. Thought I was seeing things at first but if there was even a chance you were a real life monster, I had to come see."

I hadn't even realised I'd wandered close enough to the road to be seen and I made a mental note to be more careful in future. Out loud I said "I didn't hear a car."

"You seemed pretty engrossed in whatever you were stalking," he shrugged.

I didn't believe him, but it didn't matter. I couldn't let him live.

The curious humans out to find evidence of the supernatural might not want to kill me, but if humanity had undeniable proof of our existence it could only make matters worse than they were already with the Slayers after us. Some would want to capture us alive and parade us like freaks to line their wallets, and others may well take the same stance as the Slayers, prepared to kill us to save human lives. They might even invest more money into experimenting on us on a grander scale than the Slayers could currently manage in secret, which had to be a fate far worse than death. As innocent as this man seemed, he posed too great a risk for me to let him walk away.

"If you had any sense, you'd have stayed in your car," I growled as I let the transformation take hold. There was no way a mortal could outrun me all the way across the field, back to the road where he must have left his vehicle. And I was eager to rediscover the dark pleasure of ripping apart flesh as I gave myself over to my bestial nature.

A flicker of fear passed across the young man's eyes but he continued to gaze at me with a sense of awe, and maybe even longing as my face bulged outwards into a snout. He raised his hands as if to show he was no threat to me and I was impressed when his voice barely shook as he said "Wait! If the legends are true, you started off human. I'm sure you were a good kid, and I think there's still some good left in you. You don't need to kill me, dude. I won't tell anyone about you, I swear. Just let me go and I'll leave you be; I won't come snooping around here again, I promise."

"Good, evil. I'm done asking those kind of questions. Maybe I was good once, but now I am a 'real life monster' and killing is all I have left. I can't let you live anyway, but even if I had a choice I would still choose bloodshed. It's what monsters do, is it not?"

"What if I could be of some use to you? I could be your, like, servant or what do the vampires call them in books and the movies? Thralls? I could be your human thrall and help you find victims. Why should vampires have all the fun? And killing people, well, everyone dies eventually anyway. I'm not really a fan of people either."

"And what's in it for you?"

"If I prove myself, will you turn me?" he asked excitedly.

"It doesn't work like that. Only certain humans can become werewolves and I don't sense the wolf blood in you needed to pass on my curse. Death is all I have to offer you. Besides, you wouldn't want this."

His face fell. "Immortality, power. Who wouldn't want it?"

"It's called a curse for a reason. But I guess I could let Lady Sarah make you a vampire, though you may die anyway. Paranormal investigators aren't the only ones hunting us."

"Nah man, vampires never really interested me," he said, but he must have felt the allure of immortality because he paused to consider his options. "Well, maybe I'll think about it but I don't want to sign up for vampirism just yet. Let me help you as a human for now. Don't you get lonely out here? Maybe a bit of human company is what you need. I'm Luke, by the way."

Unwittingly, he'd struck close enough to home for me to hesitate. If I let him go he was a liability, but my heart ached for greater companionship than Lady Sarah could offer and if there was even the smallest possibility he could help fill the growing emptiness of the void, I was sorely tempted to take that chance.

"How do I know I can trust you?"

"And who would believe me if I told them what I'd seen?" he laughed. "Other than the few who want to believe so badly that they're already planning to come look for you. I'm sure you would be long gone from here before any of them could arrange any kind of search in this area, though. I'm really no threat to you."

"You remind me of the boy I used to be, when I was stupid enough to wish for this cursed life," I growled, which was true. He even wore the same kind of gothic shirt I'd favoured and dark jeans. "So this time I'll let you live. But I can't trust you, so if you come looking for me again, then I will kill you."

Luke didn't seem overly happy with my answer but no matter how badly I wanted a friend, I couldn't trust him. Letting him live might be a mistake but I reasoned that the Slayers seemed good enough at covering up our existence that the risk of leaving the odd witness alive was probably fairly low. If anyone talked, I felt I could rely on my enemies to contain the damage. They'd cleaned up my messes often enough, or at least I assumed they had since I'd not had any similar encounters with humans prior to this one. And killing him was also risky if we didn't want the Slayers back on our trail. I had to assume the police would come looking for him, some of whom were bound to be Slayers. If I let him go and he kept his word, our enemies need never know we were in the area. And besides, my bloodlust remained dormant. I needed to feed after transforming part way but I wasn't ready to shatter my hopes by taking large prey, only to find the kill remained just as unsatisfactory. That small hope was the only thing keeping me going through the long days and nights spent with only the vampire and my own inner demons for company.

My thoughts turned to Lady Sarah and what she'd have had me do. I doubted the vampire would approve of my decision to let him walk away but I had no intention of telling her about the encounter. Maybe it would have been wiser to keep the human nearby till nightfall, when she could have used her powers to make him forget about what he'd seen. But I didn't want another lecture on how careless I'd been through the rage driven nights that had probably led to this, so I dismissed that idea, childish and reckless though it was.

"Go, before I change my mind," I growled. "I need to feed now."

I turned my back on the guy before he could say something that might prove too great a temptation, but I was aware of more grass trampling beneath his feet as he walked away. Satisfied that was the last I would see of him, I focussed on the natural world once more and resumed the hunt for prey.

I couldn't escape Lady Sarah's lesson that night.

"We now have only three weeks before the moon grows full again and it is becoming vital you learn to control the overpowering urge to feed on humans it awakes in you, if you wish to remain in one place for any length of time," she said. "Wait here while I find prey for us to work with. You might want to transform at least part way to raise your hunger. We need you able to resist even the strongest of bloodlusts if you are to ever have any hope of surviving the full moon without my intervention."

I still wasn't happy about being put through this new trial but deep down I knew she was right, so reluctantly I took my hybrid form while she went to hunt. I didn't have to wait long before she returned with a sheep and the length of rope from the nearby barn we'd been using as shelter. The animal was docile enough that it seemed she'd used her powers to place it under her spell.

She tied the sheep to a tree and released her mental hold over it, the animal suddenly going into a panic over our very presence. "Now, let the bloodlust rise up."

I focussed my senses on the terrified animal straining to break free of its tether and let my mind fill with thoughts of ripping into its soft flesh and gulping down chunks of meat. But no matter how hard I tried to reawaken my bloodlust or how much my insides ached with hunger, only the empty chasm gaped within. I was hungry enough to desire the meal in front of me but not to the point that it was an urge I was struggling to resist.

"It's not working," I growled.

The vampire opened up a gash in the sheep's side and I breathed in the scent of fresh blood, but still I felt nothing.

"Then either change forms a few times to make the hunger more powerful or let the wolf take control. Both of you need to learn to show restraint in the face of your bloodlust; I can work with him first if you'd prefer."

I took the transformation fully to wolf form but I was all too happy to let her train my wolfish half first. Even if I hadn't been particularly feeling the need to satisfy the hunger with the prey in front of me, the wolf wanted to gorge himself on its flesh. He felt like a caged animal pacing on the edge of my consciousness and he eagerly rose up when I surrendered control to him, while I was glad of the reprieve I'd been offered.

Even though the bloodlust was born of the human within me, it was there alongside the hunger the instant I took control. With a ravenous snarl, I readied myself to lunge at the wounded prey before me.

"I take it the wolf is in control now," Lady Sarah said. "Let your hunger and your bloodlust rage through you, but I want you to try and channel it if you can. Focus on the tree your prey is tied to and imagine that tree is an enemy. Your bloodlust can be useful in battle but only if you can learn to channel it – become too focussed on a single target and it could cost you your life. The tree is the threat: make that your target, not the prey you truly desire."

Her words sounded far away, my senses focussed so completely on the pounding of the sheep's heart and the blood pumping from the gash in its side. Drool leaked from my maw, slimy strings hanging down in anticipation of the meal the sheep presented, and my mind became clouded by the red haze of my bloodlust once more. My hunger would not wait for the vampire and her lesson, and with barely a conscious thought I bounded forward to claim my prize.

My jaws snapped on thin air as the vampire held me back by the scruff of my neck. I slavered and continued to snap at the meal that stood just within reach, straining against the vampire's grip in vain.

"Focus, wolf. Let reason guide you, not your instincts."

Her words held little meaning as the bloodlust turned my mind to its most primitive state, that base need to hunt and to kill making me no more than a mindless beast as it had so many times before. Her language meant something to my suppressed thoughts but it was like a niggling little itch at the back of my mind, swept aside by the force of the urge to feed, growing ever stronger with my prey so close, its presence occupying every one of my senses until the world around me ceased to exist and there was only the hunger and the wounded animal that would satisfy it.

"Control yourself, wolf!" she commanded. "Fight these urges and channel the bloodlust into striking at your enemy. This tree is the threat, not the sheep."

Still I continued to struggle, until weariness began to creep in and I relaxed in the vampire's grip, panting heavily. She led me back to my original position a few feet from the sheep and released me, watching closely to see what I would do next.

Twice more I went for the sheep and was held back just as my jaws were about to close on its throat. Then came the sound of footfalls and while the vampire turned her attention to the potential threat I struck again, and finally succeeded in tearing the life from my prey. She left me to investigate the approaching humans and greedily I tore into the carcass, ripping off great chunks of flesh and swallowing ravenously. But once my reason returned I realised I'd failed the first test the vampire had given me, and I knew I was going to have to try harder next time.

The two humans were not Slayers as the vampire had feared and she was able to use her hypnotic powers to persuade them to turn back to the town they'd come from. She came back to find me stood over bloody bones and shreds of fleecy skin, and I sensed she was disappointed we hadn't made any progress.

"I suppose that concludes your training for tonight," she said. "We are out of time now as I still have to feed, but we must continue tomorrow night if you are to have any hope of mastering your urges before the next full moon."

I buried the remains and relinquished my control back to the human as Lady Sarah went off to hunt, to avoid further temptation. My hunger was bearable after feeding on the sheep but I could still have eaten more, and I was craving human prey.

The wolf might have considered the hunger bearable but my stomach was still rumbling and I wanted more. But I didn't want to hunt small animals that night, though I had enough sense not to turn to human prey either.

The more I'd thought about the lack of pleasure I'd derived from killing the rabbit and other small animals, the more I felt it was the size of the prey that was the problem. I might not have felt anything when I'd faced the human earlier, but that didn't mean I wouldn't have felt any thrill if I'd decided to hunt him. I just needed to kill something big enough to spark my bloodlust again, and give me some dark thrill to drive away this emptiness that I'd so quickly fallen back into. And hadn't I sensed a lack of satisfaction from my wolf half when I'd touched upon his consciousness after taking that first rabbit in our temporary new territory? If a bigger kill brought him more enjoyment, hopefully the human part of me could share in that.

While Lady Sarah was busy hunting her own prey, I went in search of more livestock. The sheep hadn't appealed to my bloodlust either and I was convinced I needed something like a cow or a horse to awaken it.

I soon found a field full of cattle and I deliberately targeted the biggest animal which would yield the most meat, and hopefully the most pleasure. She was a fine specimen, one any farmer would be angry to lose, but obsession with the idea of bigger is better drove me on.

It didn't take long for the herd to sense my presence, even before I was on my chosen prey, and they began to panic. A brief image of the cows stampeding through the town flashed through my mind, but it didn't bring me any amusement as it once would have done. Despite what I'd just imagined, they headed in the opposite direction, away from the town and towards the patch of nearby woodland, terror allowing them to break through the fencing fairly easily. I focussed on my target and struck her with all my raw strength and power. My jaws locked on a hind leg and I wrenched her to the ground, her good legs kicking uselessly in a futile attempt to rise and flee with the others.

Attempting to awaken the bloodlust so I might lose myself in it once more, I struck again at her belly, ripping off a great chunk of flesh in a spray of blood and spilling her organs onto the grass into one soft, squishy lump. Yet the dark desire to continue to rip and tear and slaughter mindlessly still would not come. If it still existed in me it was now locked deep inside, and if the act of killing didn't give rise to it, I was at a loss. The chasm of emptiness gaped wider than ever and I felt the same sense of despair descending on me that I'd had nearly a year ago. Though before it had come with the realisation that I would continue to kill and there was nothing I could do to stop it, short of committing suicide. And now I would gladly spill more blood, if only that life could flow into the empty husk I'd become.

In the absence of the bloodlust there was no joy to be had in the cow's death and I struck a third time at the throat, to end the animal's suffering. I ignored the rest of the fleeing cattle and began to feed, feeling resigned to my fate of a pointless, empty existence.

Chapter Eight – Return to the Lunar Madness

Once my hunger was satisfied, I transformed back to human while I had enough food to replenish the energy required for the second change and picked more meat off the bones.

Having eaten my fill, I looked down at my bloodied body; so much blood on my outstretched hands. Another meaningless death so an equally meaningless life may continue. I hadn't yet regressed to the state of guilt and remorse I'd been trapped in after the death of Fiona at the jaws of my wolfish half, but there was no escaping the knowledge I was a killer. One who had left so many bodies in his wake he couldn't even remember how many there'd been. And those deaths were beginning to seem more and more pointless as time went on.

The sound of footsteps creeping towards me brought me out of my dark musings. Instinctively I ducked, sinking into a crouch just as a bullet tore through the air where my head had been only seconds before, the gunshot ringing in my sensitive ears. I hadn't been in the field of cattle that long; how had the Slayers found me already? For that's who it had to be, surely. There'd been no indication the farmer had been alerted that anything was amiss yet, and who else would be wandering the fields, or carrying a gun for that matter? Unless it was more curious humans like Luke but it was highly unlikely they'd have come with guns. And besides, they'd be more interested in me alive.

With one fluid motion I stood and turned to face my opponent, before they could fire off another shot. He turned out to be the same man I'd seen that night they'd set the trap with the help of the spellcaster, the one who'd been retreating when it had started to go so wrongly for them. He carried the same air of experience and lack of fear as before, though age had already begun to slow his movements.

I hesitated as he pointed the gun at me once more. My will to fight seemed to have gone the same way as my rage and bloodlust, either sucked into the void of my empty soul or locked away so deeply that it would take a lot to spark the smouldering remains and rekindle the fire. But had I also returned to the point of losing the will to live? My existence felt worthless once again, but was I ready to give it up yet? I'd already discovered I didn't have the strength to end it myself, but perhaps if the Slayers were to do it for me, there lay my salvation.

I couldn't do it. I knew Hell existed: Lady Sarah had told me as much, and I knew I must surely be headed there. That meant no peace for me in death, and if that Hell was as bad as the one I currently resided in, or quite possibly worse, I wouldn't go there willingly.

I turned and ran to find Lady Sarah, ducking a second time as the old Slayer fired again. A stinging on my scalp and the trickle of warm blood down the back of my head told me I'd been too slow in my hesitation. The aim of this guy was better than many of the Slayers I'd faced over the last year, who were too undisciplined and gave in too easily to fear, or simply too inexperienced, to land a killing shot. It suddenly struck me how lucky I'd been whenever I'd faced the Slayers before. Lucky they'd always missed my heart or my brain, sometimes only by millimetres. But I knew eventually my luck would undoubtedly run out, especially if I grew careless. I was far from faster than a speeding bullet, especially in human form. I would've been faster if I'd remained in wolf form, but there was no time to transform back and it would mean depleting my energy reserves yet again. Though in human form I was still much faster than most mortal animals and that made me a much harder target to hit, so long as I kept moving. With that in mind I tried to zigzag as much as I could, doing my best to avoid running in a straight line, and heading towards the woodland. It was a relief to reach the cover of the trees, and I allowed myself to pause and glance back towards the fields. The Slayer still stood there, an air of calm patience about him. There were no sounds of cursing or frustration and he didn't immediately call for back up, which I thought was odd. I pushed on before he could spot me, turning my attention to locating the vampire and wondering how I was going to explain this to her without sparking her own anger.

"Foolish boy!" she said as I came to a stop just in front of her. "I warned you against hunting large prey but did you pay heed? And now they're on our trail again, are they not?"

I opened my mouth to make excuses but the icy look she gave me killed the words before I could give them sound, and instead I stared at the floor like I was just a little kid again being chastised by a parent or a teacher. I briefly wondered how she'd known exactly what had gone on that night, as if she'd read my mind. She'd named telekinesis as one of her abilities not long after we'd first met, even if it was fairly limited compared to her other powers, or so she'd implied, but she'd never mentioned having telepathy. She must've guessed from the smell of the fresh bovine blood on my body and the fact I'd been running to find her, I decided.

"I only hope you learn from this experience," she continued. "Certain aspects of this way of life may be less than ideal, but I insist on it for a reason, born of centuries of experience. But enough of that for now; we must make haste if we are to lose the Slayers again long enough for the necessary rest through the daylight hours. You'll be better off returning to your wolf form and don't even think of moaning when your own recklessness is to blame this time."

I remained silent, so empty that her lecture didn't even stir any arguments born of that rebellious nature that comes with being a teenager. Further proof my anger seemed dead, and in its absence her words just fell into the void, instead of landing on the fires of my rage, and fuelling the need to argue which would have come from knowing she was right.

In hindsight it would've been better to keep my wolf form after killing the cow, and gorging myself while I had the chance, instead of wasting energy changing back only to have to waste yet more energy transforming again to flee the area. But I hadn't expected things to happen so quickly and I'd not exactly been thinking clearly. It was too late to go back and undo my mistakes so I had little choice but to do as Lady Sarah instructed and manage the weariness and the hunger as best I could. Then we began the long, seemingly endless run of the hunted, putting as many miles between ourselves and humanity in general as we possibly could before the dawn.

The next two weeks were a blur. With the Slayers back on our trail we weren't safe in any one place for very long, and I quickly grew weak and exhausted without sufficient time to feed. The hunt seemed even more intense than the last, and I had no energy to spare to transform. The wolfish half of my mind was growing stronger and the constant, aching hunger was playing havoc with our instincts. Even worse, once the moon was waxing again it began calling to our dark desire for human flesh. Since there'd been no time to continue with my training whilst on the run, it seemed my fate lay in the vampire's hands once more when the full moon came.

Due to my increasingly feral state, Lady Sarah had us stay as far from humanity as possible, having to make do with natural shelters from the sun. She wasn't entirely confident she could keep me in check with her power this time – the hunger had grown so powerful that my current state of mind rivalled the madness of the full moon, meaning it was possible I might be able to break free of any hold she placed over me. But seeking shelter in caves and other such places in the natural world was in some ways more dangerous, as there were fewer places to hide which made it easier for any Slayers in close pursuit to find us, and they could come in greater numbers. It wasn't until we were attacked one day and I was shot several times and stabbed twice that she resigned herself to having to sleep in the ground without the luxury of a coffin. It meant she was better hidden through the sunlight hours, and staying out in the open made an ambush impossible. I would sense any approaching humans long before they could get in position to lay a trap.

It also meant I had the option to run from any hunting parties, rather than having to fight my way out of a corner as I'd been forced to do in the last cave we'd made use of. I'd been lucky once again that the Slayers had been too undisciplined and inexperienced to aim well enough to land a killing shot, but in my weakened state I'd also been slower to kill the group. The one good thing to come of the latest skirmish was the chance to feed on my desired prey, which helped calm my urges and replenish enough energy to allow me to transform back to human before I began to completely lose myself. The vampire was also glad of the chance to feed on human blood when she awoke, from another Slayer I'd kept alive till nightfall for her.

As the full moon drew nearer, Lady Sarah led us further and further into isolation. We had to be in one of the remotest areas of the country, moorland stretching in every direction as far as the eye could see. Even my sensitive ears had trouble detecting any human life in the distance, and the Slayers had difficulty following except by air, which they seemed unwilling to do for the time being. They seemed to be counting on us growing hungry enough to venture back towards civilisation, at which point they would no doubt have set several traps in any nearby places we might visit to hunt. And it was quite likely they might finally succeed in killing us if they were able to catch us unawares. Fully aware of this, the vampire was insistent it was imperative I learnt more self-control, especially with the next full moon only a week away.

Using the same training methods as before was harder in our current surroundings, and we had to traverse miles of uninhabited moorland before Lady Sarah could find another sheep to use. She also found more rope and a wooden post to tie the terrified animal to, and had me transform and allow the wolf to take control again.

Fighting my instincts was not made any easier by the moon growing ever fuller overhead, and I spent more time fighting to free myself of the vampire's grip to get at my prey. A fury was rising in me again and the vampire's words were becoming meaningless as she tried to help me channel my bloodlust into attacking the post instead of the sheep. There was no room in my mind for reason and as the night wore on, the lesson seemed just as pointless as the first time. But the vampire refused to give up on me. She was determined to teach me this skill and so I continued to

85

struggle in her grip, growing hungrier and more miserable the longer she kept me from my prey.

The night was almost spent when finally, as the vampire led me a few feet away from the sheep for what felt like the hundredth time and instructed me to focus on the hunk of wood instead of the animal, I lunged forward and snapped at the post out of sheer frustration. The wood splintered in my jaws as they closed around it, and I attacked again and again as if it was a living animal, until my mind cleared once more.

"Finally, we are making some progress!" Lady Sarah said. "You may feed on the sheep now, and then we must return to the heart of the moors before dawn."

The vampire seemed happy with the apparent headway we were making in my training, but I wasn't entirely convinced her lessons had been particularly helpful in this area so far. Still, I followed her without complaint for similar sessions, which she held in a different place each night, careful not to take livestock from the same farm where possible. It was something to break up the long days and nights of emptiness and despair if nothing else.

And then the full moon was upon us once again, forcing us to take a break from my training. I was already miserable from the days spent in our secluded surroundings, which only served to make the emptiness gape ever wider. The full moon had become a glimmer of hope again, as I'd thought it might awaken something inside of me after the hours my lupine half had spent in the grip of the bloodlust during Lady Sarah's lessons. But so far all the two had done was to heighten the hunger and my cravings for raw flesh, much to my dismay.

When darkness fell I gave myself completely to the transformation once more, glad of another chance to escape that nothingness building inside. I could hear the soil shifting beneath hands that were fast becoming paws, but the change completed before Lady Sarah could claw her way to the surface. And as the wolf rose up, I felt the bloodlust already gripping him. With new hope I fought to keep joint consciousness with him, praying it would allow the bloodlust to spill back into the human part of my mind once again.

Whether it was due to the training the vampire had been putting me through or something to do with my human half I didn't know, but the moon called to that red haze of madness once more and I still hadn't learnt to resist it. I scented the air and pricked my ears for any hint of my favoured prey, but there were no sounds of human life for miles around. I snarled in fury as the vampire's hand broke the surface of the soil, and bounded off before she could break free of the earth and stop

86

me. For all her precautions in trying to isolate us so completely from the human world, everything was still about to fall apart that night.

I ran for miles over the open moors until finally I came to human taint, cutting its way through the countryside in the form of a road. It seemed this area was favoured by walkers, the ground made muddy by the daily tread of boots upon it. And sure enough, I heard the pant of a dog straining against his lead and the woman foolish enough to walk him on this night I'd claimed as my own. Lady Sarah was probably out looking for me and if she had her way there would be no killing, but she had to find me first and until then I had free rein to answer the moon's call. I had eagerly awaited the month when my time would come again, to run and hunt freely until my bloodlust was satisfied and the hunger satiated, and all sense of caution lay forgotten in the chaos of my urges currently ruling me. My time had come, and this human and her pet would be the first to fall to my lupine fury.

I was downwind of the dog so they never had any warning before I struck. I slunk through the shadows, mouth watering as I watched the two of them head away from the side of the road where they'd parked their car, striking out across the moors. When the woman let her dog off his lead I made my move, lunging from the shadows and knocking her to the ground. She raised her arms to try and protect her throat and her face whilst she screamed for her dog's help, and I savaged the limbs until bone splintered beneath my fangs and flesh shredded to bloody tatters. The dog had bounded too far away to run back in time to intervene, not that he had any hope of saving his human from an immortal predator like myself. I'd already crushed her skull like a bloody eggshell when the dog entered the fray, and my contempt for their kind drove me to greater savagery when I turned on him.

Canine yelps of pain filled the night as we clashed and I wrestled him to the ground. He tried to snap at my throat but I clamped down on his side and shook my head violently, my fangs slicing through flesh like a living saw. Blood spewed out and mixed with that of his master as I released my grip and struck again at his belly, spilling guts into the mud around us. Finally he lay still, but the bloodlust had truly overpowered me and I continued to attack the two corpses and gulp down chunks of flesh and viscera, until it drove me to lope off in search of more victims.

I have no further memory of that night, so lost in the bloodlust as I was once again. Only with the approach of dawn did my mind clear, and I found myself back in the heart of the moorland where I returned to human form as normal for the day.

The next two nights passed in much the same way, the vampire unable to rise early enough to keep me from going off alone. What I did during those blackouts I can't say; I know only that there was more bloodshed. But when my mind cleared after the third night I willingly retreated into our subconscious with the dawn. Losing control so completely was too dangerous, and I had to hope the vampire could help prevent more blackouts during the next full moon. Until then, or until she tested me during another of her training sessions, I would gladly let the human suffer for us both.

Despite the complete loss of control again during the full moon, there wasn't even the faintest sense of my rage or my bloodlust each day when I transformed back to human. That morning after the third and final full moon for the month I felt as low as ever, and the daylight hours dragged by. I spent a few hours hunting for what little wildlife I could find in such desolate surroundings to satisfy the hunger from the change back, but I was becoming increasingly cold and miserable as the days wore on.

When darkness fell I didn't go straight to find Lady Sarah, too lost in my own despair as I walked across the moors. It was she who sought me out, running to meet me with a sense of urgency.

"You could have picked a better night for a stroll," she said. "Come, quickly."

"Why, what now?" I asked, wondering what could be so pressing. A new format to her survival lessons perhaps?

"There is no time. Take your wolf form and follow me as fast as you can; they are waiting."

I wasn't sure what to make of this sudden turn of events or who the 'they' could be that she was referring to. Lady Sarah refused to say anymore so I had little choice but to follow, and trust that the vampire was doing what was right for both of us.

Chapter Nine – A New Threat

After traversing what felt like the entire length of the Pennines, Lady Sarah led us cautiously down to lower ground and towards an abandoned warehouse. There she had me change back to human form, passing me a couple of dead rabbits to help replenish my energy and keep the hunger in check for the time being. She left me to eat and returned moments later with a bundle of garments.

"Now dress and try not to look so feral," she instructed me.

"What's going on?" I asked, reluctantly accepting the clothes she handed me.

"There is no time. You will find out, soon enough."

The clothes felt strange after the three months spent roaming the land completely naked, and I felt uncomfortable at the touch of the material on my skin. They were also less warm than my own fur coat and they didn't fit particularly well, but if the vampire wanted me dressed for whatever meeting was about to take place, it seemed I would have to endure it. She'd only use her hypnotic powers again if I tried to argue.

"I'm not going in there till you tell me what's going on," I said stubbornly as I pulled on a hoodie several sizes too big.

Lady Sarah sighed but took a moment to respond. I got the impression she was debating whether to use her power to make me more co-operative or if it would be just as easy to give me a quick explanation of what we were doing there. Whatever she was going to do, her sense of urgency wouldn't let her delay long before she acted, and I only had to wait a couple of minutes. She must have decided some information on who was waiting for us couldn't harm because she chose to answer "We have been summoned here by the Elder vampire, Ulfarr."

"What's an Elder?" I asked, before she could say anything else. She'd spoken the words with such respect and reverence that I immediately got the impression 'Elder' was some kind of a title among vampires, like the title 'Lady' she still used from her human life. But I also sensed a measure of fear in there, despite her insistence that she feared nothing, and that made me uneasy. I wasn't sure if she was afraid of the vampire himself or the fact that he'd summoned us, but either way it was looking like I was in for another rough night.

"They are amongst the oldest and most powerful of our race. We vampires might be solitary hunters, yet we do have a society of sorts. And when times force us to unite, it is to our Elders we look to. That is all I will say for now. Ulfarr is considered one of our greatest leaders, even amongst the other Elders, and it would be unwise to keep him waiting. He is to be treated with the utmost respect, understood?"

"Why? I'm not a vampire. I'm not part of your society so he has no hold over me."

"Just do it, Nick," she snapped. "There is no more time for your questions."

It seemed I had no choice but to follow her inside, where we found other undead waiting for us and talking amongst themselves; mostly vampires but there were a few ghouls. There were no wraiths this time, for as I would soon find out – this was a matter that concerned those with a corporeal body.

There was no light inside the old building, as was befitting for a gathering of creatures of darkness. If humans had abandoned it for long enough there might not be a power supply for the electrical lights, if they even still worked, but the vampires hadn't provided any candlelight either. Not that we had a great need for it like mortals would've done; with the moon only just waning from full, our supernatural eyesight had no problem penetrating the shadows.

I could see well enough to make out the faces of the other undead, and I thought I recognised a few of them from the battle in my hometown that night before I left; those that survived the fight against the Slayers. I began to realise I was about to discover what the conversation between Lady Sarah and the other vampire had been about, that morning in the barn we'd been sheltering in two months ago.

A male vampire stood at the front of the gathering on a dusty workbench. Everything about him spoke of power and age, from his body language and fierce appearance to the respect he clearly commanded among the other undead. Piercing green eyes surveyed us with disapproval as we entered, gazing out from beneath a wolf's head. He wore the pelt like a sleeveless jacket, the wolf's forelegs draped over his shoulders and resting on either side of his chest and down to his waist, the back cut short so that it also came down no further than his waist. Beneath it the pale flesh of his upper body was bare. He had the kind of muscular form I could only dream of, stuck with the skinny frame of my youth as I was.

Where the other vampires tended to give off an aristocratic air, regardless of the era they'd lived in, there was something more primal about this vampire. If I didn't know any better, I could even have mistaken him for a fellow werewolf. The head of the wolf pelt obscured much of the man he'd been beneath it, but I could just about make out a length of wild black hair, and he had a short beard. There was still the same unnatural beauty to him as the rest of his kind possessed, but this was more of a rugged handsomeness than the sophisticated beauty of the younger vampires.

One hand rested on the hilt of the sword at his hip, attached to a leather belt, and on his legs he wore plain black trousers. His grip tightened around the weapon as we briefly locked gazes, his eyes shining with unconcealed loathing in the moonlight and his bicep bulging beneath his skin, making it look like the muscle was trying to tear free. There was a sheer presence to him as if his power was a physical thing, seeking to bend us all to his will, and I was forced to look away. I guessed he must be the Elder vampire who'd called the meeting and I was starting to sense why Lady Sarah had tried to impress upon me the need to act as respectfully as possible. He would make a formidable enemy, of that I was certain.

Even Lady Sarah seemed wary of him. She had me stand with her near the doorway at the back, where we could keep an eye on the entire room and make a quick exit if we were forced to flee. And given the nature of the conversation I'd overheard in the barn, that seemed a likely outcome.

I'd barely had chance to take in my surroundings before the male vampire called for order, the room immediately falling silent. Given what Lady Sarah had told me before we'd entered and the control he held over the assembly, I had to wonder if he was one of the oldest surviving vampires still in existence.

"My fellow undead, I have called this gathering here today to discuss some grave tidings," he began. "Matters that concern us all and which must be dealt with swiftly. What I am about to reveal to you is most troubling, and requires the co-operation of each of our great races."

His attention turned to the workbench, and I rose up on the tip of my toes and craned my neck to see over the others. I hadn't noticed when we'd first entered, but there was something laid across it, which he was stood just in front of. The thing was covered by a sheet, and I began to dread where this was going. And sure enough, the vampire jumped down and pulled back the sheet to reveal a humanoid body.

I couldn't see much from our position at the back of the room, but it seemed the torso had been ripped open, shards of the broken ribcage poking up like the fingers of two outstretched hands waiting to receive something. And yet this victim had received only death, his killer taking more from him than they'd given. It was hard to tell without getting any closer and without a clearer view, but I got the impression of an empty cavity where the organs should have been, the bloody mess appearing black in the moonlight filtering through the dusty windows.

"Behold, the corpse of our fallen brother. No bullets felled him, nor any other tool used by man. Savaged as if by an animal and yet no mortal animal could ever hope to prey on us, we who are the ultimate hunters. That leaves but one explanation as to the gruesome fate that befell him; that he was killed not by the Slayers but by one of our own!"

The room immediately erupted into chaos, various groups of raised voices sounding in indignation. The gist of which was that the ghouls had better taste than the cold dead flesh of vampires and the vampires had more class than to rip apart their prey with their teeth, let alone to lower themselves to acts of cannibalism. And in the midst of all this the dark haired vampire stood at the front, his gaze settling on me. Lady Sarah had told me before of the nature of the relationship between vampires and werewolves; that we were once enemies in the days before the Slayers and how some of the older ones had never let go of their old prejudices. I guessed that was why Lady Sarah had wanted me to present as something more human. Eventually he held his hand up for silence and the others obeyed, respecting the power of an Elder.

"Even more troubling – this is in fact the second body to be found in such a state, both with their hearts missing. But fear not, my friends! I will find whichever one of us is guilty of this crime and he will be brought to justice. We will not tolerate the deaths of our own, for we are better than humanity and we do not slaughter others mindlessly, least of all our fellow brethren. I ask those of you who were able to gather here today to be vigilant, and to spread the word to those who are absent so we may hunt the culprit as swiftly as possible, before he can strike again as I believe he will. I do find it most interesting that both these deaths occurred on nights of the full moon."

His eyes were on me once again, filled with a hatred to rival that of the enemies I'd faced – even the loathing I'd encountered in Vince and Aughtie. Several of the other vampires turned to glare at me as well. I was about to say something in my defence but Lady Sarah shot me a warning look. Finally the Elder vampire let his eyes wander over the rest of the gathering as he brought the meeting to a close, the others turning back round to face him.

"That is all for tonight. I will send word if there is a need to discuss these matters any further."

There was an air of distrust as the various undead left the old warehouse, mostly from the vampires whose eyes were invariably on me as they stalked out. Try as I might to look more like my old human self, the attempt to hide the true essence of my bestial nature wasn't fooling anyone, especially when my skin was still splattered with dried blood. They knew who and what I was and it seemed they'd all seen enough centuries to remain prejudiced towards my kind. I was suddenly glad Lady Sarah was still with me, in spite of the trouble I'd given her whilst my rage had controlled me. I might have had more than just suspicious looks to contend with if I'd been alone.

Lady Sarah seemed to feel I was at risk even with her protection, for I could sense she was anxious to return to the isolation of the moors. But she didn't want to turn her back on the crowd, which forced us to wait for the ghouls to slink off and the vampires to stalk out. Once the last few undead began to trickle out, she deemed it safe to fall in behind them but, before we could take our leave, the dark haired Elder strode over to us.

"Lady Sarah, a word please," he said.

She hid her irritation, and was that a brief sense of unease I'd detected in her as well? If she was uneasy that put me on edge, wondering if Ulfarr would execute me just on the chance that I might be the killer, even though he had no evidence.

He spoke to her as if I wasn't there, or as if I was merely an animal, too simple to understand the troubles of its masters. "We both know the most likely identity of the killer. If I find it to be your pet wolf I will kill him, regardless of whether he is truly the last or not."

"I am stood right here you know," I growled. The emptiness still wouldn't allow for anger, but if I acted like he'd angered me then maybe my rage would return.

"You dare talk to me like that," he hissed. "I'll have your throat right now and we shall revel in the extinction of your species, vermin!"

Lady Sarah quickly positioned herself between us before I could say anything else. "You say the murders happened during the full moon; I have been by his side keeping him in check, ensuring he would not unwittingly deliver himself to the Slayers, nor create a fresh trail for them to follow."

"So you can account for everything he did after he lost his control to the call of the moon?" the Elder asked disbelievingly.

"I give you my word he is not the killer."

"If I find out you are lying to me, I will have your head as well, Lady Sarah," he said. At me he spat "Get out of my sight, beast."

I wanted to react angrily again. Maybe another fight was what I needed to finally awaken my rage from the depths of that gaping chasm in my soul. Lady Sarah knew me too well by this point, however, and pulled me away, keeping a firm grip on my arm to force me to walk with her. Once outside I shook her off and ripped away the stolen clothes, glad to be free of the uncomfortable material, before transforming back to wolf form. I let her lead me back to the moors we'd made our current territory, mulling over this latest turn of events as we ran.

"What was the point in taking me there just to be accused and have my life threatened?" I growled in human form again, still looking for a fight even though the emotions still wouldn't come. "If it was so dangerous to be around a bunch of vampires that clearly don't need much reason to kill werewolves, why go there in the first place?"

"Did you kill him, Nick?" she asked, ignoring my question.

"What? No! Of course I didn't; why would I kill a vampire?"

"You were out of control for those first two months after the battle, and again this full moon. We cannot be sure where you went or what you might have done. Let the wolf answer me: did you kill the vampire?"

Reluctantly I called out mentally to the wolfish half of my consciousness, but in those full moon nights spent completely lost in the bloodlust it had been as much a blackout period for him as it was for me.

"He doesn't know. That need to kill we were feeling was like a drug or booze or something; it just took over and everything went hazy till it wore off again."

"I feared as much. It is possible a werewolf might turn on another undead in such a state and even succeed in killing some of us, especially if you caught your victim unawares. In a crazed state you would be a formidable opponent for even the more powerful of vampires like myself."

"Great. So for the older vampires who are still prejudiced there's no doubt in their minds I am guilty, simply because of what I am, and now even you aren't sure of my innocence. Looks like I'm screwed then."

"I do not want to believe you are the killer but we know of no other surviving werewolves, and I must admit this does look like a werewolf attack. If they find it was you who killed one of our own I can't protect you," she said sadly.

I wanted to argue further but there was no real anger as I'd hoped, no matter how angry I tried to act. Even accused of murder I was sure I hadn't committed, those fires of fury that had burned so strongly a couple of months ago still wouldn't rekindle. Defeated, I turned away from her to stare out over the barren landscape, or what little of it I could see in the darkness.

And how could I be sure it wasn't me? Without a way to fill the gaps in my memory, I could no more answer where I'd run off to or what I'd done than Lady Sarah could. I knew I'd killed and I had some vague memories of people screaming and blood running freely, their flesh tearing in my jaws. But there was nothing in those few brief snatches of memory to suggest any of them had been vampires. And even if the two vampires had been among my victims, could I be held guilty for crimes committed when I wasn't in control of my actions? The vampires had already demonstrated they didn't need any real reason to kill me so I supposed that wouldn't matter to them. I was no more than a savage beast as far as they were concerned. They viewed me the same way mankind viewed large predators – as ferocious brutes. Which brought me back to my original question.

"Why take me to that meeting if there was a risk they'd kill me without waiting for any evidence?"

"They demanded our presence there," she answered. "Had we not have attended as requested, it would have given them more cause to distrust us."

"To distrust me, you mean. You could always leave me to my fate; there's no reason for you to die as well if they're intent on blaming me for this."

Lady Sarah shook her head. "I will not abandon you now. If you did kill the two vampires I can at least try to prevent the loss of more lives, though honestly I would highly doubt you would make a habit of killing undead, let alone develop a liking for vampire flesh. The curse causes you to crave humans, or other mortal animals as necessary. You hunger for living prey, and even a vampire who recently fed would be a poor substitute for the true warmth of live flesh. We are, after all, the living dead. Not to mention the risk to you of attacking creatures stronger than yourself, something that goes against every predator's instincts. It is unlikely you would continue to be successful, even in the grip of so powerful a bloodlust. No matter what Ulfarr may think, if you were the killer I believe these to be isolated incidents, and something you are not likely to repeat in the months to come, even if you do manage to run off on your own again. For now we will continue to keep a low profile and hope they find evidence to incriminate another undead."

I fell quiet again, thinking over what she'd just said. Despite the reasons she'd given, I didn't feel entirely sure why she was helping me as I still knew so little about her. But I needed an ally more than ever, so I had to trust she knew what she was doing. There was something else that was bothering me though.

"I know you said vampires and werewolves are never going to be best mates given our long and bloody history, but why does this Elder vampire hate us so much? I was sensing the same level of hatred from him as the Slayers have for us, and it felt like more than just prejudice or a grudge dating back to the war our races waged against each other. Why was he looking at me with so much loathing?"

"Ah, there is still much you do not understand, young wolf," she said with a sigh. "Very well. You wanted a story of ages long past? I will tell you the saga of Ulfarr, our living legend. But you may not like what you hear.

"In a time when mankind was still evolving, when men were still very much a part of the natural world, this legend was born. As a child he was no different to the other boys of his tribe, but he would grow to be a champion of his people, a great hunter and mighty warrior, renowned for his prowess in battle against men and beast alike.

"As a man, it is said he was every bit as fierce as the great predators of the land. He made his first kill when he was no more than seven years of age, and he would fearlessly drive off dire wolves and wrestle bears with his bare hands. But no mortal is invincible and no matter how great the man he once was, his downfall was inevitable. Whether to the ravages of time or to the claws of a beast, even this mighty champion would someday meet his end.

"And that end came on the fateful hunt for Dread-Tooth, greatest of the mighty sabre-toothed cats of their time. Dread-Tooth was a fearsome predator, biggest of all his brethren with eyes that shone like fire in the night, fangs thicker than a man's arm and like great daggers, and claws sharper than any crafted knife or spear. Many fell to those cruel teeth and claws, Dread-Tooth developing a taste for human flesh and returning to the tribe night after night to prey on the people. He bore the scars from previous encounters with man, yet no matter how many spears found their mark, it seemed nothing could stop him. The wounds healed and the beast returned, as powerful as ever.

"Long was Dread-Tooth's reign of terror. Fear for him grew amongst the tribesmen, until only one dared stand against him. Their champion stood alone, as strong and impressive a figure as Dread-Tooth himself, and driven by that dark human need for revenge. For among the victims were none other than his wife and son. And when the beast charged, he didn't even flinch.

"Dread-Tooth pounced but this champion of men moved with greater speed than the beast had encountered before, and his fangs snapped shut around nothing but air. A terrible pain stabbed through his flank, another spear biting into his flesh. It was enough to drive the beast off, and he limped away to lick his wounds and regain his strength.

"The champion saw his chance for vengeance and also to rid his people of this threat, and he set out to hunt down Dread-Tooth and finish what he'd started. But even wounded the beast remained a formidable opponent, and the sun had already risen before this great hunter finally tracked down his quarry. The beast sensed him coming and there was another struggle, Dread-Tooth more wary of the man now – he would not be so easily defeated a second time.

"Six times the champion jabbed at his foe, opening up six more wounds, but they only angered the beast. With the seventh the spear finally found its mark in the beast's heart, those two fiery eyes glazing over, his jaws slackening, his fearsome fangs no longer a threat. But this victory came at a terrible price. Mortally wounded, the man stumbled away with four deep gashes across his abdomen. He struggled on in an effort to make it back to his tribe until he could go no further, collapsing from loss of blood. And there he lay, his strength slowly fading, yet still he continued to fight for life long after night fell.

"But even in such primitive times, all those millennia ago, there were far worse than mortal beasts stalking the night. It was of course a vampire who would claim this man's human life, drawn by the scent of his blood. And weakened though he was, when the female vampire began to drain what little of that crimson life force he had left, still this champion of men attempted to fight. It is said the vampire was so impressed by this show of bravery and strength that she could not bring herself to end his life, so instead she passed on the gift of vampirism, and so a mortal legend passed into immortality.

"Unable to return to his tribe, their champion became their worst nightmare. For thousands of years he stalked the long hours of darkness, the greatest of predators. But the world began to change as mankind evolved and shaped the land around them, and even in those days long before the Demon Slayers formed, the undead were forced to be more careful. We vampires will always be vulnerable during the day, and man's reach was extending ever outwards, invading the old haunts of our race.

"With the rise of Lyacon and his dread pack, the balance of power shifted and for the first time since the dawn of civilisation, men were again no more than prey for the beasts that stalked them. Many of the younger vampires still bore the human desire for conquest, and for the first time in our history we were no longer solitary hunters of the night, but instead we began to ally together as a race so we might wrest the land from Lycaon and his wolves and claim it as our own. Yet every faction needs a leader, and too many of those with a thirst for power wanted the position for themselves.

"And so the idea of the Elders was born. Only the eldest of our race had the power to unite us in the fight against the werewolves, and we turned to them for leadership. But most of the older vampires had no interest in waging war on the wolves, content to keep to the shadows as they had always done. They were of another time, before the need to dominate corrupted the heart of mankind. Though there was one who would fight.

"Once a champion of men, he would now become a champion of vampires and the first to be given the title of Elder. And this first Elder vampire was every bit as ruthless and ferocious in battle against the werewolves as he had been against mortal beasts as a man. Lycaon met his downfall when his pack turned on each other, but for each new werewolf seeking to follow in Lycaon's footsteps, the Elder would be there to crush them before they could rise to power. He had retained his feral nature from the life he'd lived as a human and he fought with a savagery the younger vampires lacked. If he had a name as a man it has long since been lost in time, but he soon earned the title of Wolf's Bane.

"Even after the Age of Men was restored and we returned to our solitary ways, still he would hunt down werewolves with a single minded ferocity and it became his custom to wear the pelts of his enemies. Even men came to respect the might of this monstrous warrior, but it wasn't until early in the Viking era when he was given the name Ulfarr, or Wolf Warrior. Originally it was meant as Wolf Slayer or Wolf Killer, until the meaning changed over time, but it suited him and he has kept that name to this day.

"Over the centuries the rise of the Slayers forced our races to become allies, weakened as our forces were from fighting amongst ourselves. Yet Ulfarr could never bring himself to trust creatures born of the same bestial nature that had claimed the lives of his wife and son. Our greatest leader withdrew into the shadows, unwilling to deal with wolves, let alone fight alongside them. But if ever a werewolf turned on us or was deemed too troublesome, it was to Ulfarr we would look to hunt them down. And it shames me to say the extinction of your race is as much my kind's doing as the Slayers'.

"So now you know why I wished to keep you away from all this.

Ulfarr will not hesitate to kill you, given even the slightest of reasons. You need to tread carefully from now on."

I listened to the saga with mixed feelings. The love of stories I'd had as a human kept me entranced, though I couldn't help but snarl through the second half of the tale. I could respect Ulfarr's deeds as a human when he'd killed the big carnivores to protect his people, but the way he'd butchered countless werewolves over the centuries seemed too much like the mindless slaughter humans indulged in, despite his insistence we were better than them when he'd spoken during the meeting. And killing animals needlessly for sport or out of fear and hatred was something I'd always loathed as much as my wolfish half, giving rise to my own hatred and creating an instant dislike for this Elder vampire. Though was I really any better than any of them when I'd also taken to killing in cold blood?

Lady Sarah seemed to sense the impact the story had made on me, and the questions it created, just as her tale of Lycaon had done on the morning after my first transformation. She waited patiently, until finally I asked "How much of that is actually true?"

"The details may have grown with the telling over so many thousands of years, but the story itself is true. Ulfarr has walked this earth longer than any other surviving undead, and though he has picked up some elements of civilisation over the years – most notably language – he still retains aspects of that primal nature of his humanity."

"If he's pretty animalistic himself, how can he hate werewolves for their bestial nature so much? It wasn't even a wolf that took his family from him!"

"Hatred is never rational. Some say he witnessed a werewolf killing a woman and child just as Dread-Tooth had done and it opened up that old wound, reminding him of the night he lost his family. Hatred became rage and rage became bloodlust, driving him to kill."

"So why doesn't he just kill me, if his hate's already convinced him I'm guilty? Why bother calling the meeting tonight?"

"The alliance between undead has always been tenuous at the best of times. Ghouls are also solitary for the most part, and it goes against our natures to band together. If Ulfarr kills you without any reason, it could cause more fighting amongst ourselves which can only lead to extinction for us all. And we also look to our Elders for justice as well as leadership. Just as humanity have their laws and customs to maintain peace, there is a need for it in our society also. It's rare for one of our kind to turn on our own but it has happened, as we both saw with Vince.

"It was Ulfarr's duty to warn the rest of our kind and our allies that there appears to be a killer among us, and if the culprit is caught alive it will fall to him to carry out the execution. So you must not give him a reason to convict you because no matter how little evidence, if there is something to suggest your guilt it will be enough to satisfy the others, especially with the prejudice most vampires still bear towards your kind. And that's all Ulfarr needs to carry out your execution, which would bring him no greater pleasure, of that I'm certain."

"Great," I said again. "There's one other thing I don't understand though. If an Elder vampire like Ulfarr is so powerful and commands so much respect not just among your kind but also the ghouls, why doesn't he lead us into battle against the Slayers? Why did it fall to me in the battle we fought back home?"

"Ah, if you think I am overly cautious, it is as nothing compared to the wariness of the Elders in the face of modern technology. Even a vampire so old and powerful as Ulfarr would perish in the blast from the bombs mankind have developed, so they will not risk open warfare for fear of leading us all to our deaths. And even the Elders remain vulnerable through the daylight hours. No matter how many victories Ulfarr could bring us, there will always be more Slayers, and though they prefer the sport of hunting and killing us through the night, they will track down our daylight refuges if necessary. As arrogant as men can be, they are not entirely stupid. They will take advantage of our vulnerability if any of us are powerful enough to pose too great a threat for them to face in the hours of darkness."

"So that's it then, we're just going to hide in the shadows until we fade away into myth and legend?"

"What more can we do?" Lady Sarah asked, suddenly sounding tired. She didn't want another argument, knowing it would get us nowhere. And without the anger driving me, I didn't have any real reason to argue either, so I let it go. It had been a long night and I soon slipped into more troubled sleep.

Chapter Ten – Dead Inside

I was back in the familiar darkness of my bedroom, the early morning light just beginning to bleed through my curtains and chase away some of the shadows. But I still felt cold, even curled up in my old bunk bed beneath my thick winter duvet, and there was none of the comfort my surroundings should have brought me.

My bedroom door creaked open and I heard footsteps approaching. With my heightened senses I knew they didn't belong to Mum or Amy, and I pulled the covers over my head. Of all the family members I wished I could see again, he was the last one I wanted to talk to. Yet face him it seemed I must, his voice sounding exactly as I remembered it when he spoke, albeit without any of the anger it had so often held.

"You can't hide behind the rage forever, son," he said. "Sooner or later you have to face what you've done."

"No!" I snarled, throwing back the covers to glare at my Dad. "Why should I feel bad for killing you when all you ever did was make us miserable?"

Mum and Amy walked in to stand beside him, their eyes still full of grief.

"How can you think we're better off without you both?" Mum asked me. "You tore our family apart, Nick. Do you really think you can ever make peace with that?"

"We will always be a part of you, son," Dad said. "I will always be a part of you. You can't keep running from that – sooner or later you have to face what you've done."

"No!" I roared, my eyes snapping open as reality crashed back over me. But try as I might to be angry, it still wasn't there. And that was exactly the problem – it seemed I had no more rage to hide behind. Without it my thoughts turned increasingly to all that pain and grief I must have caused my family, and I was growing more and more homesick. Depression was filling the emptiness inside, the emotion I least wanted to feel, but without my bloodlust to offer me a way back out I was becoming trapped in that dark pit. Despair weighed me down, crushing in the knowledge that I couldn't go back, no matter how I longed to do something for my family, to help ease their pain, and no matter how great I desired to return to my old life. I could never go back.

"You murdered me, son," came my Dad's voice. "Even if you could go back, how can you ever make that alright?"

I looked around in the early morning light but I couldn't see him. I was coming to the conclusion that my brain was my own worst enemy. It seemed my mind was especially good at tormenting me with the things I just wanted to forget, and since I no longer felt any horror for the victims I'd so brutally murdered, it had turned to twisting the knife in the one wound that could still cause me pain. My family were my weakness and my mind wouldn't let me move on, no matter how I tried. I couldn't help but beat myself up over the things I'd done, even though I knew it was pointless. I couldn't change the past. I couldn't bring my Dad back, even if I really wanted to. And did I want to take it back? I'd been so sure we'd be better off without him, but my treacherous mind kept showing me images of Mum and Amy, broken by the sudden loss of both me and Dad. I wasn't sure of anything anymore. All I knew was that my family must be suffering, and it was because of me.

Lady Sarah was quick to notice this latest deterioration in my mental state when she rose at nightfall, but she didn't have the patience for my self-pity.

"You're still mourning for your old life and it's doing you no good! How will you ever find peace if you don't move on? That life is over; you must accept who you are now and adapt to this new life you've been given. It doesn't have to be a curse if you look for the positive, instead of focussing on the negative all the time."

"And how long did it take you to move on?" I growled, trying once again to rekindle my anger, despite the message in my dream. I'd happily lose myself in it to escape the guilt of what I'd done to my family. "Oh that's right, you didn't till you had to for your own survival; you told me the night we first met! You got to carry on as if everything was normal, till your immortality became too noticeable. So forgive me if I don't jump to take your advice. You don't understand what I'm going through and your sympathy is as dead as your humanity!"

"You do not have the same luxury I did," she snapped. "And do not assume it was any easier for me, just because the threat of the Slayers was less. It was equally as hard for me to relinquish my humanity as it is for you, even if I was able to cling to it for longer. I am trying to help you adjust to this life as quickly as possible without making the same mistakes I did. But if you don't want my help then fine. Go and get yourself killed by the Slayers or Ulfarr."

"No," I replied, defeated. The depression only weighed on me all the heavier when my rage didn't even stir within. "I know I'm not ready yet and I know you're only trying to help. I'll try to concentrate."

With the vampires looking for even the smallest excuse to blame me, she was growing more determined to carry on in her attempts to teach me greater control over myself.

"Then come, you still have much to learn if we are to ensure your survival should we ever become separated," she said.

I was already growing weary of her lessons but it seemed I didn't have much option, so I trudged after her.

"It's about time you learnt to tread lightly," she observed. "You might be able to rely on the wolf to guide your paws when hunting, but you need to be equally light on your feet as a human."

I knew she was right but I was too stubborn to admit it. I had always had heavy feet as a human – the traitor Vince had said as much the second time I met him, making a joke out of it. I also knew what was coming next, and I knew once again she was right, but I was also too stubborn to act on her advice. Especially when she was asking me to embrace the very thing that had ultimately brought about the destruction of the life I found myself missing more and more as time went on.

And just as I knew she would, she said "Of course, this would no longer be a problem if you'd just allow your mind to become whole again. All those skills each half instinctively possesses, or has learned over the years, would be at your disposal. With your combined skills you could become a far more successful predator, better than either half of you will ever be alone."

So I was forced to spend each night with her, breaking off only to feed. I was starting to hate it. The daylight hours offered little respite, the weather growing colder as time wore on, making it increasingly hard to sleep. The nights taxed both my body and mind and I was becoming exhausted, but there was no peace to be had when I laid my head down to rest on the cold, hard ground, far removed from the human comforts I used to know. It was yet another reminder that the simple pleasures most people take for granted would forever be denied to me. Just when I thought I had come to terms with the fact I was no longer human, I found myself longing to be amongst them once more.

How long had it been now? It was hard to say. The nights all bled into each other until it became just one continuous period of darkness with the occasional bit of daylight thrown in. It had been some time since we left my hometown but not that long, I knew that much. There'd only been four full moons so it couldn't have been more than four months. And already I missed my old way of life. Surprisingly it was the little things I often missed the most. Obviously I missed my family and my mates, as evidenced by the torment I faced both awake and asleep, but I also found myself longing for a good book to read, or my video games, or more often than not my music, which wasn't mainstream enough for me to have heard from human buildings in the distance or the occasional passing cars on quiet country roads, before we'd been driven to our present surroundings.

I even missed the seemingly mundane aspects of my old human life, like transport. Unless I'd been itching to get back to my games either on the internet or the PlayStation, I usually wouldn't have minded an hour or so travelling in the car, watching the world rushing by and allowing my imagination to run wild. Or maybe it was just my aching paws that missed it. My stamina might be greater than any mortal creature, but even a werewolf has his limits.

Winter began to extend its frosty claws over the land. Whichever part of Britain we'd ended up in, it had to be high above sea level, and the weather's icy bite came so much stronger as a result. I was getting less and less sleep as the temperature continued to drop and conditions worsened, not only uncomfortable on the hard floor now, but cold and miserable without any shelter to protect from the elements, even when curled up in wolf form, and often hungry with the lack of prey to feed on in the area. I knew I was tired but the cold was keeping me wide awake, and I took to wandering the moorland in that halfway state between boy and wolf, hoping the simple act of moving would help bring some warmth back to my numb body.

God how I missed my old life. It had begun to seem increasingly like no more than a dream as my current reality grew ever harder, as if it had never been and there was only the miserable existence which I'd found myself trapped in. What I wouldn't have given to see my family and my mates again, to hang out with them and enjoy human pleasures. Would I have given it up so freely if I'd truly realised the harsh nature of the world I'd chosen to embrace? No, had I known the reality of life outside of the human world I wouldn't have so readily left it all behind. I'd thought I was embracing the new world to which I now belonged, but it seemed there was no real place for the undead, no world of their own. Just as we were forever trapped between the realm of the living and the dead, so were we caught between the worlds of humanity and nature. Once our humanity was gone we could never truly be a part of their world again, yet neither did we belong to the natural world. It seemed we were doomed to forever be the outsiders looking in, living in places such as this, on the fringes of the human world but never quite a part of the natural one either.

Gales began to roll across the country. The wind ruffled my fur, seeking to drive the icy cold of winter past my thick coat and through to my very bones. When it failed there came a stronger blast, assaulting me with such force that it became a struggle to breathe. Now that winter was fast advancing I was forced to spend as much time in a more lupine state as possible just to stay warm, and even with a body designed to withstand such harsh weather I was still miserable.

We were exposed out there on the moors. There was no shelter from the raging winds, not like humans safe behind their four walls, warm within their homes. It was okay for the vampire, hidden away during the day. In protecting herself from the deadly sunlight she would also be protected from the elements, at least to an extent. Did she even feel the bite of the icy cold wind upon her equally cold skin? She hadn't sought out any warmer clothes, seemingly content to roam around in the same black dress she'd worn ever since I first met her. Clearly vampires didn't sweat like mortals, for I hadn't noticed the dress beginning to smell at all. But I was sure it couldn't offer even the slightest bit of warmth, which made me wonder if she felt any change in temperature at all.

I, on the other hand, was all too aware of the drop in temperature. Having spent most of my life inside wherever possible, it was something of a shock to my system to suddenly find myself out in such unforgiving conditions. Though common sense told me to keep moving to generate body heat and thus provide a line of defence against the cold, all I wanted to do was curl up into a tight ball and lay there shivering and pathetic.

And finally when I felt I couldn't go on, an aching throb deep in my calves, pulsing with every step I took, and the cold seeking to drive me back to the ground, I caught the sound in the distance of the human world I longed to know again. I knew if I allowed myself to get close not only did I run the risk of the Slayers finding us once more, but also that of the temptation to walk among them and seek to be closer to that world again becoming too much. Yet after the time I'd already spent in total isolation, I couldn't seem to help myself.

Like so many of mankind, the human in me longed for that which was to remain firmly out of my grasp, the very things that were denied to me. The more time I'd spent fleeing from place to place, following the instruction of Lady Sarah and struggling to survive, and now suffering in the cold on top of that, the more my heart ached for the human life I had once known, until I'd been so cruelly torn from it by the curse. The closest I could hope for was a solitary walk on the fringes of their society, snatching glimpses of lives similar to my own prior to all this madness.

Lady Sarah probably would have told me I was doing myself no good by spending so much time looking and obsessing over what I could no longer have, had she known, and she would have been right. It was only feeding the depression which had been growing inside me, and I couldn't help but feel doomed to walk this world alone for all eternity. The vampire could never be the companion I sorely needed, and there were none of my own kind left. Humans were too frail with their own mortality, and anyone I allowed myself to grow close to (assuming I wasn't too damaged to feel anything like love or friendship) would only end up dead one way or another. Wasn't that why I'd left everyone I'd once cared about in the first place? I knew all this, but still I mourned everything I'd lost, and allowed my mind to torment me with these feelings of longing.

So I stood on the highest hilltop, looking down into the valley where a small rural village lay before me, somewhat humble and more modest when compared with the urban sprawls I had grown up with. I could tell it was the kind of place where everyone knew everyone else and one neighbour's business soon became the business of the entire village. The kind of place where a stranger would be instantly recognised as an outsider, and even instantly mistrusted by some of its inhabitants. The kind of place Lady Sarah would tell me to avoid.

As I watched, a break in the clouds allowed a shaft of bright winter sunlight to touch down upon the valley floor as if the heavens were offering the villagers a ray of hope in an otherwise hopeless world. The surrounding countryside and woodland that bordered one side of the village seemed all the gloomier for it.

That the sun's beam should just happen to illuminate the settlement seemed symbolic to me, though whether it was a sign I should stay clear, plagued by so many nightmarish memories and shrouded by the darker side to my nature as I currently was, or a sign that here was a source of hope for even a monster such as myself, was debatable. I chose to believe somewhere in that village I would find some comfort of some kind, no matter how small, because I felt I badly needed something to keep me going after everything I'd been through and all the changes in my life that had happened over such a relatively short period, changes I still struggled to adjust to. Lady Sarah definitely wouldn't be happy with me if she were there to witness my decision, but how much risk could the village really offer? Such a small settlement was unlikely to get much attention from the Slayers, surely. Less inhabitants and a smaller area to patrol suggested to me that they would be few in number. If I were to linger for too long, word would soon reach them of the presence of an outsider and I knew they'd likely be quick to investigate, but I felt certain I could have a quick look round and be long gone before they found me.

And there was another reason I felt compelled to approach that village in that particular moment. With the growing resentment I was currently feeling towards Lady Sarah and her lessons, the fact the village was currently bathed in sunlight and therefore a place vampires couldn't currently enter seemed like another sign I was meant to go there. Not to mention the fact she would be so against it meant that an echo of the rebellious teenager I once was wanted to go there all the more.

At first I intended only to watch from the cover of the woodland I'd seen. Even though I returned fully to human form, out of that desire to be closer to the world I was once part of, I knew I couldn't actually enter the village without washing the dried blood from my body and finding some clothes. But then my thoughts turned darker, hunger for both flesh and to feel something once again steering them in a certain direction. That same obsession that had driven me to kill the cow now made me wonder whether human prey was what I needed to restore my bloodlust. And if these were relatively safe hunting grounds, this was surely the place to try.

I circled round the village, keeping to the gloomy cover of the woodland, such as it was now the trees had shed most of their leaves. I watched from between the trunks as the village's inhabitants went about their business, to and from work and their other mundane daily tasks. As an outsider looking in their entire existence seemed so pointless. The majority of them hated work or school, and they spent the whole week looking forward to the weekend, only for Monday morning to come and the monotonous cycle to start over.

Once I would've thought escaping the human world would be a dream come true. I was free of the chains human society placed on their people, free of the arduous routines they were forced to repeat day in, day out and the hours they wasted on work. So why did I want to return to that life so badly?

Every creature must fight for survival, and yet humans had created so much more work for themselves just to survive in their own world. And here I was, free to do as I pleased and spend my time as I wished. Surviving wouldn't have taken much work if it weren't for the Slayers, my supernatural speed and strength ensuring my place at the top of the food chain. Short of any threat posed from any fellow undead, I'd have had nothing to fear. Time was mine to do with as I pleased: no authority or law governed me. Yet as much as I had always hated the thought of a lifetime stuck in the same old routine – whether that was due to education or employment – was freedom really worth it without the human comforts I had always taken for granted? Freedom had come at a high price, one I wouldn't have been so quick to pay if I'd truly understood the cost. I watched them go about their business, feeling I would gladly go back to the monotony of that existence if it meant having somewhere warm to sleep and hobbies to occupy my mind, half-heartedly wrestling the hungers fighting to rob me of the last of my self-restraint. The hunger for the life I had once known was not enough to combat the hunger to feed and, I hoped, to feel, and with a snarl I withdrew deeper into the woods, moving on in search of the perfect opportunity to hunt as safely as possible, knowing it would only serve to widen the divide between myself and the village.

The sound of children playing relatively close was unmistakeable to my sensitive ears. They had to be young, no more than six or seven years of age. To the predator in me they only represented one thing – prey. I tried to lose myself in those predatory instincts, even though my lupine half wanted nothing to do with this hunt. Like Lady Sarah, he was too cautious and cared too much for our survival. The recklessness and risk taking lay solely with the human side of my nature, the part of me that no longer cared if I lived or died, so long as I escaped this depression I'd sunk back into, one way or another.

I let the change take me back to that halfway point between man and beast, in a further attempt to lose myself in my primal urges. It felt much smoother than usual, as if my body was responding to the anticipation I was trying to build inside, trying to induce the bloodlust so I could lose myself in the violence.

I was able to keep off the streets as I circled round towards the kids, guided by the sound of their laughter. The landscape was very hilly, full of little valleys that provided further cover as well as the trees themselves.

My destination turned out to be a park. Luckily the woodland bordered it on two sides, and the street running round it seemed quiet. There were six children playing: four girls and two boys. Two women stood watching over them and chatting, their backs to the woodland I lurked in. Seeing the families brought another stab of grief for all that I had lost, and the depression and despair threatened to overwhelm me again. I shook my head as if that would clear it and tried to focus on the hunt.

Even though I'd been taking my hybrid form most of the time, it still required a great amount of energy, and the hunger was there, the craving for raw flesh, to replenish my reserves. It was never quite as strong as after a full transformation, but it was still a potent force, all the worse for being unable to satiate it properly, and I let it drive me towards my prey.

The humans had been completely unaware of me as I lurked between the shadowy trees, and I moved so fast my first victims didn't know what had hit them, until it was too late. The mothers died too quickly to raise the alarm for their children, and then I was on the first of the kids.

Laughter turned to screams and with screams came tears. Fear was thick in the air, contagious amongst my prey and almost suffocating. Once I would have revelled in it, but my dark pleasures remained lost to me. I released the first little girl with her leg almost completely chewed off, and grabbed one of the others as he tried to flee. It became less about satisfying the hunger and more about the brutality of the attack, in a desperate attempt to spark those emotions a kill used to bring me.

I bit down on the throat of the little boy, intending to rip it out. He was so small that I bit clean through his neck, sending blood spraying over the concrete of the play area. His head rolled to a stop by the swings he'd been enjoying just moments before, and blood pooled around his corpse.

Before his body hit the floor I'd already lashed out at one of the other girls, ripping a gaping wound in the soft flesh of her belly and sending her crashing to the ground, screaming in pain and shaking uncontrollably. I left her bleeding out and lunged at my fourth victim. Catching her by the arm in my jaws, I tossed her around like a slab of meat, because that's all that she was to me in that moment. My fangs ground against the bone of her small, fragile arm with every movement of my head, but I gripped the limb tight and wouldn't let go. It snapped with the force of my attack, her blood spraying into my mouth and dripping down my jaws, matting my fur, while the shock proved too much for her small body. Finally I dropped her still form to the concrete, her blood running to join that of the decapitated boy.

The other two had started to run but I was upon them before they'd barely gotten to the edge of the playground. The fifth received a swift and merciful death as some rational part of my mind knew they couldn't be allowed to leave and alert the village. The screaming would bring more humans soon enough, of that I was sure, and I had to act fast now.

Wolves don't use their paws to swipe like cats but I was also part human, so I slashed my claws across the final child's throat before she could scream again, then proceeded to savage her body. I ripped off her arm and bit through her leg, tossing the body parts with each mighty shake of my head. When finally I resigned myself to the fact my bloodlust still remained silent, I began to feed, ripping chunks from her torso and gnawing the remaining limbs. Though the screaming had stopped several minutes before, the shrill sounds continued to ring in my ears, until eventually all was silent.

The world took on that unnatural stillness that follows certain atrocities. There weren't even any birds singing in the trees, or rodents rustling through the undergrowth; no dogs barking in the distance. It was as if the entire area had felt my presence and its inhabitants had fled before me. Most noticeable was the absence of the children's laughter that had so saturated the air before my arrival, and the silence was all the more oppressing following the screams I'd elicited from each victim before stealing away their final breath.

I knew I should be feeling the guilt and remorse, and the horror, that I'd felt in the beginning. But there was only that emptiness, that gaping wound in my soul much like the one I'd ripped open in the body of the little girl. I truly was one of the undead. My body continued its mockery of life but inside I was every bit as dead as the tiny carcasses I'd surrounded myself with. Their small, ruined frames continued to ooze out blood, once a substance that had seemed to fill me with the life force of my prey, back in the early days when the curse had made me feel truly alive, before I'd come to realise the true cost of my newfound powers. But now it only ran cold and dead into the void, offering no comfort or brief reprieve from my own inner state of death.

"God, Nick, what have you done?" a voice said, making me jump.

"Lizzy! You can't really be here..."

"Are you really so desperate that you must turn to such mindless slaughter?" the apparition continued, as if I'd not said anything.

"I just wanted to feel something," I answered miserably. "I can't take any more of this nothingness inside. I need something to give my life meaning again."

"And did their deaths hold any meaning? Can there be any meaning from brutal murder?"

I remained silent and crouched over the little girl I'd been feasting on, staring at the bloody remains. The small limbs scattered around and the severed head were like gruesome doll's parts, but the mutilated torso bore little resemblance to anything human now.

"What have I become?" I finally whispered.

The hallucination didn't answer this time, so I continued along my line of thought. "Pathetic. A lost, wretched soul, intent on killing

110

for no reason other than in an attempt to combat his own misery. And for what? It seems my rage is truly spent; I don't even feel pleasure in this like I did just a couple of months ago. No wonder the wolf part of me hates me. I'm no better than the human hunters I once despised for slaughtering animals for 'sport'. How did it come to this?"

"Yes, you who has the blood of wolves in you, who could be so much greater than either man or wolf if only you'd look to the best of each half, yet still you continue to let the worst rule you. That darkness that lies at the heart of mankind that once you hated, that a part of you still hates."

"So what do you want from me?" I snarled. "To ask forgiveness, seek redemption from some silent God who doesn't even care, if He even exists? I'm a killer now and my soul is dead; how do I come back from that?"

I tried to be angry but still it would not come. Then a fresh scream brought me back to reality, the first adult to find the horrific scene. I like to think now that I looked at her with those same soulful eyes a dog gives his master knowing he's done something wrong, but in reality my gaze was probably as cold and empty as I felt inside. There seemed little point in killing this other human so I slunk off into the woods, stringy bits of the children's flesh caught between my teeth, and their blood staining my fur and the skin beneath, as if death now clung to me, as meaningless as my own pitiful existence.

I returned to the remoteness of the moors, the place so virtually devoid of life as the state I had regressed to. It would be dark soon and I knew the vampire would only look for me if I didn't return to her before she rose from the ground. But I couldn't face her in light of the sheer hopelessness of my situation that came with the realisation that not even human prey could renew my bloodlust. And I wasn't in the mood for her lectures about my recklessness in taking human prey. Instead I continued to wander the moors in search of a water source big enough to submerge myself in, and finally found a large glacial lake.

The liquid was icy cold but I gritted my teeth and forced myself to immerse my entire body in its cleansing waters, trying to wash away some of the blood to help hide what I'd done. I let the liquid pass through my jaws and lessen the metallic, salty taste that suddenly seemed foul, though the water couldn't take it away completely. A part of me wanted to just close my eyes and let the water take me, but still I couldn't bring myself to end it. And even if I had tried, no doubt my lupine half would have prevented me from dying. Short of destroying my heart or my brain, I would never be able to manage suicide without him bringing me back from the brink of death. Eventually I felt a presence at the side of the lake and I dragged my numb body back onto dry land, to find it was of course Lady Sarah.

I could tell she disapproved of my decision to take a bath as I lay shivering violently at her feet, but she wouldn't let me escape another night of training. So my misery continued.

Chapter Eleven – More Confusion

By the next full moon, Lady Sarah had grown yet more cautious. Despite her conviction that it was unlikely I would kill another vampire– if I'd even been responsible for the deaths of the other two – she wasn't taking any chances. She was determined to keep me close this time.

I had enough sense not to give into the transformation too early, so she had a chance to rise before the temptation to run off and kill took hold of me. But with no cloud cover to hide the moon, I couldn't fight it for long.

My teeth lengthened into fangs, my amber eyes burning with hunger like two powerful flames in my skull, which was already stretching outwards into a snout. Digits lengthened, hard pads forming beneath, while other bones, most noticeably my femur, seemingly ground together as they shortened. Internal organs shifted and also changed in size and possibly shape, my ears grew pointed and shifted to the top of my head, and fur now covered my body from head to the tip of the tail growing at the base of my spine. As the human part of me sunk down towards our subconscious I briefly wondered if this transformation would be my last, and whether I was destined to die a lone wolf, shunned even by my supposedly 'fellow' undead. Then the wolf took over and I surrendered control of our body to him.

I was aware of what had happened during the last full moon and why the vampire was so afraid to let me out of her sight that month, but I could already feel my bloodlust stirring.

Though I hated the human for killing the children for little reason other than in an attempt to feel something, deep down their deaths had excited me and left me hungry for more, even if I wouldn't let the human share in that. And with the full moon overhead, the hunt called to me.

Lady Sarah had evidently decided it was better to risk the Slayers' wrath than that of her fellow vampires, for she took her wolf form and bade me to follow her. She didn't trust me not to wander off if given the chance again, and with the moon calling to my most primal instincts, I didn't trust myself either. I was still as much a slave of the moon and the hunger as I had been during the first few months of my initial wakening, and I didn't possess the strength of mind needed to fight its hold over me.

I could hear the sound of cars in the distance and smell the toxic fumes that meant we had found our way back to the human world. Judging from the wall of sound assaulting my ears the closer we drew, this was a larger settlement than the village where the human had committed its latest massacre the previous month. It was fortunate she hadn't taken us to the same one, perhaps unwittingly leading us to our deaths as the Slayers must surely have been alerted to that most recent attack by now, or at the very least the villagers would have no doubt made some preparations for the 'rogue wolf' as I'd been named after the discovery of my kills in Yorkshire.

Eagerly I ran towards the sound of humanity at the vampire's side, no thought in my mind except the need to hunt, to kill. I would've lost myself in the bloodlust within minutes had I been on my own, falling upon the first hapless victim unfortunate enough to cross my path. But the vampire was still cautious, and her powerful presence kept me in check this time.

Footfalls sounded from a street nearby, causing us to turn as one towards the sound of prey, ears pricked and snouts raised into the wind. We caught the scent of two female humans out jogging, but no other scents to cause alarm. As the prey came closer I could hear their hearts pumping frantically like two caged things, begging for me to set them free, rip them from their bony prisons and let the blood flow freely. I whined and looked to Lady Sarah for permission to give in to our desires. She didn't answer but began to bound towards the approaching humans, and excitedly I kept pace at a loping run.

The humans were soon within sight and we were on them before they'd had chance to fully comprehend what was happening, sending them crashing to the ground. I had longed for this and now finally I could rip into living flesh again, feel my prey die so that I might live. Her death came in a blur of movement and savage abandon, my powerful jaws ripping her throat out, exposing her spine in the gaping hole I made, blood spraying everywhere. My first satisfactory meal in weeks, I ravenously tore into the fresh meat and greedily gulped it down, spattering the pavement with blood and entrails, the less palatable organs such as the stomach bitten in two and left in a slimy lump as I greedily hunted for the most prized offal – the heart, liver and kidneys. Beside me Lady Sarah was human once again, drinking deeply from her victim and making considerably less mess as she fed.

Once I'd finished feasting on the fresh kill there was little left, and still the hunger burned within. I glanced at Lady Sarah's victim but knew better than to encroach on the food of my alpha, and besides, she was draining the blood so quickly from her corpse that the dry meat would bring less satisfaction than I'd just experienced. The moon and the hunger screamed at me to find more, and while the vampire was lost in her own bloodlust as she fed, I forgot the dangers the night held and slipped away from her yet again.

Some small part of my rational mind appealed to my sense of caution and I wasn't yet completely consumed by the bloodlust, so I was careful to keep to the shadows. There I waited for the perfect opportunity to make a second kill without immediately drawing attention to my presence.

On the fringes of the human world the night was silent, unnaturally so. Humans may have considered it eerie but I was used to it. Not even the local

114

wildlife stirred. They knew better; death had come within their midst, and death awaited them. To do anything but hide and cower in the hopes they wouldn't be discovered spelt certain doom. I inspired fear in the living, it was my curse. The only sounds my sensitive ears detected came from the town centre, where humans indulged in their nightlife. They were so easily taken, the one species ignorant enough not to recognise me for what I was and hide with the other animals. And I hungered for their flesh above all others...

Growling, I tried to fight the urge to slink deeper into the town and slaughter to my heart's content, but something was wrong. Though the human part of my mind had been growing increasingly stronger during the full moon and lurking much closer to the surface of our consciousness than ever before, I suddenly felt thoughts running through my mind that weren't my own. It seemed the mental wall dividing our two personalities was collapsing. But I despised the human race in general, not to mention the human half of me and its complete disregard for the sanctity of life, and it was the last thing I wanted. I had only ever killed for survival before the human's rage had let the bloodlust grow to new heights, while it had mostly killed for pleasure like all of its wretched kind. And now its thoughts were invading my own and I could feel it clawing at that invisible barrier separating us in its desperation to let the bloodlust fill it once more.

I was no longer merely struggling to control my urges empowered by the moon overhead, I was fighting to keep myself apart from the human in me. But all the human wanted to do was embrace our dark desires, and it started to throw itself at the wall between our minds. And like any wall, it could only take so much...

I must have blacked out because when I came to, I was no longer entirely in wolf form, despite still being in the grip of the power of the full moon, though it was now hidden by clouds. However, my body was the least of my worries.

Apparently I'd collapsed but when I tried to stand, my body didn't seem to want to react like it should and moving my head was a mistake. It wasn't as if I'd banged it at some point in the blackout because it wasn't exactly pain, it was more like my head felt too full, as if my mind had grown and it was too big for my skull to hold. I felt like it would spill out onto the street if I moved. But it wasn't just that, I couldn't think clearly and it was as if my thoughts had slowed. Thinking was an effort, each thought slow to form, and my mind seemed to be in a state of confusion.

It took some time before I could get as far as my hands and knees. I stared blearily at bloodied hands that swam before my vision, or were they paws? Blood pooled around them, leaking from a body that lay nearby. Apparently I'd managed to kill during the blackout, probably out of instinct because I'd had to feed and replace the energy that had been lost to another transformation. I was still weak with hunger and I struggled to crawl towards the body, but after a few mouthfuls I could already feel my strength returning. I left little but as always the hunger was not satisfied when I had done and I snarled at the small patch of light breaching faintly through the clouds. It called to me and there was only one way to answer it, through blood and death. With another snarl I tried again to stand, though my mind couldn't decide if I should be upright or on all fours. Eventually I managed to stand upright, clinging to the wall for support. It felt wrong and I wanted to drop back onto all fours but at the same time it felt right. And the loudest part of my brain screamed I didn't have time for those feelings, the hunger had to be obeyed.

So I lurched unsteadily away, not knowing whether I was man or beast. I don't simply mean physically, but mentally as well. My sense of self had altered in some way and it was affecting my grip on reality, making it impossible to tell whether my body was human or wolf, or a combination of the two. But I didn't know which it was meant to be either – I felt like I was both at the same time. All I knew was the hunger and my basic animal urges, which at that point in time were simply hunt, kill, eat. There had been times before when the carefully defined edges between human and wolf had blurred, but not to this extent. Even when the Slayers had locked me up and the remainder of the boy I had once been had temporarily become a primitive beast, the wolf was still there in my sub consciousness, a separate entity. The sudden collapse and merging of our two identities seemed to have caused a shock to my system, one that was a great deal more damaging than even my first transformation. It was exacting a greater toll on my mind than any other trial I had endured and surely led the way to true madness and my eventual demise. Not that I was really aware of this at the time; my thoughts were still slow and a struggle to form. My mind spoke to me in simplistic images driven by the hunger, images being the only thing it could grasp, a universal language. So I staggered away towards the sounds of life and prey and the next meal.

As I drew closer to the building that was soon to be a slaughterhouse, a new sound reached my ears. Before it had been simply noise, discarded by my brain since it was neither threat nor prey. Yet the closer I got, the louder it became, and the more meaning it held.

The beat pounded against my ears, working its way through to a specific part of my mind that had nothing to do with the hunger. Music that had meant so much to the boy I used to be called to a part of me, a call to rival that of the moon. It reached that part of my brain and it grew stronger, strong enough to free itself from the confused mess my mind had been reduced to. The wall slammed back into place and clarity returned.

I fell against the building from the second shock of suddenly being cut off from the wolf, but quickly recovered, though I was somewhat confused at the sudden turn of events. I looked down at my body to find it human, naked and covered in fresh blood. Confused, I looked back up at the night sky but the moon was now completely hidden behind the cloud cover. My memories of the brief merging of our minds were murky and in many ways my mind remained in disarray, so I was unsure why I'd changed back.

Still puzzling over the early transformation back to human, I had the sense to retreat into the shadows and head back towards the outskirts of the town where I had a vague memory of leaving Lady Sarah. I knew I should find her and travel back to the isolation of the moors, which I assumed were far enough from the town to help keep the Slayers off our trail. The village I'd visited and killed in had been much closer to the area we'd taken up residence in, but as far as I knew she still hadn't found out about my latest murders, so I guessed the only other reason she'd deemed it too risky to hunt in was its closeness to our current territory.

The memories might not have been entirely clear, and those from when our minds had temporarily become whole before splitting back into the separate personalities of boy and wolf were the most confusing, but I had a sense of which direction to head towards for the side of town I'd left the vampire in. As I drew closer I could smell where we'd made our kill, but Lady Sarah had long since gone. And just as I was processing this information a bullet thudded into my shoulder, my own blood mixing with the blood of my victims already staining my skin. It seemed the Slayers had caught up with me, and I wasn't in the right frame of mind for a fight. My only hope was to lose them and flee back to the moors, and just pray the vampire would be waiting for me when I returned.

Chapter Twelve – Last Orders

My shoulder throbbed where the bullet had torn a hole in the flesh and blood continued to leak from the wound, but with my higher pain threshold it was tolerable for the time being. I didn't trust myself to start transforming enough to heal it with the Slayers on my trail, fearing I'd once again be at the mercy of the full moon's hold over me, even if it still remained out of sight. If I lost control and allowed my bloodlust to rule me it might give me the strength to emerge victorious from another skirmish, but I knew my luck would run out eventually as the gunfire continued to tear through the night. And I might not possess the cunning needed to evade my pursuers if I gave in to my lunar madness.

There were only two Slayers so far but the town was large enough that it seemed only a matter of time before more appeared. So I endured the pain of the bullet wound and I ran. Only once I lost the Slayers would I allow myself to heal and possibly feed again to recover some of my strength, before finding my way back to Lady Sarah.

Bullets continued to rip through the night but even in human form I was able to move quick enough that no more had found their mark as yet. I weaved through the network of deserted streets, hoping to put some distance between them before heading for the surrounding countryside where there would be less cover. Just as the sound of my hunters began to grow faint, another pair appeared from an alley, and with a curse I was forced to push myself to greater speeds, more bullets thudding into the walls just seconds after I'd moved out of the way.

Even with my great lupine stamina and supernatural powers I couldn't keep this up all night. The bullet wound was beginning to sap my strength and my breathing was growing ragged. I needed to lose them before I used up the last of my reserves so I forced myself to keep going, deciding the countryside was my only option while I could still run with enough speed to present a harder target to hit.

I raced through the streets towards the edge of the town till finally I seemed to have succeeded in losing the Slayers on foot, but to my dismay I could hear a helicopter slicing its way through the blackness of the night sky, and it wasn't long before I could see it heading towards me. I had no choice but to keep going and find some place to hide, and just hope the search would eventually be called off. The Slayers didn't want either ours or their existence to be public knowledge, which meant surely they would have to call it off before the night was over, or they risked drawing too much attention to themselves. If I was wrong I would potentially pay with my life, but without my full speed and strength I couldn't outrun them, and it was better not to be caught out in the open.

So I pushed on, trying to ignore the persistent throbbing of my shoulder and the burning of my aching muscles. Yet losing the chopper closing in overhead proved much more difficult than evading the Slayers on the ground. It followed me everywhere I went like on wildlife programmes I'd watched in my human life where camera crews would film wolf hunts, following the entire pack so the viewer could see how they worked together to bring the prey down. Except this was no camera crew observing from above and for all I knew they had a sniper attempting to line up a shot and take me down in the safety of their machine.

I was so intent on trying to escape the helicopter's sights that I took little notice of any potential dangers on the ground, and I blundered onto streets where more of my enemies lay in wait. Before long it seemed there were teams of two or three Slayers waiting for me at every twist and turn, and I was heading deeper into man's domain as they shepherded me back through the town. I knew then that this was a trap and it might as well have been a wolf pack hunt, one in which I had become the prey. But with every possible escape route blocked by members of this pack of human hunters, what more could I do other than keep running in the direction they were forcing me in? I didn't think I had the strength left to fight my way through the streets of armed Slayers, though a part of me knew that running was only putting off the inevitable now. I would have to make a stand eventually and no doubt that would only grow harder the closer I ran to the centre of whatever trap lay in wait.

In the back of my mind I was vaguely aware that there were no civilians around, which might have helped my plight if there had been. Not all the Slayers were comfortable with innocents dying for 'the greater good' and I could have used some as human shields, but it seemed my hunters were one step ahead of me in every sense of the phrase that night. They must have found a way to close off the section of town they were forcing me through, and I had to accept I was truly on my own this time. There would be no help from anyone, voluntary or otherwise.

Just as I felt I could go no further, I found myself forced to run down an alley with a wall in the middle that would have presented a dead end for a human. I could hear the Slayers closing in behind, but with a wave of despair I also picked up the scents and sounds of more heading to block off any escape from the other side of the wall as well.

My blood was still flowing freely from the bullet wound in my shoulder as I stood there panting and trying to think of a way out. The Slayers on my side of the wall would be on me in minutes, but on the other side they seemed to be a little slower getting into position and there lay my best hope, I decided. Climbing over the wall was a desperate move since I'd be vulnerable while I clambered up, but what choice did I have? I was in no shape to make a stand against a group of armed humans, and there was nowhere left to run. I had to at least try to reach the other end of the alley before my enemies could trap me in there from both ends. If they did, then they would see just how dangerous a cornered animal can be and I'd take as many down with me as I could. But I would go down eventually, of that I was certain. First I needed to heal the damage to my shoulder though, or I didn't think I'd have the strength left to do anything.

Acutely aware of what precious little time I had trickling by, I risked starting the transformation. I was still wary of the hold the moon had over my lupine nature and I remained tense while the flesh flowed back into the flawless whole it had been before the bullet did its damage. The wound throbbed more powerfully through the healing process as a result of me being so tensed up, and it seemed so painfully slow when time was of the essence. But finally the pain eased as the bullet was forced out and all trace of the injury was gone. The moon stayed hidden behind the clouds and my self-control remained, for now at least. The Slayers were almost on me – I could hear them advancing more cautiously as they drew nearer to the mouth of the alley, probably well aware I would put up a fight to the bitter end. It was now or never if I wanted to seize my chance of survival, no matter how slim. So I began to climb, allowing my nails to become claws which sunk into the brick with ease.

I made it to the top before the humans appeared and opened fire. Bullets thundered towards my prone form as I swung myself over the wall, and I just managed to drop to the other side before they could hit me again. But it was to find I wasn't alone.

One of the enemies advancing from the opposite side had already reached the alley, and her allies couldn't be far behind her. As she raised her gun, I realised my time would soon come. All I could do was make one last stand and try to drag as many of them into the darkness with me before the life drained from my cursed body. I'd been born into a bloody fate and reborn through violence, so it was only fitting it should end this way I supposed.

I boldly locked gazes with my would-be killer as I prepared for my final battle, expecting her to squeeze the trigger at any moment. We could have been frozen in time then as the minutes dragged on, yet she didn't shoot. A flicker of something passed across her eyes. Uncertainty perhaps?

From the other side of the wall came the shouts of the others. It seemed they knew she was already in position and could guess something had stalled her, because one of them was screaming "Take the shot! What are you waiting for?"

The woman seemed not to hear and I thought I could guess what was holding her back. She'd joined the Slayers to fight the monsters that had probably taken someone close to her, but even though I still presented a horrific sight with my naked skin stained with so much blood, I still looked human in form. I didn't look as much the monster I would've been if I'd changed back to either my full wolf or hybrid form. No, it seemed this woman was far from the psychopath Aughtie had been. Her empathy allowed her to see only the fifteen year old boy, and realising that I was careful to keep my features as human as possible, letting the bestial snarl that came so easily melt back into my human face.

"Take the shot!" a man yelled at her again. "Come on you silly cow, take the shot!"

The gun began to shake in the woman's hand and I knew it was time to make my move, while her inner conflict still raged. So I lunged forward, the movement causing her to squeeze the trigger in reflex but her hands were shaking so badly that her aim was completely off. For once the bullet didn't come anywhere near to hitting me.

I landed on the woman, pinning her gun down with one hand and striking her with my other. My hunger roared for her blood but for once reason ruled me, so I left her lying unconscious and intact, and I resumed my flight just as the other Slayers caught up. They swore when they realised what had happened and more bullets tore through the darkness as I ran, but having healed the damage from the hit I'd taken to my shoulder, I was able to move fast enough to avoid any more wounds that night.

Free of the trap the humans had tried to ensnare me in, I made my way back to the open countryside once more. The Slayers couldn't cut me off quick enough and there was nothing they could do to keep me in the labyrinth of streets where they might have backed me into another corner. My feet left the rough surface of the tarmac and the concrete, landing on the soothing softness of grass which felt much more pleasant, despite the hard soil beneath. It looked like I might survive the night after all.

The powerful, wintry winds were more noticeable out in the open than they had been in the town, especially to my naked human form. I'd not dared to head straight back to the moors where Lady Sarah hopefully waited for me, for fear of leading the Slayers there, and my current direction had taken me so far out from the town that I was nearing another rural village. I knew it would be safer to keep to the wilderness and find some natural cover, but I was beginning to tremble with cold and exhaustion, and the warm glow of buildings in the darkness looked so inviting.

I became aware of music blasting out from one of these buildings; a pub set a little way out from the houses, but just within staggering distance for the locals. Despite the fact it could be no more than a couple of miles from the village itself, there was a remoteness about the pub that instantly drew me to it, though I should've known better. I was so cold I just wanted to feel the comfort of human shelter, greater than any nature could offer me, and the man-made warmth and light. And besides, I knew that song they were playing; it had been a favourite once. One of Metallica's rather than Alice Cooper but still an awesome song, and suddenly I felt a yet greater longing for the life I'd left behind. I suddenly realised how much I missed drinking (on the few occasions I'd been allowed alcohol, underage as I was) and my music. Then the song ended and I turned away, as if coming to my senses, until a new song started, another I knew. Whatever this place was they were playing rock and metal: my kind of music. The irony; I used to moan at the lack of good music anywhere when I was free to come and go in human places as I pleased, but now I was forced to live as an outsider I'd discovered not one but two pubs playing exactly what I wanted to hear, and I wouldn't be able to frequent either often enough to enjoy it. As it was, I found myself unable to resist the allure of this pub and the offer of a temporary return to my old way of life. No matter how dangerous, the temptation was just too much.

As if the music placed a spell on me as powerful as the call of the full moon to my lupine half, I found myself approaching the front of the building. The helicopter hadn't continued to follow me since their trap had fallen through, and a part of me wanted to believe I would be safe inside, sheltered from both my pursuers and the elements, at least till the pub closed. I felt like that dream of a human life held me in its grip once more, so strong that I forgot about my feral appearance, wishing only to be a part of the human world I'd known seemingly so long ago. So I pushed open the door and took that final step inside, knowing it was too late to turn back then.

The inside of the pub had been lively with the banter and laughter of the locals, but the moment I entered silence immediately fell, broken only by the sound of someone receiving a text. It was only a small pub but there were still around fifteen to twenty humans crammed inside, propping up the bar or crowded round the small tables, nursing pints of beer and cider. Every one of them turned to stare at me framed in the doorway.

Too late, I remembered I was still naked and covered in blood. Living with lycanthropy for over a year had removed any inhibitions I'd had about being nude in public, and I made no attempt to cover myself. But I was conscious of my bloodstained skin which revealed me for the monster I truly was.

"Oh my God, you poor boy!" the landlady cried, grabbing a blanket from beneath the bar and rushing forward to wrap it round me. To the drinkers she snapped "Stop staring at him!"

I hadn't expected to be treated with kindness after having seen so much of the darkness of humanity, and given my current appearance. But it seemed she had immediately assumed the blood was my own, and as with the female Slayer who'd hesitated to shoot me, she saw only the adolescent boy of my physical form, not the monster. And I looked young enough for her mothering instincts to kick in.

"Now you take a seat here by the fire and warm up. Whatever were you doing out in the cold, and where are your parents?"

"Dead," I lied.

"Oh I'm sorry, love," she said. "All this blood; how did you hurt yourself?"

I remained silent. The emptiness gaped ever wider in my soul, all the more noticeable now for the brief mingling of my two personalities, which had allowed me to briefly feel the bloodlust once more. That darker, brutal side of my nature awakened by the curse was better than this nothingness I'd fallen into, but with my mind firmly split back into the two separate personalities of boy and wolf it lay out of my reach once more, and the emptiness that belonged to my human half resumed its reign. It must have given me a haunted look, for the landlady didn't press me for any more information at that point, instead bringing me a glass of water and then returning to her place behind the bar.

"And what do you plan to do with the boy now?" one of the men asked her. He spoke quietly, but with my sensitive ears I had no trouble hearing every word that was said.

"I couldn't just turn him away Jim; the street's no place for children. He looks like he's been through Hell."

"There's something not right about him," Jim insisted. "Covered in blood like that – he should be dead by now if it's really all his. And what happened to his clothes? Something is very wrong here; we shouldn't get involved. At least call the authorities and let them deal with it."

"He doesn't even look sixteen yet. I won't turn away an innocent boy," she said stubbornly.

I stared down at my drink while they talked, wishing it was something stronger, but I lost track of the conversation when one of the other humans approached my table. I looked up and was shocked to find it was Luke, the same guy who'd found me that day I was out hunting in the area near the barn Lady Sarah had been hidden in.

"You again," I said in a low voice. "How did you find me this time?"

"Never mind that. I know you're in trouble and I know the people hunting you have been out in force tonight."

"How can you possibly know about the Slayers? Have you been following me too?"

"There's no time for questions now. I meant what I said before, I want to help you."

"Why? I already told you I can't pass on the curse."

He shrugged. "I'm a fan of werewolves. A werewolf friend is cooler than nothing, even if I can't be a werewolf myself. Let me help you."

I was still wary, and I became aware of eyes on me. Jim and the landlady were casting me suspicious looks, but I pretended not to notice. "It's not safe, you'll only be putting yourself in danger. Should we even be talking? I've already caused a stir with my inhuman appearance. The fact that there just happens to be someone here who seems to know me is only going to raise more questions."

"Maybe, but I think you have bigger problems. See over there, that guy sat right by the door? He's one of the Slayers."

"And how could you possibly know that?"

"Use your nose if you don't believe me," he answered impatiently. "Surely you must be able to smell the gunpowder with your wolfish senses."

I glanced across at the man Luke had indicated and tried to be subtle about scenting the air. There was something there I thought I recognised as a scent I'd noticed around guns before, but if he was indeed a Slayer then why hadn't he made a move and why were there not more of them? Unless he just happened to be in the pub that night and it was coincidence we'd crossed paths. I assumed they must take nights off hunting us since they easily had the numbers to patrol in shifts and they had to sleep some time, but even if he was just in his local for a pint he must know who and what I was which still made him a threat, especially if he'd come out armed. Then I remembered the text I'd heard come through as I'd entered and the thought crossed my mind that even if he had been on his own enjoying a night off, he could well still be in contact with others in the area. They could be moving into position for another co-ordinated attack even as I sat there thinking about it.

"I should go," I said.

"Don't you think it's too late for that?"

"And what would you have me do, attack him? I'd have to kill them all, or at least incapacitate them and leave the wounded for the Slayers to deal with in the cover up."

"You already have blood on your hands, what does a little more matter?"

"Why do you care?" I asked suspiciously.

"Maybe I just want to see you in action," he replied with a sly grin.

Before I could ask him anything else, something drew my attention back to the humans at the bar.

"Don't say I didn't warn you Janet," Jim was saying to the landlady. "I'm off. I want no part in this. It's getting late now, anyway."

The man turned to leave, glaring at me as he headed for the door. The warmth of the pub might have chased the numbness from my limbs, but I still felt cold and dead inside, and this latest brush with humanity wasn't helping. Lost in the music when I'd first approached the pub, a part of me had dared to hope I could re-join the human world, if only for a matter of hours. Had I been thinking clearly I'd have realised that, aside from my nakedness and bloodied body, I would've been out of place due to my apparent age and lateness of the hour. If the curse hadn't halted the ageing process with the constant regeneration of cells every time I transformed, maybe I could've passed for eighteen, but as it was, even clean and fully clothed I would still have been treated as an outsider. It didn't matter. The reaction of the locals only served as a harsh reminder that I would never be one of them again. I was the outsider and would be forever more, and whatever hopes had been called forth by the rock and metal music I once loved now fell into that gaping chasm of my soul, leaving me emptier than ever. There only remained the bloodlust, and with the full moon still overhead maybe it would allow me to tap into it this time and lose myself in it once again.

"Do it," Luke mouthed at me, as if he could read my thoughts.

I glanced at the Slayer still sat by the door, but he remained impassive, giving no sign he'd recognised me or intended to mount his own attack. Maybe Luke was mistaken and he wasn't one of them after all. In any case, he didn't seem a threat in that moment so I didn't make a move straight for him. If there was to be more bloodshed that night then I would start with this man, Jim.

I cast off the blanket like I cast off my brief pretence at humanity and leapt from my seat, crashing into the man before any of the others had chance to react, my weariness all but forgotten. He landed face down with me crouched over him, but managed to kick out, dislodging me long enough to twist around in an attempt to defend himself. If I'd been mortal he would probably have succeeded in fending me off, but with my supernatural strength it was all too easy to pin him back down.

"Your instincts were right, I am a monster," I whispered into his ear, before balling my hands into fists and proceeding to beat his head into the wooden floor. I tried so hard to be angry, to act as violently as I knew how so the bloodlust could take over again. I hit him hard and fast with all of my unnatural speed and strength. The instant my fist connected the blood ran down and he started to gurgle, blood streaming from his eyes, his nose, his mouth. He was already choking on his own blood. His nose was a mess, his teeth falling out, his eyes bruised and bloody. That first blow would have been enough to keep him down while I dealt with the others, but I continued to hit him until his head caved in from the impact and he lay twitching, brains exploding out from his ruined skull. Yet still the dark pleasures I so desperately sought remained lost in the nothingness within.

Out of the corner of my eye I was aware of Luke quietly egging me on. Shock held some of the others frozen in place but a couple of younger men around Luke's age had taken their phones out to film the violence, while others rushed over in an attempt to pull me off of Jim.

I roared and lashed out at one of the first to grab me, sending him crashing into a nearby table. His head struck the edge of it, fracturing his skull and rendering him unconsciousness. I sunk fangs into the arm of a second man, ripping away a chunk of flesh and causing him to fall back, clutching his arm and screaming in agony.

It was in that moment the Slayer finally made his move, while everyone else's attention was on me. He stood and I heard him slide the bolt across the doors, before shoving the table over to bar them. That wouldn't be enough to keep me in the building but I assumed he meant to slow me, giving him longer to attempt to make a killing shot.

And with the first of my victims to go down, it was then that the screaming started and chaos ensued.

Most of them began to run for the door but I caught several with ease, ripping limbs from their sockets with my bare hands and splattering blood over the walls, floor and ceiling. It sprayed out in high arcs and gushed to form pools round my feet and the carcasses I was quickly surrounded with. Others would have made it to salvation, if it hadn't been for the makeshift barrier slowing them down and the Slayer himself. They desperately tried to push the table out of the way, only for the man to cut them down with a long knife he'd somehow concealed in his jacket. Bodies piled up and added to the blockage by the main escape route.

Some had the sense to try and call for help on their mobile phones but they barely had time to dial the emergency services before I intervened, crushing their phones and then their lives. Some merely cowered under the tables and prayed I would pass them by, but there was nowhere to hide and I would spare none of them.

Only Luke stayed in his seat, watching the horrific events unfolding as if this was no more than a horror movie to be enjoyed. I sensed no fear or revulsion from him in the face of such bloody murders, and he didn't seem worried I might turn on him. He had spoken the truth about the Slayer at least since the man had shown himself to be one of my enemies, for who else could he be? It was only a matter of time before we faced each other, but until he made a move to attack I would continue slaughtering in an attempt to summon the bloodlust.

One woman tried to run past but I swiped at her with a clawed, mostly human hand, carving deep furrows across her abdomen. She crashed to the floor where she lay screaming in agony, blood welling up in the gouges I'd made in her flesh. It soaked through her top and spilled onto the floor, mixing with the pools already made from my other victims.

Despite the agony of her wounds and the growing barrier by the door, she tried to claw her way to the main exit, whimpering with fear at her agonisingly slow progress as much as with the pain. There was no way she could have found the strength to break through that way, but she struggled on regardless, only to be pulled back to the slaughter when I roughly grabbed her legs, digging my claws into that smooth flesh as I dragged her back to me.

I dug my hands into the gashes my claws had made and pulled until muscle tore and blood gushed more freely, my hands slick with that crimson life force as I grabbed hold of slippery guts and ripped them out, trying to find savage joy in such brutality. But still I felt nothing, even as her body convulsed violently before growing still in death's embrace.

Others soon realised running for the door was a lost cause, and they grabbed the chairs to try and break the windows so they could clamber out of this abattoir. But between myself and the Slayer, none lived long enough to create another escape route.

A man found the courage to charge at me with an empty glass in hand, swinging it at my head. I caught it with ease and tore the glass from his grasp, throwing it aside where it landed amidst the carnage, broken glass shattering over the broken bodies. The man's courage failed him and he whimpered, which soon turned to a scream as I plunged a hand into his chest, grabbing his heart and pulling it free. I bit into the slimy organ as his body collapsed to the floor, fresh blood oozing out and spilling down my jaws. Then it was just me and the Slayer, and Luke who still sat taking it all in, though he was now splattered with blood just as I was. The Slayer was also covered in the blood of innocents, a reminder that he and those like him were every bit the monster I was.

The Slayer drew his gun and took aim, but there was a grim look to him that suggested he expected to die. I wondered if he'd meant to sacrifice himself all along, so as to buy time for the large force hunting me to move in. If they had the place surrounded they stood more chance of killing me than he ever would have done alone. But just as I wasn't prepared to go down without a fight, I guessed it was the same for him and he succeeded in firing off three shots before I was on him. None of them hit me and he didn't bother with Luke either, which seemed strange when he'd been so intent on helping me butcher everyone else in there. Not that it really mattered in that moment. I was too focussed on savaging him, until the last agonised breath rattled through his body, almost leaving that same stillness and quiet as the one which had immediately followed my last massacre of the children, if it hadn't been for Luke and the music still coming from the speakers. Still the bloodlust had not taken me as it had under the full moon's influence just hours earlier, and with another bestial roar I fell to my knees, defeated.

"Are you really so lost that you must continue to kill, even after confirming it won't waken your bloodlust?"

I opened my eyes to find the vision of Lizzy stood over me once more. Maybe vision was too grand a word for the product of my own tortured mind as I teetered on the brink of insanity once again, no more than a hallucination to give voice to my innermost thoughts.

"What else is there for me now?" I said bitterly. "My life has no purpose, so I might as well turn to death."

"You who could be so great yet you continue to wallow in self-pity and slaughter needlessly. You have lost your way. Find new purpose, find the path you must walk, and perhaps at the end of it you will resurrect those emotions you believe dead to you."

"Like the real you ever talked with such wisdom," I growled and swiped at the image. She vanished as soon as my bloodied hand passed through her. With the hallucination gone, I realised the pub wasn't as completely still and quiet as I'd thought. From behind the bar I could hear the pounding of another heart in the grip of fear, and a faint whimpering. Still on my knees, I rose and strode round the bar, to find the landlady, Janet, cowering beneath it.

"Please," she pleaded. "Please don't kill me. I have a family. It's the season of goodwill to all men, please."

Only then did I notice the little Christmas tree in the corner. Time had long since lost all meaning and I'd had no idea it was that season again, too lost in my own inner darkness to think about what time of year it might be. The knowledge only added to my sense of longing for my old life. I should've been back home with Mum and Amy, trying to guess what the wrapped presents under the tree could possibly hold and counting down the days till we could open them. Christmas Day would've been a time for double the celebrations, since it would also be my seventeenth birthday, despite the fact my body was still stuck at fifteen. I turned back to Janet.

"I'm not a man," I said, letting a growl creep into my voice and my eyes turn to amber. Before she even had chance to scream I snapped her neck, as quick and painless a death as I could manage in return for the kindness she'd shown me, but in no mood to let her live.

With the last of the locals dead I helped myself to a beer and sat for a while in the warmth, listening to the music and talking to Luke. But there wasn't even any pleasure to be had in that. The beer didn't mix well with the taste of blood so thick on my tongue, and the air was thick with the smell of the latest bloodbath I'd created, the room a gory mess no matter where I looked. Dead eyes seemed to bore into me, still wide with terror, mouths still fixed in silent screams. Severed limbs reduced to no more than meaty bones lay scattered around, one with a hand still attached looking like it was reaching out to me, as if its owner was pleading for mercy. Guts lay strewn around, intestines like macabre party streamers and, with some imagination, other organs could have been balloons. And yet I could find no enjoyment in the bloody festivities I'd created.

Luke couldn't offer much comfort either. He still seemed to be in awe of me, exclaiming "Wow man, that was the coolest thing I've ever seen!"

"I'm glad you enjoyed it," I growled.

"Really, you didn't? You looked to be having a good enough time of things."

"I told you before, you don't want this life. The curse has taken everything from me, even my ability to feel things normally like most people. There was a savage joy to be had in all this for a while but even that seems gone now. This was a mistake, I should never have come here."

"Don't be too hard on yourself, bro. That Slayer killed almost as many as you. He seemed a bit psycho to me; who's to say he wouldn't have killed them all on his own if you hadn't been here?"

I shook my head but didn't reply and we fell quiet. I didn't even care about all the unanswered questions I had for him at that point, like how he just happened to be in the pub and how he knew there was a Slayer in the room, or even how he knew who the Slayers were to begin with. None of it really seemed to matter in the aftermath of all the carnage.

I forced down more of my pint but I'd only managed half of it before the gruesome decorations became too much, and I didn't recognise the latest song blaring through the speakers. There was nothing more for me in that place, not even the warmth bringing me any comfort in the wake of this latest atrocity I'd committed. So I allowed the transformation to take hold, though I only took it halfway again. I chose to spend the remainder of the night in that most monstrous form between boy and wolf, because a monster was what I truly was.

Despite my earlier concerns about changing while it was still the night of the full moon, the human half of me remained in control. I still needed to feed and replenish my energy, so I ate my fill from the bodies surrounding me while Luke continued to sit enraptured by the impossible sights taking place right before his eyes.

The first corpse I ate from was the man who'd turned out to be a Slayer. A phone fell from his pocket as I ripped through parts of him still left intact from the initial attack, and with some difficulty I grasped it in my clawed hands. I didn't really know what I hoped to find and there wasn't much that made sense to me or gave me any fresh insight into how my enemies worked, but I did find the text he'd received when I'd first entered. The chilling message read 'Target entering your location. Contain the damage.'

So that was the real reason why he'd joined me in the slaughter and taken measures to prevent anyone escaping. It hadn't been to slow me down so reinforcements could have another shot at me before I had chance to lose them again, and his death hadn't been a noble sacrifice for the countless lives that would be saved if they did succeed in killing me. No, the Slayers seemed to have given up on killing me that night, perhaps feeling the need for a rethink of tactics after I'd slipped through another of their traps. The events in the pub had all been about keeping their precious secret from the rest of mankind, nothing more.

Once I'd eaten, I grabbed the blanket Janet had wrapped me in when I'd first entered. I'd already lingered too long and there were probably more Slayers on the way, who obviously felt a pile of dead bodies was easier to cover up than dealing with any living witnesses. I didn't feel like fighting my way through more of them that night.

I said nothing to Luke as I prowled over to the doorway. I wasn't sure why I was letting him live when I'd just killed so many others and I still didn't trust him. A part of me wanted to place my trust in him, I think, but something about him didn't feel right and I had enough sense to listen to my gut, for the time being at least. I could feel his eyes on me as I left, but he also remained silent.

The winter seemed all the harsher when I ventured back out, even with my fur coat. But at least the blanket would provide some added warmth when I eventually settled down to sleep. It was a small comfort and one I didn't really feel I deserved, but I knew I would be grateful for any added defence against the cold once I was back on the moors. So I kept the one Christmas present I would receive that year, forcing myself to focus on finding my way back to Lady Sarah and trying to forget the carnage I'd left behind.

Chapter Thirteen – Anger Rekindled

Even though the Slayers probably had some kind of clean up crew in each area to hide their activities and evidence of our existence from the rest of the world, there was no evidence of any nearby humans when I stepped out of the pub. It seemed it was safe to head for the patch of moorland where I hoped I'd find Lady Sarah, so I made my way back there.

She had indeed decided to return to the area and wait for me, and to say she was not happy at my reckless decision to run off on my own was an understatement.

"You fool," she hissed. "How can I protect you when you continue to be so reckless?"

"Why do you care?" I retorted. "It seems like the rest of your race hates me. Why are you so interested in helping me?"

"After giving up so many of my nights training you, I'm not about to abandon you now."

"And what would you do with those nights if I wasn't around?" I pressed.

"This is a discussion for another night," she said, and I knew better than to push her when she was already angry with me. So I let her change the subject. "What happened after you left me feeding? How many did you kill?"

"It was weird, the wolf left you wanting to make another kill and feed on more fresh meat, but then I blacked out and when I came to I had this weird feeling like I was both human and wolf at the same time. There was a body lying nearby so I ate, but I seemed to have shifted at least partially and my hunger was stronger again. I went off in search of more prey but everything was confused, until finally the human me was in control again and my body was completely human."

"Your two identities merged as I've been urging you to do, but without the mental preparation it was too much," she said, somewhat calmer now. "This is normal, but as you were not prepared you returned to a more manageable mental state. However, it is unusual that your human half asserted himself given the phase of the moon, even if it was hidden behind thick cloud cover."

"Well whatever the reason, when I came to my senses I knew I should try to find you, so I went back to where we made our first kill. But then the Slayers found me," I continued, but then hesitated. I knew she wouldn't approve if I gave her the full tale of the night's events, but I had a feeling she'd find out anyway. Though I'd not sensed any other undead around while I was indulging the darkness of

132

my human side, they were sure to be watching after the murder of the vampire the previous month, and they were obviously in contact with Lady Sarah since they'd ordered her to bring me to the meeting they'd called. "It seemed they'd set a trap for us, or at least for me. I don't know if you slipped away before they could move in on you as well. I escaped and managed to lose them before I came back here but I couldn't resist the temptation to kill again. I was drawn to this local pub, almost in the middle of nowhere if it hadn't been for the little village down the road. There was a Slayer in there but I killed him and I made sure there were no others lurking outside. I left no witnesses."

"Fool!" she said again, but she kept her temper in check this time. "The Slayers may well renew their efforts now you've given them good reason to. I had hoped if we went far enough a field we could minimise the risks. But after this latest slaughter I would not be surprised if they decide to actively hunt us again, instead of waiting for us to reappear in a populated area and setting another trap. I believe the moon will affect you as normal these next two nights, but once the full moon has passed we must resume your lessons and make the most of the time we have here, before we are forced to continue our flight and seek out a new safe haven."

I wasn't happy to hear her say that but there didn't seem much point in arguing. I supposed I should be grateful she didn't insist in continuing on that night, and I was glad to settle down to rest after the night's exertions. The floor was still hard, cold, and uncomfortable, but at least I had a blanket to curl up in. Sleep came a little easier, and I surrendered myself to the usual nightmares.

The next night I experienced the normal full moon transformation as Lady Sarah had predicted. After the unpleasant experience of our identities merging during the previous night, I gladly sank into the darkness of our subconscious, where I would be dead to the world until the new day dawned.

It was too dangerous for us to hunt anywhere near the same area we'd gone to feed in the night before, but Lady Sarah still considered it a possibility that I could be the killer of the two vampires who'd been found savaged. And if she couldn't help me satisfy my bloodlust on mortals, she feared I might take a third undead victim. She decided the safest option this time was to find a farm and steal cattle, hoping if she covered our tracks the attack would go unnoticed by the Slayers.

My control was greater after a night of being allowed to gorge myself, even if the human did most of the killing and feasting on their flesh, but still I hungered for humans over animals. And it was more than just the desires caused by the curse now: the more insight I gained into their species, the more I grew to hate them.

They would condemn an entire predatory species just for being predators. Preying upon a human carried a death sentence, regardless of the beast in question, close to extinction or not. And yet, their own species could take other human lives in cold blood and still be allowed to live. Granted, they may spend some time behind bars, but often, it seemed, they were released on supposed good behaviour, only to repeat past crimes. How could they justify culling any animal they deemed to be a problem species, when they were so loathe to take the lives of human killers who were arguably more dangerous, and a much bigger threat? The thought angered me, though I was determined not to take any more lives other than those I needed to survive. I was better than them. I was better than the human half of me, who, true to its nature, had just last night indulged in mindless slaughter to feed that darker side of humanity that lurked in every last one of their wretched species.

They wouldn't even allow the sick and the disabled a dignified death through assisted suicide, if they so wished it, despite the fact their numbers just kept on growing, at the expense of every other creature on the planet. Ultimately, all they caused was death and destruction, to themselves and their environment, or so it seemed to me. They should have been thanking the likes of myself and Lady Sarah for helping to keep their numbers down, and restoring some natural balance in doing so, but instead they'd hunted us to near extinction, like so many of the world's natural predators.

I found myself hating them more than ever, and the idea of joining with the human half of my mind to become one again filled me with disgust. The brief collapse and merging of our separate identities that we'd experienced the previous night had only served to force us further apart once more, which would be much to Lady Sarah's dismay I was sure. But I was grateful to remain free of all those traits the human possessed which I despised, and virtually untainted from them. The curse might set me apart from any other mortal wolf, in that I would always crave human flesh rather than our natural prey, and I would always need more to satisfy my unnatural hunger, but I would fight to stay true to our nature and apart from the human, even if it meant never finding peace with myself.

As if Lady Sarah knew what I was thinking, once again in her wolf form, she muzzled me to remind me of my place. As much as I hated the limitations she placed upon me when it came to feeding, I knew her methods were the best chance for our survival. As long as I didn't lose control under the full moon again I would remain by her side and feed as permitted. There was more than one reason I'd chosen to see her as my alpha, and it wasn't purely because of the greater speed and strength of powerful members of her race such as she.

We'd set off in the opposite direction to the night before and found a farm she deemed to be a great enough distance from where we'd been sighted to offer as safe a feeding ground as possible. Lady Sarah ordered me to wait just downwind and out of sight of the cattle so as not to cause the herd to panic, while she slunk under the fence to select our meal.

Again she used her hypnotic powers to keep the animals from panicking, which seemed to be just as effective on the livestock as it was on humans. For not only was she able to lead the largest specimen away from the rest of the herd in her human form, she also kept the others docile while she did so. This meant we avoided detection by the farmer.

She fed on the cow first but didn't drain all its blood as it was so much bigger than a human. Still, the cow was dead when she'd finished and she carried the carcass with ease back to where I waited. The meat wasn't completely dried out like her smaller kills and I was able to enjoy the meal, even if it wasn't the human flesh I craved. It would have been more satisfactory to answer the moon's call and make the kill myself, of course, but compared to some of the other miserable nights where I'd had to feed on less desirable prey, and not entirely satisfy the hunger, it was an acceptable compromise. Once I'd stripped the bones of meat we buried the carcass, then returned to the moors without encountering any humans, Slayer or otherwise.

We risked managing our hungers in the same way the following night, but after burying what was left of our latest kill we were not permitted to spend the remaining hours of darkness as we pleased.

Our heads turned as one to the sound of approaching footsteps. I growled, expecting another fight with the Slayers, but then I caught his scent and realised he was another vampire. He stalked forward cautiously, deliberately allowing us to sense his approach so as not to catch us off-guard. He was wary of me, it seemed. And though he addressed Lady Sarah, he kept his eyes on me as if he thought I'd suddenly lunge at him.

"Lady Sarah," he said, with a respectful nod of his head. "I've been ordered to bring you and the... wolf to another meeting."

I was no fool. I knew he'd hesitated before settling on wolf because he'd wanted to insult me, but had clearly thought better of it. I growled louder, tempted to attack him even though I knew I wouldn't win in a fair fight – it was doubtful one of the lowly vampires would act as a messenger with the recent murder, so I had to assume he was at least as strong and powerful as Lady Sarah, if not more so. Unlike the human, I knew better than to give into that temptation, so I held my ground.

"Why, what's happened now?" she asked him.

"Come, and you will see for yourself. Ulfarr didn't make it a request."

She glanced at me, clearly worried for my safety, but obviously felt we had little option but to go back to the abandoned warehouse.

"We should do as he says," she said to me, a warning in her eyes. I knew what that warning meant – follow and for God's sake don't run off! But she

135

daren't vocalise that warning and reveal I'd been left to my own devices at all. Not when the rest of her kind already distrusted me.

Whether it was because the male vampire didn't possess the ability to shapeshift, or due to his feelings towards werewolves, he led us away in human form, so Lady Sarah followed suit. I bounded along just behind them, forced to run at a full sprint to keep up, but well fed enough that it wasn't a struggle to maintain that pace as it had been with the Slayers on the trail of the human, when the bullet wound and unexpected transformation had weakened us. The night was still fairly young when we reached the vampire's chosen meeting place.

We were led inside, the Elder vampire again stood at the opposite end of the building ready to address his audience, but this time the rest of the gathering had yet to arrive. He beckoned us over and dismissed the other male vampire. I could sense Lady Sarah was uneasy and I remained alert, most of my senses focussed on Ulfarr but also keeping an ear cocked for any sounds of danger outside.

The Elder's eyes had been fixed on me from the moment we'd appeared in the doorway, making no attempt to hide his hatred and distrust for a werewolf once again. I growled at him, but the moment I bared my fangs he turned the full force of his power as an Elder on my mind. Instantly I was frozen in place as if paralysed, unable to attack, even if I'd truly been intending to.

"You remember our last conversation, Lady Sarah, and my promise of what would happen if I found you were lying to me?" Ulfarr asked her, but his eyes never left me, his control never lifting.

"Please Ulfarr, I swear to you I have spoken only the truth," she said. There was a hint of fear in her voice which put me on edge, powerless to act though I currently was.

"Yes, you also swore to me he is not the killer," he hissed, and she flinched as if he'd physically struck her. "You claimed you could account for his actions under the full moon, and yet the Slayers were out in force just two nights past hunting this same beast, who by all accounts was alone, running rampant in a town. Did you really think all of this would escape my notice?"

Lady Sarah remained silent. I hoped she was calculating, but there was something different about her now. Before she'd defended me, putting her life on the line in the process, but that night she was subdued. I still didn't understand exactly how vampires worked since they were solitary predators for the most part, but if they'd been pack animals I would've said he was her alpha and she was clearly unwilling to challenge his dominance over her this time. Perhaps it was because, in his current mood, he was likely to make good on his threat to execute the both of us. Whatever the reason, she made no attempt to defend either of us.

"Be grateful I am feeling generous enough to spare your life, for now, but do not test me or that may change," he said, before finally turning his attention to me. "You may not be so lucky, dog."

Silently I strained against his control over my body but it was no use — he was too powerful. If Lady Sarah could hold me under her spell, what hope did I have against an Elder vampire, one who was clearly among the most powerful of his race? For he had to be considered all powerful in the vampire world to command so much respect.

The same male vampire who'd brought us to the warehouse reappeared, carrying something which he laid on the workbench as before, with the utmost respect. Adrenalin flooded through me in response to my fight or flight instincts when I realised it was another body, the sheet covering it bloody this time, the stench of decay worse than that of a human corpse, making it hard to tell how long the body had been truly dead, or even how many centuries old the vampire had been. Lady Sarah had moved out of my sight and, still held in place by the Elder vampire, I couldn't see her reaction to the latest body.

Moments later the first of the vampires and ghouls began to arrive, and Ulfarr forced me to jump up on the workbench beside him and turn to face them, before freezing me in place once more. When the last of those he was expecting filtered in, he greeted them in a similar fashion to the first meeting he'd called, wasting no time explaining why he'd called them back.

"There has been another murder, a third vampire felled by another undead. You will recall I promised to find the killer and bring him to justice, and that is the very reason I've called you all back here today," he said, his eyes settling on me as, after a brief pause, he continued "And thus, I give you the murderer!"

Suddenly he released his hold on me but his mind brushed against my own, reaching out to various parts of my nature – namely my hunger and bloodlust – as if beckoning to them. Both had been controllable after feeding so well this full moon but he called to them, exerting a power over me as complete as that of the moon itself. Enslaved to my most primal instincts once more I let out an angry, threatening growl and readied myself to fall on the masses, wanting to indulge in the same mindless slaughter that the human part of me committed time and again. No matter how much I hated it for such acts, the bloodlust was tied to that part of the human, and that in turn was tied to the curse and my unnatural hunger brought on by each full moon. When I truly lost control I could no more fight it than the human could fight the transformation induced by the full moon, and I'd just had that control ripped from me by the Elder vampire.

As powerful as the vampires were, uncertainty rippled through the crowd. The ghouls were ready to flee, knowing they stood no chance against me with the power of the moon overhead and my own bloodlust driving me. In my most mindless state I would become a force of raw power and fury, virtually unstoppable unless one of them could deliver a killing blow. Even vampires with the same level of power as Lady Sarah were unsure of their chances against me, knowing their ability to hypnotise victims would be useless whilst I was at my most primal. However, I never had chance to attack, finding myself frozen in place again, though this time it was different to the mind control Ulfarr had placed me under before. Meanwhile, the

Elder vampire just laughed.

"You should have more faith in your Elders. Did you really think I would present him to you for a trial without taking any precautions?"

As he talked I found myself forced into the transformation back to human. If I hadn't been so overwhelmingly in the grip of the bloodlust, I would have been afraid then. Ulfarr was demonstrating how he was more powerful than the moon, and just as I was still very much a slave to the full moon and my own primal instincts, I was no more than a mere puppet to him either. He could kill me at any moment he pleased with no more effort than it took to lift a finger, and he probably would before the night was through, but first he wanted to enjoy humiliating me in front of his audience.

The change was the most violent I'd ever experienced, pure agony even compared with my first transformation just over a year earlier. Despite the higher pain threshold I'd developed, it was so intense that it was no longer the Elder vampire's hold over me keeping me frozen in place, but the pain itself, and I couldn't help but cry out. If I'd been in human form I'd have been screaming, but instead, as my lupine self, my cries were the canid high pitched yelps and whines of an animal in suffering. The crowd only jeered at my cries. Even the ghouls joined in, though they had no reason to share the vampires' prejudice against me, as far as I knew.

My innards seemed to twist and writhe as if they'd turned to snakes. Breathing was painful, each breath shallow and quick as if my lungs were damaged and unable to fill to their full capacity. My chest felt tight, my heart hammering against my ribcage in an irregular rhythm, seemingly struggling to continue to pump the blood boiling in my veins round the rest of my body. Bones ground together as they grew shorter while others lengthened, and there was a blow to my spine where it reversed direction, becoming convex. Just as I felt like my body would be ripped apart by this brutal transformation the Elder vampire was forcing me through, it stopped. I knelt on humanoid hands and knees panting heavily, weakened enough that I couldn't immediately attack the crowd as I still wanted to.

Ulfarr clicked his fingers purely for show, using telekinesis to move the chains which suddenly whipped up to bind me, shackles snapping shut round my wrists and ankles. The chains binding my arms wrapped themselves round hooks in the wall, forcing me to my feet so the assembled undead could see me clearly, now in my hybrid form and straining against my chains with renewed fury, snapping at the air and howling and snarling in frustration.

"You see, werewolves would have us believe they are like us, and indeed have even convinced some of us of this over the years," the Elder vampire said. "But, no matter how civilised they can be, they will never be anything more than savage beasts at heart, a danger to all others, living or undead. The Slayers have done us a favour hunting them to extinction; it's time we put this last dog down before he turns on any more of us."

138

There were calls of agreement from our audience, but I was too lost in my instincts to really be aware of what was happening. Ulfarr turned to me and again took control of my body, forcing my jaws shut, as he placed a hand on my shoulder as if to calm me. I felt his mind brush my own once more and he swept all my rage and bloodlust away as if they were no more than cobwebs, restoring my self-control. The hunger was there after being forced to transform, but it was manageable once more. Then he forced my body to resume the transformation, this time forcing me all the way back to human, and calling the human half of my mind back to the surface. I blacked out temporarily from the pain, the human back in control when I regained consciousness…

As the room swam back into focus I became aware of the same Elder vampire we'd met the previous month speaking to someone. My brain slowly registered the chains holding me upright, in front of a crowd of undead. I realised I was in the same warehouse the last meeting had been held in, and instinctively looked for Lady Sarah. It didn't take long for my eyes to settle on her in the first row. She was staring up at me in horror, but had made no move to put a stop to any of this.

"Beast!" Ulfarr repeated, commandingly. I realised he was talking to me and looked away from Lady Sarah, letting my eyes focus on him. "Have you nothing to say for yourself?"

I felt the wolf stir in my subconscious, filling in the blanks for me only out of concern for our self-preservation, the memories shared almost with the thought of 'don't screw this up'.

"I didn't do it," I said, even though I knew it was entirely possible I'd killed more than just the human victim when I'd blacked out two nights ago due to the brief merging of our split personalities. I looked back to Lady Sarah for help but she continued to just stand there. Why wasn't she defending me like she had before? And why was she letting them torment me like this?

"Lies," the Elder hissed, his hatred rearing its ugly head again. He was about to say something more when another male vampire spoke up.

"What proof do you have, Ulfarr? I for one would like to see some evidence as to why you are so convinced the werewolf is to blame."

"I have a name," I growled, but no one was paying me any attention anymore.

"Both murders happened during the full moon and they were torn apart as if savaged by a beast," the Elder vampire answered. "What else could it have been?"

"You allow your prejudice to blind you, Ulfarr. The timing could be coincidence, and we all know there are more than just werewolves that would attack with such savagery. The work of demons, perhaps?"

"Demons have not been this active on Earth since the rise of the Slayers, as you well know," the Elder vampire replied impatiently.

"That may be, but the possibility exists, no matter how slim, and it is but one possibility. I for one would like to see some proof the werewolf really is to blame before we condemn him. With the threat of the Slayers and our eventual extinction growing with each passing year, can we really afford to turn on each other? In a time when we need allies we must put the past between our races behind us; this werewolf has already proven himself on the battlefield and may prove invaluable if we find ourselves engaged in open warfare."

Ulfarr was not happy to cut me loose but reluctantly he used his telekinetic ability once more to snap open the shackles. I'd been slumped in them after the brutal transformation I'd been forced to undergo, which had drained my energy and left my limbs trembling with fatigue. Unprepared for my sudden release, I fell to my hands and knees where I shook violently. Some of the vampires laughed but some seemed to be at least open to the possibility that the timings of the killings could be coincidental, and that maybe I was innocent and useful enough to be kept alive, at least for now. The ghouls were indifferent as far as I could tell. When the real killer was found they'd be happy to participate in his or her execution, but until then it didn't matter to them what happened to me.

"Get out of my sight, dog," Ulfarr spat, kicking me when he thought no one was watching and leaving me sprawled on the floor. I felt the fires of my rage flare up at last, even if it would only prove to be temporary, and let my eyes burn amber as I met his gaze with an equal level of hate. He turned away from me in contempt, making it clear he considered me too weak to prove a threat to him, and too unimportant to take up any more of his time, at least for the remainder of the night. Somehow I knew he would continue looking for an excuse to 'put me down', as he'd phrased it. I could even feel hate towards him from the lupine half of my mind. To the wolf he embodied all that he hated of humanity in the form of a vampire – namely the complete disregard for the sanctity of life in other species. The Elder vampire didn't need a reason to kill me, and the wolf hated him for it.

Finally, once Ulfarr had moved away, Lady Sarah came to my side. While my rage was burning I let my anger direct itself towards her, too. She'd let him humiliate me and accuse me when we couldn't know for sure either way whether I was the murderer or not. I didn't know why she hadn't come to my defence this time but I wasn't happy at the way she'd just watched me suffer, without even trying to intervene.

"I don't need your help," I snarled, struggling to my feet.

She backed off and let me stand on my own. I could feel my bloodlust rising again, so tied in to my rage as it was, and wrestled with the desire to lunge for the Elder vampire. He'd proven he held more power over me than the full moon, and considering it was this time of month I was at my most powerful, if he could control me as easily as most vampires could control mere mortals I stood no chance of beating him if we ever came to blows. But still, my anger made me irrational and the temptation was there. Lady Sarah's training finally proved to be of some use as I succeeded in channelling it into my hunger instead, which raged just as strong after the change, and turned my mind to thoughts of hunting humans.

"Come, let us feed together again," Lady Sarah said.

"Oh now you want to help me," I growled. "Bit late now, isn't it? Well I told you, I don't need your help."

She knew better than to argue and any emotions she might have been feeling she kept hidden from me. She merely nodded and said "Very well."

With that she withdrew from the building, leaving me alone, except for the last of the crowd still trickling out. Then I noticed the one vampire who'd stood up for me, though why he'd chosen to help me I had no idea. Even though he was a potential ally I wasn't in a trusting mood, and Vince's betrayal only months earlier had taught me to be cautious. I now lived in a world where it seemed everyone was a potential enemy. Even Lady Sarah had let me down that night, and with the vampires I was starting to think they all had ulterior motives. For some reason it was in this vampire's current interests to keep the Elder from executing me for the time being, but I felt that could easily change, and I needed to keep my guard up around them if I was to survive.

Now I could see him clearly I noted he was slender in build like myself, but I guessed he must be strong or he wouldn't have dared speak out if he was one of the lowliest vampires. He moved with a certain grace which wasn't unusual for vampires, but there was something about him which reminded me of a big cat. A mane of dirty blond hair which fell to his shoulders added to the feline effect, and there was a calculating, predatory look in his greyish blue eyes. I couldn't even begin to guess his age as he wore modern clothes – a dark blue denim jacket over a white shirt, and black jeans – and there was nothing to tie him to whatever era he was originally from.

As if he could read my mind, he nodded to me but let me approach him. I felt I should at least thank him for stepping in and putting an end to my 'trial', if you could really call it that when there'd been so little about it in the way of carrying out true justice.

"Thanks, I guess," I said. "You probably saved my life back there."

"Ulfarr was being cruel and unfair. It was nothing," he replied. "I have a mansion less than fifty miles north from here; come find me if you wish for some company other than Lady Sarah."

I wanted to ask him who he was and why he'd taken a sudden interest in me when we'd only just met, but before I could say anything more he was gone, moving at that unnatural speed we all possessed. I wasn't about to follow a vampire I didn't know I could trust, especially not when I didn't know how powerful he might be or how big a threat he might pose if he decided to turn on me as well. Fifty miles was nothing to our kind but I was unsure of the wisdom in accepting his invitation. Maybe Lady Sarah would be able to tell me who he was, when I'd calmed down enough to talk to her. But I would worry about the vampires later. I still needed to replenish my energy and I wanted to feed the bloodlust before it faded again and left me empty once more, so I went in search of more prey.

Chapter Fourteen – Stoking the Flames

Already weakened from the brutal transformation the Elder vampire had forced on me, I couldn't afford to change even halfway again without weakening myself so far as to be helpless if I ran into any more Slayers. Hunting more humans would be risky, but while the anger and bloodlust ruled me I was feeling especially reckless, and in my current mood I would welcome a fight if it came to it. Though a part of me wanted to transform back to a more powerful form, I wasn't quite reckless enough to waste more energy in doing so until after I'd fed. I would have to kill again as a human, but once I'd eaten I could revel in either my hybrid or full wolf form as I saw fit, for as long as my newfound rage lasted. I couldn't know how long that would be, so I intended to make the most of it before I fell back into the empty abyss at the core of my being once more.

Despite the fact I was still naked and bloody as I set out from the warehouse for the nearest city, the cold didn't bother me as much while the fires of the rage burned inside. But as it happened I came across a bin bag full of unwanted garments which I decided to raid, to make me stand out less as I wandered the streets of the human world if nothing else. I was still on the outskirts in a housing area, and these had been left out on a driveway for a charity collection next morning. I was able to rummage through the discarded clothes without being disturbed, finding a fleecy jacket, shirt and jeans. They fit well enough, though the material still felt strange against my skin as it had when I'd dressed for the first undead gathering Lady Sarah had taken me to. But it would allow me to wander the city more freely so I tolerated the discomfort of wearing them, for the time being. I took consolation in the knowledge that, not only would I soon kill again and find some pleasure in it this time, but also after feeding I could transform again, and there'd be no further need for clothes.

Once I'd dressed I stalked deeper into the city. Even though it must have been the early hours of the morning by that point, there were still people on the streets. None of them paid me much attention so I guess they didn't notice my bare feet, the blood stained skin that wasn't covered, or the murderous look in my eyes, which I'd allowed to revert to human again while I walked among them. Some of them were probably too drunk to register anything strange about my appearance, and these I let stagger past unharmed. I didn't want alcohol to dull the pain I would elicit from my next victim.

As I walked, I had the sudden feeling someone was following me. I paused to listen and scent the air. Nothing. If it had been the

Slayers trying to encircle me and ensnare me in another trap I'd have sensed at least a few of them, even if some had been downwind, and their hearts might have given them away – the stronger beat pumping adrenalin round bodies fired up for fight or flight, as opposed to the normal rhythm of the humans ignorant of my true nature. But I detected nothing out of the ordinary, and the street was currently empty as far as my eyes could see.

I continued on my hunt for suitable prey to feed my rage, yet still the sense of being followed persisted. The rage left no room for uneasiness, otherwise I might have turned back and returned to the safer moorland. But as it was, only Death would stop me from taking my next victim. So I pressed on.

Prowling through man's concrete jungle, I finally heard the sound of someone approaching. Her footsteps sounded more regular than the drunken swaying of the clubbers I'd encountered staggering from place to place, and I knew she would be mine. Besides, the bloodlust and the hunger couldn't wait any longer. I was quickly losing my self-control and I knew if I didn't feed my desires soon, I'd lose all sense of caution, and that could potentially lead to my doom. The feeling of being followed was swept away as the world narrowed down to me and my next victim.

I stalked towards my prey, my face twisted into a snarl, bestial and inhuman, teeth and nails lengthening to become fangs and claws. Minutes later she was within sight. She was blonde, medium height, and fairly skinny. I didn't care about the lack of meat though; I just wanted to kill. She wasn't particularly attractive, and I wouldn't have spared her a second glance had I been human, but to the monster I'd become she was no more than flesh and blood to brutally savage, and eventually feed on.

There was something else about the woman my crazed thoughts barely registered. The glint of metal from her belt in the dim streetlights revealed a partially concealed weapon, a knife of some description, and there was the crackle of a walkie-talkie, both of which marked her as a Slayer. I couldn't see a gun and I didn't recognise the smell of gunpowder, but she no doubt had one somewhere about her person, maybe hidden under her jacket. I let this knowledge fuel my rage to new heights. They'd given me plenty of reason to hate them in my relatively short time as a werewolf, and it was easy to blame them, in part, for the loss of my human life I now mourned so deeply. If they hadn't been hunting the werewolf that bit me that fateful night maybe our paths wouldn't have crossed, or he wouldn't have been driven into seeking me out in a desperate attempt to keep the curse alive, so it wouldn't die with him. Of course, if the Slayers hadn't been keeping our numbers in check there was every chance I would have been bitten anyway, and the world might have been very different to the one we know, but I chose to ignore that fact. I wanted to believe that my lupine half would have remained dormant if only we weren't so near to extinction, if only we'd numbered enough that there was no real need to create any more of us. And even if I had still been turned, if it weren't for the threat of the Slayers maybe I wouldn't have had to leave my old life behind. Knowing they would happily go through my family and friends to get to me had been part of the reason why I felt I could no longer be part of the human world, and I'd sacrificed everything in the hopes those closest to me would remain safe. Yes, I had every reason to hate them, and that made this woman the perfect target to unleash my fury on.

My face was hidden in enough shadow that the woman didn't instantly recognise me, and by the time she did it was too late for her to draw a weapon or call for backup. I pounced on her with all my inhuman speed and strength, the weakness and fatigue I'd been feeling swept away by the bloodlust, anger making my limbs burn with a new, if only temporary, strength.

I could've killed her quickly but only violent deaths would feed the bloodlust, and I was keen to obey it, intent on keeping the emptiness at bay for as long as possible. Pinning her down, I forced open her jaws and ripped out her tongue before she could call for help, her blood gushing down the back of her throat and spilling out over my hands and onto the pavement. Suddenly finding herself choking on her own blood, she wouldn't even be able to form the most basic, wordless screams of agony.

Most people would've been too lost in pain and shock to put up much of a fight after so brutal an attack, but this woman was tough and it was easy to see why she'd volunteered to take an active part in the Slayers' 'defences' against us. Despite the throbbing pain she must be battling with, she still had the sense to reach for her weapons. But I was already aware of her hands scrabbling at her waist and with my supernatural powers she never stood a chance. I smashed the bones from her wrist all the way to her fingertips on both sides until they were utterly useless, and then, in a fit of rage, proceeded to grab her head by her hair and smash it into the concrete until blood and brains oozed out. Even though she was dead I continued to savage her body, ripping her torso open with my bare hands and lowering my face to the bloody hole, still human in form except for my fangs and claws. I ate her organs to replenish my strength, each one slippery and oozing fresh blood and other juices, dribbling down my chin and staining my skin and the stolen clothes. When I was done feasting on the organs I gnawed at her limbs, stripping them down to the bone. Her tongue lay by her body like a slug with a bloody trail, and I ate that too. Then the walkie-talkie crackled to life again and I crushed it.

Finally I rose from the bloody mess I'd left on the pavement, anger blazing in my eyes which I instinctively knew had turned amber once more, despite having been unaware of the pain that accompanied any part of the change I underwent. I didn't know how long it would take for more Slayers to come looking for her, but with my energy restored and still in the grip of the bloodlust I felt invincible, stalking off at a leisurely pace.

The sensible thing would have been to return to Lady Sarah after feeding, but I didn't want to face her again that night. So I deliberately remained in the city, wandering the streets and embracing my reawakened rage for as long as it lasted. I still wanted to transform now I'd fed and enjoy the feeling of my body growing stronger and more powerful, developing into a killing machine, all the more dangerous for the fury that powered it. But even with the full moon still overhead, something held me back, keeping me in human form and the human part of my mind in control, at least for the time being. It wasn't for fear of being sighted by anyone, Slayer or otherwise, since anyone close enough would instantly notice the blood soaked clothes I still wore, identifying me as the monster I was.

The shirt which had already felt strange and uncomfortable now stuck wetly to my skin. I considered ditching the clothes, but as with the desire to transform something held me back. Maybe I liked my prey to be mostly unsuspecting, subconsciously aware that something was amiss yet not quite grasping it until I drew too close. If I looked too much of an outsider, which I obviously would wandering around naked or partially transformed, I'd lose that. Though in wolf form I could potentially have passed for a large stray dog, so perhaps that wasn't quite it either. I didn't really know my own mind that night or why I was choosing one decision over another, and looking back now I still don't have any answers.

That sense of being followed only grew stronger the longer I walked the streets, until I finally heard the footfalls of some human foolish enough to tail behind. My rage blazed in response, expecting to find another Slayer trying to take me by surprise, and I spun round to face them, fangs bared in a snarl.

"Woah wolf boy, take it easy," Luke said.

"Tell me again why I shouldn't just kill you. How do you even keep finding me?"

"You're not a happy wolf, I can see that. Do you want to talk about it?" he asked, ignoring my question.

"No," I growled, turning my back on him and resuming my hunt for more victims to feed my rage.

The human ran to catch me up and fell into step beside me. "Let's talk about other stuff then. I don't even know your name yet!"

"Nick," I grunted, without looking at him. In my current state of mind he was an annoyance, one I was sorely tempted to obliterate. And yet, again, something held me back.

"That's cool, do you have a wolf name as well?"

"No."

"You should call yourself Darkfang or something. That would be a cool werewolf name. Or not!" he added, when I glared at him.

"I need to kill again. If you won't leave me in peace then at least be quiet and stay out of the way, or I will make you my next victim."

Luke took the hint and fell silent, but I could tell his curiosity was far from satiated.

I killed twice more in the early hours, though the third murder was less savage than the other two, and to my dismay the fires of my anger had already begun to die down. I continued to wander the streets with Luke by my side, keeping my thoughts on how Lady Sarah had let the Elder vampire torment me and accuse me, and trying to focus my anger towards the both of them, as well as my similar dark feelings towards the Slayers. But it wasn't enough to reignite my rage.

"Are you sure you don't want to talk, dude?" Luke asked. "You seem even more troubled than that night in the pub."

Still unsure whether to trust him, I didn't reply straight away. I couldn't deny the need for a friend, and so it was I found myself finally opening up to him, my latest problems breaking free of the dam I'd tried to wall them behind and gushing out.

"Have you ever been betrayed by someone you thought you could count on?"

"Yes," he said simply, waiting for me to go on.

"I don't know how much you know, or how it is you could possibly know about the Slayers. Unless you're one of them, but then, why would you be letting me kill without trying to intervene?"

"Relax man, I'm not with them. Werewolves are awesome; I wouldn't want to see you get killed by those misguided bastards."

Whether it was wise to confide in him or not, I couldn't seem to stop myself once I'd started. I told him everything from the torment

I'd suffered at the hands of my 'fellow' undead and how Lady Sarah hadn't even tried to help me that night, to my struggles to adjust to my miserable existence trapped between the human world and the natural world. "The only good thing to come out of tonight was my rage being brought back to the surface, but now I can feel it slipping away again and without it I'm nothing. See what I meant by you don't want this? I was always a fan of werewolves an' all, but if I could go back to that night I was bitten and change things so I never crossed paths with the werewolf that turned me, I'd do it without a second thought."

"Hey, freak!" a boy shouted, interrupting us.

A large group of school kids had appeared on the opposite side of the road, and I'd been so caught up in trying to explain things to Luke that I'd barely noticed. The boy who had shouted out couldn't have been any older than twelve, but he was looking for a fight and, with all his mates around him, clearly he felt unbeatable. There were a couple of girls in the group he was no doubt looking to impress, or why else would he pick on someone nearly twice his height? Having suffered at the hands of bullies for most of my human years, there was little wonder why the Elder vampire had re-awoken my rage earlier that night, and I tried to embrace it once more to brandish against the insolent little kids stood facing me.

"What did you call me?" I asked him with a snarl. Dawn was fast approaching which explained why the kids were out on the streets, though it was still a little early for them to be setting off for school. Common sense should have told me to flee the city before I lost the cover of darkness and the streets became alive with thousands of witnesses. Regular police officers didn't worry me; even if they succeeded in locking me up, there was no normal cell that could hold me. However, I'd already seen evidence of the Slayers working within the police and other authorities and, even if they weren't the ones to oversee my immediate capture, in all likelihood they would find a way to move me to one of their bases like back in my hometown, if they didn't just kill me first. Common sense told me that was a likely outcome if I didn't return to exile soon, but I was too desperate to rekindle my anger before the emptiness engulfed me once more, and these school bullies seemed my best hope at that point.

"You starting on me now?" he challenged, strutting across the road as if he seriously thought he could beat me in a fair fight. There was a time when I might have found it funny, and I did laugh but there was no humour in it. If the kid had any brains he would have backed off at the harsh sound, but of course he didn't, instead continuing to goad me. "Hey, where are your shoes, freak? And what's all that spilt down you, weirdo?"

"You started it, you little prick," I said, ignoring his questions. "Now fuck off back to mummy and daddy before I send you home crying."

"Oh yeah? I'll break your nose, dickhead," he threatened.

"Do you want a stepladder to do that or shall I kneel for you?" I sneered. I might not be the tallest of guys, but he really was that short. A few years can make a big difference in height at that age, after all.

Clearly a good comeback was beyond him, since he tried to kick my feet out from under me. Presumably so he could reach my nose which he was so intent on breaking. Maybe he would have succeeded if I'd been human, especially if his friends joined in. But with all my supernatural power, even in human form, he would meet the same end as my other prey that night.

I easily dodged the kick he had aimed at me, the group gawping as I moved faster than they knew should be physically possible. I grabbed him by his collar and threw him to the ground, where he came to a stop a few feet away. He hit the concrete hard and I smelt blood as the force ripped away layers of skin. He screamed and started to cry, his friends still stood in shock opposite us. As with any bullies they were cowards, unwilling to go to his aid now they knew they were no match for me.

I pounced on top of my latest victim, pinning him to the ground. He shook and sobbed beneath me, pathetic now he was on the receiving end of pain. My teeth had elongated into fangs once more and I tried to be especially cruel to keep the anger alive for a while longer, but my heart wasn't really in it anymore.

"You've got balls kid," I whispered in his ear. "Maybe I'll rip them off."

His face turned paler and he screamed again, louder this time, while fear robbed him of control of his bladder. I forced another harsh laugh and rose off him as he wet himself, turning my gaze on the rest of the group. Some part of me continued to nag about the danger of lingering in the human world any longer, and again I thought of what would happen if hundreds of witnesses began to appear on the streets. I glanced at Luke who stood back, seemingly happy to watch me commit more murders. The kids were all focussed on me, perhaps having just enough brains not to goad a fully grown guy who was even taller than I was.

"Do what you need to do," he said quietly, so only I could hear.

I hesitated, still aware of the dangers of being caught out on the streets. Aughtie had been conducting horrific experiments on any undead she'd captured alive back in my hometown. I was willing to bet there were plenty of facilities just like the one I'd briefly been imprisoned in. Maybe not every leader among them would agree with her methods, but there was enough fear and hate among their ranks that the majority would be quite happy to carry out such torture in the name of 'science'. More likely it was revenge that drove them since they generally became Slayers following encounters with a member of the undead. And such encounters usually meant the death of someone close to them.

So I was wrestling with some part of me that still cared about survival, or at least not meeting a particularly painful and bloody end at the hands of the Slayers, and the need to find a way to allow the tide of my bloodlust to wash over me once more, before the emptiness could re-open enough for me to fall back into it.

Lizzy appeared beside the boy's prone form. "Just walk away, Nick. You know killing him won't bring you any enjoyment now the rage has died back down. Just walk away this time."

It was at that point one of the girls found the courage to shout out to me, but she made no move to help the pathetic boy still sobbing and whimpering at my feet.

"Oh my God, what's wrong with you?" she said. "He never even did anything."

That should have been enough to feed the rage. How could she defend him when he'd started it? He was the one who'd provoked me. He'd been the one to physically lash out first. And I'd spared him his life, what more did she want? He'd been lucky not to encounter me a few hours earlier, when I wouldn't have wasted time with threats, simply acting on my darkest desires to rip and tear the entire group apart.

"How old are you?" she continued.

"Nearly seventeen," I growled as I turned to face her, which was true, even if I hadn't aged physically at all since being bitten the previous year. "Why, what's it to you? Are you into older lads?"

She knew something was very wrong, even if she didn't really understand what was happening, yet still she wouldn't just walk away, and the rest of the group seemed frozen in place. Light was just starting to spill onto the street. I was still in shadow but soon they'd clearly see exactly what was staining my clothes and skin.

"I think you should grow up," she said, trying to put on a brave face even though her doubts and her fear were evident.

"Mouthy little gits, take your friend and go before I tear out your tongues." I wished I felt the anger I tried to maintain in my words.

"Go on bro, it'll make you feel better," Luke whispered.

"Not helping," I growled at him, while Lizzy continued to play the role of my conscience and I still struggled with conflicting thoughts of survival versus more bloodshed.

"Freak," the girl shouted again, but she finally ran over to help the boy up and they fled. I watched them go. Despite my best efforts my rage had left me. My anger had burnt out again and my bloodlust was but a distant memory.

"I have to go," I told Luke.

"No worries man, I understand. I'll find you again."

There was nothing more for me in the city, so at last I ripped off the bloody clothes and transformed, taking it all the way to wolf this time. Without the rage to drive me and lend itself to recklessness, I listened to both the voice of my conscience and common sense, and took my leave as swiftly as I was capable of, knowing I'd already stayed too long. There were less shadows to hide in so I relied on speed rather than stealth. The hunger was back after transforming again, but it was manageable. Feeding on any more humans would be risky, so I would find other prey once I was a safe distance from the area. Then I knew I should return to the moors and reunite with Lady Sarah at nightfall.

Dead inside once again, my anger reduced to ashes, I was no longer mad at her, but I still felt I couldn't forgive her for simply standing by as the Elder vampire tortured and humiliated me in front of our 'fellow' undead. He might have been the most powerful being in the room, one she couldn't hope to stand against if it came to a fight, but she could have spoken out for me at least, if only to be shot down and left resigned to watch events play out. The fact that she would have at least tried to help me would have meant something. And who could say whether any attempt to defend me would've been unsuccessful? She seemed to be treated by other vampires with respect, which suggested her words would carry some weight at any gathering, yet she'd remained silent and unwilling to take any action on my behalf. It had taken a stranger to save me, one whose motives were even more puzzling than Lady Sarah's were, and even without any feelings of anger towards her at that point, I couldn't just forget the night's events and carry on as if nothing had happened. Yet even though part of me consequently wanted nothing more to do with her, I knew she remained my best hope at survival for the immediate future. I'd already established I wasn't willing to die at the hands of either the vampires or the Slayers if I could help it, and I had even less reason to trust the new vampire I'd met that night, even if he had saved me by speaking out where no one else would, so that meant I was stuck with Lady Sarah for the time being.

I made it out of the city without event, glimpsed only by the general public once or twice and mistaken for a large stray dog. Once I was back in the wilderness I caught a deer to help keep the hunger at bay, then I found my way back to the area we'd made our territory. I settled down for more troubled sleep with only the blanket for shelter, which I'd weighted down with rocks the previous night to keep it from blowing away. It wasn't much but I was grateful for the added warmth, and it wasn't long before the nightmares took me once more.

Chapter Fifteen – Chained Fury

I was aware of the shifting of earth beside me that meant Lady Sarah was awaking from the vampiric sleep of the dead, dragging me out from my own slumber. I waited in wolf form for her to emerge, knowing she would want to continue her attempts to teach me greater control, and unwilling to waste energy changing before finding out which form she wanted me in, depending what she had planned.

Remaining in wolf form also spared me from having to talk to her. Through her own ability to shapeshift she could communicate with wolves and had spoken to my lupine half in what he'd called the wolven tongue, but that wasn't a language I understood. She could say all she wanted in English, it just gave me the perfect excuse not to answer her while my jaws and vocal cords were fully wolfish, and forming words was therefore too difficult. I'd just about managed some speech in my hybrid form when I'd needed to, but somehow it was harder with my body completely lupine.

"Come, you still have much to learn if you are to survive in our world," she said, making no mention of the previous night.

You say that like we have a world, I thought to myself. When in reality we lived on the fringes, caught between the natural world and the world of men, just as we were forever trapped between the living and the dead, so long as no one put an end to our unnatural existence. If the anger had still been there maybe I'd have changed back to point that out, and how we lived in isolation without even basic shelter, our only contact with others of our kind through murder, and only then to give the prejudiced older vampires an excuse to execute me, guilty or not. How could she call that our world? Even if vampires, and possibly ghouls, had some form of society which went beyond meeting merely to deal with any new perceived threats, it seemed there was no place in that world for me. But try as I might to call on my anger again, the emptiness was just as complete as it had been before the brief resurrection of my rage. I resigned myself to enduring the vampire's latest trials.

She was still focussed on teaching me to master my hunger and my darker urges, probably hoping the killings would stop, if I was indeed to blame. We were making some progress, as I learnt to channel my bloodlust into attacking the 'enemy' as instructed. The next stage was to try to hold the bloodlust without letting it take over and drive me to attacking anything, and then let it drain away, but that was proving far more difficult. Lady Sarah kept pointing out it was becoming more important than ever for me to learn these skills, to avoid any more nights of me growing completely uncontrollable.

It wasn't particularly comforting that she was starting to seriously consider me a suspect, and I began to have my doubts about continuing to trust her, fearing she might turn on me if the other vampires had her convinced of my guilt. I knew I wasn't ready to make it on my own though; not when I would be hunted by both the Slayers and the vampires if I ran. Besides, the vampires had proven they didn't need any evidence to reach a guilty verdict and running would just provide them with another excuse to execute me. So I forced myself to stick with Lady Sarah for the time being, feeling I had little choice, but I was fast beginning to lose any faith I'd had in her.

As the nights wore on, the lessons continued. The Slayers hadn't forced us to move on yet, much to Lady Sarah's surprise, and she was determined to take advantage of whatever time we were to be granted. She didn't mention the last full moon and that began to bother me almost as much as her unwillingness to help had. It wasn't exactly anger since my emotions were still lost to me in that empty void, but there was almost some resentment there. The incident with the other vampires was the beginning of it, but also when you're around someone day in day out (or rather night in night out) for long enough they begin to grate on your nerves, no matter how well you once got on, and as long as she insisted on staying by my side every night for the rest of the month, the feelings, for want of a better word, were building.

Little things start to annoy you until you can't wait to get away for an hour or so. Granted we weren't quite stuck with each other twenty four seven. The daylight hours were mine to do with as I wished, while she was of course forced to remain shrouded in darkness, protected from the sun's deadly rays. But such freedom was short lived and once darkness returned I was forced to endure another night with her. I had no choice if I wished to survive, I knew that. And it seemed she was only trying to help, for which I supposed I should be grateful, despite what had happened under the last full moon. She was under no obligation to help after all. Yet annoy me (again, for want of a better word) she did. I found myself longing for a new companion who truly understood me, almost as much as I longed for my old way of life.

Despite the dangers, I would soon take to spending my days wandering human streets, whenever I was restless and unable to sleep. I would manage to wash the thickest of the blood from my skin in the

154

icy cold waters of the glacial lake, focussing mostly on my hands, neck and face. But first there was a matter of finding more unwanted clothes, which I was able to search for on the occasions Lady Sarah left me to do whatever she spent her nights doing when she wasn't feeding or supervising me. For the most part she didn't leave me alone too often or for too long, which again suggested she was starting to think I had been the one to kill the three vampires, but there was one night where she left me to my own devices, despite the distrust evident in her eyes. She wouldn't say why she needed to go off alone and I didn't press her, simply glad of more time away from her and a break from her lessons, and as soon as she'd taken her leave I seized the opportunity to hunt for clothes again.

I'd already spent a few nights of foraging for more clothes left out for charity, as I'd found before, and I was able to gather some of the garments I needed to at least pass for human, and ensure I didn't instantly stand out in a crowd. But I was still missing shoes and a jacket that fit well enough so as not to cause suspicion.

I'd been searching in one of the nearby towns we'd not visited yet and it was to there I headed again. I fed first to help maintain my hard earned control, forever tested by the trials Lady Sarah insisted on putting both me and the wolf through. Even though I knew by then slaughtering the townsfolk was not the way to fill the emptiness, if the hunger plagued me my instincts would undoubtedly take over (the wolf might even gain hold of our consciousness as he'd often fought for in the first few months after his awakening) and I could end up killing humans before I was even aware of what I was doing. If I thought I could truly lose myself in the bloodlust as I had during the last full moon I might have been reckless enough to allow it, but I knew there would be no more pleasure in killing that night than there had been any other time while feeling so dead inside, so there was no sense in endangering myself any more than necessary. So, by the time I struck out for the town it was in the dead of night. Frost covered the ground and an icy wind raged. I slunk across the frozen landscape in wolf form, undeterred by the bite of the wind, sure footed on the layer of frost where a human would undoubtedly have slipped.

Once I reached the town it was clear there were no more charity collections due that week, and it was of course too cold to find washing hung out to dry. I wasn't sure how else to steal anything without attracting unwanted attention from the locals, but I wasn't just going to give up. In the end I decided to wander the streets until a better idea hit me.

The world was quiet, most people asleep in their beds, though I could hear the sounds of the town's nightlife coming from within its heart. Even though I'd eaten well enough to take the edge off the hunger, the need to hunt came again, the wolf closer to the surface than he had been in some time. The next full moon couldn't be far off and with the constant changing Lady Sarah put me through to force me to battle my urges and learn to control them, my predatory instincts were closer to the surface than ever. I was able to fight it and avoided wandering any nearer to the town centre, not trusting myself to resist the temptation if I drew too close. I just wished I could rediscover the thrill of the kill, but as far as I knew it was still denied to the human part of me, and with all the kills I'd made since we'd settled out in the moors, the Slayers would surely be as vigilant as ever in their hunt for me. The risk was too great.

Sometime later I found myself on a back alley and came to a stop, able to smell prey. Struggling as I was with my need to hunt, a sudden movement made it harder. Before I knew what I was doing, I had taken several steps towards it, drooling at the thought of fresh meat, feeling the wolf's mind alongside my own, almost one again but still separate, only a thin wall separating our two different personalities.

A homeless man lay beneath a makeshift shelter of rotting cardboard and a thin sheet of plastic. He had curled into the foetal position against the cold, with only the old tattered rags he wore to protect him. He was muttering to himself under his breath, an empty bottle of whiskey beside him. He stunk of alcohol and death. I could almost sense the cold slowly creeping into his veins and freezing the life out of him. I don't think he was even aware of me stood over him.

The movement I had seen, however, came from rats, not the man. They were everywhere, crawling through the rotting garbage strewn around, sleek bodies snaking in between the junk with ease, bald tails whipping in and out of sight. As I drew nearer they scurried away, hiding in cracks in the walls or amongst the garbage. I turned back to the man and considered ending it for him, but there was no way I could think of to kill him in wolf form without it being an obvious attack from a large canid, and besides, the moment I tasted his blood I knew I would lose control and my wolfish half would take over, and he would lose himself in the bloodlust. If I allowed that to happen it was surely only a matter of time before the Slayers would find the body and be on the alert, and I had no desire to spend another night being hunted through the streets and the surrounding countryside. So with a force of will I pushed my wolfish half back down into our subconscious and turned away, the desire to taste human flesh lessening.

I could've taken the vagrant's clothes, but the whole point of stealing any in the first place was to allow me to blend in. If I'd taken his rags I would've still looked an outsider, and my journeys to the town would've been pointless. With the longing for my old life came a desire to connect with the human world once more, and that was what currently drove me. With nothing else to live for I just wanted to walk among them again and maybe feel a part of their world, if only for a few hours at a time, even though I knew I could never truly be part of the human world anymore. So I continued my search.

Sometime later I came upon a drunken guy, passed out on the concrete. The streets were otherwise deserted and there was no one to come to his aid. His leather jacket was only thin and would no doubt have proven to be inadequate protection from the wintry weather if he spent the remainder of the night in the cold, but it looked roughly my size. As long as I had a jacket to help me blend in, people would just see me as another youth daft enough not to wrap up properly, so I transformed halfway back to human, able to grab the jacket with my hands rather than my jaws to avoid ripping it, as well as his trainers. Unfortunately for the man, he hadn't drunk enough to make him dead to the world, and he stirred while I took what I needed, not quite fully conscious of what was happening.

"What the fuck do you think you're doing man," he slurred, somewhat aware of the fact he was being robbed. He peered around blearily and laid eyes on my monstrous form for the first time. "What the fuck are you dressed like that for; it's Christmas, not Halloween!"

Quicker than a snake striking, I thrust a clawed hand at his throat, instantly crushing the windpipe before he could make anymore noise and attract unwanted attention. My stomach rumbled, the hunger back with a vengeance, and I weighed up my options. It would be safer to leave the town back in wolf form. Not only was my body at its fastest and most powerful when fully lupine, but it attracted less attention than either my current hybrid form, which was obviously instantly recognisable to anyone as a werewolf, or changing all the way back to human, given that I'd be mostly naked again, with only the jacket and shoes to hand to dress in. Unless I took the rest of the man's clothes to change into, I supposed. I needed to feed but I was also beginning to feel I'd been in the town too long, so it was probably safer to take my kill back into the wilderness and eat in an area where there was less threat of the Slayers finding me. That meant I needed to be humanoid to carry the carcass and the stolen clothes, but even if I took the transformation back to fully human and dressed, I'd still attract attention carrying a corpse around. The only other option was to leave the body and feed on animals, but I couldn't decide if it was better for the Slayers to find it or for the man to simply disappear. My hunger made itself known again and my decision was suddenly made; I stayed as I was and carried my meal and the clothes, keeping to the shadows and trusting my superior senses to warn me if anyone came close, even if I hadn't mastered the skill to pick out the myriad of scents and sounds which was second nature to the wolf.

I made it back into the wilderness without being seen and ate my fill, burying what little remains were left, then I took the jacket and trainers to the same place I'd stashed the rest of the clothes I'd found, where I'd also taken to storing the blanket. It was only a shallow, rocky fissure in the landscape, but it was the best hiding place our current surroundings had to offer. Hidden beneath the rocks, at least my current link with humanity, tenuous as it was, wouldn't be taken from me by nature. It wasn't particularly well hidden if Lady Sarah had any reason to come poking around, but it would have to do. Once I was satisfied my prizes were as safe as they could be, with only an hour or so of darkness left there was nothing more to be done that night other than wait for the vampire's return.

As reckless as I could be, I decided it was better to get the next full moon out of the way before venturing into the town again. Once it had passed the wolf should be quieter, and there was less risk of him taking over and losing himself in the bloodlust in a fit of hunger, surrounded by the prey the curse caused him to desire as we would be. I also knew that, in the absence of the predatory instincts which were beginning to spill into the human half of my mind that month, I would fall completely back into the emptiness and the sense of loneliness. I just hoped that being able to temporarily reconnect with humanity would go some way to easing the loneliness, and give me a brief sense of being back in my old life, after the miserable existence I'd been stuck in since.

The night before the full moon, we were called back to the old warehouse the Elder vampire had been using as a meeting place. I started thinking to myself that surely he must have somewhere grander for this kind of thing, like a mansion hidden away from humanity or even a castle. Maybe he'd always preferred to live in the wilderness, given the primitive life he'd led as a human, but surely one of the other older vampires had somewhere they could use. The vampire who'd stood up for me during my 'trial' had told me he had a mansion, so clearly not all of them had been driven from any such places they'd made their home. Maybe they preferred to meet on neutral ground, which made the warehouse as good a place as any I supposed. I would have liked to be summoned to a mansion though, if only to enjoy some warmth while being accused of crimes I didn't even know myself if I'd committed. Not that Ulfarr would care what I wanted.

As we made our way back to the abandoned building, I wondered whether there'd been a fourth murder. If there had at least I would know it wasn't me after all, since I hadn't completely blacked out at all in the weeks after that last full moon. I wasn't looking forward to seeing the Elder vampire again so soon after our last encounter, but if I could find a way to clear my name then I hoped I wouldn't have to endure any further torment at his hands. The Slayers were a big enough threat without the vampires to worry about as well.

Similar to our last visit to the warehouse, we entered to find we were the first to arrive, other than Ulfarr himself. I was in human form again when we went in but unlike our first trip there, I was given no clothes to make me appear less feral, and I was soon shivering at the cold air brushing across my bare skin. The Elder's attitude towards me and werewolves in general clearly hadn't improved, as he didn't deign to acknowledge me once again, initially addressing only Lady Sarah.

"My Lady," he said. "I trust you understand the necessity for this."

"I do, but that does not mean I am happy with it," she replied.

"Happy with what?" I asked her, curiosity overriding any need to goad Ulfarr just to get him to speak to me, as stupid as that would have been. "What's going on?"

Lady Sarah wouldn't even look at me then, let alone reply. The Elder simply continued as if I hadn't spoken. "Good. Bring it over here then."

"Bring what? Don't just ignore me, what the hell's going on?"

Ulfarr strode over to the other end of the building where the same chains I'd been bound with last time had been fixed to the floor and wall, the workbench removed from the room. Lady Sarah motioned for us to follow him and curiosity kept me from arguing as we made our way over to the Elder. Too late I noticed the bars that had been added to the windows and the reinforced door ready to seal the building they'd turned into a cage. I'd barely had time to make the connection as to why we'd been brought back here when Ulfarr forced me into a state of paralysis much as he had the previous month, and telekinetically bound me once more with an additional chain round my neck this time, freeing me from his mental grip only when I was secured. I thrashed against the chains, shouting at the both of them, but I couldn't quite find the strength to break free. Either the vampires had found some kind of supernatural reinforcement capable of containing my own supernatural strength, or the Elder had found some subtle way to weaken me without me realising. However he'd done it, I wasn't going anywhere anytime soon.

"Be still, beast," he commanded, and even though I wasn't aware of his power this time, I began to quieten, panting heavily. "We will hold you here till the full moon passes. Though doubtful, if there should be another murder in this time we will consider you innocent and you may walk free. If, however, there are no further bodies discovered it may not prove you guilty beyond doubt, but you can be certain we will be watching you much more closely. Understood?"

"Yes," I growled, feeling the same hate as before stirring within.

"If you behave I will slacken the chains so you can make yourself more comfortable, but give me reason to treat you like no more than the feral dog you are and your stay here will be most unpleasant."

I chose not to answer this latest threat, instead looking at Lady Sarah who refused to meet my gaze. How could she continue to let them treat me like this? I felt betrayed, and I couldn't understand why she was suddenly so unwilling to even attempt to put a stop to it. The Elder was at least as good as his word, allowing the chains to slacken so I could move around and sit if I wanted to. Then they left me before dawn, alone with my anger.

As soon as they'd gone I began to struggle against my shackles again, driven by my rage. There was also the vague hope it had been Ulfarr's power preventing me from breaking free of them and that he wouldn't be able to hold me while he slept through the daylight hours. But the chains held fast even after the Elder vampire had gone, and I soon gave up wasting my energy.

The hatred and anger Ulfarr had once again re-awoken in me didn't last, soon lost in the emptiness which gaped ever wider as time crawled on. I had never felt so utterly alone as I did then. Even if she'd been there, Lady Sarah was no company, not when she was always so reserved and offered little in the way of comfort or companionship. She couldn't visit me in the daylight hours of course, but with the greater sense of isolation that came from being locked in my makeshift cage, I was reminded of the fact she still couldn't really be considered a friend. And with the deep ache resonating from the chasm in my soul, I knew I needed a friend more than ever, someone to share the burden of my lycanthropy and everything the curse had brought upon me, even if they couldn't fill me with life once more. Or if that was too much to hope for, someone to help pass the time and break up the monotony of the meaningless nights my existence now consisted of would have been nice.

My thoughts turned to the human world I longed to return to and I started to investigate the inside of my cage as much as the chains would allow, looking for any weaknesses that might offer a way out. That also proved pointless, my claws unable to gouge deep enough into the brick to pry the brackets I was shackled to loose, and the wall held when I threw myself against it. Both of which seemed to confirm there was a supernatural element to my prison, keeping me from breaking free through brute strength. So I turned my attention to searching the floor for anything that might have been left lying around. I didn't know the first thing about picking locks, but if there was anything I could use to give it a go then I felt I might as well at least try. If nothing else it would help pass the time.

It was then I noticed the bowl of fresh water they'd placed nearby and a bucket to relieve myself in, which was a slight improvement on the facilities provided when I'd been imprisoned by the Slayers, or lack of. But otherwise the room was empty, no rusty nails or other small objects I could have used left lying around. I wasn't entirely surprised by that fact, knowing a vampire as old and powerful as Ulfarr was unlikely to be so careless, though I still felt a little disappointed. I really was stuck there until the Elder chose to free me, with no one but my own tormented mind for company and the growing sense of loneliness dragging me further under the drowning waters of my despair.

The human world felt even further out of reach as the day wore on and I remained trapped in the building they'd abandoned, but after a while I heard the sound of approaching footsteps. Daylight still reigned outside so it couldn't be any vampires coming to check on me, which could mean only one thing – humanity had found me, as if drawn by my longing to reconnect with them. But who could possibly be lurking out there? The warehouse hadn't been used in years as far as I could tell and from what I'd seen of the surrounding area each time Lady Sarah had brought me to it, we were pretty isolated. No doubt Ulfarr had picked it as a meeting place because he felt it was a safe enough distance from any other human buildings to minimise the risk of discovery by the Slayers. So what was a human doing out there, and what reason would they have to visit the old building?

A rush of adrenalin flooded my system as the person drew closer. My heart pounded with the realisation that, whoever it was, I was at their mercy whilst chained at the back of the room. And since I could think of no other reason for anyone to be here other than to kill me while I was cornered and unable to escape, it seemed that in all likelihood it was one of the Slayers approaching. Somehow they'd found me again and they'd come to take advantage of the restraints the vampires had placed on me.

The footsteps stopped on the other side of the door, the handle turning. I struggled to hear anything over the beating of my own heart, desperately trying to think of a plan but knowing full well I was doomed. There was nowhere for cover if the human had brought a gun, and the chains didn't stretch far enough to allow me to reach the door and attack before the Slayer could make their move. There was no way out this time, yet still I couldn't bring myself to just give up on life, as miserable as I was.

The door swung open and a woman entered, carrying a long metal pole with a hook on the end. That puzzled me. It didn't look like a weapon and while I'd expected them to come prepared to deal with me at arm's length, surely a gun would have been so much easier. It wasn't like the Slayers had any trouble acquiring guns, since most of them I'd encountered had been armed with one.

I tensed as the woman drew close enough to stab at me with the length of metal, but she remained just out of reach for me to lunge at her. My only hope was to try and grab the pole and pull her to me, and I readied myself to make my move. Time seemed to slow and as the seconds dragged on I noted how she had an odd vacant expression. Her glazed eyes seemed to slide over me as if she was unaware of her surroundings, like she was sleep walking. Could it be a trick to catch me off-guard?

The attack never came. The pole wasn't a strange type of weapon after all but merely a tool for the woman to reach the bucket without having to get in range of the dangerous animal they were treating me as. I should have known the vampires would consider such menial tasks beneath them. They must have placed the woman under their spell, which explained the vacant expression and the lack of reaction to a naked, feral looking boy. But I also wondered if they'd sent a human because they knew it would add to my torment, and sure enough my hunger grew more powerful in response to her presence. So close to the full moon I briefly lost control, straining to break free again and snapping at the prey just out of reach.

The woman didn't even flinch. She turned away and walked back towards the door, retrieving a clean bucket from where she'd placed it just outside. She used the pole to place it close enough for me to use it, but the length of metal remained as frustratingly out of reach as the woman herself, and when she took her leave moments later I slumped back to the floor, defeated.

Ulfarr's hospitality hadn't extended to any fresh water and I spent the rest of the day thoroughly miserable, plagued by the discomforts of thirst and hunger, and shivering in the cold building. At least it was sheltered from the elements but the air was just as chilly inside as it had been outside. And to top it all the depression weighed even heavier on my mind as my longing for my old life resumed, try as I might to focus my thoughts elsewhere.

When the day finally came to an end and the full moon rose, I welcomed the transformation. I was glad of the reprieve I would be granted while the wolf took control, and I offered him no resistance as he rose up, sinking into the blissful darkness of our subconscious, free of my mental anguish till morning at least.

The transformation complete, I had become a force of uncontrollable power, a thing of almost un-containable rage, except they had found a way to contain me, and I became all the more frenzied for it.

I strained against the chains, furious that the vampires would dare to deprive me of my freedom to answer the moon's call and the burning hunger once again. My restraints held, so I snapped at them instead but even my powerful jaws couldn't break the cold metal. Sounds of prey in the distance caused me to resume my struggle at the end of my tethers, despite the discomfort as the chain around my neck choked and bit into the soft flesh of my throat.

As the night wore on the hunger fed the rage and the rage fed the bloodlust, which was in turn tied to the need to hunt and kill, and taste warm flesh. Like a snake eating its own tail the three ruled me, each bleeding into the other and growing ever stronger, once again robbing me of my sanity and sense of self. I had no hope of controlling it, and if it weren't for the chains that bound me I would have attacked the first being I came across, even if they'd been a vampire. Indeed, part of me still wanted to kill the Elder vampire who had given me new reason to hate him. He'd demonstrated just how powerful he was during the last full moon, but instead of using that power to keep me placid so as to ensure I couldn't possibly hurt any more vampires, he'd chosen to let me suffer.

Sometime before dawn a new vampire appeared, approaching cautiously and careful not to get too close. He tossed me a severed arm which I snatched from the air in my jaws, dropping it between my paws to gnaw on hungrily. The scrap only served to heighten my frenzied state, probably exactly why the Elder had arranged the snack for me, and I continued my useless struggle to break free. Only when the sun rose did I feel the exhaustion from my exertions, and once I was forced back to human form I was weakened considerably.

That second day was equally as miserable as the first. In my weakened state the fury that had ruled my wolfish half all night under the full moon seemed to instantly burn out, the bloodlust fading away as if it had never been, despite the hunger still being there. The scrap of meat I'd been fed was far from enough to replenish the energy from each transformation, and I felt drained. Continuing to struggle against my restraints was pointless, and in the absence of the rage I had no reason to do so. Even when the woman from the previous day returned with another clean bucket and more water this time, I made no attempt to get at her. I merely sat hugging myself against the cold, pathetic and dejected.

The second night would pass in much the same way as the first, with another severed limb the only offering to appease my hunger and keep me from becoming too weak to struggle even in wolf form (and I guessed the Elder vampire wanted me in that frenzied state as further evidence I was no more than a wild beast in need of putting down). And only after another lonely day, in which the emptiness filled with ever greater depression and despair, a deep pit like that I'd been stuck in after first learning the wolf hungered for humans and not animals as I'd originally assumed, did something happen to break the pattern.

Once more a thing of rage, again I struggled to break free of my chains and unleash my fury on the world. Despite being weakened by the transformation I'd been forced through at each rise and fall of the full moon without enough sustenance to replenish my energy each time, I continued to pull against my tethers and strain for freedom. It was as if my rage gave me renewed strength.

The sound of approaching voices caused me to grow still. I caught the scent of humans carried in on a draught and eagerly waited to see if they would be foolish enough to enter the old warehouse. Some part of my crazed brain knew they'd only get close enough if I remained quiet, so I ceased my pointless struggling and stayed crouched in the shadows like a coiled spring, waiting for the moment to pounce.

There were three male youths who it seemed had heard me raging and had dared each other to investigate. A small part of me wondered if Ulfarr had planted the idea in their heads, or at least encouraged such thoughts, but I was too hungry and devoid of self-control to show any caution. If the Elder vampire had arranged for them to find me it surely was not out of kindness, but I was too lost in my hunger and rage to give any real consideration as to what his motives might be. All that mattered was the fact that humans were nearby, each one representing a potential kill. My mouth watered in anticipation of the taste of their flesh, threads of saliva dripping to the floor. When the warehouse door creaked open I almost tried to bound forward, which would have resulted in the chains holding me back and the boys no doubt fleeing in terror, but somehow I managed to remain patient and keep quiet and still.

To my pleasure, the ringleader turned out to be the same insolent schoolboy who'd dared to challenge the human the morning after the last full moon. He'd obviously recovered from the incident since he was full of the same swagger he'd exhibited when the human had first encountered him weeks ago and he boldly entered the building ahead of his mates, the beam of his torch sweeping the area in front of the door. It wasn't strong enough to penetrate the darkness at the far end of the building where I lurked, and satisfied whatever beast had been heard must have moved on, he told the others to 'stop being pussies and come take a look'.

The boys kept the torch beam on the ground ahead of them so as not to trip over any debris that may have been lying around, as well as to look for evidence of some monster having been there. Finally they drew close enough for me to strike, and I did so with all my supernatural speed and strength, knowing if any of them had time to react they'd soon be out of reach, the chains stopping my jaws short of the kill.

I latched onto the leg of the nearest prey and bit down with such force it caused the bone to break, pulling him to the ground where he stayed screaming in agony, blood gushing from the broken limb and pooling around us. It happened in seconds, the other two barely able to register this horrific turn of events before I lunged again, disabling my second victim in a similar fashion. I don't remember consciously leaving the bully my human half had already had dealings with till last, but once again the colour had drained from him as he took in the damage from my fangs inflicted on the other two, and his bladder failed him once more at the low growl that rose from my throat.

He turned to run but I caught him by the ankle before he could clear the area of the room the chains would let me reach, and I dragged him back to lie screaming by his mates. Then I truly lost myself in the grip of the bloodlust, savaging the first body to attempt to move until it was unrecognisable as human, blood and guts spilling out around my paws and arterial blood spraying out over the walls, severed limbs lying twitching and convulsing in a mockery of life. So great had my rage become by that point that I was more concerned with the need to kill than to eat and I left more of my kills than usual. If I'd been thinking clearly I would have been sure the Elder vampire had indeed toyed with my mind, for the bloodlust should have been satisfied without the added rage and bloodlust from the human half of my mind feeding my frenzy. I had been much more like my old self that month, before the human had caused us to lose control so completely that it had led to the blackouts of previous months. And that meant once I'd gorged myself I should have grown calmer despite my restraints, instead of remaining frenzied and eager to kill again.

I was so crazed I didn't notice I'd left the lead bully alive. The scent of so much blood and death masked any scents of life, and I resumed my struggle to break *free while he tried to lie still, somehow having realised in my fury I was drawn to movement more than anything. Only when the first light of dawn spilled into the warehouse and I was forced back to human form once more did I finally cease my struggles, the pain of the transformation causing me to temporarily forget the chains.*

I wasn't really aware of it at the time but the boy watched me with wide eyes, one of the few humans ever to witness me transform and live to tell the tale, though for how long was now in the hands of my human half. I retreated into our subconscious but having been given the opportunity to eat more that night and thus be free of the weakness and exhaustion that had plagued my human self over the last two days, my rage remained. It blazed across our mind and fed the dark hunger for violence and murder born of the human in me, and despite being forced back to human form my other half was as feral as ever.

A part of me was glad to feel the darker side of my human nature, the rage that was tied to that violent part of me preferable to the emptiness and feelings of misery. But the chains the vampires had placed me in still held me back and prevented me from satisfying my bloodlust, which I wanted to make the most of again while it lasted. Knelt in a pool of gore, I let out a bestial roar of fury, the threat of the Slayers forgotten in my desire to visit the nearest human settlement and commit more massacres. If only I hadn't been restrained I could have slaughtered to my heart's content. Since I couldn't have that I made do with the leftovers of the wolf's kills for the time being, enjoying the rich organs and tender meat almost as much as my lupine half. Movement out of the corner of my eye distracted me from my bloody meal and I finally became aware of the one victim to have been left alive.

"You," I snarled, and lunged at him with bloodied hands.

The boy had evidently decided it was time to make his move while I was busy feeding, but he was too slow. I was able to catch him by the ankle much as my lupine self had done in his jaws, sending him crashing to the ground once more and dragging him back into the bloody pool of his friend's remains, where I pinned him down on his front.

"Please don't kill me; I won't tell anyone, I swear!" he pleaded, sobbing and pathetic.

"Do you know just how many I've killed? No? Well I'm not sure I know either. Let's just say there's been lots of them, including some I once considered friends and even my own blood. So tell me, what reason could I possibly have not to kill a bully like you? Someone who reminds me so much of the bastards that made my human life Hell. Why should I spare you?"

166

"I don't want to die, please."

"But everyone has to die eventually. I still see no reason why I should let you go."

He didn't have much to say in response to that. I was growing bored with him and the pleading was doing nothing to help keep the rage burning, so I whispered in his ear "I could make good on my threat from last month now. But I won't 'cause I don't really want to touch your balls, even to rip them off. I will kill you though, and it will be painful, I promise you that."

His screams rang out as I ripped his shirt apart and bit into the muscle of his lower back with teeth that had lengthened into fangs once again, piercing the flesh and trapping it in my jaws. I deliberately pulled backwards at a more leisurely pace so that the stringy flesh was slower to tear away from the bone it clung to, drawing out his suffering. As I took another bite, I remembered a programme I'd seen once on cannibalism and how some expert had said it was the ultimate taboo and the one that fills humans with the most dread and disgust. I hoped the bully was horrified to find himself being eaten alive by a monster that currently looked like a fellow human in form.

I didn't want to do too much damage round his spine and kill him too quickly, so after a third bite I forced him to roll over onto his back.

"My dad will find you, you freak," the boy yelled in panic while he'd been offered a temporary reprieve from the agony, resorting to the one last defence that had no doubt saved him from a beating in the past whenever he'd been prey to bigger bullies than himself. "He'll get his mates to help him kill you slowly, so you better let me go!"

"Then I'll kill your dad as well."

But it was what I needed from him, the rage latching onto the word freak. The old anger that had built up over the years at the bullies I'd once been powerless to stop fired up. And the rage had no time for slow, painful deaths. It wanted violence and it drove me to greater brutality as I committed this latest bloody murder, and gave me what I needed to revel in it.

I gave voice to that renewed rage in another bestial roar and lashed out with a clawed hand, raking the flesh from the top of one shoulder, right down to his hip on the opposite side of his body. The boy screamed again and returned to pleading with me, but when I rose from him it wasn't to grant the bully mercy.

Shaking and crying, he curled into the foetal position as I stood over him, his hands pressed to the gashes across his torso in a futile attempt to stop both the pain and the blood flow. There was something extremely gratifying about seeing him in the same position he'd no doubt had many of his playground victims in as he and his mates beat them. So I proceeded to smash his fragile mortal body with my fists, shattering bones and splitting skin. I'm not sure at what point he died but eventually my rage burnt itself out again and I fell to my knees by his corpse, weariness creeping in.

"Did I really deserve that, just for being a mouthy little git?"

I looked up to see the dead bully stood over me and his own broken body.

"Yes, for all the pain you've no doubt caused your classmates," I growled.

"And what about the pain you've caused my family?" he asked me. "Don't you care about that?"

"Mortals die and their loved ones move on. Their wounds will heal."

"And what about your wounds, son?" Dad said, appearing beside my victim.

I closed my eyes tiredly, hoping they'd go away. But my mind was never going to let me off that easily, so I answered "It's too late for me. The curse is going to keep on making me kill so why shouldn't I embrace that? I'm tired of fighting. And even if I choose to let go of the anger, I'm sure my lycanthropy would find some way to resurrect it eventually."

"Do you really think that anger is just the curse? My blood runs through your veins, whether you like it or not, and my anger is also a part of you."

"I'm nothing like you," I snarled. "If I'd stayed human I could have been happy."

"But you are more human now than ever," came a third voice, another face I'd never wanted to see again. Aughtie appeared, giving rise to a growl deep in my throat. "This darkness that drives you to kill, that is part of your humanity. If you truly want to be human again, you should continue to embrace it. Murder is what sets us apart from all other living things."

Murder, is that what it means to be human? Or was my brain simply trying to justify all the horrific acts I'd committed? I didn't know what I was trying to tell myself but I felt too drained to play my own mind games. "Just fuck off and let me sleep."

"I'll still be here, son," Dad said as I closed my eyes. "Awake or asleep, you can't escape me. We're bound by blood. Killing me hasn't freed you from that."

168

I tried to ignore him and let sleep take me, though it didn't come any easier now I was lying on a floor that was no longer merely cold and hard but also slick and sticky with blood. The scent of the death and carnage filled my nostrils, which would only call to the nightmares when I finally nodded off. But at least there were no more voices troubling me while I lay there, and eventually I drifted off.

I awoke to find night had already fallen. The vampires hadn't yet returned but I felt certain I would have to face them again that night, and I was surprised to find that thought had already summoned my anger back into being, even though I hadn't been consciously aware of it.

What meat was left on the three carcasses was cold and stiff, but I forced myself to eat and keep my strength up while I waited for my captors to come back. I didn't have to wait long before Ulfarr appeared in the doorway, stalking towards me as if he meant to kill me that very night, Lady Sarah following just behind him. I crouched in the pool of gore, my anger smouldering in the depths of what had once been my soul. I didn't raise my head to look at them until they came to a stop in front of me.

"Was there another murder?" I growled.

"Unsurprisingly, no there was not. Mark my words wolf, I will find such undeniable proof of your guilt that no one could possibly find any further reasons for me not to have your filthy head for the deaths of our brethren. And you will be revealed for what you are; nothing but a wild beast in need of putting down. Even now you crouch before me naked and bloody, every bit as savage as you were under the full moon. The Slayers did us a service by wiping out your kind, and it shall be my pleasure to finally rid the earth of you once and for all!"

"Not if I end you first," I snarled. "You should kill me now because if you don't, I swear one day I'll hunt you down while your corpse lies dormant and all the power you wield by night is out of your reach, and I will rip your rotten flesh from your bones like the beast you believe me to be."

"Don't tempt me, dog."

He dismissed me once again by turning his back, gave a nod to Lady Sarah and disappeared into the night, undaunted by my angry eyes following him until he was out of sight. I turned my glare on Lady Sarah but before I could do anything she placed me under her spell, my mind instantly calming. How could I be angry at a creature so beautiful as she? I was released from my chains and I obediently fell into step behind her as she led me back to the moors.

Once she deemed it safe, she released me from her hypnotic power, knowing I had no hope of tracking the Elder vampire if I'd been stupid enough to do so. The rage immediately spilled back into every fibre of my being.

"I am sorry for all this Nick, but I had no choice," Lady Sarah said, before I had chance to say anything.

"Really? Ulfarr might be so powerful he can control all beings around him but he didn't hold your tongue last month when he humiliated me in front of all the others. You had a choice to speak out on my behalf, so why didn't you? Or this full moon you could've at least tried to persuade Ulfarr to allow me peace while I was imprisoned, even if the chains were deemed necessary. Either one of you had the power to calm me but instead you let him trigger my rage. You chose to standby and let him torment me!"

"There is more at work here than you could know," she replied, her emotions impossible for me to read.

"Know what, I don't want to know," I growled. "You're not my friend and you're becoming even less of an ally. I don't know why you've helped me at all or what's suddenly changed, but I'm done with you."

"You are free to do as you wish, of course, but I would beg you to reconsider. Whatever your feelings towards me, you must realise you are still not ready to survive on your own."

"I'll take my chances."

I stormed off, cursing every last one of them. I'd had no reason to hate the vampires before I'd met the Elder, but after the way he kept treating me and the way it felt Lady Sarah had betrayed me, not to mention everything with the traitor Vince the previous year, I hated them then. I was done with vampire kind, sick of being treated as something beneath them, as if I was a lesser creature. Not all vampires were more powerful than me, and yet even the lower ones would receive better treatment than I had, or so it seemed. If I had truly been responsible for the three deaths I'd been accused of I was glad. Given the attitude of those I'd met, every last one of them deserved it, and I was not going to mourn for the loss of any more.

Though it hadn't been a conscious decision, I found myself at the same rocky crevice where I'd hidden the stolen clothes I'd gathered in the nights leading up to the full moon. If there was no world for me among the undead, other than as the outsider on vampire society (such as it was), no place for me in nature and none of my own kind left to seek out, where else could I go but back to the world of man? Even if I couldn't live among them, they at least had no supernatural power to subdue me with, and I was suddenly confident I could continue to elude the Slayers, even if I'd be hiding in plain sight. It wasn't like I was planning to go back to my hometown, where they could use my friends from my old life and my family against me. And still I dared to hope being back among humanity would go some way towards easing the loneliness and filling the empty void once I fell back into it, as I had to assume I would, the rage likely to burn out again before the night was through.

Chapter Sixteen – A Wolf in Human's Clothing

After washing the thickest of the filth from my skin, I set out in the opposite direction to the warehouse, determined to put as many miles between the vampire's preferred meeting place and myself as possible. I also wanted to be as far from Lady Sarah as I could get before weariness took over and I was forced to stop to rest.

I wandered towards lower ground in wolf form, leaving the barrenness of the moors for farmland which eventually gave way to man-made landscapes of concrete and tarmac. As tempting as it was to find a local hotel or bed and breakfast and steal enough to spend the night in the comfort of a warm, human bed, I hadn't quite grown reckless enough to disregard everything Lady Sarah had impressed upon me in the last few months together. I found shelter in an old shed on a property that was for sale. Whoever had lived there previously had already moved on and though it was still fairly risky, sleeping in an area surrounded by humans, I felt it was as good a place as any to spend the early hours of the morning.

Compared to the harshness of the moorland and the discomfort of my makeshift cage during the full moon, the shed might as well have been a five star hotel. I'd carried the clothes and blanket in my jaws and I was able to curl up in relative comfort and warmth, quick to fall asleep.

Shards of daylight penetrated the dusty, cobweb lined glass, uncomfortably bright against my eyes. I growled and tried to doze back off, but the sound of human footsteps made me instantly alert.

"I'm telling you, there's some kind of wild beast in there," a woman's voice said. "I came to unlock the property ready for a viewing this afternoon and when I stepped out into the garden for a smoke, I could hear growling coming from that shed."

"Probably just some stray dog. We'll take a look," a man assured her. "You did the right thing calling us – can't be too careful after all that nasty business with the rogue wolf running loose in Yorkshire last year."

I tensed, ready for a fight. The man could have just been some kind of wildlife official sent to investigate the call the estate agent must have made, but at worst he was a Slayer who knew full well any report of a wild beast could be something more. And if he was a Slayer he'd no doubt come prepared for the possibility of finding the supernatural, werewolf or otherwise, which meant I needed to be equally prepared.

The shed door was opened cautiously and I made a split second decision to kill them both before either could call for help. But first I had the sense to quickly push the clothes and the blanket under some of the junk left by the previous owners, in the hopes they'd be protected from the worst of the blood I was about to spill.

As the man peered round the door I lunged, grabbing him by the throat and silencing the scream before he had chance to form it. He fell to the floor, clutching at the torn flesh flapping about in ragged strips as air passed through it, panicking as he gasped for breath, his brain quickly becoming starved of oxygen. Even as he fell I was on the woman, ripping the life from her in a similar fashion. Blood and gore sprayed the inside of the shed but I felt nothing this time as I killed them, and I didn't immediately cause any further damage to their dying bodies.

I checked the pile of clothes lying towards the back of the shed and was able to rescue them before any blood soaked through. Luckily I'd shoved them under an industrial quality plastic bag which had protected them from the worst of the arterial spray. My skin was another matter and I was going to have to find another pond or lake to wash in before I could pass for human, so with that in mind I decided to gorge myself while I had the chance, ensuring I had plenty of energy to support the transformation back to human later.

I made sure to push the clothes just outside, hoping no one was watching, and then fed as quickly as I could. It was messier than usual because I was rushing, trying to chew off bigger chunks than I could manage and dribbling chunks of flesh and blood everywhere as a result. I was able to finish without being disturbed and did my best to lick the worst of the blood and gore from my lips and my fangs, hoping I could bundle the clothes in my jaws so the blanket would protect them from becoming covered in suspicious looking stains.

There was no evidence either of the humans had been Slayers but I knew I would be better leaving the area and moving on to another town or city, since it would only be a matter of time before the bodies were found. I'd find somewhere to wash along the way and dress, then I could return to the human world for a time, as I was suddenly so desperate to do.

I was forced to remain in wolf form until nightfall, when I was able to wash under the cover of darkness in a stream, ribbons of blood twisting and dancing out from my filthy body, contaminating the otherwise pure water. I was right in the middle of more farmland, the stream cutting through the surrounding countryside and rushing on towards the coast. During the day I would surely have been seen and driven off or worse, but hidden in the shadows I was relatively safe, and the main cause for me to hurry my bath was the bite of the cold.

Once I'd dressed I headed back towards civilisation, but it was dawn before I took to wandering the streets of my latest chosen haunt. Once there I started out simply taking in the sights and sounds, as if I was a traveller from some strange lands experiencing British culture for the first time.

Though the term concrete jungle was often applied to the built up world humanity lived in, a part of me liked exploring this new place I'd found myself in. There was a certain sense of history to the old town, despite all the modern developments. It wasn't joy as such since that gaping chasm still remained where once my emotions had been, but I guess you could say I found it interesting, if nothing else. It wasn't that I'd ever had any particular passion for history or anything, I just liked the atmosphere to the place that was lacking from newer settlements, and those that had changed so much over the years as to be barely recognisable to what they once were, so modernised they might be mistaken for being completely new.

At first the streets were quiet and mostly deserted, only the occasional early riser passing me by. They didn't even spare me a sideways glance and like a ghost I roamed through housing estates, working my way to the centre. However, the town soon started to come to life as various businesses opened their doors to customers, and for the first time in months I found myself in a throng of people. The lupine part of me hungered for them, but it was the fast food and other eating places dotted around that made my mouth water. As much as my lycanthropy caused me to crave raw meat, it seemed some part of me still desired the cooked food I'd been accustomed to as a human.

Other scents permeated the air, overpowering and alien to me after the months spent in the natural world, even though they'd once been so great a part of everyday life as to be barely noticeable. There was a certain novelty to it all after months of solitude and I spent most of the day trying to immerse myself in that world and blend in with the crowd. I allowed myself to step inside some of the more interesting shops, where I wouldn't appear out of place. Looking round them meant I could escape the cold and it helped pass the time.

I checked out a few of the latest DVDs and games, careful to keep my head down so the security cameras didn't capture a clear image of my face. But it didn't really help the depression that was creeping back in, knowing I would most likely never get to watch or play them. I kept to wandering between the three bookstores after that

174

unhappy thought, killing time by reading different sections of the same book in each store, moving on after each chapter so as not to overstay my welcome or invite awkward questions. Luckily it seemed to be a weekend, as no one challenged my presence like they might have done on a school day.

When Luke appeared again, I wasn't even surprised to see him by that point. Whatever it was that allowed him to just happen to be in the same places I turned up in, I felt sure I'd find out eventually. Until then he at least made for better company than the vampires.

"Hey bro," he said. "There's something surreal about seeing you in here."

"I wasn't always a monster, remember. I used to have a normal human life, like everyone else."

"Yeah, but knowing who you really are and after seeing you at your wildest, I never expected to see you clothed and browsing bookstores," he laughed.

"Even monsters get bored," I shrugged.

"I see you had good taste in your human life. I've always been a big horror fan as well."

"Yeah, I never thought my life would turn into a horror story though. You know, if you keep hanging round me you could end up dead or worse yourself. The Slayers will quite happily go through humans to kill me and there's the vampires – if they come for me, they may well decide to execute you as well if they see us together and I can't protect you from them."

"I understand the risks, don't worry man. I'm not going anywhere."

"You better not, you crazy bastard. I've got too many questions for you now so no disappearing on me without answering them, okay?"

"Deal," he said, grinning.

I bid him goodbye and ventured away from the town as it was growing dark, hungry again and knowing I should find somewhere to rest, if only for a few hours. I caught a rabbit which was enough to keep me going if I kept the number of transformations to a minimum. For the time being I had no real need to change to wolf form again so I remained human, returning to the farmland with the stream cutting through it where I'd hidden the blanket in a shallow hole with a large rock to cover it. I undressed and changed the clothes for the blanket so as to keep the garments as clean as possible. What I would do when they started to smell I hadn't thought of, but I would worry about that later.

175

I also briefly wondered what I'd do during the next full moon, as I had no intention of returning to Lady Sarah. Ulfarr's argument for my guilt might be circumstantial evidence at best, but even I had to admit I was the most likely suspect. There was every chance I had indeed killed the three vampires during a lapse in my self-control, and the fact there'd been no further murders while I'd been locked up for the last full moon suggested it wasn't the work of some supernatural serial killer, or another surviving werewolf the vampires didn't know about. After the way I'd been treated I really didn't care if I'd killed any of them, or if I killed any more of them next month, but if Ulfarr was keeping a closer eye on me as he'd said he would, then they surely would execute me the moment I attacked any more of their kind. I pushed that thought away as well, hoping a solution would present itself when the need arose.

That night I rested in a patch of woodland, behind a fallen tree. It wasn't much in the way of shelter but the thick trunk went some way to keeping the wind off me. I was able to doze for a few hours, waking again early morning while it was still dark. Another rabbit served as breakfast, then it was back to the stream to wash and dress, and find another town to spend the day in.

A few days later the novelty had already begun to wear off. As I sheltered in one of the bookstores, I was aware of the staff talking amongst themselves in low voices and I overheard one of them say "There's that boy again. He's been coming in here all week, hanging around when he should be at home or in school. Something's not right about him."

"Yeah, it does seem weird," her colleague replied. "We better keep a close eye on him; wouldn't surprise me to find him shoplifting."

So I abandoned the book I was reading and retreated back out onto the streets, suddenly noticing how the humans were giving me a fairly wide berth and sometimes casting me suspicious glances. I wasn't sure whether that was because, unable to wash the clothes or give my skin a proper wash in soapy water, I had indeed begun to smell, or the fact that people thought I should be in school and knew something was amiss, just like the staff in the shop. Or maybe people simply sensed deep down that I was different from them. Whatever the reason, I was back to feeling like the outsider. Maybe I'd never passed as human during this brief return to their world, and I just hadn't wanted to see it until it reached the point where I was no longer able to deny it. I didn't know but the more I was made to feel apart from them, the greater the depression that began to envelop me, every bit as bad as the emptiness I'd been existing in over the last few months.

Even Luke's company couldn't ease it that day.

"You could just kill them all," he said.

"How come you're so okay with killing? Most people would call that insanity."

"Don't worry about me. But you're hurting and they're only making things worse, right? Teach them a lesson. It's not like you haven't done it before, so what's stopping you?"

I shook my head. "Not this time."

I didn't immediately return to the natural world, but the longer I lingered in the town, the more paranoid I grew. People seemed to be staring and I saw several whispering to each other, too quietly for even my acute sense of hearing to catch what they were saying. I started to feel on edge, wondering how many of them could be Slayers, and my eyes constantly darted from face to face, searching for any potential threats.

Loneliness washed over me, surrounded by people though I was. I knew I could kill any one of them and feel nothing, not even bat an eyelid. After all, what was one more lost soul in the endless sea I'd created, so many ripped from their bodies long before their time? Yet I looked around and realised I didn't want to kill them anymore, not even the potential enemies. I no longer wanted to be this dead thing surrounding himself with more death. I just wanted to live again, even if I couldn't truly be part of their world anymore. You see, there's a big difference between living and existing, and I can barely remember now the last time I felt truly alive.

I might have been born a killer, but there is also a huge difference between a killer and a murderer. I used to despise human hunters, yet in indulging mindless slaughter had I not allowed myself to become as bad as them? By embracing the darkness maybe I'd sealed my own fate, setting myself apart from most of the law abiding citizens as surely as if I'd walked among them as a wolf. Maybe they could sense I'd given into it and feared me like other animals did, even if they weren't consciously aware of that instinct that screamed predator.

And yet, how much could the curse really be blamed for? Of all the atrocities I'd committed, when I'd murdered out of rage or massacred simply to try and feel something, how much of that was born of my curse, and how much was purely that inner darkness that existed at the heart of humanity? How many of those killings had been the work of my darker side, which would have been there independent of the curse? Without the curse maybe that darkness would never have been unleashed, but once it had its first taste of blood, I was quick to fall into it. And how much could I blame on humanity itself? My rage was tied to the curse, but it had been made all the more potent over the years for the way I'd been treated at the hands of my playground tormentors, as well as the anger my own Dad had fed me by bullying me in his own way during his own fits of anger. And maybe some of that anger had been passed on from him through blood, as my brain had suggested through that latest hallucination of him I'd seen in the old warehouse.

How much of that rage had humanity created, or at least shaped? Maybe if they'd treated me better I wouldn't have been so quick to indulge the dark desire to kill on so many occasions. But human darkness and cruelty will always be quick to spread, even to those that think of themselves as the purest of souls, where it will fester and breed and infect others. How many of my crimes could I blame on them for sculpting me in their own image? Even my lupine half was afflicted by the human darkness to some extent, the bloodlust stemming from our humanity.

Another voice brought me out of my dark musings, making me jump.

"Did you even stop to think what fate you forced those poor souls into? Oblivion, Purgatory, Hell? Which is worse do you think?"

The hallucination of Lizzy had reappeared. I growled as if to make her go away but she only continued to torment me, like an echo of the conscience I'd assumed dead.

"Your two latest victims; they were innocent and yet you chose to kill them instead of running. How might they be suffering now because of you?"

"I didn't know they were innocent though, did I?" I argued, while Luke gave me a concerned look, but he seemed to know I wasn't talking to him and didn't interfere.

"You knew it was a possibility. How many more must die because of the darkness you continue to allow to rule you?"

"And what would you have me do, huh?"

It came out as another growl and I turned to glare at her, only to find she was gone. More of the townspeople were staring now I was acting even stranger and I was forced to leave. I found an alley in a quieter part of the town and ripped off the stolen clothes, all desire to appear human and walk among them suddenly gone. The transformation back to wolf form came quicker and more smoothly than during a full moon, and I slunk off back into the wilderness without even saying bye to Luke, alone once more and unsure what to do.

Chapter Seventeen – Blood Festival

The loneliness weighed yet heavier upon my heart with the renewed realisation that I was as far from human as I'd ever been, while the winter grew harsher. I was growing delirious in the unforgiving conditions, my mind made more fragile by the physical hardships I continued to force my body through. I should have sought out shelter now that there was no Lady Sarah to insist we remain exposed on the moors, but instead I stayed shivering under my blanket in wolf form (having retrieved it after leaving the town), cold despite my fur coat and the extra man-made layer.

Lizzy began to appear more frequently, though the apparition only fed the loneliness and allowed it to grow even more.

"You're supposed to be dead," I said to her one night.

"I could be for all you know, thanks to you."

"No, you're not her ghost. Not the flesh and blood you, I meant my conscience. That's what you are, right? But you're supposed to be dead."

"Perhaps your emotions are not as dead as you let yourself believe. You buried them to cope with all the deaths you caused, the atrocities you committed, and continue to commit. But you're not so damaged as to be left with nothing at all."

"What does it matter; happiness is out of reach now. Completely empty or depressed: both are equally as bad. The only thing worth feeling is the anger which keeps me going, but I just can't hold onto it whenever it does temporarily spark back to life," I said bitterly. "You were one of my closest friends, Lizzy. I wish you were really here now, even if you'd hate me for the monster I've become. I wish I could go back home. My heart aches for everything I left behind, for all of you who I left behind. What's the point in feeling unless I were to go back to you all?"

"But you know you can't go back. I almost died once because of you," she answered. There was no emotion in the hallucination's voice; it was merely a statement, one of the many hard truths that had led me to make the decision to leave my old life behind in the first place. The hallucination changed, taking on the appearance of Lizzy that night when I'd found her deep within the local base the Slayers had imprisoned us in, bloody and beaten. She held up her left hand where the little finger had been cut off, the one wound the Slayers had inflicted which was truly irreparable damage. Maybe if I'd had enough sense to grab the severed digit and make sure the hospital staff would find it along with the rest of her they could have reattached it, but the thought had never occurred to me at the time. The other wounds she'd suffered had no doubt scarred, and it pained me to think about the mental scars she might also have been left with, invisible but just as severe.

"No, the Slayers did that to you. I did try to keep you out of all the madness the werewolf passed on when he bit me."

"Yet you still blame yourself," she replied. "You know it was you who did this to me. If you were to return to us now, do you truly think we would welcome you back with open arms? Maybe if you'd told me the truth when I asked you what was going on we could have avoided this, instead of keeping me in the dark of my ignorance where I was easier prey. Do you think I've forgiven you for just leaving without at least explaining to me who Aughtie really was or why her people did this to me?"

"How could I tell you the truth? Even if I transformed to make you believe me you'd have soon realised I was the 'rogue wolf' that killed Fiona and the others. How would that have helped?"

My conscience did not deign to answer me. Lizzy had vanished, leaving behind a dull ache for the life the curse and the Slayers had torn me from, like a steady throbbing deep within that empty chasm that had once been my soul, an ache even the winter couldn't numb.

Snow came down thick and heavy, the wind driving it against my pitiful body. I hadn't eaten in days yet I was reluctant to hunt, curling into a tighter ball under what little warmth the blanket had to offer. The hunger would not be denied, however, and eventually it drove me to my feet. Stiffly I rose and began to wander in search of prey, a dark shadow prowling the whitened landscape.

I used to like snow when I'd been mostly human, but whilst I remained caught out in that frozen world it made me thoroughly miserable. It fell thick and fast, the wind driving it into my face. Flakes caught in my fur, specks of white against the dark greys and browns of my coat. One flake found its way into my eye, hard enough to make it sting. I squinted, trying to protect them while I searched the bright whiteness for any signs of prey, but the snow made it almost impossible. With my eyes squinted, it was harder to focus on anything but the little flecks of white falling around me. As a wolf my eyes were designed to pick up signs of movement. The snow made it hard to differentiate between the movement of animals and the movement of the snow itself. I was having to rely on scent and sound, neither of which my human self had mastered, sight remaining my primary sense I relied upon. It seemed the only way I would make a kill would be if something came and offered itself to me, which of course was never going to happen.

I felt so lost and alone, I was losing my will to live. Part of me was ready to just collapse and let the cold steal the last of the warmth from my limbs until it drained my life with its icy fingers. Yet still a part of me fought for survival, and I struggled on. It became clear there was no prey to be had out on the snow covered moors, no life in this barren landscape, this wintry realm of the dead. To the realm of men I knew I must turn once more, despite the unhappy endings in each area I'd visited over the last few months. It was either that or starve.

Finding my way to the nearest town was easy enough. Whether it was the same place that had become my haunt for a brief time or not, I couldn't say. The snow hid most landmarks I might have recognised and my current state of mind continued to weaken my grasp on reality. But before long buildings loomed overhead, marking my return to civilisation, and it didn't matter if this was a new place or somewhere I'd explored before. There was food to be had here to fill the emptiness in my belly, even if there was nothing to be had for the emptiness in my soul. So I padded down the streets in search of my next meal.

That pure white snow of the wintry world I'd come from had already been turned to dirty slush on many of the streets, symbolic perhaps of mankind's polluted stain on the world. After spending so long in the purity of the natural world, or as pure as it could ever be in this modern age, it might seem odd to some that I had been so desperate to return to the smog of man's domain. And yet it was all I'd ever known and all I'd longed to know again, before my latest attempt to reconnect with humanity had crushed that desire through the realisation that I would always be the outsider, never to be accepted in their society again.

Hard though it may be to believe, I had no intention of taking human prey. The curse hungered for human flesh, the wolf stalking restlessly in my subconscious, waiting for a chance to take control and revel in the hunt and the kill. As cautious as my lupine self usually was, hunger was stripping him of rational thought until he was reduced to his most primal state. My poor mental and physical condition was taking its toll on both parts of my identity it seemed, and while he hated me for usually being so careless, our personalities continued to shift, ever changing and swapping traits. As reckless as I could be, caution ruled me in that moment and I fought the wolf and the curse's lusts, determined not to succumb to such cravings.

I would have been content to take a stray cat or dog, or even to scavenge what I could from the rubbish bins, but the bins must have been emptied recently for I found no carcasses to pick at, and the streets were just as deserted of animal life as the countryside had been, most creatures having the sense to shelter from the cold. Only one creature braved these conditions, always seeking to defy nature as they went about their hectic lives.

I heard the man long before I saw him. There'd been sounds of a car attempting to battle its way through the snow covered roads, then the slam of a car door as the driver was forced to abandon his vehicle and continue on foot. I could hear him trudging towards me as I fought my own inner battle. Briefcase in hand, he refused to be beaten by the weather, some urgent business requiring him to brave the blizzard and journey to the office. It was growing dark by this point and the working day must surely be drawing to a close, yet whatever his business was, it seemingly could not wait till the next day. He was so intent on his own battle with the elements that he didn't notice me watching hungrily, fighting my instincts and the wolf. In the end my hunger won out, as it always did, though I wouldn't let the wolf or the bloodlust completely take over, wanting only to feed and move on.

As I advanced on the latest hapless mortal to cross my path he remained unaware of me, his head bowed against the cold, the wind howling in his ears. I fell on him like the ravenous beast I was, sending him crashing to the ground face first. His precious briefcase was torn from his grasp, the catch flying open, but the man could do nothing to save his documents or his life. He screamed as my fangs tore into his muscular shoulders, ripping the meat free of the bone and gulping it down eagerly. His blood sprayed out, warm as it splattered my face. The man continued to struggle but I was too strong for any mortal to overpower. I moved from his shoulder along his arm, cracking bone in my jaws and leaving the limb hanging on by a thread of tendons and ligaments. More warmth splashed across me and I abandoned the meat in search of offal, biting into the flesh around his spine and burying my snout in his abdomen as if I could steal the warmth from him, as well as the flesh I needed to sustain me.

The sound of more humans from somewhere in their town centre distracted me from my meal. It sounded like they were holding some kind of festival, and though I had far from eaten my fill the loneliness rushed back in, more powerful than the hunger. Despite my earlier caution I howled as if to tell them I was coming, the sounds of human laughter calling to me as surely as the howling of a pack would call to the wolf. I abandoned my kill, suddenly convinced I was meant

183

to be at the event this town was holding, as if it would give me the connection to humanity I so sorely longed for. In my current delirious state of mind I was foolish enough to think I might laugh along with them and rediscover how to fill that void with something other than anger, as there had been once, before I fell victim to the curse. Behind me the man lay dying, his life fading as fast as the blood leaking from his ruined body. He shook violently from the pain and the cold, powerless to do anything but wait for death to take him. Papers were blown from his briefcase and scattered by a gust of wind, as insignificant now as the man's life I had ripped from him. Then the street grew still and quiet once more, fresh snow falling quickly enough to cover the corruptive stain I'd created on that pure white blanket.

I transformed back to my human form but similar to that full moon night when I'd entered the pub, my feverish mind failed to consider the problems this appearance would bring, with my lack of clothes and blood stained skin.

"You know you can't go back, Nick," the hallucination with Lizzy's face said, my only constant companion. "Why do you continue to torment yourself with these false hopes?"

I was barely aware of her as I stumbled into the town square where the humans had gathered despite the heavy snow, oblivious even to the cold on my bare skin in my desperation to join them, to be one of them and enjoy their world as I once had.

Luke was quick to find me, and he eagerly asked, "On the hunt again?"

"You're even more bloodthirsty than I am. Why do you enjoy all this slaughter so much?"

"You're not the only one to suffer people's hatred of anyone they see as different from themselves. There's a few I'd kill myself if I could but, unlike you, I have to answer to the law."

That might be partly true, but I wasn't entirely satisfied with his answer. Bullying alone wouldn't have made me a killer, if it hadn't been for my lycanthropy. There was much more to this human than he was letting on, and I was determined to discover his secrets eventually. But I was more interested in the town event taking place to press him for answers right then.

A local band played on a stage directly in front of me and burger vans lined either side. Hundreds were packed around the stage and crowded round the burger vans, waiting to be served. Those on the stage noticed me first. The bassist's eyes met mine as he scanned the crowd, his fingers fumbling his guitar as if his hands had suddenly forgotten how to play while he gawped at me in shocked silence, taking

184

in my naked, gore spattered body. The rest of the band soon followed suit and the crowd turned to see what they were looking at with shouts of "What the hell?" but they too fell silent when they caught sight of me. They stared as the customers had in the pub that night when my mind had briefly become whole again, but there were no kindly women to mother me this time. Worse than the silence was the jeering that came soon after, kids of all ages pointing and laughing and shouting freak, while most of the adults just continued to stare in horror or morbid fascination, though some of them joined in the childish laughter. Always it came back to the cruelty of mankind, and their intolerance for anyone who differed in any way to what was considered 'the norm'.

"See, they don't deserve to live," Luke whispered in my right ear. "Your pain should be clear to see but instead they just point and laugh, and stare at the freak among them. No one cares enough about you to come rushing to your aid, no one wants anything to do with someone who doesn't fit into the nice little box assigned by society."

As I looked back at them I began to see the school bullies that had tormented me through my mortal years, and between their behaviour and Luke's words, something in me snapped. My rage blazed into life, roaring through the emptiness until the fury filling my core must surely have given me a fiery glow, my veins alight with blood turned to something molten, my eyes replaced with fiery pits, the snow turning to steam on my bare skin. My bloodlust was re-awoken, wed so closely to that rage as it was, and it was pressing for the change. I gave into it gladly, welcoming the power and the greater strength of my lupine form, and revelling in it. But as had become my wont I only took it halfway, letting the townsfolk see the true nature of the monster I had become.

"Don't do it, Nick. You know this is wrong," Lizzy said, appearing on my left side.

The jeers soon died in the throats of the crowd when they realised they were witnessing the impossible. I fell to my hands and knees while the change took hold, the shifting of bone and flesh too uncomfortable if I remained standing. As always when it was brought on by rage the pain felt good, and I ignored the voice of my conscience as I embraced the transformation taking place. The changes were not as dramatic as when I took it fully to wolf form, and it was over quickly. I rose back onto two legs and turned my fiery gaze on the now silent crowd, horror and disbelief holding them in place.

"Teach them a lesson, Nick," Luke urged me. "They deserve the same cruelty they just showed you. Let them feel your pain."

"No, Nick," Lizzy implored. "It's time to put a stop to the needless slaughter. Just let go of the anger and turn back. You don't have to do this."

"You know it will feel good this time. It's what you've been waiting for, and it's too late to turn away now. Unleash your fury on them. Enjoy the slaughter while your rage lasts."

A wordless roar of anger rushed out of me in response to his words, and then the screaming began and they scattered like any panicked herd before a predator. My heart sang with their terror and I fell upon them, slashing with clawed hands which ripped through cloth and flesh, exposing bone and spilling guts. My jaws snapped around the leg of a woman trying to flee and sent her crashing to the ground. She'd been carrying her young boy in an effort to save him but my bloodlust would not be denied, my rage directed at all of them and demanding the lives of every last one. I killed man, woman and child alike, exulting in their screams of pain and terror and the deaths I tore from them all.

The image of Lizzy looked on disappointedly until she began to fade, drowning in the darkness I'd fallen back into. Luke stayed to watch as he had every other time he'd been around to see the gruesome spectacle my rage created, though I soon lost sight of him in the chaos. Most of the terrified humans were fighting against each other to escape the monster in their midst, crushing each other in their mindless panic. Any who fell were quickly trampled into the snow beneath the feet of their fellows.

Bodies quickly piled up in the square, my supernatural speed allowing me to kill dozens in the blink of an eye. Some I made quick work of, ripping out their throats with tooth or claw, some I left broken and bloody but still alive when they hit the ground, in the grip of a slow and agonising death. One of the men in the burger vans was too slow to make his escape from the vehicle and I leapt up on the shelf beneath the counter where the sauces were laid out for customers, reaching over the counter to grab his head. I pressed his face against the grill where burgers were still sizzling, steam rising up as his skin touched the hot metal. He screamed and his body jerked violently but I would not let go until finally he went still, a smell like roasting pork filling my nostrils and making me drool hungrily, though it was tainted somewhat by the sulphurous stink of his hair sizzling. Regardless of how tantalising the pork smell was, I would not eat until the last one was dead, determined none would escape my wrath.

As I'd seen in the pub, some of the humans were stupid enough to film me with their phones and digital cameras they'd brought to the event. I wasn't too concerned with any footage they'd captured, trusting any devices that survived the chaos to be taken care of by the Slayers. I was more infuriated to see them standing there when they should be fleeing before me with the rest.

The band hadn't yet had chance to exit the stage and join the stampeding throng. The crowd had been most packed around there, the ones nearest the front pushing through those slower to react, fighting for their lives. There were a greater number of casualties in that direction, before I'd even got to them.

I turned my attention to that area and bounded forward, killing several in the crowd as I made for the stage. Some human part of me, remnants of the boy that had once longed for fame and fortune, wanted to stand in the spotlight where the crowd could see the glory of my bestial form, singing with a strength and speed they would never know as it crushed their fragile mortal bodies, magnificent but deadly. In reality the humans were too busy trying to escape to pay much attention to the bloody spectacle now taking place on stage, but still I dealt the band especially grisly deaths.

The singer I impaled on his own mic stand to keep his body propped up, then grabbed his lower jaw and ripped it off to leave his tongue lolling out. Finally I pried open the skin and flesh around his voice box, moving on once his natural instruments were laid bare.

The soft flesh of the lead guitarist's belly I tore open as easily as a knife through butter with the claw of my left index finger, while I held him by the throat in my right hand. I ripped out his entrails and stuffed the body of his beloved guitar in the hole, then turned to the bassist who'd been the first to see me. Since he'd been the first to stare I gripped his head in my hands and drove the claws of my thumbs into his eyes while he screamed and writhed in my grasp. I dropped him to the floor, still alive, where he tried to weakly crawl away, so I stamped on him hard enough to shatter his spine and render his limbs useless. Finally I advanced on the drummer who I seated back behind his drum kit, ripping open his chest to break two ribs off and force them into his hands like drumsticks. This was some of my bloodiest, most brutal work, but still the bloodlust was not satisfied. With another roar I leapt from the stage and back into the now lifeless crowd. The living had finally made their way out of the town square, but they would not get far. Still the snow fell around us, too deep for them to escape by any method other than on foot, and even that was made hard enough.

The massacre spilled into all the surrounding streets, as if the first blood spilled in the square was the bleeding heart of the town and now it was being carried into the connecting veins and arteries. Young and old fell before me, strong and weak. If we lived in an age of heroes then perhaps this tale would have a different ending and I would not be here to tell it myself, but the Slayers are far from heroes and there were no others to stand against me. In stories they say evil never wins, yet in reality evil, if that's what I am, triumphs just as often as good. The real world is harsher than those of fantasy, though monsters like myself are real enough. But in reality heroes do not miraculously appear to deliver the townsfolk in their hour of need, and prey fall before predators, both natural and unnatural. My rage claimed them all, and no rescue came. Though it was a wonder no Slayers had shown up to disturb me from my carnage. Either any that happened to be in the area already lay dead before they'd had chance to draw a weapon, or they had forsaken this particular town for some twisted reason. So there would be no help for these people. All they could hope for was a quick death when I caught them, for die they would that night. Even those who'd been quickest to react and had managed to put some distance between us while I slaughtered in the town square, even they could not escape. If it hadn't been for the snow maybe some of them would have stood a chance, but it slowed them too much and none made it far. And then finally I was advancing on the last of my victims, a group of the school children who had mocked me so, and thus unwittingly brought about their own doom.

They heard me coming and turned to look, their hearts pounding faster with renewed terror. Even with the scents of blood and death so thick on the air, I could still smell the stink as one of the boys lost control of his bowels. I slashed open his throat in disgust and focussed on the other three, intending to make a meal of them. They were running again and I gladly gave chase, bounding over the snow on all fours. One of the girls fell and cowered before me, the other two never even slowing or looking back. I leapt over her, deciding to kill her last, and continued to close the distance on the other two. The other girl was slightly slower so I caught her first, grabbing her meaty calf in my jaws as I drew level and pulling her to the ground. She screamed and cried for help, reaching out towards the kid who might have been her boyfriend. I left her on the floor and pounced on the boy. He'd ignored her cries and was still running, until I landed on his back and sent him crashing to the floor. His screams joined her own as I snapped one of his arms in my jaws, ripping it from the socket and crunching hungrily. He died soon after, his back torn open to reveal the bone of his spine and ribcage, the flesh shining brightly beneath the streetlight. I didn't eat my fill from the first one, turning back to the girl struggling to rise with her ruined leg.

She fell back down, onto her side, and covered her head in her hands as if that would protect her from this living nightmare. I grabbed her good leg and chewed on that, moving up to her abdomen and the rich organs that lay just beneath that smooth skin. Her heart beat its last as I wrapped my jaws around it, pulling it free. Blood oozed down my throat, spilling over my jaws and onto the snow. The markings of my coat which resembled a mortal timber wolf were no longer recognisable, the lighter fur darkened and stained from the slaughter. My fur was matted with blood and gore, which must have made me look even more fearsome. When I'd eaten my fill from those two I hunted down my last victim, the girl her friends had left behind.

She'd picked herself up from the spot where she'd fallen and pushed her cold, aching body onwards, back down the street. The snow was quickly covering her footprints but she would not be hard to track down, even with my inexperience at using my enhanced sense of hearing and smell. The sound of life was unusually loud in this town of the dead, as if she belonged here no more than I had when I'd first entered and it had still been the province of living men. There was no challenge in hunting her down but that didn't matter. I soon had her in my sights once more and this time there would be no escape. She knew as much, her despair plain to see on her face, and her terror of the pain and death that was soon to come, as it had for all the others. Yet still she struggled when I bore down on her, her punches growing weaker as the cold stole the warmth from her body and I savaged her flesh, until finally she grew still and all was quiet, save for my panting.

"Must it always end in blood?" Lizzy asked sadly.

Blood and death, that seemed to be all that was left to me. But I didn't say it out loud. Even my anger was draining back into the emptiness that was once my soul, and I knew better than to try and cling to it by then. I would only fail as I had so many times since leaving my hometown, so why bother to continue in my struggles to hold onto it? I let it fade away, staring down at the tattered ruins of yet more lives my rage had claimed, flaps of torn flesh blowing freely in the wind, a ghastly flag proclaiming my savagery. Maybe the vampires were right, maybe I was no more than a beast, feral and brutal. I stared down at my bloodied, monstrous hands as if, even more than a year after falling victim to the curse, I still could not believe they were my own.

Whilst no mortal could ever match the beauty of the vampires I'd beheld during my 'trial', as cruel and merciless as they had been towards me, the girl I'd slaughtered had been quite pretty by human standards, which I noticed in a detached sort of way. Half her face remained untouched, the right eye still whole and not yet dulled, the flesh pale in death but unmarred by even the ravages of acne suffered by most humans her age, perfect and unblemished like a porcelain sculpture. The rest of her was unrecognisable as male or female, or even human, her body so badly mutilated that she'd been robbed not only of her life but of that beauty she'd once held.

My rage might seem dead to me once the gaping chasm engulfed it and the emptiness returned, but, when it did rekindle, it seemed nothing could withstand my wrath. I'd once thought to become a werewolf would be a gift but I had soon learnt why it was always talked of as a curse. This power I'd been granted was destructive and nothing good could come of its ravaging nature. I'd known that when I'd come to realise I could no longer live among humans, unless I wanted more people I cared about to get hurt. And I was reminded of it once again. I wasn't safe to be around mortals, the Slayers posing as much threat to any around me as my curse. It could only ever end in death, either at my jaws or at the hands of the Slayers who had already proven they would go to such lengths to end the curse for good. The hallucination of Lizzy was right; how many more must die before I surrendered myself to my lonely fate?

It seemed I couldn't tear my gaze from that one perfect eye staring at me out of what remained of her beauty, and in that instant she was no longer some unfortunate stranger that happened to cross my path, but Amy's friend Mel, as she'd lain in the frozen ground just over a year ago, her once beautiful form similarly mutilated. It had snowed that night as well, a night that now seemed a lifetime ago.

In the midst of all the grief and the guilt I'd probably thought about how the world would never know such beauty again, but that was foolish. There were billions of girls on the planet, many of them blessed with good looks. There would be more, just as beautiful as the girls and women I'd stolen such beauty from, along with their lives. Was that all mortals were, just another of their species briefly walking upon the earth until death claimed them, each just another face in the crowd, unremarkable and so very alike hundreds, thousands, maybe even millions of others around them? And what did that make me, a being with no foreseeable end and no others of his kind? I had never truly been one of them, the blood of wolves making me different to the sheep I'd tried so hard to imitate and fit in with. So why did I still torment myself with that which was denied to me, even before my wolfish half was awoken?

"It's a terrible thing, to walk this world alone," came a male voice from somewhere behind me, as if he had heard my thoughts. But it wasn't Luke this time. I hadn't noticed the human since I'd lost him in the chaos I'd created. "Do you not tire of it?"

"Better this way," I grunted. "I can't control it. Friend or foe, my bloodlust claims all. This world holds no place for one such as me. I have no place among humans, nor among wolves. The vampires shun me. So who else can I turn to? I am the last of my kind. To live in this void, between worlds but never truly a part of any of them, is to be alone."

"You need not be alone," he replied, walking into my line of sight so I could see that he was the same vampire who had saved me from Ulfarr's judgement, and the execution he had been about to sentence me with.

"Look at the carnage surrounding us. I destroy everything around me. For all I know I did kill those vampires last time I lost control. You should leave, before I kill you too."

"Do not mistake me for some weak human or lowly vampire," he said coldly.

"And what would you care of a lowly beast?" I asked, as if he'd not spoken. "That's all we are to you vampires, right?"

"To some, yes," he answered, his voice growing warmer again. "Ulfarr is a fool, however. I do not believe you killed those vampires, no more than I believe you are nothing but a beast. Even the mortal predatory animals are more than savage killers. Is it not humans that are the true savages?"

"Now you sound like the wolf part of me," I growled.

"Maybe you should listen to him."

"Yeah right, next you'll be telling me to make my peace with him, like Lady Sarah kept nagging me to do for so long. Is it so wrong to want to cling to my humanity, however little there is left? Maybe eventually I've got no choice but to let my mind become whole again and embrace my wolfish half. But I'm not ready yet."

The vampire held his hands up as if he didn't want to fight. "Forgive me, I meant no offence. I offered you the chance of some company other than Lady Sarah's before, if you recall. It seems to me you are more lost and alone than last we met. These bodies speak of your anguish. Both wolves and humans are social animals. You cannot endure while you remain alone. Whether in a year or a hundred years, it will eventually be the end of you. Both parts of you yearn for companionship, and I would offer it to you again. Come with me and I can teach you more than Lady Sarah ever could."

"Why do you care?" I asked again, not bothering to hide my suspicion. The more I was forced to deal with vampires, the warier I became of them. Once again I thought about how it seemed they all had some ulterior motive, as Vince had proven when he'd sought to hand us to the Slayers, and then Lady Sarah had betrayed me to Ulfarr just months later. I might never even know why she'd turned on me, but that didn't really matter. For some reason she'd seen fit to help me in the beginning, until eventually it had served her purpose to give me over to Ulfarr to abuse and torment as he saw fit. Though Lady Sarah had never really been a friend, there was still some anger and feeling of betrayal smouldering beneath the emptiness that currently smothered it, and when we next crossed paths as I believed we would, if it saw fit to flare up again, I knew my wrath would seek to destroy her too. I had no wish to go through another betrayal with this new vampire, or any others of their wretched kind. "Maybe it's better to die alone."

"As you wish, but know that my door remains open to you, should you change your mind. And as a show of good faith, I will clean up the mess you created here. You should tread carefully for the Slayers have likely already caught your scent, but I can at least take care of any video footage captured of your transformation, so the world at large does not learn of the existence of our kind outside of myth and legend."

I frowned, but before I could say anything more he was gone. The cold had crept back into my body and I knew I would only grow colder the longer I remained there. I turned away from the body of the girl and loped off on all fours, forced to keep moving in a desperate bid to fight the cold. I couldn't stay in the town if I didn't want the Slayers to find me, for surely it would not be long before humans discovered the bloodbath and the Slayers came to investigate. My thoughts turned to the blanket and the little extra warmth it had to offer, and so I found myself out on the moors once more. The blanket had long since been buried in the snow, however, and for hours I searched in vain for the spot where I might have left it. Finally I was forced to admit defeat, cold and weary. I sat down in the snow and hugged my knees, the loneliness and despair smothering in its intensity, leaving me utterly dejected.

"How many more must die?"

I looked up to find Lizzy had reappeared, but didn't answer.

The apparition changed as before, this time becoming Fiona, my brain making the image exactly as I remembered it the morning I'd found her dying from the horrific wounds the wolf had inflicted on her. Her leg was in tatters, scraps of flesh hanging off the bone and dripping blood, her stomach red raw, the muscle beneath the skin glistening and wet.

"No!" I screamed, rising to my feet. "Don't appear to me as her, not her!"

"What's the matter, Nick? You can't face me?" the hallucination said. "Are you going to continue blaming my death on your wolfish half? He might have been in control, but it was still your teeth that ripped through my flesh. It was still your body that murdered me, that murdered them all."

"No, you won't do this to me again," I snarled. "I'm done feeling guilty over you. It wasn't murder; I needed to feed and you were simply in the wrong place at the wrong time. I didn't choose you as my prey: that was the wolf."

"Is that all we are to you, prey to your predator? I was supposed to be your friend. If you truly cared you would have protected us from yourself. And you want to go back home, for what? So you can prey on more of us under the full moon and slaughter us in the daylight hours when your anger gets the better of you? Do you even remember the faces of all the people you've beaten and savaged in the grip of your own rage?"

My anger flared up again and I roared at her, lashing out with those bloodied claws. My hand passed through her and she disappeared, but a noise from behind caused me to turn and find Luke stood watching again.

"Don't feel bad, Nick. There's nothing wrong in indulging guilty pleasures when the need arises," he said.

I didn't answer, trying to work out how he could possibly have just turned up in the middle of nowhere. I was starting to wonder if he was even human. Or could he be some kind of supernatural being as well, one I couldn't detect as being something more than human?

"I was human," he answered the unspoken question. "Don't you remember me? That month where you gave yourself so completely to all that delicious rage that you spent the entire cycle in wolf form. I watched in awe as you tore through the town, much like the massacre you committed today. And then you turned on me even as I begged you to turn me. That wasn't cool, bro."

Gashes made by my fangs slowly began to appear on him while he talked, shredding through his clothes and his skin, blood welling up and soaking through the ruined material. Ribs streaked red were visible in his chest and half his face peeled away, revealing bare jaw bones grinning morbidly.

"Don't feel bad man," the embodiment of my inner darkness continued. "Just remember how good it was to embrace your bloodlust, the primal ecstasy of savaging prey with tooth and claw.

Don't listen to the other voices. With me as your guide, you're truly unstoppable. I'm the only one you need."

"No," I breathed, unable to believe my mind had fooled me so completely into thinking he was a real human.

"Come on, there's more towns just waiting for you to unleash your rage on them. Already it bubbles back to the surface. Time to feed it with more blood."

"No!" I roared, and again I lashed out at the hallucination. He also disappeared, leaving me to rage and wrestle with old emotions I thought I'd lost. I howled in anguish, overwhelmed with a new wave of guilt and despair, the threat of the Slayers and the vampires forgotten in the grip of my latest emotional turmoil. The thought about how far the sound carried never once crossed my mind. I lost all sense of time while I raged and grieved and indulged my re-awoken conscience, the murders I'd committed still weighing so heavily on it. But my latest breakdown was brought to a sudden end when the sound of gunshot rang in my ears, just as an explosive pain ripped through my chest, and in the shock of that thud from the impact I felt my heart stop. The world seemed to spin as I crashed backward, still conscious.

Blood pumped out of the hole from my ruined heart and pooled on the ground where I lay. The Slayers had found their mark at last and I knew I would never be able to transform quick enough to save myself. There was a reason we could be killed by destroying the heart or the brain – it was the only wound the change couldn't repair before death claimed us. But even though my heart could no longer function, my death wasn't instant. I remained conscious as my body grew weaker and the agonised seconds ticked by. And as I lay there helpless and unable to escape the end drawing ever nearer, I was aware of my killer standing over me. The same grizzled old Slayer I'd encountered before raised his gun a second time, now aiming it at my head. It seemed they hadn't completely forsaken the town I'd brought death to after all. I assumed he'd tracked me from there, though why he hadn't appeared sooner to put a stop to the carnage was anyone's guess.

So this is how it ends, I thought to myself. I was going to die alone and unloved, my body left to rot in a shallow, unmarked grave. Maybe it was a fitting end for a monster such as me, and no more than I deserved, but in those final moments I just wanted to see Mum and Amy one last time, to tell them I was sorry for what I'd done to our family and to have the comfort of a hug goodbye. Instead there was only the loneliness and the face of my enemy staring down at me.

Even if it hadn't been too late for me and I could have somehow repaired the damage from the first bullet, there was no escaping the second he was about to put through my brain. Fast as I was, the older man was disciplined and had mastered his fear. He wouldn't panic if I found the strength to lunge for him, and there was no hope of him missing his target at so close a range. Even if that first bullet hadn't sealed my fate, there would still be no way out. My luck had finally run out and I was going to die at the hands of my enemies.

My vision was growing blearier with each passing second as my brain struggled to keep its hold on reality, the lack of fresh blood being pumped to it starting to take its toll. But beside the blurry form of my killer, the hallucination representing my conscience reappeared, still in the form of Fiona. She crouched over me with a sad smile, the last clear image I had of the surroundings that were fading away as quickly as my life. Her injuries were gone again and so was the accusation from her eyes.

"Just let go, Nick," she said gently. "It's time to stop fighting now. Let it wash over you and find peace in death."

I tried to reply, to tell her I couldn't just give up even though I knew there was no way out this time, but I couldn't make the words form. There was too much blood in my throat and I was growing too weak from the blood loss.

"Just let go," she repeated, as I slid into blackness.

Chapter Eighteen – Cheating Death

I floated there in the blackness, a stream of consciousness seemingly cut off from both the mortal realm and the afterlife. Where was I? Lady Sarah had once explained that some souls made it to some form of afterlife, while others stayed on the Earth to become wraiths or ghosts, and others faced oblivion. But how could this be called oblivion when I still had some form of awareness? Yet it didn't seem to fit any form of an afterlife I'd been given reason to believe in, and I certainly wasn't still trapped on Earth. Even if I'd become a spirit too weak to manifest as a ghost, I would surely still be able to see the mortal realm if something kept me bound to it. But there was just nothing other than my thoughts, as if I'd fallen into my own inner void, lost in the emptiness that had claimed me in the last few months of my cursed life.

You might think this situation would have been terrifying, to be faced with an eternity of nothing but my own thoughts, completely independent of any other part of the universe. But I was surprisingly calm and felt a sense of peace as I drifted in the darkness, soon losing interest in trying to fathom where exactly I might be. Some part of me continued to exist, free of the pain life had held, and for that I felt a sense of gratitude.

"Wolf," came the alien voice in the blackness. It was female and not part of my own consciousness, so it seemed I wasn't alone after all. But it felt like it didn't belong in that little pocket of reality I'd found myself in, a place that was mine alone to exist in as this small part of me lived on, even after my earthly remains rotted and eventually crumbled away to dust. "I need you to come with me now. Follow my voice, and I will guide you back."

Back where, a part of me wondered. I found I didn't really care, and I continued to float in that peaceful state.

"I know you can hear me, wolf," the voice said again. "This is not your path. Come to me and I will help you rise up, to face your true destiny."

My curiosity got the better of me and mentally I reached out to that voice, wanting to find out more. There was a brief sensation that felt like our thoughts touched, and the next thing I knew that blackness turned to a blinding white light, pain crashing back over me as nerves reconnected with my mind. It was as much of a shock as the initial impact of the bullet had been, and a part of me wanted to fall back into the darkness where I'd been blissfully free of the agony of my flesh. But instead my eyes snapped open to find a blonde haired woman leant over me. I was still lying on my back and my heart was just as ruined as it had been before I'd lost consciousness, incapable of pumping the lifeforce through my arteries which my body needed to keep my brain alive. The woman was speaking to me, but I struggled to make sense of her words through the agony of my damaged chest.

"I have to take the bullet out now, then you must transform or you will die."

I didn't know it at the time but the bullet had ricocheted, causing damage to more than just my heart, and it was still lodged somewhere in that mass of screaming nerves and ruptured tissue. It had embedded itself in such a way that it no longer lined up with the entry hole it had created, and the shifting flesh wouldn't be able to push it out as it had the last few times I was shot.

I'm not sure I was even truly aware of what the woman had said to me and whether I willed the transformation, or whether it took hold regardless like any of the body's natural responses designed to ensure its survival. But as she drew the bullet out, the fur began to sprout along my skin and flesh and bone started to shift and become lupine. And as my form grew more wolfish, the bomb site the bullet had made of my chest began to rebuild as tissue knitted itself back together, my heart becoming whole again and fully functional. That first beat of renewed life felt like an explosion of blood rushing through my arteries, but it was a relief to feel it pumping stronger than ever as my body sought to repair the damage.

The last of the pain faded away as the change completed and I lay on my side on the luxurious softness of a proper bed, panting heavily. I tried to growl questions at the woman who'd saved me like who was she, and how was it possible for me to have survived a mortal wound to my heart, but I couldn't form the words with my lupine vocal cords, and even though the transformation had healed the damage, I was still weak.

"Easy, wolf. There will be time for questions later. Rest now, and recover your strength."

Drowsiness crept over me, giving me little choice but to do as she said. I gave in to the beckoning darkness once more, falling into a deep, dreamless sleep.

I don't know how long I laid there, slipping in and out of consciousness, but when I opened my eyes for long enough it was to find the woman sat watching over me. I was more aware of my surroundings this time and it seemed I'd been taken to a little cottage which had an old world feel to it, as if I'd somehow gone back in time to the past Lady Sarah and several of the other vampires I'd met seemed to be stuck in. But the woman's scent seemed human and daylight was streaming through the window so whoever she was, she couldn't be a vampire. She offered me a chunk of raw meat with a kindly smile on her pretty face and a warmth in her turquoise eyes that most vampires were lacking.

I felt some of my strength returning as I gulped down the meat, but my eyelids still felt heavy with tiredness. Much as I wanted to learn more about this woman and how she'd saved me from certain death, I couldn't keep myself from falling back into darkness. Except this time I wasn't alone. Like a parasite bound to its host, my nightmares latched back onto my weary mind and I didn't have the strength to fight free of their clutches.

I found myself back on the moors which should have been my final resting place, but this time it wasn't the Slayers hunting me. A dark shape was stalking towards me, one that filled me with a sense of dread. I tried to run but every time I twisted my head round to look back at it, the thing was drawing ever nearer. Until I looked behind and it was no longer there, but stood blocking my path when I turned back round. I came to a sudden stop, feeling my heart thudding in my chest as I panted for the oxygen my body craved. And as I looked at that robed figure, a beam of sunlight revealed the face of my adversary from within the depths of his cowl.

The grinning skull looking back at me was no worse than any other horror I'd faced over the last year, and yet the cold stab of terror turned my blood to ice. Sockets empty of eyes somehow still held the weight of time and a force so utterly unstoppable that none could hope to stand against it. My despair returned stronger than ever, along with a sense of sheer hopelessness at my plight.

"I will not be cheated!" Death thundered, and my terror reached new heights as I felt my heart stop again.

I fell to my knees, clutching my chest with one hand and reaching out as if for help with the other, but there weren't even any hallucinations to accompany me in my final moments now. Was I to die here, truly alone this time, cut off from everyone and everything I'd ever loved before the curse robbed me of my human life?

Again I felt that longing to see my family just one last time before I slipped away from the mortal coil, but Death's skeletal fingers were reaching for me and there was no escaping his grasp this time…

Still in wolf form, I broke free of the nightmare with a pitiful whimper and just as my mind cleared of that terrible image of Death's grinning skull bearing down on me, I heard his voice in my head once more.

"Are you so arrogant as to think your wolf's blood will protect you from ME? I will claim you eventually, and next time you will not escape."

A shiver ran through my lupine body. I couldn't even console myself with the thought that it was only a dream, knowing as I did that dreams were far more than random images conjured by the brain while we slept. Was it just a nightmare, or was it something more than that? I had no way of knowing, but even after I'd fully woken, I still felt like Death was coming for me.

I couldn't explain why the dream unnerved me so, especially as I didn't exactly fear dying, even though I'd already found I couldn't just let myself give up on life. Yet my heart still pounded in the grip of fear. What had the woman done to me?

It had grown dark in the time I'd spent in my troubled sleep and the cottage was now empty. A fire burned in the hearth, casting eerie shadows that seemed to dance and mock the terror I'd allowed the nightmare to inspire in me. But I was grateful for its warm glow, especially once I returned to human form and the cold air slid over my skin in an icy embrace.

Another wave of exhaustion hit me as the change completed and I had to lie back while my body recovered, until sleep threatened to creep over me again. Perhaps it was a mistake to transform but I'd been feeling stronger for the meat I'd eaten earlier and the rest I'd had, and I was determined to get some answers. Whoever the woman was, she appeared to have gone off on some errand while I slept, but I would insist on speaking with her when she returned. In the meantime I planned to have a look around, and it would be easier to explore the room on two legs instead of four.

I didn't want to nod off again until I'd had chance to try and find out a bit more about what was going on, so I forced my weary body upright into a sitting position, feeling my heart pounding in my chest as if that simple act had been a great exertion. I welcomed the feeling after the unsettling sensation of it stopping, and I looked down at my body to find it as flawless as ever. The transformation had repaired the damage as normal, leaving no trace of the wound that had almost cost me my life. Yet so dire a wound should have killed me quicker than my body could bring on the change to heal itself. Again I had to wonder, just what had this woman done to me after I'd been shot?

She'd left me a blanket folded on the end of the bed, which I wrapped around myself for warmth, then with another effort of will I got unsteadily to my feet. My muscles protested but I ignored the aches and pains shooting through my legs as I shuffled around the room, searching for any clues as to who my saviour might be and why she'd gone to the trouble of saving my cursed life.

My curiosity only grew as I took in shelves lined with herbs, incense, candles, and vials of what appeared to be various oils, and cupboards containing more of the same. I could see no evidence of the modern world – no gadgets lying around or batteries to power them, and there were no electrical sockets, which again made me feel like I'd travelled back in time. There was even an old wooden mortar and pestle for grinding the herbs, and as I made my way over to the table in the far corner I could see a stack of parchment and a quill dipped in an ink bottle. There looked to be an open book on there as well, which might give me the answers I craved, but as I drew closer I thought I could see something moving out of the corner of my eye, like a shifting of shadows. The nightmare still fresh in my mind, I couldn't help but replay the image of Death's skeletal fingers reaching for me and I half expected to find myself facing that robed figure stalking out from the gloom. But when I looked around for the source of the threat, it was to find – nothing. The only movement came from the twisting shadows cast by the writhing flames, the cottage still empty of anyone other than myself. Somehow that wasn't as comforting as it should have been, and when I turned back round my eyes continued to dart nervously around the room, as if I could penetrate the shadows and force them to reveal their secrets. But the cottage remained shrouded in mystery, until I reached the wooden surface covered with the clues I'd been hoping for.

Even in the dim light from the fire the pages of the book were clear to see. Passages in a foreign language lined the aged paper, formatted in a way that at first made me wonder if I was looking at poetry. But there were a few small bones scattered around the table and as I turned the pages it was to find most of them were covered in occult symbols, clearly for the use in various rituals. I'd seen all I needed to guess the woman's true identity, and I fell back from the table in shock. She was a witch!

Chapter Nineteen– Danger in the Shadows

My mind raced as I stumbled away from the table, towards the door. Lady Sarah had told me on the morning after my first transformation that witches were 'in decline in this modern world'. I knew a little about some of the infamous historical witch trials and I supposed in a way I couldn't really blame them for joining the Slayers if it was their one chance to live. They were only human after all. Even though they'd gained supernatural power through the practice of magic, that didn't make them either undead or demonic in nature. They remained human, and though I'd thought of them as traitors before to turn their backs on the supernatural world they were a part of, there was no real reason for them to turn against humanity. If there were so few of them left as Lady Sarah had once suggested, it seemed likely they'd all chosen the side of the Slayers, and that meant I had to assume this new witch was also an enemy. Whatever twisted motives she had for saving me, it couldn't be anything good, and I felt my only chance was to get away before she returned home and I found myself at her mercy.

I didn't have enough strength to run from the cottage. The best I could do was a fast shuffle but it felt painfully slow. And much as I would have liked to keep the blanket for warmth, it soon became a hindrance, slowing me even further, and I was forced to drop it and suffer the sting of the bitter air on my bare skin once more.

As I passed through the doorway, I again had the unnerving feeling something was hiding in the shadows, but my nose couldn't detect any strange scents and my ears picked up no sounds other than those made by my own body. I tried to focus on my escape but I had the nagging feeling there was something I was missing. Was it Death coming for me, just like I'd seen in the nightmare? Or were more apparitions conjured by my own mind on their way to haunt me? At least the latter couldn't physically hurt me, and I half hoped it was no more than another hallucination, though I wouldn't exactly welcome the torment they often brought me.

Once outside, I found I was still in the middle of nowhere, out on the moors. Even with my enhanced senses, my eyes struggled to penetrate the darkness, especially after being around the fire in the cottage. Any natural light was hidden behind a thick layer of clouds, and I was faced with a wall of blackness so complete, it seemed almost like a solid barrier which my sight struggled against. I had no option but to run blindly through the darkness, my uneasiness at the feeling that something was lurking in the shadows mounting with every step.

But still my other senses failed to pick up any signs that I wasn't alone, and still that brought me no comfort.

I hadn't gone far from the cottage when a slither of the waxing moon broke free of the clouds, providing just enough light to break up the shadows. And once again I was sure I could see movement in the darkness. Something was out there with me, I felt certain of it then.

The moon would soon be full again and as it continued to break out of its cloudy prison, it illuminated the area around me, the ghostly light so strong that I could see my own shadow. But that wasn't all I could see. Directly in front of me there was another shadow, a patch of darkness the light couldn't touch. And the moonlight revealed that on this night the shadows had teeth, bared in a feral snarl just like my own in wolf form.

The creature looked like a huge black dog with glowing red eyes, but I knew it couldn't be a mortal animal. I felt my wolf half reacting to its presence, and he was just as uneasy as I was at how it had so suddenly appeared, without any warning. There should have been the sound of its movement or a scent for me to detect, yet even though my eyes could see it, to my other senses there was still nothing there, as if the dog was made from the very shadows it hid in. And if this thing wasn't a flesh and blood animal, what chance did I have against it? At full strength I am one of the greatest predators to stalk the Earth. You know this: you've felt the power in my jaws when I ripped the life from your mortal body. But that night I was still weakened from the mortal wound that should have killed me, and the transformation I'd undergone without the energy needed to support it. There was no way I could transform again without feeding first, not even partway to wolf form, so I was forced to face this thing as a human. And in my weakened state I was no longer the predator, but the prey to this other beast. My only hope was to push my body onwards, even though I knew I would never outrun the thing if it decided to give chase.

I tried to keep from staring into those demonic eyes as I stumbled on, wanting to give the dog as little reason as possible to attack. And I knew all too well the workings of the canine mind – direct eye contact was a challenge to dominance. I was also careful not to completely turn my back to the creature, taking a path that I hoped would allow me to go around it, without directly turning away and behaving like prey. Though there was no way of telling how the thing would react. Since it was supernatural in nature, its mind might not bear much resemblance to a mortal dog, even though it looked like one.

At first it seemed my ploy was working. The creature made no move to attack, though its eyes never left me. But then it charged, and still lacking the strength to run or to fight, once again it seemed I was doomed.

The beast leapt and sent us crashing to the ground, pinning me under one of its huge paws. As I lay there resigned to my fate, I found myself back in the night I'd been bitten by the black werewolf who'd awoken my lupine nature. I'd thought I would die at the jaws of the black wolf, though it turned out I'd never been in any real danger – he'd recognised me as a fellow wolf descendant and deliberately passed on the curse as a last desperate act to keep our race alive. But at the time I'd expected him to kill me, and so had Lizzy, the one friend who wouldn't leave me to die as the others had, those four who'd been more concerned with saving their own skins. No, Lizzy had refused to run even when I told her to leave me, and she'd helped drive the wolf off. But I'd left Lizzy behind with the rest of my human life, and there was no one to save me that night.

The dog lowered its great head towards my throat, but there was no warm breath on my skin which again made me think it was made of nothing more than shadow, even though physically it was very much there. It had a weight to it like a real animal, and in my current state it was beyond me to push it off my prone form and make another bid for freedom. I'd used up too much of my body's reserves already and unconsciousness beckoned again, so I gratefully slipped into the blackness, knowing I would at least be spared the same pain I'd visited on my own victims. Then I knew no more.

I awoke to find I was back on the bed in the witch's cottage, the blanket I'd discarded now draped over my naked body. The witch was sat watching over me and the huge black dog lay on the floor on the right side of her chair, glowing eyes fixed firmly on me. I yelped in shock and sat up, but when it became clear my life wasn't in any immediate danger, I settled with my back to the wall and eyed the two suspiciously. I still wanted answers, so I started by asking "Who are you?"

"I've been called many things over the years. Satanist, pagan, witch. But my name is Selina."

"So you are a witch!"

"I am, and you are right to be wary; too much trust will get you killed in our world."

"Yeah, especially when every other kind of spellcaster I've met has been working for the Slayers. So why did you save me?"

"It was not your fate to die out there on the moors."

Real or imagined, the grim reaper I'd been seeing seemed to disagree with that. But I didn't voice the thought out loud, instead replying "The way you talk about my fate, it's like you've seen my future or something."

"Indeed I have. You have a great destiny ahead of you, young wolf. Would you like to hear it?"

"I make my own fate," I growled.

"As you wish."

"Why am I here anyway? Am I your prisoner?"

She shook her head. "You are free to leave whenever you choose, but I would advise you recover a little more of your strength first. Here, I brought you some more meat."

"How do I know you haven't poisoned it?" I asked, sniffing the raw flesh and eyeing her suspiciously.

"Why would I make the effort to save you, only to kill you myself? I admit, I did task my familiar with watching you and keeping you here," she said, gesturing at the shadow dog. "But only because I knew you would not be strong enough to leave too soon. However, if you are truly determined to leave now, I will not stop you again."

Her words did nothing to ease my wariness, but the meat was too tempting to resist. My hunger overruled my sense of caution and I tore into it ravenously, feeling more of my strength returning as the raw flesh slid down my gullet and into my stomach. Once I'd eaten, I was able to stand again without too much protest from the muscles in my legs, and I strode almost effortlessly towards the door. Selina was as good as her word, making no move to prevent me from leaving or to take her blanket back from me. I looked back at her, a part of me wanting to stay and potentially make a new friend. But she'd neither confirmed nor denied any involvement with the Slayers, so how could I trust her? For all I knew, the Slayers had decided they wanted me alive again for some twisted purpose, or maybe this 'great destiny' she kept speaking of was as a sacrifice to fuel some powerful ritual. She'd not given me any real answers about why she'd saved me and I knew that no matter how badly I wanted to find a new friend now the vampires had turned against me, I had to assume the worst. Though if she did mean me harm I couldn't explain why she was letting me go, unless she was really that confident she could recapture me when she needed to. There were no clear answers, so I turned away and stalked off into the night and the isolation of the moors once more, still wrapped in the witch's blanket.

Uncertainty nagged at me as I trudged across the seemingly endless plains, Selina's words reverberating inside my skull as if they'd become trapped in there. Who wouldn't want to believe they were destined for great things, and had I not wanted to be famous while I was still a part of the human world? Yet I found that I no longer had any desire for fame. I still felt dead inside and I knew the limelight would bring me no pleasure. And with greatness there would no doubt come responsibilities, which was the last thing I wanted. Better to endure in the shadows and remain the mere beast the vampires believed me to be than become a figurehead and take the weight of everyone's needs on my shoulders. I could barely cope with my own troubles, let alone those of others. Whatever destiny Selina had seen for me, I didn't want it.

My thoughts turned to my latest brush with Death. I felt emptier than ever and not for the first time I couldn't help but think how it would have been better if my wretched existence had been allowed to come to an end. This was the second time I should have died. First the curse had brought me back and now witchcraft had pulled me from Death's clutches. If the grim reaper of my nightmares was real, there was no wonder he felt cheated, though it wasn't like I'd had a say in the matter either time. Somehow I couldn't find any kind of gratitude towards Selina for saving my life, and when my path took me back towards civilisation and I found myself prowling through another village, it was little surprise I felt drawn to the local graveyard, outside a church.

I gazed at the tombstones as if transfixed by them, a part of me wishing I could join the dead and finally know peace. But I knew myself well enough by then to know I couldn't simply let go of my grip on life, and if Death was truly coming for me, he would have to take me by force. As much as I hated my meaningless existence, I couldn't just give up. Still, there was a sense of peace to the graveyard that kept me there for some time, even though it was another place I didn't belong. I only stirred from my dark musings when the rain started to fall. Only then did I turn my attention to the church.

The grey stone walls loomed cold and uninviting in the gloom, yet I found myself approaching this unwelcoming structure as the light drizzle quickly became a heavy downpour. The wooden door swung open for me, even though I could see no one inside. It wasn't much warmer within the old building but at least it provided shelter from the elements, and I hoped I might find sanctuary there till the rainstorm passed. You might wonder how it's possible for a place of worship to provide sanctuary for a monster such as me, but even though Lady

Sarah had once said I was one of the eternally damned like the vampires, I had no trouble walking over holy ground. No invisible force repelled me, no divine power caused me to burst into flames. Maybe it was another sign God didn't care for humanity, or maybe there was some hope for me yet.

The pews were far from comfortable but I sat down anyway to rest my legs, warily scanning my surroundings for any hint of danger. I tensed as the one other being in the place strode towards me, the vicar of this parish I'd been drawn to. I'd not noticed him when I first entered, too focussed on the desire for shelter.

"Are you lost, child?" he asked, taking a seat beside me. There was a kindness to him that I had not encountered in mankind for some time and I felt myself relaxing in his gentle presence. He made no comment on my strange appearance, probably assuming I was a homeless orphan or a runaway. He didn't seem to recognise the dried blood on my skin for what it truly was, and I doubted he would ever have guessed I was naked beneath the blanket I hugged around me.

"I think I must be; I'm no Christian," I replied, giving him only a brief glance before fixing my eyes on a large wooden carving of Jesus nailed to a crucifix.

"God finds us at the most unexpected of times," he told me. "Perhaps He brought you here to show you the way through your troubles, or so that we might guide you down a lighter path."

"I never used to believe in God but I have had cause to question certain beliefs recently. I've done terrible things, Father."

"The Bible teaches us God is merciful and forgiving of even the most heinous of sins, if the soul is truly remorseful and seeks redemption. You are young," he said, smiling. "And I doubt your sins can be so terrible as to place your soul beyond salvation."

As little interest as I'd had in religion in my human life, I couldn't help but want the vicar's words to be true. If God did truly exist He'd never listened or helped me before, but I had a sudden need to believe divine intervention was possible to free me from my curse. I just wanted to return home and enjoy the human life I'd been forced to leave behind, the life I'd lost to my lycanthropy and the war with the Slayers. I wanted it so badly that I raised my eyes to meet the kindly gaze of this so called man of God and asked him "Can you truly offer me salvation?"

Something in my eyes must have repelled him, for he drew away from me then. The warmth drained from his countenance until he grew as cold as the old stone building and he said simply "I see only darkness."

206

"But you said even the worst men can be saved. Isn't there anything you can do for me?"

"There is nothing to save. You should leave now."

The storm still carried on its relentless attack outside, the wind driving the rain in a battering assault on the land. I thought about killing the vicar. Gruesome images played in my mind as I imagined my claws raking bloody furrows in his throat, blood splattering the wall and dripping down the crucifix hung there. And in my mind, the carving stared accusingly at me through a mask of blood. But despite that mental accusatory glare, part of me wanted to act on those dark impulses, and to say something like "Then if you can't guide me back to the light, let me drag you into the darkness."

Luke reappeared, bearing the same wounds I'd apparently dealt the human whose face this apparition had taken.

"Do it," he urged me once again.

There was no supernatural vampiric power to hold me back, nor any of the hallucinations conjured by my newly awoken conscience. No visions of close friends or family appeared with more words of wisdom. It would be so easy to claim this man's life, to take him as my latest victim. Yet something held me back. Though my inner darkness wanted more bloodshed, my rage remained a dormant volcano and my bloodlust was equally as quiet.

"Maybe it's what you need to bring them back. Think how good it felt when we massacred the town and how good it will be to embrace that again."

But I ignored him this time. Until the two erupted and flooded my consciousness anew, there would be no pleasure in killing. If I indulged in more mindless slaughter it would only leave me feeling all the emptier for the lack of the savage joy I'd come to crave in such bloody violence. The last thing I wanted was to leave the shelter of the church and venture back into the rain, but I found that preferable to waiting in the dark pit of emptiness and despair for the storm to pass.

I felt the vicar's eyes on me as I walked back down the aisle, and I wondered if he sensed the wolf threatening his flock. Would he report me to the authorities? It didn't really matter. I would need to feed again soon but I had the strength to put enough miles between myself and the village before I was forced to stop for the day. Even if the Slayers picked up my trail, I was confident I could lose them again.

Reluctantly I stepped back out into the downpour, squinting my eyes to protect them from the icy drops of water being blown in my direction. It seemed brighter than when I'd first entered the church and

I guessed the sun had now risen, but the early morning light was grey and dreary.

Once again I looked on at the rows of tombstones, wondering how many had been sent to be buried here in early graves by monsters like me. I thought I could hear the anguished screams of the dead as they writhed in torment, their rest disturbed by my very presence. Even though it was no more than my own treacherous imagination troubling me, I felt just as unwelcome as I had inside the church. The graveyard no longer felt peaceful but instead it became the embodiment of my own despair in such dismal light, no rays of hope breaking through from the dark clouds overhead.

Shadows lingered, and between the torrents of rain I caught a glimpse of a dark form with glowing red eyes. The witch's familiar. Despite letting me leave, she'd still had the creature follow me, and I felt a brief glimmer of anger. She truly believed in this great destiny she'd seen for me, and though I'd told her I'd make my own fate, it felt like I was being steered in the direction others wanted me to go in. Did I not have a say in which path my own life would take? It seemed not, since she'd already interfered by keeping Death at bay long enough for me to heal a wound that would otherwise have killed me. But I hadn't asked her to interfere. As terrible as the loneliness had become over the last couple of months, I wished she would leave me to my lonely existence, her and the vampires. I wanted a friend, but I needed someone I could trust, and I didn't want anyone meddling with my life.

I snarled at the shadowy canine, expecting it to respond to my challenge, but to my surprise it vanished. One minute it was stood amongst the tombstones and the next its shadowy form collapsed into a kind of black mist, before fading away, seemingly to nothingness. Whatever the thing was, it seemed it wasn't of the mortal realm and I suspected it had returned to wherever it came from, until its mistress called it back to our world once again. But I made my way over to the grave it had been stood by to check if it had truly gone, and as I drew closer I could see something lying in the mud where the dog had been.

There was a corpse lying between the graves, and I wondered if it was another offering from Selina to help me regain my strength. But when I crouched over it to investigate I found a bloody mess of shredded flesh and shattered bones much like one of my own kills, the heart ripped out from the open ribcage, and four gashes across the woman's face and through her lips which revealed her to have been something more than human. Some of her teeth were visible in the gouges running over her mouth, including one of the upper canines, lengthened into a fang. A vampire fang. And this definitely wasn't my work this time, since I'd had no blackouts that night. But why had the black dog been stood over the body? Then it hit me. Ulfarr had been right to assume this was the work of a supernatural beast. Selina must be the real killer, and she was using her familiar to frame me. Maybe that was why she'd saved me, as a convenient way to cover up her own murders. Was she in league with the Slayers after all? It could be another grand scheme they'd cooked up to try and quicken our seemingly inevitable destruction, perhaps because they wanted to avoid another big battle which would cost more lives. Maybe they were hoping we'd turn on each other and make ourselves easier targets.

The why didn't really matter. I'd been given proof of my innocence. If I could clear my name, maybe there was some hope for me after all. I could try to mend my alliance with the vampires and perhaps forge the new friendship I so badly needed, if not with Lady Sarah who had always been too distant before then maybe with one of the others. I just had to find a way to prove my innocence to them, which would be easier said than done.

Chapter Twenty – New Purpose

I spent the day back in the remoteness of the moors, where I could rest in relative safety after hunting more rabbits and eating enough to keep my strength up. Once night fell, I attempted to retrace my steps back to the area Lady Sarah had chosen for us before I'd gone off on my own. I had no way of knowing if the vampire had kept to the same stretch of moorland since I'd gone, but it seemed the best place to start looking. If she had moved on I'd have to hope the wolf could track her, and that he would be willing to co-operate with me since it was in the interests of our self-preservation.

Trying to find the exact area I'd last been in with the vampire proved a challenge. I had no idea how far we'd travelled since leaving my hometown, or whereabouts in the country we'd been when I'd gone off on my own, or where that was in relation to my current position. Using nature or the stars as a guide was not a skill I'd been taught, and consequently it meant I was lost without the aid of any human signs or landmarks.

The wolf seemed to have an inbuilt sense of direction, but I had no idea how to use it. And after the brief merging of our minds, he was even more reluctant to have anything to do with the human half of me, which meant I had only my human instincts at my disposal. As tired as I'd become of Lady Sarah's insistence that I needed to allow my two identities to merge and become one again, I knew this was one situation where it would have been a big advantage. In the end it was only down to luck that I found the vampire and it took a few nights of aimless wandering. I was trying to find a familiar looking area that might indicate I was heading in the right direction, when I came across Lady Sarah feeding on the blood of a large stag.

"You should not have come," she said, looking up from her meal.

"You found the latest victim already then."

"Yes, another body was discovered, mutilated like the others. Your cries of rage and anguish carried across the moors and now Ulfarr has thrown your sanity into question."

"Of course he has," I growled. "I didn't black out this time though, and I think I know who the killer is. I met a witch with a huge black dog for a familiar, and it was stood over the corpse of a female vampire."

"It doesn't matter," she said sadly.

"How can you say that? Of course it matters!"

"Do you have any proof?"

210

I didn't answer, but I felt my anger stirring deep inside. It felt like not even Lady Sarah believed me, and it was enough to awaken my rage once more.

"Without proof, no one will believe you. If you can find something, I will take it to the other vampires. But until then you should go. Ulfarr will have you stand trial again if he finds you, and I do not believe he will listen to reason this time."

"Oh come on, don't you think it's convenient how, after getting you guys to rally against the Slayers and battle against Aughtie's forces, suddenly so many of you have turned on me? Don't you think the Slayers could be behind this? The witch is probably working for them! Sure, some of them might prefer to personally kill me and wipe out werewolves for good but I'm sure there's plenty of them who'd gladly let others do their dirty work, especially if it means a few of us end up killing each other in the process. What if they feel threatened by me after the battle – you said yourself how we undead need a leader, and it seems I'm the only one who's managed to get a force onto the battlefield in the last couple of centuries since the Elders are so unwilling to fight. They've hunted us on and off since that night but no matter what they've thrown at us, so far we've escaped. What if they're desperate to get rid of me and wipe out werewolves for good?"

"It's plausible, but it's still only a theory. Ulfarr will not be swayed by anything short of undeniable proof."

"For fuck's sake, whether the Slayers intentionally caused it by framing me for the deaths of the vampires or not, the murders have us divided and fighting among ourselves when we should be united against our common enemy. Can't you make him see sense?"

"Have you not been paying attention these last few months?" she hissed, the flames of my rising anger leaping across to ignite her own once again. "He's an Elder vampire. No one can 'make' him do anything."

"But don't you think it's time we prepared for another battle?"

"Again, they will not listen to your theory without proof. You're hardly in a position to unite them again when they suspect you of turning on our own."

"You told me another big battle was coming. Well the battle for my hometown could hardly be called big. If the end truly is inevitable for us why not make a last stand and take down as many of them with us as we can, instead of allowing them to hunt us like animals? I hate running. We're wasting time; we should at least be trying to do something with however long we have left! Maybe we could even find a way to win. But if there really is no hope, at least we'll have died trying."

The anger suddenly drained from her and she sounded tired. "And just what do you propose, Nick? How can you hope to win a war against our enemies when you still fight a war with yourself? Whether you want to hear it or not, we are doomed. You should try to find some purpose out of the time we have left."

"Like what? I had to leave my human life and hobbies behind. I'm a killer, and it seems killing is all that's left. The fight against the Slayers is the only real purpose I can find."

That wasn't quite true since I'd already set my sights on proving my innocence and trying to fix things with the vampires, and as if to drive the point home Lady Sarah said "Focus on clearing your name or it won't just be the Slayers hunting you. That should be your purpose for the time being."

"Fine; I should have known this was a waste of time. When you and all the other bloody vampires are ready to listen, I'll be back."

She gave me a sad smile but said nothing when I turned to go. I'd expected her to be more willing to aid me, but it seemed she wasn't even going to help find something concrete to prove my innocence, let alone talk to Ulfarr on my behalf. I felt a mixture of anger and disappointment as I stormed off. If I didn't even have Lady Sarah on my side, who had been so set on keeping me alive before she'd turned on me to help the Elder imprison me for the full moon, then who else could I turn to? Every time I thought I'd found an ally, they'd all betrayed me in the end. First Vince, now Lady Sarah, and Selina seemed to have helped me only because it was in her own interests, so she could continue to frame me for the murders, whether at the request of the Slayers or for her own twisted reasons. I couldn't go back to any of the humans I'd been close to, since that would only put them in danger. It seemed I had only one option, one last hope, and I didn't even know if I could trust him, or if he would also turn out to be false. But he had stood up for me when no other vampires would during the first trial Ulfarr had put me on, and he had helped a second time when I'd massacred that entire town and had been in no frame of mind to clean up my own mess. He was the only potential ally I had left, and with nowhere else to go it seemed I had no option but to place my trust in him. I had to find the mansion he'd invited me to, and pray he would be more willing to hear me out.

Hours later, I'd been trying to find my way back to the old building the vampires had used to put me on trial without success. If I

212

could just find my way back there and then head north, I should be able to find the mansion. But I seemed to be lost in the heart of the moorland and I suspected I may well have been going in circles. It seemed I had to rely on the lupine half of my mind after all, so I came to a stop and mentally reached out for him.

"What do you want, human?" he snarled.

"I know you lurk and watch on the edge of my consciousness; you're well aware what's going on. If you still want to live, you need to help me find this vampire's mansion."

"And what makes you so sure he will help us?"

"I'm not," I sighed. "But if we go to Ulfarr alone, he's not going to listen. Lady Sarah seemed pretty certain of that. Our only hope is to get another vampire on side and find some proof they can take to him, and it doesn't look like we can rely on Lady Sarah anymore. What choice do we have?"

"I don't like this," he growled. "We know nothing about this vampire."

"No, but he stood up for us when Lady Sarah wouldn't."

"Very well," the wolf said reluctantly, and he rose up to take control. I retreated into our subconscious, trusting his survival instinct was still strong enough for him to go along with my plan.

When the wolf surrendered control back to me, I found myself in a big clearing in a patch of woodland, stood before the gates to a large building. Still in wolf form, I padded cautiously forward. The gates swung open for me even though the grounds seemed deserted. I assumed there was a hidden camera somewhere, and it was still dark which meant the vampire would still be up. He was probably watching as I prowled along the path towards his mansion, but no undead came running to drag me away for another trial, nor did any Slayers appear with more guns. Emboldened by the lack of any kind of ambush, I made my way up the stairs to a front door flanked by two huge stone lions. Whoever this vampire was, I guessed he'd been around for a few hundred years and had therefore acquired vast amounts of wealth over the centuries. Clearly he wasn't afraid to live with the human luxuries he'd become accustomed to in his mortal life, though I had to wonder how he'd lasted so long in this place when most of us had been forced into hiding on the fringes of the human world. Granted the mansion was hidden by the woodland surrounding it, but it would still be visible from the air. It seemed unlikely the Slayers wouldn't know of its existence, and the true nature of the man residing within.

I transformed back to human but just as I was about to pound on the door, the vampire opened it and gestured for me to enter. I didn't waste any time with pleasantries.

"I don't know if I can trust you, but it sounds like Ulfarr is convinced I'm guilty and I guess that means he'll be looking to execute me again before long. I know who the real killer is, but I need your help to clear my name."

"Of course. I will do everything in my power to save you from the others," he said.

That raised my suspicions again. I'd been expecting to have to convince him to help, but this was beginning to seem all too easy. "Wait, why are you so keen to help me?"

"You are believed to be the last of your kind, and it was you who led a force of undead into battle against the Slayers. You have become the object of much curiosity amongst our kind, despite the hatred so many feel for your race. I offered you my companionship merely with the intent of satisfying that curiosity. And while there is much hatred for werewolves among my kind, I have only ever had respect for you. It would be a shame to see your race die."

"Come to think of it, how is it you just happened to be in the town to clean up after me when I was in no state to do so myself?"

"I was out hunting and I sensed you in the area. Again, curiosity led me to you and I realised you were on the verge of a breakdown. I hoped by helping that it would sway you to accept the hand of friendship I'd offered you, and here you are. I simply want to learn more about the werewolf who successfully united our races on the battlefield and led us to victory."

"No," I growled. "There's always some fucking ulterior motive with you vampires. Forget it, this was a mistake. I'm done with the lot of you!"

I was about to retreat back outside, but he pointed out "You are hardly in a position to refuse my aid. You know this, or you would not be here. If you leave, the others will hunt you down eventually. It's only a matter of time before Ulfarr gives the order, if others don't take it upon themselves to kill you first."

"So what is this, some glorified prison? Did Ulfarr talk you round to seeing things his way? Has he put you up to luring me here while he decides when to execute me?"

He shook his head, his expression neutral. "You are free to leave, if you wish, but I would advise against it. And I believe we can be of some help to each other if I could persuade you to stay. I realise you have little reason to trust us vampires given the recent

214

mistreatment you have suffered at our hands, but I assure you I am sincere in my offer to aid you. Ask yourself why I would go to the trouble of standing up to Ulfarr if I bore you any ill will."

I couldn't argue with that but I was still filled with doubt and perhaps a touch of paranoia after so many had turned against me. In the end I had to remind myself that I'd come to him of my own free will because he'd seemed like my best hope if I didn't want to die at the hands of Ulfarr, for crimes I didn't commit. And at least I could be certain he was real, and not another product of my tortured mind like Luke had turned out to be.

"Come, spend the day here at least where you may rest in comfort."

I let him lead me to one of the many guestrooms. It was much larger than my own bedroom had been back in my family home, which had been a good size for a growing teen. This room was luxuriously big, with enough room to fit a king size bed, what looked to be a wardrobe along one wall, and a desk and drawers on the other wall, as well as a bookshelf, and there was still plenty of floor space to walk around. I gazed in amazement at the number of human comforts I'd never expected to see again. Not only did the bed look soft and inviting after so many months sleeping rough, but the room was warm compared to the wintry world outside and the bookshelf looked to be lined with several interesting titles. There was also a TV on the desk and a door to what turned out to be an en suite.

"Dawn approaches and I must retire to my own chambers. I will leave you to consider my offer. My home is yours to explore as you will, or if you wish to venture out there are towels in the en suite and clothes in the wardrobe which should fit well enough. I ask only that you try not to slaughter the locals in the nearby village. I would hate to have to abandon this place, and a massacre in the area may be all it takes to bring the Slayers to my door," he said, and with a sly smile added, "It might be as well if you avoid the human world for the next few days, with your time of the month at hand."

"Really, time of the month jokes?" I growled. "I'm not some bloody girl due a period."

"I'm sorry, it was just too easy," he laughed. "Anyway, you will find plenty of prey in the surrounding woodland, should you wish to hunt. Whatever you decide to do with the day, I hope to find you here come dusk. There is much I'd like to discuss if you'll hear me out, before we lose you to the moon's clutches for the three nights it's full."

With that he stalked out, so silent he might have been no more than a shadow. I watched him go, still wondering if I'd made a mistake in coming here. But the temptation of all these things I'd been missing from my human life was enough to keep me in the mansion for the day, and I wasted no time in making use of the en suite, in which I found a large bath and a separate shower. After months of living like an animal and having to wash in icy cold waters when the need arose, I was going to enjoy washing the filth from my body. It would probably be the first shower I ever truly appreciated, since in my human life I'd still been young enough that it had always been a chore. But having been deprived of so many of the things humans take for granted, I was going to make the most of the comforts the mansion had to offer, for as long as it lasted.

I enjoyed a hot shower first to wash the thickest of the dried blood and gore off my body. My skin was so caked in it that the water ran red down the drain, and when I stepped out I was still not entirely cleansed of it. I felt the need to bath as well, even though I'd hated bathing in my old human life even more than I'd hated showering.

I filled the tub high enough to immerse my body in its warm embrace from the neck down. I could easily have nodded off in the soothing hot water, but when I closed my eyes I could still see the corpses I'd made during my last massacre. Fresh torment awaited me if I gave into sleep, where they would rise and condemn me for their murder, and as tired as I was after spending the night running across miles of open moorland, I didn't want to face the nightmares just then. So I opened my eyes before sleep could take me to find the water in the bath had also turned bloody, and I felt new despair creeping in. What meaning did life hold for me when the only true companion left to me was death?

"So find a new reason to fight," the hallucination said, reappearing as Lizzy once more. "Rekindle your anger and let it grow into rage, then channel it into a purpose and put all this senseless slaughter behind you."

"And what am I supposed to do?" I asked her. "March on back to Lady Sarah and try again to get her to arrange another meeting to rally what little forces we can muster?"

"Maybe that's exactly what you're meant to do," she replied. "You led them into battle once before; you can do it again. You can't just give up because she wouldn't hear you out last night."

"It won't make any difference, their minds are made up," I answered, somewhat bitterly. "Even Lady Sarah didn't seem convinced of my innocence without any proof."

"And what do you have to lose by trying? Your freedom? You're hardly free. Your life? You already admitted to yourself you're no longer living. You need a reason to live and killing is all that's left to you. You might as well kill with a purpose. You know you have to try."

"I am tired of running, that's for sure. But I don't really feel like fighting anymore either, despite what I said to Lady Sarah last night, and I sure as hell don't want to hand myself over to the vampires so they can chain and torment me some more, nor the Slayers for that matter."

"Then what reason do you have to go on? Part of you must have come to the same conclusion or you wouldn't be having this conversation. I'm not her, remember? This is all coming from you."

She had me there. If the hallucinations I'd been having over the last few months were my brain's way of working through my innermost thoughts, then deep down I knew I needed to embrace the war to give me something to exist for. Otherwise I'd just carry on in the same vicious cycle, letting my inner darkness tempt me to shed more innocent blood, only to feel worse for it afterwards. And why else would I have raised it with Lady Sarah when I'd gone to see her about clearing my name? But when my situation seemed so hopeless, my will to fight had been crushed again. Even proving my innocence didn't seem so important in that moment.

"Bollocks to it all," I growled. "I'm done with the other vampires, and I'm done with the Slayers. I'll stay here for as long as I can, then at least if this new vampire proves to be untrustworthy like the rest, I'll have enjoyed some of the human comforts I've been missing."

Once my mind was made up, I climbed out of the bloodied water and dried off, not worrying about staining the towels. The vampire was no doubt used to blood stains, and he clearly had enough wealth that replacing them wouldn't be much of an issue.

Though the walls of the mansion provided welcome shelter from the elements, the air was still chilled enough to raise the hairs on my skin. As unaccustomed to wearing clothes as I'd become, I searched the wardrobe for the warmest garments it had to offer, finding fleecy jogging bottoms and a jumper, and socks in the drawers underneath the desk. It felt so good to be warm again that I almost wanted to throw caution to the winds and place my trust in the vampire completely if it meant I could spend the rest of my days as a guest in his mansion, but I knew that was one luxury I didn't have. It would be hard to give up human comforts a second time, yet I had to remain wary in case he also proved to be false, and be prepared to return to my exile at a moment's notice. If it came to that I could only hope it would be when the weather had turned warmer, though my loneliness would be no easier to bear.

I was hungry after transforming back to human when I'd first reached the mansion, but I was curious to see the rest of the building that was to be my haven for the time being, and curiosity overrode my hunger. So I left the bedroom to explore the building, hoping I might also learn more of the vampire and the wisdom in placing any trust in him.

As I padded down the corridor, I took in more of my surroundings than I had when the vampire had first led me to the guestroom. The building had a sense of history to it, though I couldn't say what era it might have been built. Despite its age it appeared to have been well kept through the centuries, though there was no evidence of any human servants within its walls. I found it hard to believe the vampire would trouble himself with its upkeep, however, so he must have some dealings with mankind. How he could live on the edge of their world and treat with them as necessary, yet still escape the notice of the Slayers was a mystery to me. Especially when it seemed I couldn't set foot within a few miles of human settlements without setting off some silent alarm to alert the Slayers to my presence in the area.

From the view out of the windows I passed I could see more of the grounds, and that they were a modest size compared to the building, surrounded by the dense woodland which no doubt helped to hide the building from most humans. Assuming the vampire had the mental power to manipulate other beings as Lady Sarah and Ulfarr did, perhaps that and the trees were enough to hide the home he'd made for himself here. Yet surely if it was that easy no vampire would choose to live the life Lady Sarah had insisted we led for the past few months, driven from town to town and sheltering in abandoned buildings and graveyards. She'd been leading that life for centuries from what little I knew of her past, sheltering in a mausoleum with not even a coffin to call her own when we'd first met. How was it this vampire had managed to make a life for himself in human comforts, as if he was still one of them, when so many were forced to live as nomads, hunted at every turn? The more I took in of the vampire's mansion, the more questions and doubts I had. It seemed the only answers I would find would be the ones the vampire chose to give me.

I paused before a large framed painting depicting the portrait of a woman and her young son. A relic from the vampire's life as a human perhaps; the family he had once known and loved? I'd always said I had no need of love, only sex, yet the thought that no wife would ever wait for me to come home to her, no children would ever run into my arms, suddenly saddened me. I would never father children, only spawn monsters that would never be permitted to reach adulthood. The loss of my family and friends was partly the reason for the hole that gaped ever wider in my soul, such a vital part of being human and one I could never know again. Even a wolf has his alpha female and his pack, but I had no one. And as the last of my kind, what hope did I have of ever finding someone? How could any human love a monster like me? To accept the bestial side of my nature and the involuntary full moon transformations was one thing, but how could anyone ever love the empty shell I had become; a being so dead inside that it was quite possible I had no love to give in return. I might have felt I had no need for relationships in my human life, but somewhere in the empty abyss within was the need for the simple comfort of the affectionate touch of another, to be held in the arms of a woman who could love me as more than a friend. The very things that would forever be denied to me.

Even though I'd never had any interest in married life before, my treacherous mind saw fit to show me a vision of what might have been if my lupine half had never been awoken and I had remained a mortal. Perhaps it was partly down to the time of year. It had to be sometime around February by then which meant it was the mating season again, though I hadn't yet felt those instincts taking over like they had in my first year as a werewolf.

A beautiful woman greeted me after a long day's work and our son dashed out, but moments later the flesh sloughed from their faces with decay, as if any such life could only ever be corrupt and rotten at the core for the monster I'd become. The boy looked at me with accusing eyes glaring out from that gruesome, skeletal face, and then I recognised him as one of the kids I'd slaughtered in the playground. I'd seen enough horrors that it no longer turned me to a shivering wreck as it once did, so I snarled and swiped at the vision, and the gruesome hallucinations vanished instantly. But the anger remained quiet in my deepest recesses and with a heavy heart I stalked away from the portrait, wondering how long this mourning for the life I'd lost and the future I could have had would go on for.

I paid little attention to the mansion after that, pacing the corridors without really taking in the layout or the furnishings. The only other portrait to really catch my eye was an artist's depiction of a male lion, majestic and regal on the African plains. There was also a life sized statue of a lion rearing up on his hind legs, with claws unsheathed and fangs bared in an eternal display of ferocity. It seemed this vampire liked lions then, and perhaps he still missed his human family. Beyond that he still remained a stranger.

After a while I found myself back in the entrance hall and hunger drove me to venture back out, into the woods to hunt. I was able to track down and kill a large stag, eating my fill before I returned to the mansion. Then I made my way back to the guestroom and turned on the TV, hoping to find something to distract me from the dark thoughts that constantly circled my mind like carrion crows. Eventually I nodded off, sinking back into the nightmares.

The vampire seemed happy to find I was still in the mansion when he rose at nightfall. He invited me into his billiard room for a drink and I seated myself nearest the door to give me the best chance to escape if he did turn out to be false, something that was not lost on him.

"I am not in the habit of harming guests under my own roof. You need not fear anything here; not Ulfarr, nor the Slayers," he promised.

"Tell me again why you're choosing to help me when it seems every other vampire out there wants me dead."

He sighed but didn't answer immediately, giving me a penetrating look that I thought would pierce right through to the hole where my soul should have been. I got the impression he was reading me like an open book, as if my every thought and emotion were open to him. I cracked under the weight of his gaze and broke eye contact, frowning down at my glass of wine. Somewhere inside the wolf squirmed, uncomfortable at what he perceived to be a challenge for dominance, though I didn't think the vampire meant it to be.

Finally he answered "You have become as infamous as the deranged Aughtie you fought! Like I said, you have become the object of much curiosity. But you are correct, I am driven by more than mere curiosity. You were right to strike back at the Slayers. Too long have we run from them, letting them hunt us down when we are alone and vulnerable. If we are to die, better to do so fighting, I think. Most of the undead might have lost their stomach for battle, but I yearn for it. Is it not our right for us to fight for our very existence? If we wait any longer there will truly be too few to wage war against the Slayers and our only option will be to fade from existence, save for in myth and legend. That is not the fate I would choose. I believe we should fight while we still can, and remind mankind why they still fear the darkness."

"So why do you need me?" I asked.

Again he studied me before giving me an answer, perhaps weighing me up against the stories he had heard from those who fought with me in the battle for my hometown. "Why? You convinced a number of us to fight once. I believe you can do so again if we can prove your innocence to the rest of my kind and gain their trust in you. I admit I offered you my help and companionship not out of kindness but because I wanted to meet the last surviving werewolf for myself – find out what has made you so intriguing to my kind and humans alike. Not every wolf could inspire a group of us to join together and fight, after all. Perhaps you are the one we've been waiting in the shadows for, these long years past."

"Even if we do prove my innocence, I'm not sure they'll trust me enough to follow me into battle again," I said bitterly. "Destroying the base back home was nothing to the Slayers. It's just one small town, a mere fraction of their forces. I'm sure they'll soon re-establish themselves there. Those undead that remained in the surrounding area may have been given a brief respite, nothing more. They'll be hunted again soon enough, just like me and Lady Sarah have been since we fled. The others know this and they'll call open warfare futile, just as Lady Sarah did when I suggested it to her, and maybe they're right. At least if we stay in hiding we'll endure for longer."

"You underestimate what it is you have already achieved," he replied. "You did us all a great service that night in slaying Aughtie and thwarting their operations in the area. It was hours before the Slayers learned of what had transpired. And once they realised the utter destruction you had wrought on the unit stationed within that particular town, it was too late to cover everything up before the bodies were discovered by those ignorant to the reality of our existence. The news reports were most amusing. They attributed it to some kind of gang war at first, but that didn't explain the desecrated graves from which the inhabitants had been 'stolen' and moved to the scene of the crime. Then they talked about a gas explosion which, I think, was too unbelievable. The Slayers attempted to take control of the situation as best they could but they didn't entirely succeed in steering the public to a satisfactory cover story that kept both our existence and their own hidden. So you see, in a single night you may have changed everything.

"And then there's all the deaths you've caused in other areas. You've been so busy over the last few months, the Slayers couldn't successfully cover up everything you've done. The public are aware something is amiss, since no mortal wolf could cause so much destruction."

221

I thought about that. If the world found out about us I doubted it would be a good thing but on the other hand, if they discovered what the Slayers had been doing in secret for all these years they would be horrified, I was sure. They would no doubt agree the monster should be slain but they may question their methods, especially those which had cost human lives. There would no doubt be an uproar over the fact they had kept everyone in the dark as well. If the world had been presented with undeniable proof that we were more than mere myth and legend then they would have had no choice but to accept our existence. That in itself could have saved lives if people were prepared.

It was fair to assume the Slayers wanted to avoid that as much as we did, if only to save their own skins. Perhaps this meant they would have to be more careful now in their quest to bring about our extinction, although it hadn't done me any good so far. But if the vampire was right, maybe I was the exception. Maybe they'd decided I presented the most danger for the time being and if there was any chance to kill or capture me their patrols had to take it, no matter the risk. I smiled to myself at that, feeling a strange pride at the idea. My ego liked the thought they were afraid of me, and so they should be, it added in Luke's voice.

"So how come you just happened to be there in the midst of my latest breakdown? Have you been following me?"

"Yes," he admitted. "That you left Lady Sarah's side is no secret. Ulfarr knows you have been wandering around unchecked, and he was not happy with your former travelling companion when he learnt of it. You should not be too hard on her – she is trapped by old allegiances that make things difficult for her."

"It took you, a stranger, to save me from the execution Ulfarr would have sentenced me with. She stood there and did nothing to prevent it!" I snarled.

"It was difficult for her to continue speaking out against him. It is not for me to explain, however. You should return to her once we have proven your innocence and make amends."

"She should be the one to come to me," I growled, and then I was forced to ask once again "What do you care anyway?"

"If we are to convince the undead to go to war we need all the allies we can get. She helped you gather a force before – perhaps she will do so again."

Silence fell while we concentrated on our drinks. I was beginning to wonder if I'd made the right decision in staying. I had no intention of dealing with any other vampires after the way they'd treated me, not even Lady Sarah who had pretended to be my ally, if not my friend, only to stand by and let it happen when I needed her aid most of all. If she'd been more willing to help when I'd visited her the previous night then maybe I would have forgiven her for everything, but her unwillingness to aid me in proving my innocence had only pushed me further away, not just from her but from vampires in general. I'd only come to this vampire out of desperation, as a last resort.

"Tell me, what skills has Lady Sarah taught you?" he asked, breaking the silence and changing the subject.

"Just stuff to help me survive in case I ended up on my own, stuff to help me pass undetected by the Slayers wherever my wanderings might take me."

"But what of war; has she taught you nothing of battle, no fighting skills?"

"No, nothing like that. I did used to do taekwondo as a human, though."

"Then in this I believe I can help," he said. "You have been lost since severing the ties with your human life; that is plain to see. I will give your life that new purpose you are in dire need of, if it pleases you, and help set you back on the path you're meant to walk. From what I have seen so far, you are like a rampaging force – a formidable foe, but lacking control and discipline, or any kind of finesse. Many of the Slayers still fight with blades as well as guns, as you have seen for yourself. I can teach you how to wield a sword. I can train you to fight, in case you should ever face opponents against whom your greater speed and strength alone is not enough to ensure victory. I can take the rough brute you are now and polish him into a warrior."

I didn't answer immediately, considering his offer. To learn to sword fight did appeal to me, even if I no longer felt like engaging the Slayers in open warfare. At least it would give me something to focus on, and it could only serve to help me survive any future unavoidable clashes with the Slayers, or even other undead. I'd already decided to give the vampire a chance, though I couldn't trust him completely, especially for as long as he remained a stranger to me, so it seemed I might as well accept his help.

"I would be grateful for any training you can give me," I answered him.

"Then we will begin as soon as you are ready."

"But shouldn't we focus on clearing my name first? That's why I came here, after all."

"Of course, but that may take time and I think it will be wiser to wait till the full moon has passed for another month."

"Okay, well we can get straight to it tonight I guess. But I have questions first. I don't even know your name."

"I've had many names, but you can call me Leon."

I didn't need him to explain why he'd taken different names over the centuries. It made him harder to track by the Slayers, and by the authorities. It wasn't always possible to hide a kill from humans, and most undead probably didn't have others to clean up after them, as I'd had. Before technology grew so advanced, the Slayers probably had a harder time of hiding our kills from the rest of humanity, and if they'd had reason to suspect Leon he would have been hunted by Slayers and the authorities alike.

"Leon, like a lion?" I asked him.

"It's as good a name as any."

"You really do like lions," I laughed.

"I have always had an affinity for cats, but if everyone has an animal, I've always felt mine was the lion. The king of beasts," he said, before correcting himself in response to my growl "The king of mortal beasts."

"And how come you get to live in a place like this, when most of us are forced to hide in the shadows, on the fringes of the human world?"

"Ah, I am quite lucky in that respect. You see, there was a time when those who practiced magic were more numerous and some of them wielded great power. Much greater than those now working for the Slayers, by all accounts. We would be doomed if they had any truly competent spellcasters among them.

"I laid claim to this place over three centuries ago, at a time when one of the most powerful witches to ever walk the Earth happened to be in this area. We struck a bargain, and she placed a spell on this building and its grounds to protect it from prying eyes. No human can find this place, unless they are led here by someone who already knows the way.

"In the modern world, aircraft passes overhead all the time, of course. But thanks to the witch's magic, the humans only see a stretch of woodlands from above. From the ground, they never get close enough to lay eyes on the clearing. The power of the spell manipulates them in such a way that they never find their way through the woods to these grounds, and any perceived strangeness around the area soon strays from their thoughts. The nearby villagers never even try to enter these woods anymore. They have too many local legends to deter them, without the need for the magic. So I am able to remain here, quite safe from the Slayers, unless something were to lead them to my door."

"So that's why you don't want me stirring the locals," I said.

"Precisely."

"But the magic doesn't work on supernatural beings?"

"No, our minds are too strong. But there has never been a need to hide from my fellow undead."

"How come this place has electric if it's so old then? And if it's so well cared for, you must have some dealings with humans."

"You are quite right, I have invited humans here who possess the necessary skills to suit my needs, and I do employ both a cleaner and a gardener who come round once a week. But you are no doubt aware of the hypnotic powers most of us vampires possess, and I have each under my spell. As soon as they leave the grounds, they forget all about this place, and it's only when they're due to come back that they feel compelled to come here, though they can't explain why and if anyone asks I've given each a cover story. I haven't lasted so long in this place by being careless."

There was more I could have asked, but we'd finished our drinks and Leon needed to feed. I paced restlessly through the building while I waited for him to return, but he was not gone long and the night was still young. The vampire had answered my biggest questions and I was more eager to start training than I was to continue talking, so he led me to a large room adorned with weapons along its walls. More weapons hung in racks within the room itself, but he ignored these, retrieving two blunt swords which had been propped in a corner of the room.

"Shouldn't we be training with wooden swords?" I asked, eyeing them with uncertainty.

"With our strength, wooden swords break too easily, and you'll learn quicker if you get the feel for a proper weapon straight away."

"But isn't there a risk of us doing a hell of a lot of damage to each other with real swords?"

"You won't hurt me – I'm too fast and too skilled a swordsman. And I'm skilled enough that I won't accidentally cut you, if you trust me to train you in such a way? The only alternative is to bring a human in for you to fight, but finding a skilled swordsman in this era will be a challenge. We'd have to try and capture one of the Slayers trained in swordsmanship, which could be dangerous. So will you trust me?"

I didn't want to place any trust in him so quickly when I was still only just getting to know him, but I could see no other way to learn the skills he was offering to teach me. And the boy I'd once been had always loved fantasy, which was probably why learning to wield a sword held such appeal. So I nodded.

"Good. Now, show me your fighting stance."

I'd spent a year training in taekwondo, and the stance I'd adapted for sparring still came naturally to me. It felt strange when Leon corrected that stance, advising me not to spread my legs too wide or place my back foot too far to the side, as a matter of balance. Once he was satisfied with the positioning of my feet and my hold on the blunted training blade, he invited me to strike at him.

I'd only ever handled a sword once before, during the fight against Aughtie where she'd almost killed me when she'd stabbed me through the chest. And as with the last sword I'd wielded, the blade felt long and awkward in my hand. I was also wary of striking too hard, despite the vampire's reassurances that his skill would prevent either of us from doing too much damage. Even if the swords were too blunt to slice through flesh, they could still break bones, and it seemed a waste of energy to have to transform multiple times to heal any serious wounds sustained during training. So when I clumsily swung at Leon, the blow was much slower than it could have been with my lycanthropic speed and strength, and with his even greater vampiric powers, he blocked the attack almost lazily.

"Come on wolf, is that the best you can do? The moon rises as full again tomorrow night. Don't you feel its power coursing through your veins?"

With a snarl, I struck again, faster but still awkwardly, and my aim was off. Leon blocked again and retaliated with a thrust to my chest, deliberately slowing his movements enough to give me a chance to parry. I barely managed to bring my sword up in time, before the vampire struck again at my head.

We traded a few blows, mine far too slow and clumsy to ever land on the target, but before long I'd instinctively reverted to the stance I'd grown so used to in taekwondo, leaning in on my leading leg to stab at the vampire constantly dancing out of my reach. Leon easily dodged and retaliated with a blow to my leg, instructing "Be careful of spreading your legs too wide. If you ever find yourself fighting in a line you don't want to step out too far or you'll make your front leg a target, and you'll find your balance is off in that stance."

I tried to follow his advice but the taekwondo stance came so easily to me, I received several welts to my leg before the lesson stuck.

With our supernatural abilities, it meant we were able to keep sparring far longer than mortal humans without beginning to tire. Obviously I wasn't going to become a master swordsman in one night, but my hand-eye co-ordination had always been good, perhaps as a result of all my human years spent gaming, and I was quick to learn. I was soon parrying and dodging Leon's blows more naturally and my aim was fast improving. I still couldn't hit him but at least my blade would have found its mark if he'd been any slower at blocking and dodging.

As the fight wore on, Leon's attacks became more frenzied, until suddenly it no longer felt like a training session but real battle. Adrenalin flooded my body and I felt more alive than I had in weeks, my rage beginning to bubble up. Even though I was outmatched, I began to attack with a new ferocity, no longer holding back.

The vampire brought his blade up in a vicious arc at my neck, but I ducked and swung at his side. If he hadn't been so fast, I would have landed the hit, but he dodged and retaliated with a blow to my own side. I blocked it and we broke apart momentarily, before attacking again. This time Leon parried my blow and then kicked me backwards, the move taking me by surprise and causing me to fall flat on my back, where I lay panting.

"That was awesome!" I exclaimed as I accepted the vampire's offered hand to help me back onto my feet.

"You did well," Leon said with a feral smile which made his fangs visible. His eyes still shone with the light of battle but even though our sparring had grown somewhat wilder, he'd remained in complete control, keeping to a speed that matched my own and never once hitting me with enough force to do too much damage. "Remember, in a real fight you can still rely on your natural weapons as much as man-made tools. Your sword should become an extension of your arm and it may be your primary weapon, but that doesn't mean you can't lash out with fists or claws, or kick your opponent back as I just did."

I nodded, grinning, and asked eagerly "Again?"

"As you wish," the vampire replied, settling into his fighting stance. I mirrored him and we began round two, which lasted a little longer and this time ended with me disarmed, the tip of Leon's blade lightly touching my throat. I insisted on a third round, but after that we were forced to call it a night. Dawn was not far off, and the sparring had raised Leon's bloodlust. He wanted to feed a second time while he still had the cover of darkness, and though my anger hadn't fully formed into the raging inferno it was capable of becoming, I could still feel its presence deep within and I decided to hunt as well. I might not be able to completely lose myself in the bloodlust that night but I hoped there would be some pleasure in making a kill while I still felt alive from the combat training.

"When the full moon rises this evening, you are free to roam the grounds and hunt in the surrounding woodlands, but if you can try to keep from taking any of the locals as human prey it will help us remain hidden here. I suspect I will see you again in four night's time, unless I happen upon you in wolf form," Leon said, once we'd fed and were back in the mansion, before departing to his room to sleep through the daylight hours.

The feelings our sparring had awoken in me soon wore off, and I was forced to re-think the decision I'd made the previous day to turn my back on the war with the Slayers. If sparring could make me feel alive once more, perhaps real battle was what I needed after all. There was still the problem of Ulfarr convincing the other undead I was guilty though, and if we were ever to have any hope of making a proper stand against humanity then I needed to clear my name. It was either that, or hope Leon would let me spend eternity hiding out in his mansion, but I doubted it would last. Sooner or later either the other vampires would find me and carry out the death sentence Ulfarr would no doubt order, or something would happen to bring the Slayers to the mansion. There was nothing I could do that day though, so I enjoyed more TV while I dozed on and off, awaiting the call of the moon.

Chapter Twenty One – A Taste of Heaven

The full moon passed without any trouble that month. My lupine half knew it was safer to prey on the animals in the woodlands than stray to the village for the humans he really craved, and there was a whole herd of deer in the woods to keep him happy. I suspected Leon had used his powers to bring the prey within his territory and keep them there, despite the terror we inspired in them, since he had to feed as well and I doubted he went into the village for fresh blood. He'd asked me to stay clear of the local humans twice so he could remain in his mansion hidden from the Slayers, and if it was that important to him surely he wouldn't risk throwing it all away just for a bit of human blood. Not that it really mattered, I was just grateful for the supply of fresh meat.

I was eager to resume my sword fighting lessons as soon as the full moon was over, and we spent the next few nights trading blows as I sought to gain some skill with a blade. The sparring sessions continued to give me a sense of being alive after the months of feeling dead inside, but a monster like me was never going to get a fairy tale ending and it seemed the enjoyment it brought me was to be short lived.

It had only been roughly a week since I'd first arrived at the mansion and our mock battle grew especially frenzied that night, when suddenly Dad reappeared.

"Don't you think this is all a bit too convenient, Nick?" he asked. "Being back in a home with everything you've been missing; how you can be sure it's real?"

As he spoke, the walls of the room fell away and I found myself back out on the moors, as if I'd never left. Sparring with Leon had felt so real, from the scent of the vampire and my surroundings to the sound of his voice, but the sudden change in reality felt equally so. I could feel the cold wind whipping across the open expanse of land and battering my body, and smell the scent of the grass covering every inch of the ground as far as my eyes could see. The waning moon was bright overhead and the night sky was clear and spattered with the shining dots of the stars. But I wasn't alone, and the blade slicing through the air towards my chest was real enough, except it was no longer Leon wielding it but a human enemy – a Slayer no doubt.

My own sword had fallen from my hand, if it had every truly existed at all, and I barely managed to dodge the blow. My opponent struck again and I grabbed his arm in an attempt to wrench it from the socket. But somehow the man twisted free and pulled me into a stranglehold. I fought to free myself, the pressure increasing on my throat until I grew light-headed. Moments later I blacked out, leaving me helpless in the hands of my enemy.

I came round to find myself on the floor and Leon knelt over me, looking concerned. I was back in his mansion, or at least I seemed to be. My grip on reality had been weak for some time but if I could no longer trust any of my senses, how could I be sure of anything anymore? For my brain to fool me with Luke's 'presence' was one thing, but this had been something else entirely.

"Easy, mate," Leon said when I tried to sit up. "Do you know where you are?"

"In your home, I think. But for a minute there I felt like I was back outside, facing another of the Slayers."

"Okay, that's enough training for tonight."

"No, I'm fine," I growled in protest. "It's just my mind playing more tricks on me."

Leon shook his head. "You're not fine but I know what might help. More wine is in order I think, or I have some beer in if you'd prefer."

I growled again but the vampire wasn't taking no for an answer, so I followed him into the billiard room where we'd talked before. He poured himself another glass of wine and offered me a bottle of beer, which I drank deeply from.

"So, do you want to talk about what's troubling you?" he asked, sitting.

I shrugged. "I guess part of me still feels guilty for all the lives I've taken and doesn't think I deserve the luxuries you've allowed me by letting me stay here."

"The hallucinations, do you have them often?"

"Yeah, but that's the first time I've felt like I was physically somewhere else. Usually I just see people and hear voices."

"It might help to talk. Why don't you tell me about everything that's happened since the night you were bitten."

I laughed bitterly. "What is there to tell? I was turned, I killed a lot of people at full moon, my bloodlust spilled into the human half of my personality and then I killed a lot more people outside of the full moon. I thought fighting the Slayers was what my bloodlust and my rage needed, but after the battle back home I realised I couldn't go on living like a human if I didn't want people I still cared about to get hurt, so I left it all behind. And I've been moving around ever since until I ended up here.

"Lady Sarah had us make the most of whatever shelter we could find – old buildings mostly before we ended up on the moors. There was an abandoned campsite we made use of and that was where I ran off to find human victims to slaughter under my first full moon after the battle. My rage and my bloodlust were all that were keeping me going; I just wanted to feed them and the only way I knew how was with fresh blood. I don't even remember everything that happened after that or everyone I killed.

"Lady Sarah found an old barn for us to shelter in at some point, out in the country. There was a town nearby and a small patch of woodland, but my rage was starting to burn out by then and I don't think I killed any people in that area. Then there were a couple more massacres after we'd moved on, including that one you cleaned up for me.

"I've been empty inside since my anger faded and I just wanted to feel something again, but it seems all it brought me is fresh guilt. So now I have to deal with whatever new torment my mind conjures up for me."

"Ah, this is the struggle we all face when we are first turned. And you've had it especially hard now the Slayers are so big a threat and there's so few of us left. But you seem strong, so you will learn to adapt."

I took another swig from the bottle before answering "I don't want to talk about it. What about you? If you've been here over three hundred years that makes you what, a few centuries old?"

"A few centuries," he laughed. "Try over two thousand."

"Two thousand?" I said, stunned. He seemed so modern compared to the other vampires I'd met that I'd just assumed he was younger. But then again, Vince had been the same age as Lady Sarah and he'd also embraced the modern era. "Wow. So how did you end up as a member of the undead and how did you cope in your first few years?"

"Ah, my tale is not so epic as Ulfarr's which I'm sure you will have heard from Lady Sarah by now. I was no one as a human really – no champion of ancient Rome, no warrior of great renown. But my name did become known in my last few months as a human when I was caught stealing and condemned to the arena, where I would spend the rest of my mortal life as a gladiator.

"For many it was a death sentence and given my slender build, no one expected me to last beyond even my first game. But I was sent to one of many gladiator schools that existed at the time for training, not because anyone wanted to give me a fighting chance but in order

231

to make a spectacle of my death. There I picked up new combat skills and what I lacked in strength I made up for in speed.

"First they pitted me against other men and I emerged victorious each time, much to everyone's disgust. They wanted to see me die in the bloodiest, most glorious fashion the games had to offer, after a long struggle against one of the many favoured champions. But against all the odds I survived match after match, no matter how great my opponents.

"It was in my time there that I saw my first lion. I'd never seen such a majestic animal before or a creature so powerful, and I was fascinated by him. Then the day came when my masters decided to pit me against one of these mighty beasts, but that match surely would have been a death sentence. I'd just been wounded in my last game – a nasty cut to my sword arm which would have caused lasting damage to the function of it if I'd stayed human. They patched me up but I hadn't been given training in the use of fighting with my left arm, because they wanted to make an example of me. I was never meant to last in the arena, only to suffer a violent death for their enjoyment. I knew I was doomed."

He paused and I couldn't help but ask "What the hell did you steal to make them so desperate to watch you die?"

"That is a story for another time. But to answer your first questions, it was the night before what should've been my last match when I was visited by the vampire who turned me. In her way, she was every bit as majestic as the lions I'd grown to admire so. And she offered me a second chance, though my freedom came at the price of my humanity."

"Why?"

"That's also a story for another time. But I agreed of course, or I wouldn't be here now. And so I became a vampire.

"It was easier to adjust back then, without the Slayers forever hunting us at every turn, and I was already accustomed to killing for survival so taking human prey was not as hard as it has been for you. I chose to live among humans for as long as possible, until eventually it became too dangerous and I was able to make this place my home – a happy compromise between hiding in the shadows and living in the world of men. I have been luckier than most to be able to stay here and it's the longest I've ever been in any one place."

It struck me then that he spoke without any discernible accent. Other vampires still seemed to have a hint of their original accent when they spoke as if, no matter how many times they may have relocated over the centuries or how far, it was a part of their never-changing, ageless bodies. I wondered if it was as a result of moving around so often and learning to blend in that had caused him to lose it, but no doubt that was 'a story for another time' as well.

I also realised the portrait of the woman and child I'd seen during my first day in the mansion couldn't be the vampire's family, as it was unlikely it would have survived his time as a nomad before he'd settled in the mansion. Unless it was an artist's impression of a description he'd given them, I supposed. But I wasn't given chance to find out any more about that either before Leon spoke again, interrupting my thoughts.

"Now, if you're sure you don't want to talk I know what will help keep your mind off things," he said, and led me to a part of the mansion I hadn't seen yet.

I looked on in awe as we entered the vampire's own personal home cinema, thinking some god must have taken pity on me and let me into Heaven after all. Judging from the stacks of DVDs lining the shelves on either side of the room, he had enough movies to open his own video store, and there were speakers for surround sound. He also had numerous games consoles hooked up to the system and they were the reason he'd brought me there that night.

"Nintendo, PlayStation, Xbox, or something more retro?" the vampire asked me.

"PlayStation," I replied eagerly, sitting back on the leather sofa.

"Take your pick," Leon said, handing me a stack of games from which I chose the game adaptation of the third Lord of the Rings movie. It was one I'd owned but never had chance to complete, thanks to my lycanthropy. "Good choice; we can play co-operatively on this one. I was impressed with these films and I especially liked the portrayal of Legolas."

Leon passed over a controller which turned out to be for player one, so I selected the co-operative mode and the first level, but once we were taken to the character select screen I deliberately picked the character he'd just named as his favourite.

"Oh really? I invite you into my home and let you stay here even through the full moon, and this is how you repay me?"

I just laughed until he grabbed me in another stranglehold, forcing me to submit. "Okay, okay. I'll play Aragorn instead."

He released me and gave me a playful shove, but then the game loaded and we were soon focussed on fighting virtual enemies.

"Do you still see the faces of your victims?" I asked him while we played.

"After two thousand years they all blend into each other and one human becomes very much the same as another. But yes, I can still see the faces of my earliest victims."

"Do they still haunt you?"

"Like I said earlier, I was already accustomed to killing for survival so their deaths had less impact on me than taking human prey has had on you. And it's literally ancient history now. We can't change the past and it does not do to dwell on it, only learn what we can from our experiences and move on."

"I wish someone would tell my subconscious that," I sighed.

We fell quiet as we approached the boss fight at the end of the level but I was out of practice, and even with my enhanced reflexes which allowed for more efficient button mashing, my character's health bar was still quick to drop down into the red.

"Oh come on, you single-handedly defeated the leader of the Slayers in your hometown and now you can't even survive a first level boss?" Leon joked.

"Fuck off, it's been ages since I had chance to play this game."

We beat the level but dawn forced us to save and abandon our adventure for the day.

"You're welcome to spend as much time in here as you want," the vampire said before retiring to his chambers for the day. "Help yourself to any of these games or movies whenever you need another distraction."

For the next two months or so I actually began to feel, if not true happiness, then at least some form of contentment. I enjoyed Leon's combat training much more than Lady Sarah's lessons in survival. He was a far more patient teacher for one thing and I was always the one to instigate a training session, rather than the vampire insisting I learn more like Lady Sarah had. And since I'd once been a typical teenage boy, learning to fight was just cool.

Once I'd learnt some skill with a blade, Leon went on to train me in hand to hand combat. I was becoming a competent fighter and if I ever found myself unable to transform and facing an opponent of equal speed and strength, I would already stand a far better chance of coming out alive for the tuition the vampire had given me. Not that such a short space of time allowed me to truly master these new skills, but at least I would be more prepared for combat when the time came to put them into practice.

The full moons that passed in that time were as uneventful as my first in the area had been. Without my rage driving my lupine half into a frenzy, he had enough self-control to keep away from the humans he still craved and he kept to the woodland each time. And with the locals already fearful of the area, there was no danger of crossing paths with any of them. Surprisingly, I didn't run into any trouble with any more vampires either.

As for my friendship with Leon, I couldn't help but grow close to him, despite my initial misgivings around his motives and the wisdom in placing my trust in him. I was already beginning to regard him like a brother and when we weren't training, we would enjoy more gaming time or watching movies in his home cinema, or simply chatting over a drink. Human luxuries I'd never expected to experience again, but which helped fill the emptiness I'd fallen into since attempting to leave the human world behind. And the vampire was much easier to get on with than Lady Sarah had been, even though he was far older. He was more open with me for a start, more 'human' I supposed, and the friend I'd sorely needed. I was content in his company, surrounded by all the comforts I'd been missing, but I had to remind myself there was a reason I'd sought him out and it wouldn't do to delay too long. The time had come to prove my innocence to Ulfarr and the other undead.

Chapter Twenty Two – Quest to Prove My Innocence

"Leon, it's been like two weeks since the last full moon and there's been three of them since I first arrived, and we haven't even talked about the real reason I came here yet," I said. "Isn't it time we started working on clearing my name?"

"Why, are you growing bored already?" he asked.

"No and I don't mean to seem ungrateful; you have no idea how badly I needed these last couple of months after struggling to adapt to being on my own and without any of the things I took for granted in my human life. That's why I haven't said anything sooner. But if we delay any longer, doesn't that give Ulfarr more time to move against us? If there's been more murders, won't he be working his audience up into even more of a frenzy? If this place is only hidden to humans that means I'm not all that safe from them here, and if they come in force the two of us can't stand against a mob the size of the crowd that came to my last trial. Isn't there a risk they might just show up one night and kill me right here, before I have chance to get away?"

"You're right, I suppose," he sighed. "Okay, you told me that first night you think you've discovered who the real killer is, but you haven't said much else about it since then. Tell me more of what you know."

"I think it's a witch called Selina, if that's even her real name. She had a black dog familiar but I've not seen owt like it before. It had these glowing red eyes and it was like it was made from shadows, but it had no trouble pinning me down and it felt to be strong. I saw it standing over the body of a vampire and I'm pretty sure something like that could easily overpower any undead. I've been wondering if this is another of the Slayers' pet spellcasters and they've put her up to framing me to make us turn on each other, so she's using the dog creature to make it look like werewolf kills."

Leon's eyes widened as I talked. "The black dog you describe sounds like a barghest. They are indeed formidable creatures capable of preying on other supernatural beings, as well as mortals. It's not the first time I've heard of a witch summon one and bind him to her will, and as far as I know only witchcraft can stop them."

"Great, so we're fucked if the witch sends it after us. All the more reason to try and stop her, don't you think?"

"Indeed, but just how do you propose we go about finding some evidence to back up your theory?"

I slumped back in my chair, suddenly feeling dejected. Why couldn't anything be straightforward anymore? To Leon I said "I'd hoped you'd think of something. We could go back to Selina's cottage I suppose and hope to find something there. You don't have to come with me though. Judging from what you just said about her familiar, it'll be dangerous going back there. I understand if you'd rather I went alone."

"No, I think I will join you. If Selina is doing this to frame you then I suspect you won't have anything to fear from the barghest, though I may well be putting my own life at risk. But two sets of eyes are better than one. If there is any proof to be found in the cottage, we're more likely to find it with two of us."

I nodded gratefully to him. "The only thing is, I'm not sure exactly how far the cottage was from here and it might take some finding. The sun hasn't been down that long but sunrise is at what, around five-ish at the moment? That's only about eight hours of darkness to find and explore the place, and then get back here."

"If needs be, I will have to shelter elsewhere through the day until we can return here tomorrow night. But I do not believe it will come to that. If you let your wolf half guide you, I suspect he will be able to find the way back without too much trouble, and in wolf form you should be able to cover the ground easy enough in the time we have. And I will have no trouble keeping pace beside you."

"Okay, but if I'm going to transform I'll need to eat first to keep my energy up. Could you fetch me a deer or something?"

Leon raised an eyebrow. "You may be my guest here, but that doesn't mean you should expect me to wait on you hand and foot."

"Yeah but we only have so long, and it would save time if you could bring me some meat while I transform. If I have to hunt for it myself, we'll be losing valuable journey time."

"True. Very well then, come outside and take your wolf form, and I will go hunt."

"Cheers mate."

I stripped off and followed him through the front door, wasting no time in starting the transformation once outside. The vampire ran off into the woods while my body shifted from human to wolf. There came the familiar stab of pain within my stomach as guts twisted, the aching of my bones as they elongated or shortened to fit their new form, and my flesh stretched outwards to cover new structures – most notably my lupine snout and tail. It was over in minutes, but that was all the time Leon needed to make a kill and bring it back to me. He reappeared between the trees just as the last of the changes completed, and I caught the scent of the fresh meat in a wave of mouth-watering hunger. I bounded across the grounds to meet him, enjoying the powerful feeling of my wolf form and the ease with which my four paws carried me over the earth.

Another deer carcass hung limply in Leon's arms, its head swinging from side to side as the vampire continued towards me. As I drew closer, he dropped the kill for me to feed on and waited patiently while I gorged myself, then it was time to call on my wolfish half to guide us back to the witch's cottage.

I was wary of the vampire, even though my human half had grown close to him. But time was of the essence if I wanted to clear my name before the rest of the vampires sentenced me to death, so I had no option but to co-operate with my human half and trust that it knew what it was doing.

Finding my way back to the witch's cottage was easy enough. It was a long run but even mortal wolves have great stamina, so I was able to cover the miles effortlessly. Leon kept pace beside me, just as graceful on two legs as I was on all fours. The land rushed by us in a blur, harried at times by strong gusts of wind but we pushed on. Fortunately it was not the constant gale I'd suffered through the winter months and so it failed to slow us.

When the cottage first came into view, it was nothing more than a dark shape almost lost in the blackness of the night, and we were also fortunate in that the witch seemed to be out again. We slowed and proceeded onwards with more caution, straining our senses for the monstrous shadow dog Leon had called a barghest. I could hear nothing besides my own panting and the steady beating of my heart in my chest, and the faint sounds made by the vampire creeping forward beside me. Nor did any scents come to me on the breeze, but after last time I knew that meant nothing. The barghest had seemingly materialised out of nowhere, without the warning signs I would have picked up from a flesh and blood creature. It seemed the only sense I could rely on was my sight, a strange feeling for a canid. My hearing and sense of smell were so finely attuned to the world around me that I was so used to detecting potential threats through sound and scent alone. Often I would be aware of something approaching long before it came close enough for my eyes to see it, and I felt uneasy facing a creature I wouldn't be aware of until it came into view. Yet in spite of feeling less than confident against the shadowy threat, there were no glowing red eyes waiting for us as we drew closer. I knew that didn't necessarily mean anything either after the way it had just appeared before, but with each step we took without any sign of the barghest, the higher our hopes that the witch hadn't left it guarding her domain.

I suspected similar thoughts were going through the vampire's mind, as he said "So far so good but stay alert. You might want to transform back while things are quiet, unless you'd rather manage searching as best you can on four legs."

Unlike Lady Sarah, this vampire still spoke in English, but I could understand him well enough. I debated the wisdom of changing back. It would sap some of my strength which I would need if it came to a fight with the shadow beast, but looking round the cottage would be easier on two legs – I'd have the advantage of height to get a good look at the shelves and on the table once we were inside. I supposed I ought to let the human take over since this was its idea to come back here, so I left the decision to my other half.

"Nick?" Leon asked, unsure if I'd understood him. "It might be an idea to transform back now while there's no sign of the barghest, unless you think it's better to stay in wolf form."

Like my lupine half, I knew I needed my full supernatural strength to face the black dog if it turned up. But the whole point of coming back was to try and find some proof that Selina was behind the killings, and it would be a more thorough search if I was on two legs rather than four. In the end I opted for a compromise, taking the transformation just halfway to my hybrid form so I didn't use as much of my energy, and so I remained more powerful than if I was fully human. The vampire nodded approvingly.

We trod carefully as we approached the doorway, and I wondered if it wasn't just the barghest to worry about. What if the witch had placed some kind of magical booby trap on the place, if such a thing existed? Could crossing the threshold uninvited trigger some kind of spell she'd placed as she left her home? If Leon had any similar concerns he didn't voice them, but I could feel the tension emanating from him like a physical force as he tried the door. It was open, which I found ominous. Perhaps the witch just didn't expect unwanted visitors, or perhaps it was a sign that there was some kind of magical security in place, something we couldn't sense.

I held my breath as we stepped inside, half expecting flames to spring up around us or some kind of curse to strike us down. My heart beat faster in response to my fears and my senses strained to pick up any hint of danger. But we passed through the doorway unharmed, and still there was no sign of the black dog familiar lurking in the shadows. Shakily I exhaled again, not yet allowing myself the luxury of relief. Just because we'd been able to enter unharmed, it didn't necessarily mean we were safe, and I wouldn't relax until we were back at Leon's mansion. And of course we had no way of knowing how long we had before Selina returned to her home. We needed to keep our wits about us in case she came back while we were still searching, though at least our heightened senses should be able to pick up her approach with enough time to make our escape.

There was no fire burning in the hearth this time and even our supernatural eyes struggled to penetrate the blackness as we stepped further into the room. Leon grabbed a candle from the nearest shelf and produced a box of matches from a pocket.

"Where did you get those?" I whispered as best I could, which was something of a challenge in my lupine state.

"I grabbed them on our way out, figured they'd come in handy," the vampire replied normally. "Why are you whispering?"

I shrugged. "It felt safer to whisper."

"If the barghest's nearby, he already knows we're here. Whispering won't save us."

"Yeah, I know," I sighed. "It just made me feel better."

I was glad of the faint glow from the candle flame which provided enough light to get a good look at the tools of witchcraft stored on the shelves, and it made watching for the barghest somewhat easier. But it also meant the shadows we cast crept around after us, and the movement only made me edgier.

There was nothing new to see when Leon checked in the cupboards, and I was disappointed to find no evidence of the witch's involvement in the murders when I searched the table. I honestly don't know what I'd been expecting to find there, that night. I examined the small bones with my clawed hands in the hopes there might be something there, but they all seemed to be from animals. No vampire fangs lay scattered among them, nor any I recognised as part of a humanoid skeleton – not that humanoid bones would have meant anything without some way to prove if they'd been human or vampire.

"Do you see anything out of the ordinary?" Leon asked. "Anything that might help our case?"

"No," I growled, rifling through the spellbook for any sign of a ritual involving the deaths of vampires on the off chance her reasons for killing them were rooted in the occult, rather than as part of some new plot devised by the Slayers. Still there was nothing. I should have known it wouldn't be that easy, but without any kind of proof of the witch's guilt to take back with us, I was at a loss for how else to clear my name.

"We should go," the vampire said. "It's not safe for us to linger too long here."

"Yeah I know. But when we get back to the mansion, what then? How the hell are we going to convince the others of my innocence now?"

"Worry about that later; we need to make it back to the mansion first. We've been lucky not to encounter the barghest, but the witch could return at any moment. We need to leave before she catches us here."

He had a point so I tried to focus on the journey back and staying alert for any hint of danger along the way, but my mind kept straying to the question of what next. Short of catching Selina or her familiar in the act, I couldn't see any other way to clear my name, and no matter how hard I concentrated on searching the shadows for more imminent threats, I couldn't keep the sense of doom from creeping over me.

Leon blew out the candle he'd been carrying, darkness engulfing us the instant the flame was extinguished. He returned it to the shelf he'd grabbed it from and we made our way back out of the cottage, my feeling that Death was coming for me only increasing once the impenetrable shadows returned. Twice I was sure I'd seen movement in the blackness and we paused, readying ourselves for an attack, but the room remained still and quiet. Despite my dark expectations, we were able to pass back through the doorway unscathed, out into the surrounding blackness of the moors.

And then we saw the glowing red eyes seemingly floating in the darkness ahead. The barghest was here after all, and he was coming for us.

Chapter Twenty Three – Enemies Abound

The black shadow dog charged us, Leon barely managing to draw his sword before it pounced on him. Taken by surprise and facing a creature possessing supernatural speed and strength similar to our own, he never had chance to slash at the barghest, and the blade clattered out of his hand as he fell to the ground, pinned down by the beast. I threw myself at the creature and succeeded in knocking it off of the vampire, the two of us rolling away in a tangle of teeth and claws. We snapped at each other but even though my jaws closed round the other canid a couple of times, my fangs could inflict no damage on the shadow dog. But its teeth were capable of tearing flesh just as effectively as any mortal beast and I received a variety of cuts in our initial struggle, though none were serious enough to do anything more than call to my rage as nerves sparked with that stinging pain of flesh wounds.

Leon retrieved his sword and regained his feet just as we two canids broke apart, before the barghest charged once more. And like the first time I'd faced it, I was reminded again of the night I'd been bitten by the black werewolf, and the way he'd singled me out. But this time it was my friend who was the target. The black dog had seemingly lost interest in me, lunging again at Leon.

The vampire was ready for it this time, his blade flashing through the air in a deadly arc intended to sever the beast's head. But as the sword passed through the shadow creature, the thing's form merely collapsed into a kind of black cloud barely visible in the slither of moonlight, before reforming in a wave of primal fury. Its jaws closed around Leon's sword arm and savaged the limb until its fangs shredded the material of the vampire's jacket and the flesh beneath, bloody strips hanging down. The barghest had made such a mess of the vampire's arm that it was impossible to tell the material from the ruined flesh in the darkness, and if he'd been mortal the limb would no doubt have been ruined beyond repair. As it was, Leon temporarily lost use of the arm and he dropped his blade a second time.

I re-joined the fray, snapping and clawing at the shadow beast to try and distract it long enough for Leon to get away. The black dog growled and released its grip on the vampire's arm, only to clamp its jaws round him again, this time sinking fangs into his right leg. Even with the near full force of my lupine strength, I strained against the beast's might in an attempt to wrestle it off my friend. I managed to prise its maw off Leon's leg and struggled to pull its head away so I could pin it down. Somehow I managed inch by inch to push it to the ground.

"Run," I grunted. "I'll be fine; it's you the barghest wants."

Leon nodded and limped off. I had no idea how vampire healing worked but if he couldn't regenerate the ruined flesh of his limbs without feeding, I needed to buy him as much time as I could. Unfortunately, I didn't think I could hold the barghest down for long, the beast thrashing beneath me as I fought to keep it there.

The vampire had just made it out of sight when the huge black dog gave a powerful jerk of its head and succeeded in shaking me loose. It sprang up to give chase, but I pounced on its back and fought to restrain it a second time. The beast twisted round and grabbed my arm in its jaw, then tossed me away with enough force to send me crashing head first into the side of the witch's cottage. I felt a sharp pain in my skull as it connected with the stone wall, then I slumped to the ground, dazed and unable to rise in time to prevent the barghest from bounding after its prey. Leon was on his own now, and all I could do was hope I'd given him enough of a head start to escape back to his mansion.

I was sat leaning against the side of the cottage for long enough that I vaguely wondered if I had a concussion. Pain blazed through my head, like someone was hammering a nine-inch nail through my skull, driving it deeper and deeper into my brain. Somewhere in the back of my mind there was a sense of the need to move, but I couldn't think clearly enough to work out why that was so important.

Precious minutes ticked by as I struggled to grab hold of the thoughts that were eluding me, until everything crashed back into place with sudden clarity. I needed to get away before the witch came home, in case she no longer needed me alive or now had orders to hand me over to the Slayers, and I had to help Leon. The barghest was no doubt already gaining on him, if it hadn't caught up to him already, and he was powerless to stop it. I couldn't lose the one being I felt close to, the only one left in my cursed life I truly considered a friend. Even if I was able to clear my name and I forgave Lady Sarah for her part in the torment Ulfarr had put me through, I didn't think she'd ever open up enough for me to grow close to her as I had to Leon. And so many of the vampires were still prejudiced enough against werewolves that true friendship would be a rarity among them. No, in all likelihood Leon was all I'd got.

At first, moving was so agonising that it felt like my brain had been liquefied and even the smallest movement would cause it to spill through my ears. But somehow I managed to pick myself up, driven by the thought that I had to save my friend. And just as I got to my feet, there came the sound of a gunshot and a sharp pain in my side. The bullet had only grazed me, but if I'd stayed slumped against the wall a minute longer, I knew I would probably be bleeding out from another mortal wound. Much as I wanted to run after Leon and the barghest, I was forced to turn my attention to the new threat.

The same grizzled old Slayer that had almost claimed my life once already strode confidently towards me, raising his gun to squeeze off a second shot. I leapt to the side before the bullet could find its mark, growling "You again."

The man responded with a third shot aimed at my chest, but I was able to dive out of harm's way once more.

"Who are you?" I snarled.

He regarded me with those cold eyes but remained silent. I was thinking about trying to force some answers out of him when a fourth shot rang through the night, from somewhere behind me. The bullet narrowly missed my head, leaving a burning hole in my right ear, and I roared with a mixture of pain and fury.

My bloodlust rose with the pain as rage and adrenalin coursed through my body, but the wind changed direction and carried the scent of more humans creeping towards me. I really wanted to kill the two Slayers who dared attack me, but it seemed they were trying to spring another trap. And there was still the threat of Selina returning to her home, her witchcraft far more deadly than the guns I was currently facing. Much as I hated to have to flee yet again, I knew it was my best option. So I turned to the second Slayer who'd fired and quickly weighed him up. He was younger than the other man who seemed so set on ending my life, and I knew from experience he was likely to be ruled by the same panic that had gripped so many of his dead comrades if I charged at him.

Aware of the older Slayer taking aim again behind me, I made my move, rushing towards the younger human with a roar of fury. He panicked as expected, firing off more shots without taking aim first. A hail of bullets sliced through the air, but only one thudded into my thigh, leaving another hole of searing pain in my flesh. Then I was on him, and I ripped out his throat with one powerful bite, leaving him gurgling as he lay dying. Much as I wanted to give in to my bloodlust and slaughter them all, I knew I needed to keep moving. Perhaps Lady Sarah's training had done some good after all, since I'd been able to resist the urge to kill for once.

I made it out of range of their guns, pausing briefly to transform fully back to wolf form so I could heal my wounds and cover the ground more quickly to the mansion. I also needed the wolf to guide me back again, and he gladly rose up, not trusting me to get us back safely.

I started running in the direction of the vampire's mansion, but after a few miles I sensed more humans, forcing me to veer off course and find a slightly longer route back. This happened a number of times, and it was already dawn before I reached the cover of the woods surrounding the mansion.

I passed through the treeline and started towards the clearing, but I became aware of more Slayers waiting for me. There was no time to question how they seemed to know where to find me; they'd obviously put some planning into the latest trap they were trying to spring and I had to assume fighting wasn't an option. If there were enough of them and they were heavily armed, I knew it was a fight I couldn't win.

I slowed and slunk through the gloom, hoping I might be able to slip past them, only to find my path blocked by a Slayer who'd been waiting downwind of me.

"Over here!" he yelled, opening fire.

I darted away, desperately searching for an opening so I could return to the safety of the vampire's lair, but the Slayers seemed to have me surrounded. Bullets flew from several directions, but somehow I managed to avoid getting hit. Not that it would save me for long — they were closing in, and if I couldn't run through their ranks I was going to have to fight my way out.

Focussing on the closest human blocking my path to the mansion, I rushed forward. Another destructive spray of bullets tore holes in the surrounding trees, and I yelped as another one found its mark, this time in one of my forelegs. But I didn't stop, limping on my three good legs and pushing myself onwards. My target was a woman this time and her eyes widened as she realised, too late, I was coming for her. Screaming, she fell to my fangs, her blood leaking into the soil, summoning the bugs lurking in that dank darkness, waiting to feed on decay. They would soon emerge to feast on the death.

I didn't have the luxury of stopping to eat, however, and I managed a final burst of speed. To my dismay, I found the gates to the mansion were closed this time, and with the wound in my front leg, I knew I'd never make it over the wall to the grounds. There was nowhere left to run, and with a sense of finality I turned to face my pursuers. I couldn't kill them all before one of their bullets found its mark in my heart or my brain, but that didn't mean I was about to just give up. A cornered animal has nothing left to lose and will fight all the more fiercely for survival, and I was no different.

The humans advanced cautiously, weapons raised. But just as they were emerging from the woodland, I heard the crackle of one of their walkie-talkies. I didn't follow what was said, but for reasons I couldn't fathom they began to retreat.

Suspecting some kind of ploy to put me off-guard, I waited for several long minutes in a defensive stance, ready to take down as many of them as I could before the inevitable killing shot. Only once I heard them crashing through the woods back in the direction of human civilisation did I relax, limbs trembling with fatigue. I'd used up a lot of energy that night and this latest bullet wound continued to sap my strength. But I couldn't rest yet. I knew I had to find the strength for one more transformation to heal the damage to my leg, and to climb over the wall. I wanted nothing more than to collapse and give in to the exhaustion, but instead I willed my body to revert to its human form, letting the human half of me take over once more.

Chapter Twenty Four – Into Enemy Territory

"Wait, they chased you right through to the clearing?" Leon asked with a sense of urgency. I'd filled him in on the night's events as soon as he'd risen, once darkness had fallen again that evening.

"Yes," I confirmed. "I tried to sneak past them but they had me surrounded, and the wolf thought the only way to escape was to fight his way through to the sanctuary of the mansion."

"You realise what this means? Now a group of them know the location of this place, the witch's spell will no longer repel them. They'll be able to find their way back and what's more, they can lead as many of their comrades here as they see fit. It's only a matter of time before a force of them come for us."

"I'm sorry mate," I started to apologise, but he held a hand up and I fell quiet.

"The damage is done now. I think it's time we put your training into practice."

I grinned. "What do you have in mind?"

"The group that ambushed you here are likely part of the force in this area. I doubt any will have come back here during the day, though they may well have shared the location with others. Just knowing the mansion is here isn't enough to pass the witchcraft that repels intruders, but if the woods are suddenly crawling with Slayers, it's only a matter of time before more of them are able to follow one of us back. We can't risk leaving any alive, so our best bet is to take out their base. We need to move quickly though, before they have chance to make a move against us."

"How big is the nearest base?"

"From what you've told me about the one you took out in your hometown, I'd guess this one's a similar size."

"So there's going to be dozens of Slayers and there's just the two of us against them. Isn't that a bit suicidal?"

"Oh come on, after the things you've done in fits of rage, now you're stopping to worry about the odds? It is a risky move I admit, but if we can catch them unawares we'll have the advantage. I'm sure we can slaughter most of them while they scramble around for their precious guns."

He was right that I'd made more reckless acts in the past, yet this time my gut was telling me it was a bad idea. Perhaps because of my latest brush with Death, my sense of caution had been heightened. Or maybe it was the wolf's strong survival instinct invading my thoughts.

But I couldn't say no when I'd been the one to lead the humans to the mansion, so reluctantly I agreed to go along with his plan.

"Good," he said, with the same gleam in his eye I'd seen when sparring. "Something bothers me though. The Slayers were waiting for you in the woods, like they somehow knew where you were going to be. It's as if they've been tracking you."

"I've wondered that, but the last man I tried to question about it bit off his own tongue to avoid giving up any of their secrets."

"Hmm," he responded, and then after a moment's pause he instructed "Take your shirt off."

"Why?" I asked suspiciously.

"Humour me."

I did as he said, but the vampire started to trace a hand along my back and I automatically started to pull away. "Hey man, I appreciate your companionship an' all but I'm not —"

Before I could finish, he pinched the skin around my left shoulder blade and I felt the sharp pain of a knife piercing my flesh.

"What the hell are you doing?" I snarled, but he placed a firm hand on my shoulder to keep me in place.

"Hold still."

Despite my higher pain threshold, I couldn't keep myself from tensing up, even though I tried to relax and trust that whatever the vampire was doing, it was for my own good. Blood trickled down my skin as the knife slid through my flesh. Leon seemed to be carving a hole in my back, and then I felt his fingers dig into the wound and I snarled again. He pulled something out as he withdrew them, and showed it to me.

"A GPS tracker. That's how they've been able to find you so easily and set up the various traps you've told me about."

I gawped at the device. The Slayers must have implanted it the previous year when I'd been imprisoned in a base just like the one we were about to march right into. "I had no idea they'd fitted me with that."

"It's a wonder it survived so long, given the number of times they've wounded you. We'll take it with us and find a new home for it along the way – maybe it will help us take them by surprise."

"Hang on, if I've been walking round with that under my skin then how come there's been times where they've left me alone for like weeks on end? Why wouldn't they just keep attacking constantly till they finally managed to kill me?"

"You'd have to ask them that to know for certain but my best guess would be that they were merely biding their time, rethinking their tactics and waiting for the perfect opportunity to strike. Plus after a quieter period they might have felt they were more likely to catch you off-guard, giving them better odds when they made their next attack. And their desire to operate in secret from the rest of humanity probably limited them at times as well."

"Yeah, I guess that all makes sense."

"Now, we should feed before we set off. Come."

I had managed to make a kill that morning after I'd transformed back to my human form, and then it had been easy enough to climb over the gate and return to the mansion to rest. But I'd not eaten since then so I followed the vampire out into the woods, where I came across the corpse of the woman my lupine half had killed. As always I wanted to make a fresh kill, but Leon was impatient to head out and he'd already caught and drained the blood from several of the bats flitting between the trees while I took my hybrid form. There was hardly any meat to be had from the tiny carcasses now littering the ground, so I settled for the cold human flesh, forcing down as much as I could stomach to keep my energy levels up for any further transformations I would need to undergo.

The vampire knew where to find the Slayers' base of operations in the area, and as he led us towards the fight which I couldn't help thinking of as our last stand, I asked him how he'd escaped the barghest.

"I got lucky," he admitted. "Thanks to you I was able to limp quite a way from the cottage before the beast caught up with me, but he was on me a third time and I was sure I was going to be the next victim Ulfarr would accuse you of killing. But I guess this witch, Selina, had need of her familiar elsewhere, 'cause suddenly he ran off. I started to make my way back and as I passed closer to civilisation, I could hear humans nearby. I was able to feed quietly in the shadows, without alerting any others to my presence, which allowed me to heal the damage the barghest had done. I had no problems after that. The Slayers you encountered must have moved into position after I'd returned, because I came across no other humans on my journey home."

We fell quiet as we drew closer to the Slayers' base, keeping to the shadows while Leon assessed their defences. He was far more experienced at it than me, and he took in security cameras I'd have missed.

It seemed they'd disguised this place as a military base to keep the public away, and the main entrance was covered by two humans dressed in army uniform. Leon assured me they were in fact Slayers, and he decided there was no way we'd slip past them without raising any alarms. If it had been just the humans to worry about we could have handled them, but the cameras were a problem.

We circled round the perimeter but the vampire could see no opportunities to sneak in undetected, without creating one ourselves. He'd already been thinking ahead as if he'd suspected as much, and he outlined his plan to me in a low whisper.

"The only way we can sneak past those cameras without raising any alarms is to cut the power. That building over there houses the generator. Since I'm faster than you, I'll take out the camera covering that area and run in to sabotage their power supply."

"How do you know the generator's in there?" I asked him, a little too loudly.

"Keep your voice down!" he hissed. "From now on we need to be as quiet as possible. I've studied the layout of this place in the past, and I've seen enough to know that building supplies the power to the rest of the base. It always pays to know your enemies."

"Okay, but if one of their cameras goes down, don't you think that will raise suspicions?"

"Yes, but I should be able to slip in before they can send any of the guards to investigate. If any enter the building it will be to our advantage – I can hypnotise them into believing nothing is amiss, which should buy us more time. But if anything goes wrong, I need you ready to create a distraction. Whatever you do, don't show yourself to them. Find an animal to send running in their direction or something, but don't give them reason to suspect you're in the area or we stand no chance. This will only succeed if we're facing a few enemies at a time. The moment the Slayers realise they're under attack and gather their forces, our chances of making it out alive will drop considerably."

As plans went it didn't seem the most well thought out, but I didn't have any better ideas so I nodded my understanding. Before I could say anything else Leon was off, moving silently to human ears and too fast for their eyes to follow. As long as he kept out of their artificial lights, to them he would be no more than a shadow, and they had no forewarning when the small stone he hurled smashed against the lens of the camera overlooking the generator room.

The sound brought two of the guards running over to investigate, and one of the men found the stone lying on the ground nearby.

"Those idiot kids again?" he asked his comrade, holding the stone up for the other man to see. I could hear them as clearly as if I was stood right next to them.

"Yeah, could be. Little shits; makes you wonder why we bother risking our lives to keep the likes of those low-life scum safe from the undead threat."

The two men surveyed the surrounding countryside, trying to find any movement in the shadows. But Leon had already slipped unnoticed into the building as planned, and there was nothing for them to see.

"We should check it out, just in case," the second man said, turning his attention back to the immediate vicinity round the broken camera. It seemed he was bright enough to realise whoever threw the stone had created a blind spot round the generator, and that if it wasn't a random act of vandalism, they needed to investigate inside. "You look in there, and I'll have a look round out here, see if I can see any sign of the bastard behind this."

As he spoke, he pointed at the building housing their power supply to the other man, and then he pulled out a torch he kept in a holder fixed to his belt and flicked it on. They split up and I watched tensely as the man tasked with checking inside the building stepped through the door. Then the lights went off, which could only mean Leon had cut the power as planned.

I felt sure then that the Slayers would put two and two together and they'd swarm out of the building like ants from an anthill, sealing the vampire's fate. But all was quiet, until minutes later the guard stepped back out, Leon just behind him, and he stood waiting for his comrade to return with a dazed expression on his face. The vampire motioned for me to join him, and I padded over as quietly as I could. It seemed the first part of his plan had worked.

As we crept towards the entrance, I heard the man searching the vicinity for the rock thrower run back over to his ally.

"What happened?" he asked. "Why's the power down?"

"I dunno, there was no one in there when I checked. Must be some technical fault or something. We'll have to get Jeff to look at it."

"Seems an all-mighty coincidence it goes down just after some bugger breaks the camera. I don't like this, mate. Something's not right here."

"Well check in there yourself then but I'm telling you, it was empty when I looked."

I lost track of the conversation after that but the man's suspicions made me uneasy.

Once we reached the entrance to their base, Leon placed both guards on the door under his spell, before they had chance to react.

"Relax. All is quiet out here. We're just two of your members checking in before we go out on patrol, but if anyone asks, you don't remember seeing anyone enter."

The men had no choice but to obey, their minds too weak to resist the hypnotic power of the vampire. And so we walked right in, unchallenged, to enemy territory.

Like with the base I'd briefly been imprisoned in, the Slayers had used some form of soundproofing, though this method didn't seem to be as effective as whatever they'd used in the other one. It might be enough to muffle the screams of any undead captives to human ears, but to our supernaturally enhanced hearing it was still possible to pick things up from the rooms around us. We could also clearly hear when humans were approaching.

Leon's plan was simple: we would systematically work our way through the building, killing any Slayers we found and hiding the bodies to help delay the alarm being raised for as long as possible. I had my doubts as to how long we could wander round unchallenged, but the vampire seemed confident we could take out enough of them before we were discovered to give us a fighting chance when facing the rest en masse. And it was too late to turn back, giving me no choice but to continue going along with his plan and praying it would work.

Stalking through the enemy base, my nerves were as taut as ever. I felt my senses were more attuned to my surroundings than they'd ever been without the wolf taking control, my ears pricked to the slightest of sounds, my nose working overtime to try and make sense of the myriad of scents passing through my nostrils. If we'd been out in the open my eyes would have been constantly scanning the shadows for danger, but sight was of little use in the corridors with so many corners for our foes to lurk around.

The immediate area round the entrance seemed quiet, but it wasn't long before we began to detect signs of life. We came to a stop by the room in which we could sense a human presence, keeping out of sight of the window set in the door. There were three of them in there, and they seemed to be arguing about something. I could hear the rustle of papers as if one of them was searching for something, and the glow of a torch was visible on the other side of the glass.

"Come on mate, we're not supposed to still be here. We have our orders," said one of them.

"Fuck our orders! I'm not a soldier – I signed on for revenge against these bastards and I'm bloody well going to get that revenge."

"Mike's right, fuck all this pissing about waiting for these monsters to come to us. Pass me that map; I say we head straight for where they were last seen and deal with them ourselves."

"I don't know guys, they came up with this plan for a reason," the first voice answered his friends, or comrades, or whatever they were to each other. "Think how many of us have died trying to kill that beast already. Do you really think the three of us can succeed where so many others have failed, in greater numbers?"

"The werewolf slaughtered my wife and kids last year and he still runs free. I won't stand by any longer and let him tear more families apart," the second man retorted, his voice shaking with emotion.

I felt a pang of guilt alongside the unease that had been ruling me since agreeing to Leon's plan. The vampire looked at me and motioned to stay out of their line of sight, my hybrid form instantly recognisable as a monster. He seemed well aware of the impact those words would have on me and he didn't want my emotions making me careless.

A part of me wanted to rush in there and let the humans face me, so at least this guy, Mike, could die trying to avenge his loved ones. I couldn't undo the horrific acts I'd committed but I could at least offer him a chance at the vengeance he craved. But for once I listened to reason, my survival instincts particularly strong that night while my body was flooded with adrenalin, and I let Leon handle it.

His human appearance allowed him to enter without being immediately gunned down, and by the time the humans in the room realised something was amiss it was already too late for them. The vampire dealt each a swift death, breaking their necks before they had chance to draw a weapon or warn their allies.

The threat dealt with, Leon beckoned me inside. It was an ordinary looking office room which could have been in any building. There was a map laid on the desk in there which I imagined they'd been looking at while they debated the wisdom of going out hunting for us.

"Help me hide these bodies. That storage cupboard should take one of them and we can probably get away with another under the desk. You deal with these two and I'll take this third next door while there's no one else about on this corridor."

I did as he'd instructed, my heart hammering against my ribs. There was something else about the conversation that bothered me and I felt an even greater alertness to my surroundings. When I opened the cabinet and a stack of papers fell from the top shelf, I winced at the noise and paused to listen for the thunder of footsteps rushing towards me. But all remained quiet in the immediate vicinity so I stuffed the body inside and shut it quickly. Only the upper half was shelved so there was just about room for the cadaver.

Once I'd dragged the second corpse under the desk where it was less noticeable, I re-joined Leon out in the corridor, doubt still nagging at me.

"I don't like this, man. The plan those three were talking about, it can't be owt good for us. Don't you think we should turn back while we still can? There's got to be some other way we can deal with the problem of them finding your mansion. We can slip back out while it's so quiet and come up with a better idea."

"We might not get another chance and I won't abandon my home unless I really have to. We can do this."

So we continued on. I kept expecting trouble but most of the corridors were empty, as were most of the rooms. That only added to my uneasiness: it almost seemed too quiet.

We did find one of them rushing down an adjoining corridor to the one we were on, and unwittingly headed in our direction. She saw us before we could move in for the kill and had time to run back the way she'd come, skidding to a stop in front of two secure looking doors. There she fumbled with the locks, throwing the doors open to reveal one of their weapons arsenals. But Leon was on her before she had time to grab anything useful, though he didn't make the kill this time.

The locker was packed so full of weaponry that her body wouldn't have fit inside, and without venturing into any of the rooms in this part of the building, we couldn't know for sure whether they'd be similar to the office type rooms we'd been in or not. There might not be anywhere close enough to hide the body, so instead the vampire used his hypnotic powers to keep her calm and docile, and to convince her nothing was amiss, like he had with the guards outside. He had to do this a few more times as we moved through the building, but those we were forced to leave alive we would come back for on the way out.

This Slayer base of operations seemed to serve a similar purpose to the one I'd been imprisoned in, however, we didn't come across any rooms containing cages, and certainly none specifically built to hold undead. Yet there was evidence of scientists performing similar ghoulish experiments to the ones I'd witnessed before – there was no mistaking the scent of blood emanating from under some of the doors we passed, and some of the rooms contained operating tables and surgical tools, and more body parts preserved in jars filled with some clear fluid. But we only came across one living test subject. Or unliving, or whatever the correct term is for an undead.

We both heard the sound of laboured breathing coming from the other side of the door and we ventured inside to investigate, but when my eyes fell on the room's only occupant I froze with shock.

A female vampire lay strapped to an operating table, weakened from starvation so she couldn't break free. Her chest had been opened up like her skin was merely a jacket that had been unfastened, the bloody flaps turned back and hanging down her sides. Her breast tissue had been removed and on one side her muscle had been cut away to reveal her lung and part of her heart, while on the other side the muscle had been left intact. Sections of skin had also been shaved off her limbs, baring more of her muscles, though for what purpose I couldn't even begin to guess at. In the darkness everything looked black instead of the lurid red the scientists would see under the bright lights of their makeshift operating theatre.

The vampire was fully conscious, and through her dry throat she struggled to form her croaked plea. "Help me."

Such cruel experiments had unnerved me the first time I'd seen them, but in the primal state I'd fallen into they'd failed to horrify me, and what memories I had of them just didn't have the same impact as actually being there. But this time I was fully aware of the atrocities the scientists were committing. Seeing my fellow undead trapped in so agonising a state, unable to die unless the Slayers granted her the mercy of destroying her heart or her brain, spoke to both my rage and whatever empathy I had left. Even after the anger I'd felt at the vampires for the way they'd treated me over the murders, I didn't want to see one of them made to suffer such a pain filled existence indefinitely.

"We have to save her," I growled, fumbling with her restraints in my monstrous hands.

Leon shook his head. "There's no time."

The pain was plain to see in her eyes, and the anguish at Leon's words as she again struggled to voice her plea. "Help me."

"Then we should at least end her suffering," I said, grabbing one of the surgical instruments laid out on a nearby table. But Leon caught my arm before I could deliver the killing blow.

"No, Nick. We can't risk alerting the Slayers to our presence here so soon. If they discover her and raise the alarm, it gives them time to mount a defence and we lose the advantage of surprise. We need to catch them unawares if you want to escape here with your life. We'll try and come back for her afterwards."

I hated leaving the female vampire to the horrific existence humanity had devised for her, but I knew Leon was right, though I suspected we wouldn't make it back. Reluctantly I turned away, trying to tune out those terrible words which still haunt me to this day.

"Help me."

We made it through almost the entire building without incident, though that did nothing to ease my tension. But the reason why we'd encountered so few Slayers on the corridors and in the rooms we'd passed soon became apparent.

Up ahead we could sense the bulk of their forces gathered in what must be a large room. I guessed it was some kind of assembly hall or briefing room, if they operated in such a way. We could hear a man, presumably their leader, addressing them all, and from the way Leon looked at me it seemed he'd anticipated finding them in such a meeting.

"This is it," he mouthed, drawing his sword and placing a hand on the door.

He didn't need to elaborate. This was where the real slaughter would begin, and our attack had to be fast and brutal to take down as many of them unaware as possible before they could react and defend themselves. I guessed there were around a hundred humans gathered inside and as formidable opponents as we could be, to attack so many at once was beyond reckless. But Leon gently pushed the door open with the intention of picking off as many from the edges as possible before they realised what was happening, and it was suddenly too late to turn back. All I could do was follow him in and pray he knew what he was doing.

Once inside, the shadowy form of the leader of the Slayers in this area barked a command and the humans turned to face us, weapons raised. Our plan wasn't going to work out after all. For all our attempts to catch them unawares, and even with the discovery and removal of the tracking chip that had been implanted under my skin, it seemed they'd still been expecting us. Instead of the bloodbath we'd intended to make of the gathered humans, unaware and too slow to arm themselves to take us down while they still had such a great advantage in numbers, we were now facing around a hundred enemies, all armed and prepared for combat. Our chances of surviving this insane mission had just dropped to around zero, and worse than the potential death awaiting us was the threat of being captured alive and subjected to the same horrific torment as the female vampire. Then the

Slayers directly in front of us opened fire, and so began the fight that was surely to be our last.

Chapter Twenty Five – The Last Stand?

I dived for the door we'd come through, but in the first few seconds of chaos one of the Slayers had managed to lock it, and I knew I'd never be able to break through before I was cut down by the gunfire. One bullet had already found its way into my flank in those precious few seconds spent trying the door, and with a roar I let the bloodlust rise on a tidal wave of fury, giving myself completely over to it. If this was to be my last stand, I was taking my enemies down with me.

Leon had already entered the fray, dodging the worst of the first spray of bullets and rushing into the gathered humans, cutting down two of them before they had chance to react. At such close quarters they couldn't all open fire or they risked killing too many of their own, but they were armed with blades as well and the vampire was soon engaged in a deadly dance of cold steel as those around him hacked and slashed with their own knives and swords. With so great an advantage in numbers, it wasn't long before cuts started to open up on Leon's limbs and sides, and for every enemy he took down, there was always another to take the place of their fallen ally.

The Slayers nearest the door we'd entered through were still trying to take me down with their guns. I charged through the hail of bullets, taking another wound to my arm. The pain fuelled the rage as I leapt on my first victim, sending him crashing to the ground and taking the woman behind him down with us. I was aware of the Slayers around me aiming their guns at my exposed back, and I sprang away just as they opened fire. Blood pooled on the floor from beneath the two fallen humans, their bodies riddled with enough bullets to seal their doom, while I grabbed hold of another man by his shirt and threw him at his comrades, buying myself some time as they went down like skittles.

A woman to my right rushed forward in an attempt to stab me, but I slashed my claws across her throat, the knife clattering from her grasp as she fell to join the others in death. I twisted to face another woman wielding a blade, catching her arm before she could bury the weapon in my flesh and crushing her bones in my monstrous hand. She screamed in agony and stumbled away once I released her, clutching her ruined limb with her other arm.

Another blade pierced my side, between two of my ribs. It was far from a killing blow and I realised the Slayers were trying to subdue us through sheer force of numbers. I could only take so many wounds before blood loss took its toll, and while I had the energy to heal the damage for the time being, if I was having to constantly use the power of the transformation to regenerate damaged flesh, I'd soon be overcome with exhaustion. And though I didn't know much about how vampires healed, Leon surely had his limits as well, which meant we could only keep things up for so long before the Slayers overwhelmed us.

I voiced my fury as fresh pain throbbed through my wounded flesh, turning to deal with the man who'd knifed me. Another swipe of my claws ended his life in a spray of blood and gore, but two more Slayers stepped towards me to fill the gap I'd created, wielding swords. I dodged one of their blades and grabbed the man's leg, pulling it out from under him so that he landed on the growing pile of bodies. But the second sword opened up a gash in my thigh, and before the first Slayer could pick himself up and renew his assault, I circled round the man still standing and lunged at him. We landed on top of the first Slayer and the numerous corpses littering the floor, and I crushed the second man's skull in my jaws, then snapped at the arm of the other man as he reached for his sword. My fangs bit down with such force that they went clean through the flesh and bone, severing the limb at the elbow. The human screamed as blood pumped out of his stump, no longer a threat, and I rose to take down more of them.

Blood oozed from the numerous wounds I'd sustained and I could feel my strength draining, but I wasn't given the chance to heal the damage. Bloody fur hung loosely from my thigh and nerves sparked as they reacted with the oxygen, stinging so badly it became painful to walk on. My rage could only keep me going for so long. Then a gap opened up in the seemingly endless sea of humans and there was Leon, faring little better than myself, despite his greater speed and strength. And as I looked over at him, I saw one of the Slayers splash his face with a bottle of some fluid, causing him to scream and raise a hand to his eyes. There came the unmistakeable stench of burning flesh as if he'd been doused with acid, and I realised it must have been holy water.

The vampire blindly swung his sword but it seemed the hallowed liquid had melted his eyes, and as I was distracted by the sight of the human nearest him raising his gun to finish off my friend, another knife found its way between my ribs. I roared with renewed rage but I had no interest in killing the enemies attacking me then. Leon was about to die unless I could reach him, and everything else around me might as well have ceased to exist.

Time seemed to slow as I bounded towards my friend, fighting my way through the humans trying to stop me. I slipped twice in the ever growing pool of blood, and yet somehow I managed to stay on my feet and reach my target before he could finish aiming and pull the trigger. He was too focussed on the vampire to realise I'd pounced until I crashed into him. I smashed his head against the floor like a water melon, spraying a grisly halo of blood and brains around what little remained of his skull. But more Slayers were taking aim at Leon, and there was no way I could take them all out in time. My friend was about to die, and there was nothing I could do.

Chapter Twenty Six – Death Sentence

Light flooded the room, whatever damage had been done to the generator obviously having been fixed. In a detached sort of way I was more aware of my surroundings, taking in the bloodbath we'd created with a vague hint of pride. Even though Death must be close again for both me and Leon, it seemed we'd taken down a respectable number of Slayers between us before our inevitable end.

In the spreading pool of blood on the floor, corpses lay with their throats in bloody tatters. Severed limbs twitched as if the will of those they'd belonged to still drove them to attempt to fight the monsters in their midst. Some of the humans had been slashed across their abdomens, and guts had spilled out, intestines coiled like great snakes amidst the gore, along with other organs. Then there was the mess of brains I'd created from the smashed skull of the corpse I was still crouched over, as well as from the man whose skull I'd crushed between my fangs.

I squinted against the glare overhead, my eyes still adjusting to the sudden brightness, and as I rose from the body of my latest victim I thought I could see the shadowy outline of the grim reaper stalking over to claim me at last. But it seemed the Slayers could see him too, the heads of those about to finish Leon off snapping round to take in this new intruder. And as my eyes became accustomed to the light, I realised the dark figure wasn't the robed skeleton wielding a scythe that I'd imagined, but Ulfarr, and he was leading a force of more vampires, including Lady Sarah. The cavalry had arrived, though part of me suspected that wasn't necessarily a good thing.

The Elder vampire strode towards us, cutting down any humans stupid enough to get in his way with a ferocity that rivalled my own, while those behind him rushed at the Slayers to engage them in combat. In that moment Ulfarr was the most impressive figure in the room, and in the primal joy of hacking and slashing his enemies to pieces, he seemed to become almost one with the werewolf pelt he wore, as if he'd transformed into one of the very beasts he hated so. He could have used his powers to deliver quick, clean deaths to his enemies, but instead he chose to wield his sword, the blade carving through flesh and bone as easily as it sliced through the air around us. Limbs flew and heads rolled, the Elder vampire fighting with a savagery I'd yet to see in any others of his kind. One by one the humans began to fall, the odds now against them. Without the advantage of numbers they were weak, too slow to stand a chance of defeating our supernatural might.

I took advantage of the distraction to charge the humans nearest me, before they could regain their wits and deliver Leon a killing blow while he was still vulnerable. In a flash of claws, two fell back clutching ruined throats. I grabbed the outstretched arm of a third and ripped it clean out of its socket, tossing it aside and leaving the woman to stumble away in shock as I pounced on a fourth. I was aware that Ulfarr had reached us which meant it was all over for the humans. And while he killed them in a similarly brutal fashion, that gave me the time to focus on healing my injuries, using the regenerative power of the transformation but without the need to actually take it all the way to either my human or wolf form. I'd long since learnt how to heal myself without having to undergo a full change, and it was only the severest of wounds that required a full transformation to heal. Then I gave in to the hunger, tearing chunks of meat from the body at my feet and gulping them down ravenously.

Finally the room was still and quiet around me, every last human turned into a part of the bloody mosaic of carnage we'd created. One of the vampires had guided Leon to feed, and with the fresh blood in his system his own healing powers began to kick in.

His face had become a hideous mess of melted flesh, the liquid creating bloody rivulets as it ran down, eating right through to the bone of his skull in places. Two gaping craters were all that remained of his eyes, and his nose was all but gone. Part of his lips were missing, revealing the grinning jaw bones beneath. But as I watched, the ruined flesh began to reform. A jelly like substance filled the empty eye sockets until it became two eyeballs, and eyelids re-grew around them. It seemed the vampire's vision had been fully restored, his new eyes sweeping across the room to take in the carnage, before fixing on Ulfarr.

Cartilage swelled up to form a new nose, skin stretching across it, and new flesh covered his skull, until the same face I'd grown to know so well looked across at the Elder, as flawless as ever. But the Elder vampire's eyes were fixed on me. The anger blazing in them was plain to see, and I felt the strong impulse to flee coming from my lupine half. I might have been spared the death I was facing at the hands of the Slayers, but I was far from safe yet.

"You fools!" Ulfarr spat. "What did you really hope to accomplish here? We have survived the last century by keeping to the shadows, only killing to feed or in self-defence. But you had to go and poke the wasp's nest and stir them into a frenzy. Now humanity will surely be more diligent in their quest to wipe us out."

He motioned to two vampires and they came forward to seize me. Instinctively I started to struggle, but they each held one of my arms in a vice like grip, the strength I could feel from them suggesting they were both centuries old. And at the first hint of resistance from me, Ulfarr once again used his powers to force me back into human form. It was just as excruciating as it had been the previous time, and I couldn't help but roar in agony until my vocal cords became fully human and it turned to a scream. I slumped between my two captors, shaking from the pain and reluctantly accepting that I had no hope of breaking free through brute strength.

"As for you, wolf," Ulfarr continued. "You are found guilty of the murder of six vampires, the penalty for which is death."

"It wasn't him, Ulfarr," Leon said. "And as for the Slayers, they will come for us anyway – it is only a matter of time. You may have lost your nerve, but some of us would rather die fighting than cowering like whipped dogs."

"You will be quiet! You have no authority here, Leon; you are not an Elder. I am this close to charging you along with the wolf. Do not test me."

Leon could do no more than watch as I was led away, and I couldn't even see Lady Sarah amongst the other vampires. It looked like I was to die at the hands of my former allies, and there was no one left to save me.

I was taken to the same abandoned warehouse the vampires had imprisoned me in before, and once again they chained me in there. Ulfarr let the two vampires who'd apprehended me fasten the shackles around my wrists and the iron collar around my neck, but he stayed to oversee my incarceration. Once he was satisfied I was secure enough in my makeshift cage, he turned to go, but I called out to him.

"If you want me dead, why not just let the Slayers do it for you?"

"And risk either of you being taken alive by our enemies?" he replied, facing me once more. "Who knows what information they could extract to use against us. Leon especially knows too much."

"So why not just kill me now, instead of going to all this trouble to keep me here?"

"Because I promised my people justice, and they are entitled to seeing that justice carried out."

"This isn't about justice. You want to make a spectacle of my execution. You want everyone to watch as you put an end to werewolf kind."

He made no reply, offering only a cold smile from beneath the lupine head of what could well have been one of my ancestors, before he swept away to wherever his daylight refuge might be. The door to my prison swung shut with an awful finality, as if it had already become my tomb. The vampires had gone to the trouble of cleaning up the mess I'd made when I'd last been chained in the building, but there still came the scent of old blood and death which did nothing to help my troubled mind.

At first the rage surged up and I embraced it gladly, though it still wasn't enough for me to break free. I was angered by the fact the vampires were so ruled by their prejudice towards werewolves that they'd been so quick to sentence me to death, when the Slayers were a far greater threat than I could ever have been, if I had proved to be the real killer. I was angry that my allies had been so quick to turn on me, especially Lady Sarah, when we needed to stick together if we were ever going to have any hope of survival at a time when the Slayers seemed to be making increasingly determined efforts to wipe us out. And most of all, I was furious that they were going to kill me and call it justice when I wasn't even the killer.

"How can you say this isn't justice?" came a voice just behind me. It was a child's voice, and yet the words felt more adult.

I turned to find one of my victims from the playground massacre. At first she appeared like a normal, healthy little girl, but then blood blossomed over the dress she was wearing, a loop of intestine slipping through a gash which opened up in the material and her flesh underneath. I quickly turned away, my head in my hands as if that was all it would take to keep the horrors of my guilty conscience contained within my skull. But more hallucinations of my victims appeared around me, torn flesh flapping as they moved to confront me. The little boy from that same day in the playground whose head I'd bitten off came forward, holding his head in front of his torso like the decapitated ghosts of horror films.

"You might not have killed the vampires, but you're still guilty of murder," the severed head said. "Do you even remember how many of us you slaughtered in cold blood? And what meaning did our deaths have, when you came to realise your existence was equally as meaningless? All the massacres you committed this past year, and they were nothing to do with hunger or survival. Why should you go unpunished for the futures you denied us, the lives you cruelly ripped from our mortal bodies?"

"What do you want from me?" I snarled, raising my head to look at the faces of so many of those I'd sent to an early grave. "My death won't bring you back, and it won't bring peace to your living relatives since they'll never know the truth of the monster that killed you, or what became of him. We don't execute human murderers in this country, so why should I pay with my life?"

My conscience didn't answer and the grisly hallucinations vanished. I turned my thoughts to how I might escape this new predicament I'd found myself in, but as before I could find nothing left lying around on the floor to use as a lock pick on my shackles. There was only the bowl of fresh water and a bucket like I'd been provided with the first time I'd been held there, so I was left praying that maybe Leon might find a way to help me. With nothing better to do, I clung to the hope he'd find a way to rescue me that night, until exhaustion claimed me and I fell through the portal of horrors, into the waiting nightmares.

I awoke to find I did indeed have a visitor, but the last vampire I'd been expecting to see was Lady Sarah.

"What do you want?" I growled.

"I came to check you were as comfortable as possible," she replied, seeming saddened by the recent turn of events.

"What do you care? You haven't bothered to help me at all since Ulfarr last locked me in here, so why bother making an effort now when I'll be dead soon anyway?"

"I did not wish for it to play out this way, but there are things you do not understand."

"If you really care, go tell Ulfarr about the witch who's really behind the killings, like I told you before."

She shook her head sadly. "He will not be swayed without any evidence. I'm sorry, Nick. Truly I am. But there is nothing more I can do for you."

"Fuck off then," I snarled. "You haven't been there for me when I needed you most, and I don't want you here now."

So she took her leave, turning to look back at me in the doorway but saying nothing. Then she bowed her head and stalked out into the night, the door closing behind her. I caught the scent of two more vampires outside, guards no doubt, which meant if I were to escape, it would have to be during the day somehow.

The next vampire to visit me was the Elder again.

"Elder Ulfarr," I said, trying to be respectful despite the rage the vampires had brought back to the surface, though I wasn't fully ruled by it that night. "You have to believe me, I didn't kill any of your kind. But I saw who did and I'm telling you, there's a witch out there with a black dog familiar – a barghest, Leon called it. She's sending that thing out to kill vampires and make it look like werewolf kills, to frame me. I'm guessing she's working for the Slayers, getting us to turn on each other when we should be allying together to fight them again."

"Is that really the best you can do?" he laughed. "If the Slayers were behind this, why would they still be trying to kill you? Do you not think they would want you alive for as long as possible if the goal was to make us fight amongst ourselves?"

I realised he had a point. "Well maybe she has some other reason for murdering vampires, but the witch is the real killer. Maybe she needs your hearts to fuel some ritual she has planned!"

"And maybe you would say anything to save yourself. But I did not come here to listen to such unlikely stories. You are to be executed in two night's time, to give the vampires who wish to be present the chance to travel here. I thought you would want to know."

"So kind of you," I growled, expecting the Elder vampire's own anger to rise in response. But he didn't reply, and soon I was alone again.

I continued to hope Leon would be able to help me escape, but when he came to visit me the next night it wasn't to bring me the news I'd been hoping to hear.

"Took you long enough," I said, as he walked over to where I was chained. "Please tell me you have a plan to get me out of this mess."

He shook his head. "I'm sorry, my friend, there's nothing I can do. Ulfarr has seen to it that I'm watched until after your execution, and I can no more walk through direct sunlight than they canto free you while they sleep."

"Can't you slip me a key for these shackles so I can break out while the sun's up, or hypnotise a human to come and free me in your stead?"

"Not without them realising what I was up to. The two vampires outside were reluctant enough just to let me in here to see you, and if Ulfarr knew I'd come he would no doubt have forbidden me to enter your cell. The best I can do for you is this."

He reached into his jacket and took out a freezer bag with fresh meat stuffed inside, which he handed over. The Elder's hospitality hadn't extended to any scraps of meat this time and I doubted I would be granted the luxury of a last meal. I should have felt more grateful to my friend for thinking of me, but I couldn't help the bitter disappointment that he hadn't come to me with some miraculous escape plan to save my life.

"Time's up, Leon," one of the guards shouted.

"Coming," he replied, before turning back to me. "It's not much but it's the best I can do. I don't know if Ulfarr has bothered to tell you, but he intends to execute you tomorrow night. Stay strong, young wolf. Don't let them humiliate you when the time comes."

"Yeah, thanks."

I was left alone once more, resigned to my fate and nursing dark thoughts. The universe was a cruel place to give me another taste of the life I'd once known during the time I'd spent with Leon at his mansion, only to snatch it away again. In the months when I would have almost welcomed death I'd been saved from a wound that should have killed me, but now I'd been given a reason to live I was going to die anyway. It was cruel and unfair that after everything I'd been through, my life should end at a time when I'd found some contentment.

Unsurprisingly, I slept little after that, and by somewhere that was around what I would guess was late afternoon, I gave up on sleep entirely. There was no rest to be had when my mind was so focussed on my own demise, which was only hours away. And I was under no illusion as to the chances of entering the gates of Heaven for a monster such as me. They would surely be closed to me, which meant there could be no rest for me in death. Not unless I was one of the souls destined to fall into oblivion, and given the cruel fate I'd been dealt, I doubted I would be that lucky. And would oblivion really be any better than the eternity of torment I no doubt faced in Hell? I would be at peace if I were to completely cease to exist forever more, yet the thought of never again knowing anything of the world around me, or to never again think or feel, began to fill me with fear. The prospect of eternal suffering was no more welcoming, but if I was truly facing Death this time then I would be dragged into one kind of darkness or another.

I took a bite of the small offering Leon had brought for me but for the first time since my last struggle with depression brought on by Fiona's death, I couldn't eat, even though I should have felt ravenous. There was only that nauseating feeling in my stomach that comes with a growing feeling of dread, my thoughts too troubled by the fate awaiting me when darkness fell once more. After chewing for several moments and trying repeatedly to swallow, the raw meat still wouldn't slide down my throat. I spat it back out and gave up on eating as well.

"You should have stayed with us, Nick," Amy said sadly. "You could have been surrounded by all of us who loved you, instead of ending up here, hated and alone."

267

"How could I if it meant any of you getting hurt? It was the right decision to make so why do you insist on beating me up over this?" I growled to myself rather than the hallucination.

Mum appeared again. "We could have found a way to manage your curse. You didn't have to go."

"You wouldn't want me at home if you knew the truth," I answered, as another wave of despair crashed over me.

"Of course I would, you're my son! I'll always love you, no matter what."

"Oh come on brain, really? Love conquers all? Since when have we ever believed that crap. How could anyone love this?" I growled, gesturing at my naked body, still spattered with gore from fighting the Slayers. "How could anyone ever find me anything other than hideous? You'd both be horrified if you knew the truth. Maybe you'd even disown me, and who could blame you. No one wants a monster in the family. No one wants to be associated with a killer, a murderer. You wouldn't love me if you knew what I'd done.

"And what future would there have been for us if I had stayed? What happiness would there have been in watching as the years passed and time ravaged all of you, until one by one you died and faded away into memory? I would still be just as alone in the end while I endured till the end of time. What life is that?"

"Maybe it's better this way," came that hated voice again from somewhere behind me. "At least you can die feeling like you've paid for your crimes, and maybe that will bring you some peace in death."

"You're the last person I want to spend my final hours with, real or imagined. Why can't you just leave me alone?"

"Because you still haven't faced what you've done, not really," Dad said. "You keep trying to hide behind your rage and bury your guilt deep down in your subconscious, but it's still there, and sooner or later you have to face it."

"What do you want from me?" I snarled, my back still turned to the apparition. "For me to admit I'm sorry? Okay, I admit it. I feel bad for what I did to our family, for what I did to you. But your anger's as much to blame as I am. If you'd treated us all better, maybe I wouldn't have turned to killing so readily. Maybe I wouldn't have been so lost in the darkness and you wouldn't have died."

"Then face me. Face what you've done."

Rage surged up again, my father calling to it as only he could. The hallucination seemed so real, like the night in Leon's mansion where I'd thought I'd been back on the moors, all my senses tricked into believing he was really there. But when I finally turned round,

268

shock froze the rage before it could take over and I fell back, unprepared for the gruesome sight that met my eyes. For the image of my Dad this time was not the man he'd been in life, but the bloody mess he'd been reduced to in death.

He had only a head and torso, his limbs ripped clean from their sockets. Strips of flesh hung loosely from the bloody skull beneath where I'd shredded his face, and entrails lay in front of him where they'd spilled from the hole I'd ripped in his stomach. And I'd done that to him; to my own father, my own flesh and blood.

"I never meant to hurt family," I said in a low voice, misery replacing my rage.

"But you did. You did this to me, son. And now it's time to face the consequences. Accept your punishment and maybe you can know peace in death."

"There can never be peace for a monster like me," I growled and swiped at the ghastly apparition. As with the visions I'd lashed out at before, it vanished, and when I turned back round the images of Mum and Amy had also disappeared, leaving me alone once more.

And then the daylight began to fade, just like my life was soon to do, and I could see through the windows that it was another red sky out there. Except this time instead of the clouds taking on the colour of all the bloodshed from lives I'd taken, it was my own blood that was about to be spilled. With dusk there truly came the end of any small hopes I may have still had that I would somehow escape my fate, and I was forced to accept I would be put to death, whether I truly felt I deserved it or not.

As day became night and my execution drew ever nearer, I began to imagine I could feel the fires of Hell reaching up for me. That was surely where I was headed after all the terrible things I'd done, and worse than the torments the demons down there would devise for me would be meeting any of my victims I'd sent there. I felt certain I would never be allowed to know peace, despite the slim hope of it that my brain had tried to offer through the images of my family. And while I suffered in that inferno below, would the vampires celebrate the end of my race, even after more victims turned up and the realisation sank in that I had been innocent after all? Not that it really mattered. Death was coming for me, and this time there was no escape.

Darkness had fallen and the door to my prison swung open. I thought I saw a robed figure enter, a reminder that the grim reaper comes for us all eventually, even those of us granted the power to withstand the ravages of time. But just like during the latest battle with the Slayers, the figure in question was in fact Ulfarr in his usual garb.

"It is time," he announced, undoing my restraints telekinetically. "Come. And do not bother attempting to escape. We both know you are powerless to resist my will."

I had no choice but to follow him. So this was it. After everything I'd been through, my life was to end not by the blades or guns of the Slayers, but at the hands of beings who should have been allies and kindred spirits. I felt strange as I walked in the wake of the Elder vampire, each step feeling leaden with the weight of my pending doom, as my feet carried me one step closer to the end of my life in the mortal realm.

Ulfarr led me out of the warehouse and into a nearby patch of woodland. He took me to a large clearing not unlike the one Leon's mansion was hidden in, and with the moon nearing full again overhead, it was a bright night once we emerged from the gloom of the trees. And waiting there were even more vampires than I'd seen at the meetings Ulfarr had called to deal with the murders, as well as a number of ghouls again. With a sickening feeling I realised that the animalistic ghouls were probably there to eat my remains once Ulfarr had delivered the killing blow, rather than out of any interest in justice. My only comforting thought was that the execution itself must surely be quick and fairly painless, rather than the long and drawn out deaths humans had devised in the Middle Ages, since only a mortal wound to my heart or my brain would kill me.

The walk to the clearing couldn't have been more than a few miles, but it had felt like an eternity to get there. I'd had a sense of going to my death the previous year, when I thought I'd foreseen my end in the battle for my hometown, and again when I'd followed Leon into the Slayers' base. But at least there'd been room for some hope in battle, no matter how slim, that I might survive. Not like this time, where I was faced with certain death. And at least if I had fallen in battle, I would have gone down fighting. To be executed was not the end I would have chosen, but it seemed it would happen anyway, no matter what I wanted or whether I truly deserved it.

I was led to the front of the crowd, where there was a large rock which I was made to climb up so that they could all see me clearly as I stood there, naked and covered in dried blood, shivering in the chill of the night air. Ulfarr followed close behind, his hand already straying to the hilt of his blade in anticipation of the blow that would put an end to the lycanthropic blight he despised so greatly.

270

"My fellow undead," he addressed the crowd. "These are grave times indeed when we find ourselves beset not by human killers intent on slaying beings they perceive as monsters, but by one of our own."

A part of me wanted to comment on the fact he'd referred to me as one of them, when before he'd made it clear he thought of me as nothing more than a beast, lowlier than the other races of undead. But I suspected he wouldn't take kindly to me ruining his theatrics, and that he could find a way to make my death more unpleasant if I gave him reason to. So I held my tongue for once, while the other undead murmured angrily amongst themselves.

Ulfarr paused while the crowd voiced their distaste, before continuing "Tonight, I present to you the beast responsible for the deaths of our brother and sister vampires. There is no doubt in my mind of his guilt now, and so the time has come to pass judgement. A few months ago I promised you all justice, and tonight you shall finally have it!"

While the gathered undead roared with approval, Ulfarr commanded me "Kneel."

"If you'll grant me a last request, I would rather die on my feet."

"Why, do you imagine that will allow you to die with some honour?" the Elder vampire sneered. "Animals like you do not deserve honourable deaths. Now, you will kneel!"

Raising a fist to motion for effect, like he was pulling downwards on a cord or a chain, the Elder vampire forced me to my knees with his telekinetic power. I tried to hide the pain of being pushed down so roughly, but I couldn't quite keep myself from grimacing and most of the watching vampires jeered. I seemed to be facing even more hatred than I'd witnessed in my human enemies, but then the undead did have centuries more to nurse their loathing than the mere mortals.

I was able to pick out Leon's face in the crowd, and he alone seemed sorry to bear witness to the death Ulfarr was about to deal me. I could see no sign of Lady Sarah, and despite how saddened she'd seemed when she'd visited me in my makeshift cell, I had to wonder if she really cared at all, or why else would she not be there for me in my final moments?

From behind came the sound of the Elder vampire unsheathing his blade with all the finality of dirt falling on a coffin lid or the flatlining of a hospital patient. And stood just to the side of me I again saw Death. Was he real?

"Does it matter?" the apparition answered to my unspoken question.

271

I supposed it didn't. Whether real or a metaphorical hallucination, either way I was within his grasp yet again, and this time he wouldn't be cheated. I was acutely aware of Ulfarr raising his sword above my head, my heart hammering in my chest no matter how I tried to calm my nerves, my lupine half's instincts screaming to run. But there could be no fight or flight this time, not against the power of my executioner, and all I could do was shut my eyes to the sight of the sea of hate I saw in the dead faces below. Yet I couldn't escape the vision of Death's grinning skull so easily, the image of the reaper still waiting patiently from behind my eyelids. Then came the sensation of the Elder vampire's blade slicing through the air as it carved its way towards my prone form, and I prepared to die.

Chapter Twenty Seven – Beneath the Mask of Sanity

I kept my eyes closed in those last few seconds before the sword cut its way through my skull and destroyed my brain beyond all repair. The shouts of encouragement from the crowd of undead were loud in my ears, but then I heard another voice, male but different to the reaper's.

"It is not your time."

I felt the blade whistle through the air just inches from my head, and the noise of the metal striking the stone with enough force that I imagined there would be sparks was unmistakeable. When the scent of humans carried to me on the breeze, my eyes snapped open again to find a large group of Slayers were approaching, and they had a spellcaster with them.

Ulfarr hissed angrily and ran past me to face the greater threat to their survival, engaging his enemies with the same feral savagery as I'd witnessed before. Why I'd been spared I couldn't say. He could have easily carried out the death sentence he'd condemned me to before running into battle, if he was that desperate to see me die. Unless he wanted me to fight with them, but the Slayers didn't yet have us surrounded and why should I help them when they'd been so quick to turn on me?

The other vampires also lost interest in me with their own existence threatened by the approaching force, except for Leon who pushed his way forward.

"Why didn't he finish it?" I asked, on the off chance my friend had enough of an idea of the Elder vampire's mind to guess what had just happened.

"It matters not. You're lucky the Slayers decided to strike now, perhaps in retaliation for what we did to their base. My guess is they also found this gathering in such numbers too great an opportunity to resist, though how they discovered us so quickly is as yet unclear. But none of that is important at the moment. You need to get away from here, before any of them decide to finish this charade Ulfarr is calling justice."

"I'll meet you at the mansion then?"

"No! That's the first place they'll look once this battle is over. If you head west of here, you should come to an abandoned barn, possibly the same one you sheltered in with Lady Sarah," he said, pointing. "Wait for me there."

I nodded and the vampire turned his attention to the battle. They were all fully focussed on the Slayers and I was able to slip away

273

with ease, into the surrounding woodland. Once I was sure none of them had followed me, I took my wolf form and set out in the direction Leon had shown me. But I hadn't gone far before I caught the scent of more vampires up ahead, and I slowed, slinking cautiously through the trees.

As I drew closer, I caught the familiar scent of blood and death, and I could see a humanoid figure crouched over something lying on the floor. I realised it was another dead vampire, and I tensed, expecting a sudden attack from the barghest again. Yet I didn't recognise a human scent that might belong to the witch, Selina. My nose only detected vampires, and when the killer twisted around with a hiss, as if suddenly aware of my presence, I was shocked to find myself facing none other than Lady Sarah. She was the murderer!

The vampire showed no sign of recognising me, looking wilder than I'd ever seen her. It was as if she'd given herself so completely to her bloodlust, just as I had done so often that year, that she had lost all sense of self until the world around her became nothing more than an endless hunting ground filled with prey. But why she'd turn to killing other vampires instead of the human victims she hungered for was something I couldn't fathom. And I wasn't going to stay to find out, the look in her eyes convincing me that any warm feelings she might have once had for me were currently lost in the chaos of her hunger for the kill. Besides, she'd been quite happy to let me take the fall for her crimes, no matter how saddened she'd acted while I was imprisoned, so she clearly hadn't cared that deeply for me.

I growled instinctively as I backed away, my hackles raised and my teeth bared in warning. The vampire remained crouched over her kill, baring her own fangs, but she made no move to attack. I risked turning my back on her and sprinted away, straining my ears while I ran for any sounds of pursuit. There were none and eventually I slowed again, to try and work out what direction I'd been fleeing in. Judging from the distant sound of fighting I could still hear from the clearing, I'd veered east, so I resumed as swift a pace as my paws could manage, in the direction I hoped was west.

Somehow I managed to find the old barn without any guidance from the wolf, and it was indeed the one Lady Sarah had previously found as a temporary shelter for us. I knew how silently she could move and as I waited for Leon, I grew tenser and tenser as the minutes dragged on, the moon now hidden behind clouds, plunging the world into greater darkness. She could have followed downwind without me realising and she might even have realised where I was headed. She could be waiting in the shadows for all I knew, and perhaps she'd already marked me as her next victim, now I knew her secret.

The more I thought about my gruesome discovery, the more it made sense. It explained why she'd always been so secretive and distant, even if I still couldn't work out what her motives might be for preying on her own kind. But what good did the knowledge do me? I still had no proof to take to Ulfarr and I doubted he would want to hear the truth, even if I had some solid evidence. Convincing him Selina was responsible for the killings would have been one thing, but to present to him another vampire as the murderer, especially one as old and as respected as Lady Sarah seemed to be, would probably be met with disbelief at best. He might well dismiss the notion out of hand, unwilling to accept the truth.

I had to survive the night first though. I'd been spared from the execution Ulfarr had sentenced me to, for the time being at least, but if Lady Sarah planned to kill me herself then it was possible Death was still nearby, waiting patiently to claim my life at last. And when my eyes detected movement in the shadows, I felt sure it would be her. But to my relief Leon had returned at last, bloodied from the battle and still drunk on the savage joy killing held for our kind.

I couldn't talk to him while my vocal cords were fully lupine, so I started to transform, deciding to go all the way back to my human form. If the battle was over and Ulfarr tracked us down, being in either my hybrid or my wolf form wouldn't save me. If the Elder vampire made an appearance I'd try talking to him again and even though I held no real hope of being any more successful in getting him to listen, I felt I had more chance if I looked human, rather than the savage beast he believed me to be. If Lady Sarah showed up I would have to hope Leon's greater age made him powerful enough to give us a chance to survive the encounter, otherwise I was probably equally as doomed.

"Leon!" I said, as the vampire walked over to me. "I was wrong, that witch isn't the murderer after all, or at least she didn't kill all the victims that have turned up. It's Lady Sarah, I saw her crouched over another dead vampire and covered in blood!"

The vampire didn't seem to hear me, simply stating "It's not safe for you here."

"Yeah, 'cause Lady Sarah could come for us at any moment. So what's the plan? I don't suppose you have another secret mansion tucked away in another corner of the countryside that the others don't know about, do you?"

Again Leon didn't really seem to hear my words. His eyes had a faraway look as if he'd travelled to another reality and was only vaguely aware of this one.

"The moon will be full again in a few days," he said. "The clouds may hide it now but I feel it, just as you do. It calls to us. We must heed its call and give in to the need to hunt."

I gave him a puzzled look. Something was wrong; vampires shouldn't feel any connection to the moon.

He closed his eyes and raised his head to the sky as if he were going to howl, but instead he breathed deep as if savouring the moment. Then he roared, seemingly becoming much more bestial in nature than the usual dignified, aristocratic, humanoid character I'd come to associate with most vampires, as if he too were a werewolf. When he opened his eyes something had changed, though they were physically still the same.

He gave a cold, emotionless laugh at the bewildered expression on my face. "Ah Nick, how well you think we have grown to know each other and how little you do not know. I feel the call of the moon, feel it bringing our beasts to the surface."

All emotion seemed to have drained from his body and his voice as he talked, to such an extent that I felt like I was talking to a stranger. And this new Leon was decidedly less stable than the one I thought I knew, that was clear.

I watched him examining his hands, as if convinced they had become paws. He roared again and shook his head like an animal, swishing a tail that existed only in his head. But his beast, imaginary or no, was nothing like mine. The wolfish part of me respected the sanctity of life while I could see it in his eyes, his beast, born of humanity, revelled in death.

"I am lion again, my true form," he growled, turning his eyes on me.

His bloodlust was already raised from battle, and I sensed it had soared to new heights, perhaps of the kind experienced by human serial killers. My bloodlust was rooted in the curse of my lycanthropy and my need to kill was tied to my predatory nature and my hunger for human flesh, even though it had driven me to take so many more lives than I needed to survive. But his bloodlust was nothing to do with the relationship between predator and prey, of that I was growing certain.

"Leon, what's going on? We're not out of danger yet, we need to get going! We can hunt later."

"The moon's call must be answered, you of all beasts should know that."

"It's too dangerous with so many enemies about. You just said yourself it's not safe! We need to go before Lady Sarah turns up, or Ulfarr, or even more of the Slayers. Come on man, quit fooling around."

"You are quite right, it's not safe for you. I will hunt now, but I'm ready for a new challenge tonight. Wolf against lion, who do you think will win?"

A chill crept through me as the terrible realisation began to sink in.

"A new challenge?" I asked, praying I was wrong.

But his next words seemed to confirm my fears when he answered "Yes, vampires have kept on proving unworthy thus far."

"It's not Lady Sarah, is it? It's been you all along."

"Indeed, I am the beast responsible for killing all those other vampires. And when I ripped out their hearts, it made such a glorious mess! Could there be any greater pleasure than ending a life?"

"Is that why you still see the faces of your earliest victims? Not because they haunt you but because of some psychopathic pleasure?" I said, hoping if I kept him talking long enough I might be able to break through to the saner Leon I'd grown close to.

"Indeed, I still remember that giddy moment when I killed for the first time, the world swimming in and out of focus as a strange dizziness came over me, and then the beauty of blood splattering as I stabbed her over and over. I can still see her eyes so wide and full of shock and pain, and the excitement of sending her there, pushing her further towards the void until she fell through into death."

"It wasn't theft that condemned you to life in the arena, was it?"

"In a way it was. What is a murderer, but a thief of lives?"

"And the portrait of the woman and little boy? Two more of your victims?"

"Yes. The mansion was theirs until I killed them and took it for myself, but I kept the painting. I guess you could say I wanted a trophy of sorts."

"But why start killing your own kind? You had to know it would cause Ulfarr to take counteractive measures, alerting as many as he could so they'd all be on the lookout for you. Even with framing me, surely you've only bought yourself more time and they'll catch up with you eventually."

"Humans die too easily, I've long since grown bored of hunting them," he snarled. "And Ulfarr is a fool. He'll never accept that a vampire could turn on his own. If he wasn't so blinded by hatred for your kind, he might have put the pieces together before now. This isn't

277

my first killing spree, far from it, and it won't be my last. Taking new names and moving around often helps alleviate any suspicions others might have, but the evidence has always been there, if they weren't too blind to see it. The time will come for me to move on again soon, though I will miss my mansion. But perhaps I will go to Africa and seek out other lions. Besides, can killing vampires really be considered murder? We are undead after all, forever caught in a state between life and death for as long as we exist. We're not alive in the same sense that mortals are, and murder requires taking the life of a living being."

"I don't think Ulfarr sees it that way."

He ignored that and continued "My other self has grown fond of you, for reasons beyond me. He wouldn't have spent so much time training you, otherwise. And he even considered taking you with us, when we leave here. But I think you will make much better prey. The last surviving werewolf will surely be an excellent victim, and with all training you've been given you will make even greater sport. And perhaps when I eat your heart, the power of your lupine half will transfer to me, and I can be both lion and wolf."

I realised then the vampire was truly insane, and there would be no reasoning with him. If his plan had been to frame me all along, the help he'd given me was probably just to buy enough time for him to indulge his murderous needs before he was forced to move on. Or maybe some part of him had formed some kind of a bond with me, though whether it could really be considered friendship was debatable if he was a true psychopath. But that part of him was currently elsewhere and if his other self had already decided the time had come to leave the UK, then I had no further use to this 'beast' alive. So I did the only thing I could: I ran.

Chapter Twenty Eight – Hunted: Part One

My mind raced while my legs pumped the earth as I pushed my body to its limits, my heart hammering furiously with the strain to meet the physical demands placed on it. And yet it wasn't enough. Leon hadn't given chase straight away, wanting to give me a head start to make the hunt last longer, but I was under no illusion as to my chances of escaping. His vampiric powers granted him greater speed and strength, and over the open fields he would easily cross the distance between us and run me down. There was the patch of woodlands I'd explored before when I'd been in the area with Lady Sarah, but I hesitated as the outline of the trees loomed ahead of me.

Moving through the woods would slow me down considerably, but it should also slow the vampire and maybe if I was able to pick the ground where I would make my final stand, I might find something that evened the playing field somehow. It would give me more thinking time at least, so with a deep breath I plunged into the blackness of the woods. The night was dark with the moon still hidden behind thick cloud cover, but impenetrable darkness pressed in all around me once I was under the trees. Humanity roamed their streets under the comfort of artificial light, breaking up the blackness into more manageable chunks for the eyes to digest, and in that unnatural world you forget just how dark the night can be. But without any natural light to see by, even my supernatural vision was rendered useless by the completeness of the darkness beneath the trees.

I was painfully aware of the seconds ticking by in which the vampire was no doubt making his move, but I came to a standstill in that blackness, panting slightly from the short sprint. Not for the first time, I cursed my decision to return to my human form. For Leon, this hunt was about the thrill of the chase, which meant he probably wouldn't use his hypnotic powers to subdue me as it would take away from the enjoyment and the challenge of hunting down and slaughtering the worthy prey he'd deemed me to be. If it was to be a struggle, pitting his strength against my own, I would need all the greater might of my lupine form, but I daren't change back without feeding again first. It would only weaken me further, defeating the purpose of the transformation for the fight ahead.

Like a blind man I crept between the trees, arms outstretched to feel around me. My hands passed over the rough trunk of a tree just ahead. Running any further was out of the question, unless I wanted to risk colliding with a tree and knocking myself unconscious, where I would lay helpless for the vampire to finish off perhaps just moments later. I tried to at least reach for the fires of my rage to grant me strength, yet even with the moon nearing full, my anger lay dormant again. So instead I tried to focus on the near full moon, hidden though it was behind the clouds, but I felt no sense of that lunar energy or the power it would soon hold over me in the nights to follow. I thought that ironic, when Leon had claimed to hear its call in his insanity, even though it held no sway for him as it did for the wolf in me.

I knew I needed the help of my lupine half to navigate the woods. I was too clumsy as a human and still too inexperienced when it came to my other senses, still too reliant on sight as my primary sense. And without my eyes to guide me I might as well have been a full human for all the good my other enhanced senses were doing me. But I was reluctant to let the wolf take control. He was intelligent enough to know the hunger needed to be satisfied before risking another transformation, yet the temptation to change to wolf form would be there. And for all his cunning, he was still guided by his animalistic instincts which I doubted would be much good against the vampire. I knew then I had but one option. It was time to let the last of the barrier between human and wolf crumble away as Lady Sarah had kept urging me to do, to let my mind become one again and embrace the advantages of each half to combine our strength.

I paused again, despite my instincts screaming at me to keep moving, and retreated into my mind where I called to him, instantly feeling his consciousness rise up towards the surface.

"I know we've had cause to fight in the past but it's time to make a pact. We are part of each other after all and we'll be stronger as one," I said.

He studied me silently and dipped his head in acknowledgement, though he didn't deign to speak.

I took a deep breath and continued "I've much to learn from you, I realise that now. That darker side of my humanity that you despise, the pointless slaughter, I will – no we will – try to keep better control of it. And while little remains of the human I used to be, anyone I still consider to be a friend from that former life, or any new friends I make, we won't hunt. Agreed?"

He studied me with those cold predatory eyes for a moment as if considering what I'd said. He didn't answer but instead, after what seemed like an age, charged towards me, his consciousness drawing closer to mine. While every instinct of my remaining humanity screamed at me to fight, I forced myself to remain passive, neither drawing away nor retaliating when his consciousness came crashing towards mine. I gasped and took an involuntary step backwards as if it had happened in the physical world and there had been an actual impact, then I was back in the woodland, back in reality.

There was the feeling of confusion again, and I was unsure whether I should be standing on two legs or four. But it wasn't as strong as the first time it had happened, maybe because I was ready for it that night.

Despite the confusion, I was aware of an immediate change to my state of being. In acceptance of who I truly was, I felt at peace for the first time since the curse had taken hold. Those I had preyed upon no longer seemed to be haunting me, and though the savage murders I'd committed outside of the need to feed were regrettable, there was no guilt. Unlike before when I'd grown numb to the tumult of overwhelming emotions, there wasn't the same emptiness that had developed or complete lack of any feelings. There was simply no need to feel guilt or remorse because I'd finally accepted my predatory nature.

The rage born of man but fuelled by the curse was still there and in embracing my killer instincts it flared up again, but with acceptance above all else came control. I would wield that brutal side to my nature, welded with the hunger born of wolf, whenever the situation called for it, and in doing so give rise to a ferocity greater than that of any mortal beast. Perhaps there might still be times when I lost myself to it – it was too early to tell yet – but without any internal conflict between the two halves of my nature, the rage wasn't able to take an instant hold like it had in the past. I held it there as it blazed at the very centre of my being, but for the first time since it had developed in the emptiness where my soul should have been, it couldn't flood my body unless I allowed it to. And I would, when the time came. The vampire might hold all the advantages physically, but in our brutality we were evenly matched. In times of such conflict my rage would prove vital to my survival, a killing tool greater than any blade. But only when I chose to unleash it.

I had kept my eyes closed in concentration of what I mentally needed to do and when I opened them it was as if I had been trapped in a dark room and someone had turned on the light.

The moon had broken through the clouds once again and it penetrated enough gaps in the canopy overhead that I could make out shapes in the darkness, outlines of the trees around me and obstacles on the ground such as logs and large rocks. I could see enough that I knew my eyes had changed colour to the burning amber of the wolf, even though I hadn't consciously willed them to change.

However, the eyes are not the wolf's primary sense. Scents were stronger and the wolf in me knew how to read them, coupled with the sounds around us. Not only did my already enhanced senses seem to have become sharper still, but I was more attuned to them than I had ever been before. As humans we rely so heavily on our eyesight that we often forget our other senses. We fail to notice most sounds or smells around us, and anything we do pick up is often filed away as background noise. I'd gradually learnt to use scent and sound to a degree, but the human part of me had far from mastered those senses.

Yet with the joining of the two halves of my mind I was picking up much more than I ever had in the past and what's more, I suddenly knew how to process the information. Enough to make a far more detailed mental picture of my surroundings than the one my eyes showed me.

I brought a hand up to scratch my ear and found it was slightly more pointed than usual, and a quick feel of my nose proved it had also subtly changed shape, becoming slightly longer and wider, the beginning of a snout. I ran my tongue over my teeth and found them to be longer and sharper, small fangs. I hoped the changes weren't permanent or it would be much harder to blend in with the human world when I wanted to, but right then I welcomed them. My senses, already sharper than a human's, had become even more so without changing too much to use up the last of my precious energy. And with the full use of my lupine instincts I suddenly knew how to take full advantage of them.

Though the vampire couldn't be far away after the time I'd wasted, there was no fear. Instead I felt a cold predatory calm, despite the threat of the more powerful predator hunting us. A mortal wolf may have been afraid, but we weren't. We were surrounded by woodland: this was home. We ruled the woods, vampires or no. If the vampire proved to be the stronger, so be it. We would fight to survive for as long as we drew breath, but we did not fear death if our end was to be the outcome.

I took a deep breath, taking in as many scents as I could, searching for any sign of Leon. I didn't detect him anywhere nearby yet and I was aware enough of my surroundings that I was able to resume running, knowing I would have to fight him eventually but determined to pick the battleground.

I was deep into the heart of the woods before I realised my mistake. The chilly night air swept over my face, cool yet fresh as I breathed in, searching for any new scents it might carry to me. It was the dead scent of the vampire rather than any sound that gave him away. He was nearby and I still had no plan to defeat him. I was hoping something would come to me while I was running but I had no destination in mind, nor had I come across any landscape that inspired me.

Knowing he was close I forced my legs to move faster, despite the burning hunger sapping at my strength. I desperately needed to feed and replenish the energy I had used switching forms earlier, but there was no time for that now.

I had just forced myself to a full sprint when without warning something landed on top of me and sent me crashing to the ground, slender fingers grasping my head, ready to crush it to a bloody pulp. I cursed myself, realising Leon had been there all along, flitting between the treetops as I ran. He hadn't needed to wait for the ideal moment, he had merely grown bored of what he deemed to be too easy a hunt after all and had gone for the kill the moment it pleased him.

"Such a disappointment. I had expected more from the last surviving werewolf," he growled, still acting like the lion he believed himself to be.

The internal monstrous form of my rage strained against the chains I'd placed on it and knowing it was my last faint hope, I finally unleashed it in a rush of primal fury, snarling and writhing beneath my opponent. It was no good, the vampire's strength too great for me to dislodge him through my own brute strength, even with the aid of my rage. Unwilling to add to his enjoyment I reined my anger back in and fell still and silent, waiting for the end. I expected to feel fear again in the face of certain death, but the cold calm remained and there was only acceptance of my fate.

"There is nothing more beautiful in life than the moment of death. I have shared more with you than I ever have with any other creature. It is only fitting I share with you your death."

His grip tightened but there was no sense of excitement or anticipation from him like he'd described in the memories of his earliest murders. Just that infinite emptiness, completely void of emotion. Still, I knew this was it. My time had finally come.

Chapter Twenty Nine – Demonic Intervention

A growl of displeasure rent the thick, putrid air of Hell, causing the tormented souls chained to the stony walls in this lair of horrors to writhe in fear, each praying not to be picked as the latest form of stress relief. Regardless of who they'd been in life and how great or terrible their deeds, each now existed purely for the amusement of the demon who'd claimed them. There was no fate worse than the eternal agony each endured, constant and unending, but their current suffering was as nothing compared with the times when He turned the full force of His anger on any of them.

Beads of blood and sweat rolled down the human souls, the heat from the fire blazing in the corner unbearable. But the demon needed the flames which acted as a window to the mortal realm, where He could watch the happenings taking place on Earth and influence them as needed. Like a puppet master, He pulled the strings of the beings who interested Him, nudging events in the direction He desired. Yet there was more at stake here than the amusement to be had from the suffering of these living souls and the dark emotions to feed on, and the time had come to act again.

Ideally He would have preferred not to have to directly influence events yet but like the rest of His kindred, He dreamt of the day when they would unleash Hell on Earth and revel in the suffering of the living as the world burned. The Demon Slayers had driven them back into Hell all those centuries ago, but one day they would return to the mortal realm in force and no man would stand in their way, Slayer or otherwise. That day was closer at hand than most of the other demons realised, too intent on tormenting the souls of the damned to notice much of what went on in the world of the living. He alone was aware of the coming shift in the balance, and the young werewolf was central to that. So He had no option but to interfere, in order to keep the werewolf alive.

The insane vampire threatened His plans but it wasn't so easy as simply removing him from the equation. The vampire's soul had already been claimed by another, one who rivalled His own power and whose wrath He wished to avoid, which meant He couldn't directly harm the vampire in any way.

The demon fixed His intent on the fire where the images of the world above danced across the flames, focussing on the vampire until it held nothing but his eyes, burning with flames of their own, the fires of madness. Despite the bestial growl He'd made, He currently looked like a mutilated, black haired man, four gashes like claw marks across

His left cheek giving Him a lopsided, skeletal grin, and another ran down over His right eye, the bone marked with a long scratch in the middle of each cut. Red slit eyes fixed on the vampire's and He whispered softly, knowing His voice would be the loudest amongst all the other voices clamouring for attention in the vampire's skull.

Once He had the vampire's attention, He raised His hand palm upwards to His shoulder, where a tarantula crouched. The spider crawled onto its master's hand and at another whispered command it rubbed its abdomen, flicking the bristly hairs into the fire and the image of Leon's eyes. The hairs didn't burn in the flames but instead passed through, into the mortal realm, and flew into the vampire's eyes.

The demon didn't wait to see what happened next, instead moving the image on to another part of the woodland with a lazy flick of His hand, in the same way a mortal would swipe a touchscreen device. He used His power to search the area until He found a deer nearby, and this time whispered a command to the boa constrictor coiled around His body. The snake slithered into the flames and also passed unharmed into the mortal world, where it reared up and sank its fangs into the deer's neck before it could bolt, wrapping itself around the animal and squeezing the life from its prey. But instead of swallowing the carcass, the snake's form collapsed into a shadowy mist, much like the barghest's had done, reappearing at its master's side moments later.

Satisfied He had sufficiently manipulated the night's events to keep them on course, He refocused the fire on the two undead and sat patiently, watching and waiting once more.

Chapter Thirty – Hunted: Part Two

The vampire's nails were starting to bite into the flesh of my scalp, slowly drawing closer to the vulnerable brain tissue. I had no doubt they would dig through my skull with ease. The pressure was building and I couldn't help but imagine the death that was surely only minutes away – seconds if he wished. I could see the moment where the bone crushed as if it were no more than an eggshell, blood and brains exploding outward, my life along with it.

Just as the pressure was becoming unbearable, something whispered through the trees – a strange supernatural force. It couldn't be felt physically and yet the woods were suddenly bursting with life, animals who'd been cowering in their dens in the presence of two unnatural predators now fleeing from an unseen terror.

Leon whipped his head round at the sudden disturbance as he listened to voices only he could hear, probably telling him to kill them all, though his grip on my head remained strong. But then he hissed in pain and his hands released their hold on my fragile skull, suddenly raised to his own face where he pawed at his eyes and shook his head to try and clear them of whatever was causing the irritation, like the animal he still believed himself to be. It was all I needed to break free.

I'd been given a second chance at life and I took it, heaving my body with every ounce of strength I had, enough to throw him off balance and wriggle free. I was up and running again before I really knew what was happening, desperately trying to think of a plan. I didn't look back but I knew I had only moments before the vampire turned his attention back to me.

Built for endurance as wolves are, my body was running too low on energy and I knew I couldn't go on for much longer. My muscles were aching with exhaustion, the cold air starting to sting, though my lungs gasped for more. I was beginning to pant heavily, my chest heaving with the exertion, and before long I started to feel a light headedness that probably meant I would collapse if I pushed myself on much further.

I came to a stop behind the thick trunk of a particularly old tree and leaned back, keeping myself as flat against it as I could. If the vampire had followed over the ground this time I should be hidden from his field of vision, though I knew I couldn't count on that, and it would only be a matter of time before he located me with his other senses. As soon as I caught my breath I had to push on.

Had he been any other creature I could have laid in wait and ambushed him this time, but he was a vampire. He had all the advantages. It wasn't just his superior senses or speed and strength but the fact that, when it came to hunting each other down, he could evade me far more effectively than I could hide from him. His body didn't need to breathe like mine did, nor did his heart need to pump. I wasn't sure if they could control it but their bodies only needed the blood of the living to keep them going, and the usual necessary bodily functions didn't apply. That meant even when my breathing grew much quieter as it returned to normal, my heart becoming calmer, no longer thudding as loudly, he could still listen for these tell-tale signs of life and pinpoint my location with ease, whereas I might as well have been blind to my surroundings again. He could be feet away, utterly silent and downwind, and I would never know he had drawn so close until he struck – again. And I knew there would be no second chance this time.

There was no hope of him brushing against a leaf or snapping a twig either. Vampires just weren't that clumsy and with his training and centuries of practice, he really was the perfect predator. The wolf in me might have felt we ruled these woods, but we paled in comparison to our adversary.

I wanted nothing more than to collapse right there on the woodland floor but to do so was certain death. With an effort of will I forced my aching body onwards, feeling the last reserves of energy burning up with every movement. I needed to pick the place I would make my final stand or I wouldn't have enough energy left to fight. Knowing my situation grew ever more desperate, I tried to think of any area in these woods I'd come across before that might offer some advantage in a fight. As I sifted through memories of the lay of the land I began to think it was hopeless, but then I settled on the one place that might offer the advantage I needed.

With a destination now in mind, I pushed myself to a full sprint, praying the vampire wasn't too close behind. A plan was forming as I ran. Foolproof it wasn't, but it was the best I could think of in such desperate circumstances. It was the only shot I had at coming out of this alive, since there was no way I could beat the vampire in a fair fight, especially when restricted to my weaker human form and with so little energy left to me. So I forced myself to keep running, vowing to myself that if it was my fate to die that night I would at least take the bastard with me; he who had pretended to be my friend, only to prove as false as the rest of them.

Just when I felt I couldn't run any further, the mental image of my surroundings indicated I had reached the right place. I sagged to my knees momentarily, grateful for the brief respite, when a welcome smell reached my nostrils.

At first I didn't dare believe my luck and was convinced my mind was playing tricks on me. But after a quick feel around on the floor my hands passed over it, confirming it was indeed real. I was surprised I'd not noticed the scent sooner, the hunger burning inside as it was. Or perhaps my subconscious had been aware of it all along and it was no coincidence I'd settled on this part of the woods for the fight. If I hadn't been subconsciously aware of it then it certainly was a hell of a coincidence to find it here waiting for me in the very area I'd chosen to run to. That said, I was too exhausted to be suspicious. If it was some kind of a trap, the odds of me making it through the night alive weren't that great anyway. I decided it was worth the risk.

I crouched over the carcass which my nose told me was that of a deer. The smell of blood thick in my nostrils, I lowered my face to where I sensed its soft underbelly was and bit into the flesh. The kill was fresh and mostly intact, though there were two large puncture holes in its throat where something seemed to have bitten it. I couldn't be sure what exactly had killed it but it didn't seem likely it was the vampire's doing, at least. He tended to be considerably messier, judging from the state of the victims Ulfarr had found and revealed to us all. I wondered if it was maybe connected to the supernatural force we had felt earlier.

Ripping my way through to the deer's organs, I knew I didn't have long to eat with the vampire surely not far behind now – if he wasn't already here. I ate the liver and kidneys as well as the heart, knowing these organs were the best source of sustenance which is why only the alpha and cubs may feast on them in a natural wolf pack. They would likely give me the greatest amount of strength and energy I needed to defeat the vampire.

As I ate, I could already feel fresh energy flooding through me. Even though my body couldn't digest the food that quick, I felt better just for having a full stomach. I didn't know how it worked since the usual laws of nature didn't exactly apply to the undead – all I knew was that I had to feed between transformations and doing so gave me the energy to change again. Once I'd eaten the organs I knew it was enough to return to my hybrid form, but first I crept into the ditch I'd been searching for, out of sight in the darkness of our surroundings and, I hoped, downwind from Leon. There was nothing I could do to hide the beating of my heart or the inhale and exhale of air through my lungs, but I tried to keep those vital functions going as quietly as possible while I crouched there, waiting for the vampire to come stalking by.

It seemed my luck was in once again. Leon trod so softly over the bed of dirt, twigs and fallen leaves that his approach could easily be mistaken for little more than the stirring of a faint breeze. But with my newly enhanced awareness of my surroundings, I recognised the faint shifting of earth under the pressure of his 'paws' for what it truly was, and I bunched my muscles in preparation for the ambush I planned to make.

The vampire came to a sudden stop as if he'd sensed my presence. I held my position, knowing he was just out of reach and if my timing was even slightly off, I would lose the advantage of surprise, which was the only thing currently in my favour. Leon scented the air like an animal while I silently willed him to creep just a little closer to the ditch where I hid, my muscles beginning to burn with the discomfort of remaining tensed up. It seemed my one chance to emerge victorious wasn't going to work after all, but then the vampire padded nearer as I'd hoped and my moment came.

In a rush of fury, my rage free again and my bloodlust roaring for the brutal death of my adversary, I burst from the shadows and fell on the vampire, taking him by surprise as I'd hoped. The successful ambush meant he wasn't quick enough to react before we hit the ground, and I was able to sink my fangs into the arm he threw up to protect his vulnerable head. Teeth tore through flesh and blood splattered my body and the surrounding vegetation, but this was no mortal victim and it would take much more than a ruined limb to stop him.

Leon threw me off of him with his three good limbs, sending me crashing into a tree. I yelped from the impact, momentarily winded which meant I was a few seconds slower to pick myself back up. The vampire charged before I could recover and he sank his own fangs into the base of my neck, but my fur offered some protection, his elongated canines not quite as lethal as the lion he imagined himself to be. They were long enough to pierce through flesh and skin, but he only had upper fangs and they would have to nick my jugular vein to weaken and subdue me, which he hadn't yet managed to do. Until then, the sensation of those two fangs tearing into the back of my muscular neck was merely a painful irritation, and I was able to twist my head round and savage the vampire's collar bone, on the side of his good arm.

Leon was forced to pull away, the blood gushing from the wounds I'd dealt him making him weaker and evening the odds. But he wouldn't give up his hunt so easily, and we circled each other slowly in the dance of the two great predators we were, each looking for an opening in the other's defences to make our next move.

The torn flesh at the back of my neck was also bleeding profusely, but it seemed vampires suffered the effects of blood loss much quicker than creatures with living bodies still capable of producing their own blood. Starving his dead heart of the blood he'd taken from his prey, the very life he'd stolen from his victims, put him in a state akin to if he'd been starved all night. It gave rise to his hunger and the need to feed once more and regain the full might of his vampiric power. Even in his crazed state, Leon was well aware that time was no longer on his side. He needed to subdue me and make the kill he craved before he grew too weak, so he lunged for me, slightly slower than he'd been when the fight began.

I was ready for the attack and braced myself, taking a defensive stance like the one he'd taught me for hand to hand combat as part of the training he'd given me. I stood firm as he came at me, grabbing his thin frame in my monstrous clawed hands. Now evenly matched, he struggled to wrestle me back to the ground so he could pin me down and rip my heart out like he had with his previous victims, or perhaps he'd smash my head open first like he'd been about to do before the strange presence had distracted him. Regardless of what he wanted to do, it was I who succeeded in throwing him back to the forest floor, and this time I was able to pin him down and keep him there. The world around us went quiet, save for my heavy panting.

"Finish it," a familiar voice hissed from behind me.

"You came back," I said, with some surprise. After the way I'd treated her over the last year, I hadn't expected to see her again, especially as she'd already given me a second chance when I'd first left her to feed my rage with more blood.

"Finish it!" Lady Sarah repeated, more urgently.

"No," I growled, after a pause. Leon remained silent, as emotionless as ever.

"He's a murderer, Nick. The only way to stop him is through death. If you won't end it then I will."

"No. I can't take back the atrocities I've committed, but I can resolve only to kill for survival from now on. If we take his life, how are we any better than him?"

"This is survival! He won't hesitate to kill us, the next chance he gets."

"Perhaps, but tonight I choose to spare him. We are not creatures of peace, but we don't have to indulge in mindless slaughter either. My bloodlust is in check, and I choose not to lower myself to this vampire's level."

I released my grip on Leon's head and stood. Lady Sarah lunged forward as if to finish him herself, but Leon found a last burst of speed in him, slipping away from her and running off into the night. I placed a hand on the female vampire's shoulder before she could give chase, and she turned on me angrily.

"This is foolish! Your actions will only lead to more deaths."

When I didn't respond she studied me as if searching for an answer, her expression softening.

"There is something different about you. Am I right in thinking you have finally seen sense? You have fully embraced your wolf side now?"

I nodded, before changing the subject. "Why did you come back this time? And if Leon was the killer, what were you doing crouched over that dead vampire? And come to think of it, why the hell did you just suddenly stop helping me when Ulfarr put me on trial, and all these times since then when I've needed you. Why wouldn't you even offer to help clear my name when it looked like the witch might be behind the killings?"

"I told you before, there is much you do not understand. But I suppose you deserve the truth.

"The first thing you should know is that Ulfarr is not just an Elder to me, and it is not the mere respect for an Elder that binds me to him and commands my obedience. You see, Ulfarr is the vampire who made me."

"What? But you told me you never knew the name of the vampire that turned you, which kinda sounded like you never even saw him again."

"I was not completely honest with you. It was some time before our paths crossed again but perhaps it was inevitable, with the blood ties that bind us, even as those same ties bound me to Vince.

"Given Ulfarr's attitude towards werewolves, I had hoped to keep you away from my allegiance to him and thus I deemed it safer to lie about this aspect of my past. But it is not within my power to go against his wishes, so I had to obey whenever he ordered you to be brought before him, and his hold over me meant I was forced to hold my tongue while you were subjected to his cruelty.

"I did try to help where I could, making sure you had some comforts while imprisoned, no matter how small. Ulfarr wouldn't allow you the luxury of fresh meat but I convinced him to at least provide you with some water and the bucket to keep the floor clean."

As she spoke, I heard someone else approaching and I caught the scent of the witch, Selina. I growled in alarm, but she came into view with her arms raised in a gesture of peace.

Lady Sarah eyed the witch, before continuing "And the other thing you should know – this is my younger sister. When you came to me before, you never gave me the name of the witch you suspected and I was not yet aware that the two of you had met. But just as eternal youth was granted to me through vampirism, so she gained power through her witchcraft to halt the ravages of time."

"But then that would make her the next in line to the throne after you had to fake your death, right? How does a queen end up turning to witchcraft?"

Lady Sarah glanced at Selina, who remained quiet, before answering me. "Her story will have to wait. Ulfarr still believes you to be the killer and there may still be Slayers on the hunt in this area. We should not linger here too long."

"Okay but answer me one more thing. I ask again, why did you come back? Why did you even choose to help me in the first place, during my first full moon and since then, before your ties to Ulfarr got in the way?"

Selina answered this time. "I told you before, you have a great destiny, should you choose to embrace it. The future is not set in stone, but I have seen many things – enough to convince me that the last werewolf must not die so young and full of unfulfilled potential. And I shared the nature of my visions with my sister, who agreed to await your coming and watch over you where possible while you adapted to your lycanthropy."

"So all those times you go off on your own, have you been meeting with Selina?" I growled at the vampire. "After letting me give up everything from my old life, you get to see your sister? How is that fair?"

"Whoever said life was fair?" Selina asked.

"So you two what, meet up in that cottage on the moors?" I continued, ignoring the witch.

"Sometimes," Selina answered. "But that place isn't my home. I go there when I need to perform rituals away from the prying eyes of mortals, but the rest of the time I'm free to live among them. There was a time when I had to isolate myself from the rest of humanity of course, just like you undead, back when the Church had people in a panic and the witch hunts began. But once mortals turned to science and forgot about the existence of the supernatural, there was nothing stopping us witches from living among them again, since we are technically still human. I'm not known to the Slayers, and there are spells that can cause illusions which allow me to 'age' over the years, then I simply fake my death and move on. I'm currently living on the outskirts of a town not far from where you grew up, and I've invited my sister over a few times to keep her updated on the modern world she refuses to be a part of. Films seem to be going down well though."

I hadn't really paid attention to how the witch dressed before but I noted that night she was wearing a modern top and jeans, which fit with her story.

"All this time struggling in a world with no place for us, when there was somewhere we could have gone to shelter after all?" I snarled at Lady Sarah, unable to believe what I was hearing. "You let me give up everything I'd ever known, when I could have at least carried on in a human lifestyle?"

"I'm sorry, Nick, but I couldn't risk taking you to my sister whilst you were still so out of control. She's the one witch still on our side, as far as I know, and if we are to fight the Slayers as you've been so desperate to do, her powers will prove invaluable. Taking you to Selina could have proven disastrous for all three of us, so I had to be sure you'd mastered your self-control first. Now please, there will be time for more of your questions later but for now we must move on, before we are discovered here."

I'd been curious for so long as to what the vampire did on a night besides feeding, but the truth only fed my anger. I wasn't satisfied with her reasons for keeping me in the dark, and we would no doubt argue again, once we'd reached safer surroundings. But no sooner had we left the cover of the woods than a shot rang through the night, and the smell of blood came from a bullet wound in Lady Sarah's chest. Before any of us could react, two more shots sounded, and two more bullets hit the vampire. Just as she collapsed, another bullet thudded into my own chest and my entire ribcage seared with pain. I was forced to my knees, struggling to breathe and trying to force the transformation to full wolf form to heal the damage quick enough before I was hit again. Selina was more vulnerable and she knew she'd never be able to invoke any incantations in time that might save her life, so she began to run. But moments later I heard another gunshot and saw her go down.

Through the pain, I sensed the approach of a human and recognised the scent – it was the same Slayer I'd encountered before, come to ensure I died for real this time it seemed. I glared up at him, knowing he'd fire the killing shot before I could do anything. But he didn't fire again, instead striking me across the head with the butt of his gun. I fell to the ground beside Lady Sarah, blackness closing in. I didn't even know whether she was alive or dead, but I had to assume the witch had been killed, her body frailer without the help of witchcraft to combat the Slayer's gun. It didn't matter. There was nothing I could do for either of them as I slipped into unconsciousness, and I knew no more.

Epilogue

Dusk approaches and I fall silent again. The full moon has passed for another month but I haven't eaten all day and I need to feed. And yes, I mean to kill again. Do you hate me for that? I can't say I blame you: I think a part of me still hates myself. I might have found peace for a time when I accepted my lupine half and allowed my mind to become whole again, but it wouldn't last or we wouldn't be here, now. All those horrific acts I've committed still burden my conscience, what remains of it, and a part of me still longs for the life I could have had if it hadn't been for my curse. Such is the nature of my wretched existence, yet I continue to kill and indulge my bloodlust.

Footsteps crunch over the bed of fallen leaves and I slink towards them, intent on my next prey. You might be giving me an accusatory glare now if you were still flesh and blood, but would you really prefer me to feed on your rotting corpse?

How frustrating it must be to remain powerless to influence the events about to unfold. I'm about to take another life and you can do nothing to stop me, except attempt to appeal to my better nature, if only I still had one. But darkness rules me and it will claim another life, this person about to meet as equally a brutal end as the one I dealt you.

A scent reaches me and I pause, listening intently. More humans, moving too stealthily for the general public. I've lingered here too long and now it seems my enemies have found me once again. My intended victim will live to see another day after all. If only the Slayers had turned up to disturb me last night, then perhaps you would have survived crossing paths with me as well.

I retreat deeper into the woods, pausing to return to my wolf form. The Slayers are on my trail and there are too many of them to fight this time, but I feel confident I can outrun them. Come with me if you wish, and I will tell the next part of my story once I've lost them and satisfied my hunger once more. Perhaps we are bound to each other now, you and I, and we must see this tale through to its end. Or do you want the Slayers to succeed this time and end it now? No matter – that is not to be my fate this night, whether you want it to happen or not.

Effortlessly I bound across the woodland floor, my enemies falling behind. I pass through the treeline and onto the streets you once called home. At least the Slayers will find your mortal remains and may grant you the dignity of a proper burial.

Soon all ties to your life are far behind us, just as it was for me when the curse first forced me to move on. But I have long since grown used to this lifestyle, despite the struggle to adjust I initially faced all those years ago, and I will find more temporary shelter where I will continue my tale. Yes, we are bound to each other now, you and I, and I feel sure you will be with me to the end.

Biography

Nick Stead began writing at the age of fifteen. His love of horror and werewolves in particular led to the creation of Hybrid, following a brainstorming session with his cousin to get him started on the first three chapters. Twelve years later at twenty seven and after two major redrafts, his dream of seeing Hybrid published was finally realised. Now twenty eight, he lives with his two cats in Huddersfield, England, where he is hard at work on the next book in the Hybrid series.

For more information about Nick, the Hybrid series, and other works visit: www.nick-stead.co.uk.

Lightning Source UK Ltd.
Milton Keynes UK
UKOW03f0607240117
292738UK00003B/94/P